"You're a minion of the Shadowlord!"

It sounded so incredibly stupid, Tony regretted the words the moment they left his mouth.

Lee stared at him for a long moment, blinked once, and started to laugh. "I'm a what?"

Oh, crap. Now he was going to have to repeat it because there really wasn't any variation on this particular theme. "You're a minion of the Shadowlord."

"That's what I thought you said." Scooping his shirt up off the floor, Lee shrugged into it, still chuckling. "You know, you're a very weird guy."

"You're not leaving this room."

"Is this supposed to be where I strike a dramatic pose and tell you that you can't stop me?" Lee leaned closer, his position a parody of his earlier seduction. "Guess what? You can't."

And he couldn't.

The shadow swept across the room, holding him against the wall. Tony couldn't move, he cou and most importantly, he couldn't breath trapped under a pliable sheet of that covered him from he g to fit up each nostril ae.

As the door ng Lee's body, the shadowom him, and slipped through the open space.

He had to stop Lehe left the building.

Also by
TANYA HUFF

SMOKE AND SHADOWS
SMOKE AND MIRRORS*

**

BLOOD PRICE
BLOOD TRAIL
BLOOD LINES
BLOOD PACT
BLOOD DEBT

**

SING THE FOUR QUARTERS
FIFTH QUARTER
NO QUARTER
THE QUARTERED SEA

**

The Keeper's Chronicles
SUMMON THE KEEPER
THE SECOND SUMMONING
LONG HOT SUMMONING

**

OF DARKNESS, LIGHT AND FIRE

**

WIZARD OF THE GROVE

**

The Confederation Novels
VALOR'S CHOICE
THE BETTER PART OF VALOR

*coming soon in hardcover from DAW Books

SMOKE AND SHADOWS

♠ ♣ ♦ ♥

TANYA HUFF

DAW BOOKS, INC.

DONALD A. WOLLHEIM, FOUNDER

375 Hudson Street, New York, NY 10014

ELIZABETH R. WOLLHEIM

SHEILA E. GILBERT

PUBLISHERS

http://www.dawbooks.com

First Paperback Printing, April 2005
1 2 3 4 5 6 7 8 9 10

DAW TRADEMARK REGISTERED
U.S. PAT. OFF. AND FOREIGN COUNTRIES
—MARCA REGISTRADA
HECHO EN U.S.A.

PRINTED IN THE U.S.A.

For Karen Lahey because until I met her I never made the connection that "people" write books. (Where I thought they came from, I have no idea.) Essentially, Karen's responsible for my being a writer so if you've enjoyed any of my books, you should thank her. Thank you, Karen.

I'd like to thank Blanche McDermaid and the cast and crew of A&E's *Nero Wolfe Mysteries*, who graciously allowed me to hang about the set. I'd especially like to thank Matt and PJ, the PAs, who were more than patient with two solid days of stupid questions. Anything I got right, I owe to them. Mistakes are all my own.

One

LEANING forward, brushing red-gold hair back off his face, he locked eyes with the cowering young woman and smiled, teeth too white within the sardonic curve of his mouth.

"There's no need to be frightened," he told her, his voice holding menace and comfort equally mixed. "You have my word that nothing will happen to you; unless—and I did warn you about this—unless you've been holding out on me, Melissa."

A full lower lip trembled as her fingers clutched the edge of the park bench. "I swear I've told you everything I know!"

"I hope so." He leaned just a little closer, his smile broadening as she trembled. "I truly hope so."

"Cut! Mason, the girl's name isn't Melissa. It's Catherine."

Mason Reed, star of *Darkest Night*, straightened as the director moved out from behind his pair of monitors. "Catherine?"

"That's right."

"Why does it matter, Peter? She'll be dead by the end of the episode."

Safely out of Mason's line of sight, the actress rolled her eyes.

"It matters because everyone else is calling her Catherine," Peter told him calmly, wondering, and not for the first time that morning, what the hell was taking the tech guys so long to come up with believable CGI actors. Or, conversely, what was taking the genetics guys so long to breed the ego out of the ones they had. Years of practice kept either thought from showing. "It matters because Raymond Dark called her Catherine the last time he spoke to her. And it matters because that's her name; if we start calling her by a different name, the audience will get confused. Let's do it one more time and then we'll rig for close-ups."

"What was wrong with the last take?" Mason demanded, fiddling with his left fang. "*I* liked the last take."

"Sorge didn't like the shadows."

"They changed?"

"Apparently. He said they made you look *livide*."

Mason turned toward the director of photography who was deep in conversation with the gaffer and ignoring him completely. His expression suggested he was less than impressed with being ignored. "Livid?"

"Not livid, *livide*," Peter told him, tone and expression completely nonconfrontational. They had no time to deal with one of Mason's detours into ego. "It's French. Translates more or less as ghastly."

"I'm playing a vampire, for Christ's sake! I'm supposed to look ghastly."

"You're supposed to look undead and sexy. That's not the same thing." Flashing their star a reassuring smile, Peter returned to the director's chair. "Come on, Mason, you know what the ladies like."

The pause while he considered it could have been scripted. Right on cue: "Yes, I do. Don't I?"

As the visibly soothed actor returned to his place on the park bench, Peter sent a prayer of thanks to whatever gods were listening, settled back behind his monitors, and yelled, "Tony!"

A young man standing just off the edge of the set, ear jack and harried expression marking him as one of the crew, jerked as the sound of his name cut through the ambient noise. He stepped around a five gallon jug of stage blood and hurried over, picking his way carefully through the hydra snarl of cables covering the floor.

"We're not going to need Lee until after lunch." Peter tore the wrapper from a granola bar with enough force that the bar itself jerked out of his hands, bounced off his thigh, and was heading for the floor when Tony caught it. "Thank you. Is he here yet?"

"Not yet."

"Fucking great." An emphatic first bite. "Have someone in the office call his cell and find out where the hell he is."

"Do they tell him that you won't need him until after lunch?"

"They remind him that according to the call sheets, his ass was supposed to be in makeup by 11:00 . . . Tina, was what's-her-name wearing that color nail polish in scene sixteen? She looks like her fingertips have been dipped in blood."

The script supervisor glanced up from lining her pages. "Yes." Looking past Peter's shoulder, she indicated that Tony should get going. "I think dipped in blood is what they were trying for."

Shooting Tina a grateful smile—it wasn't always easy to tell when Peter's abrupt subject changes were, in fact, a dismissal—Tony headed for the office. A muffled shriek from the actress playing Catherine stopped him at the edge of the park.

It seemed that Mason was getting playful. Testing out his teeth.

As the gaffer's crew adjusted two of the lights, shadows danced against the back wall of the set, looking on their own regard if not ghastly then strange. Forming shapes that refused to be defined, they moved in weirdly sinuous patterns, their edges overlapping in ways normal shadows did not.

But this is television, Tony reminded himself as he left the park, cut across Raymond Dark's office, and hurried past the huge mahogany coffin on his way to the production office. *There's nothing normal about it.*

The studio where CB Productions shot *Darkest Night* had been a box warehouse in its previous incarnation and much of it still looked the part. Chester Bane, creator and executive producer of *Darkest Night,* as well as half a dozen other even less successful straight to syndication series, had gone on record as saying that he refused to spend money the viewer wouldn't see on the screen. His comments off the record had been more along the line of, "I'm not spending another cent until I start seeing some return on my fucking investment!" Since CB had only one actual volume and that volume had been known to send the sound mixer running for his board to slap the levels down, *off the record* essentially meant that no reporter was taking notes within a two-kilometer radius.

Leaving the sound stage, Tony pushed his way through racks of clothing—the wardrobe department's solution to a ten-by-sixteen office and no storage space. Given the perpetual shortage of room, he was always fascinated to note that many of the costumes hanging along both sides of the hall were costumes that had never been used on the show. Granted, he covered enough second unit work that he wasn't on the set all the time, but he somehow doubted he'd have forgotten the blue taffeta ball gown, extra large, with size twelve stiletto-heeled shoes dyed to match. Assorted World War II uniforms had been used for a flashback sequence two episodes ago, but he had no idea when or if they'd ever needed half a dozen private school uniforms. And he couldn't help but wonder about the gorilla suit.

Maybe a few shows down the road they were going after a whole new demographic.

He'd been with the series as a production assistant since the beginning—thirteen of twenty-two episodes in the can and word was they were about to be picked up for a second season. There was no shortage of television work in the Vancouver area—half the shows that filled the US networks were shot there—and there'd certainly been more high profile production companies hiring, but *Darkest Night* had piqued his curiosity and once hired he found himself unable to leave. Even though, as he'd told Henry, some days it was like watching a train wreck.

"They don't know shit about vampires," he'd complained after his first day on the job.

Henry had smiled—his teeth too white within the cupid's bow of his mouth—and said, *"Good."*

Henry Fitzroy, writer of moderately successful romance novels, had taken Tony Foster, a nineteen-year-old street kid into his home, his bed, his heart. Had moved him from Toronto to Vancouver. Had bullied him into finishing high school, had provided stability and encouragement while he worked in a video store by day and attended courses at the Vancouver Film School by night.

And although Henry Fitzroy, bastard son of Henry VIII, once Duke of Richmond and Somerset, had, in the end, allowed Tony to leave and live the life his protection had made possible, he'd refused to cut all ties—insisting they remain friends. Tony hadn't been sure that would work, the whole Prince of Man thing made Henry frighteningly possessive of those he considered his, but however unequal the relationship they'd had, it turned out that the friendship they'd built out of it was solid.

Henry Fitzroy, vampire, Nightwalker, four hundred and fifty odd years a member of the bloodsucking undead, wavered between being amused and appalled about *Darkest Night*.

"They seem to know less about detectives than they do about vampires."

"Yeah, well, it's straight to syndication . . ."

Tony'd learned early on that no one wanted to hear the opinion of a production assistant so, after a few aborted attempts, he surrendered to the inevitable clichés and set about making himself indispensable.

Which was the other reason he stayed with CB Productions. Chester Bane was notorious for hiring the minimum crew the unions would allow and, as a result, his PAs ended up doing a wide variety of less than typical jobs. This resulted in turn in a higher than usual turnover of PAs but Tony figured he'd learned more about the business in thirteen shows than he'd have learned in thirteen seasons elsewhere. Granted, some of it he'd have rather not learned, but after spending his teens on the streets—not to mention unmentionable experiences with demons, mummies, zombies, and ghosts—he had a higher tolerance for the unpleasant than skinny blondes out of West Vancouver by way of UBC who apparently thought themselves too good to empty vomit out of Raymond Dark's file cabinet. He hoped she was very happy being the TAD at the honey wagon on *Smallville* location shoots.

The dressing rooms were just past makeup which was just past the bathrooms. Tony figured he'd check them first in case Lee'd arrived while he was on the set. As he passed the women's washroom, he reattached a corner of the frayed sign covering the top half of the door and made a mental note to remind the art department they needed a new one. The sign should have read, "DON'T FLUSH WHILE RED LIGHT IS ON—CAMERAS ARE ROLLING" but had been adapted to read, "DON'T FUCK WHILE RED LIGHT IS ON." Fucking was not actually a problem, but air in the pipes made them bang while flushing and the sound mixer had threatened to strangle the next person who ruined her levels.

He stuck his head into makeup, covering all the bases.

"Lee?" Thumb stroking the graying line of his thin mustache, Everett blinked myopically at Tony from behind his glasses. "I haven't seen him, but I'm almost positive I heard him out in the office. Don't quote me on that, though."

Someday, when he had the time, Tony was going to find out just when Everett had been misquoted and about what.

Lee's dressing room was empty, shadows fleeing as Tony flicked on the lights. He frowned past his reflection in the mirror. Were the shadows pooling in the corners? Lingering past the time the overhead lights should have banished them? But when he turned . . . nothing. Lee's wardrobe for the day had been laid out on the end of the couch, his Gameboy left on the chipped garage sale coffee table, two cushions tossed on the floor . . . but nothing looked out of place. Any strangeness could be explained by a bulb missing from the track lighting.

Chatter over his radio suggested the camera crew had gotten involved in the lighting debate and that problem of shadows marring Raymond Dark's youthful yet patrician features was unlikely to be resolved any time soon.

Four phones were ringing as he opened the door to the production office, the usual chaos cranked up a notch by their current lack of an office PA. He'd been sent out for coffee a week ago and no one had seen him since; his resignation had been written succinctly on a Starbucks napkin and stuffed through the mail slot late one night.

". . . understand why it might be a problem, but we really need that street permit. Uh-huh." Rachel Chou, the office manager, beckoned him toward her desk. "Tell you what; I'll let you talk to our locations guy. No, we totally understand where you're coming from here. Hang on." She hit hold and held the receiver out toward Tony. "Just listen to her, that's all she really wants and I don't have the time. If she asks you if it has to be that street at that time, say yes. You're very sorry but you can't change anything. I doubt she'll let you get a word in edgewise, but if she does, be charming."

Tony stared at the receiver as though he were likely to get a virulent disease from it. "Why can't she call Matt?"

"She tried. She can't get through."

They used the services of a freelance location finder—who no one could ever find.

"Amy . . ."

"Is busy."

Across the office, Rachel's assistant flipped him the finger and continued convincing someone to do something they clearly weren't happy about.

He sighed and wrapped his fingers around the warm plastic—as far as he could tell, the office phones never got a chance to cool down. "Who is it?"

"Rajeet Singh at the permit office." Rachel had a second receiver halfway to her ear. "Just let her talk," she told him again, reached across to hit the hold button on his phone, and snapped, "CB Productions."

Tony moved as far away as the cord allowed, and turned his back. "Ms. Singh? How can I help you?"

"It's about that night shoot you've got lined up on Lakefield Drive . . ." Everything after that disappeared into the argument coming through the jack in his left ear and the ambient noise in the office. Resting one cheek on the edge of Rachel's desk, Tony did as instructed and let her talk.

From where he was sitting, he could see the front doors, nearly blocked by a stack of cardboard boxes, the door leading to the bull pen—the cramped hole that the show's three staff writers called their own, although not in CB's hearing—and CB's office.

If he turned a little, he could see Mason's office and through the open door, Mason's personal assistant, Jennifer. Snide remarks about just what exactly her job entailed had ended the day she'd pushed past a terrified security guard and strong-armed a pair of Mason's more rabid fans off the set and back into their 1983 Dodge Dart. She rode with the Dykes on Bikes during Pride Parade and someday Tony promised himself he'd find the guts to ask her about her tattoos.

Next to Mason, the art department—one room, one person, and a sideline in erotic greeting cards everyone pretended they didn't know about. Then finance, the kitchen, and the door leading to post production. Somewhere amid the half dozen cubbyholes crammed with equipment, Zev Sero, CB's music director, had an office but Tony hadn't yet been able to find it.

Behind him and to the right, the costuming department. Directly behind him, the stairs leading to the basement and special effects. Given CB's way of making a nickel scream, Tony had been amazed to discover that the FX was done in house. He was more amazed when he found out Arra Pelindrake was a middle-aged woman who'd been with CB—through bad television and worse—for the last seven years. Safer not to think of the possible reasons why.

". . . so does it have to be that street at that time?"

He glanced over at Rachel who appeared to be attacking a pile of order forms with a black magic marker. "Uh, yes."

"Fine. But I'm doing you guys a significant favor here and I want it remembered on election day."

"Election day . . . ?"

"Municipal elections. City council. *Don't* forget to vote. I'll send your permit over this afternoon."

"Thank you." But he was thanking a dial tone. He handed Rachel the receiver in time for her to answer another line and turned to see Amy's shadow come out of Mason's office.

Or not.

His own shadow elongated and contracted again as he walked across the office and by the time he reached Amy's side, he'd almost convinced himself that he'd merely seen Amy's do the same thing. Almost. Except Amy had been standing, essentially motionless, beside her desk.

"You okay?" she asked, sitting down and reaching for her mouse.

"Yeah. Fine." Her shadow reached for the mouse's shadow. Nothing overtly strange about that. "Just having an FX moment."

"Whatever. What do you want?"

"Lee's not here yet and he was supposed to be in makeup at eleven."

"Do I look like his baby-sitter?"

"Peter wants you to call him."

"Yeah? When? In my copious amounts of . . ." She snatched up the ringing phone. "CB Productions, please hold . . . spare time?"

"Yeah."

"Fine." She reached for the rolodex. So did her shadow. "What are you looking at? I got a boob hanging out or something?"

"Why would I be looking at that?"

"Good point." Glancing past his shoulder, she grinned. "Hey, Zev. Tony's not looking at my boobs."

"Uh . . . good?"

Tony turned in time to catch the flush of red on Zev's cheeks above the short black beard and smiled in sympathy. On her good days, Amy went about two postal codes beyond blunt.

The music director returned his smile, hands shoved into the front pockets of his jeans as though he suddenly didn't know what to do with them. "You're off set? I mean, I know you're off set," he continued before Tony could answer, "you're here. I just . . . Why?"

"Peter sent me out to have someone call Lee. He's not here yet."

"He is. I, uh, saw him from Barb's office."

Barb Dixon was the entire finance department.

"What were you doing in with Madame Number-cruncher?" Amy asked.

Zev shrugged. "She gets swamped at the end of the month. Sometimes I help her out; I'm good with numbers."

"Yeah?" Tony'd been leaning out around the boxes, watching for Lee to come in the door, but that got his attention. "I totally suck at math and I'm trying to come up with a budget. I've got to buy a car—the commute's fucking killing me. Maybe you can help *me* out sometime."

"Sure." Zev's cheeks darkened again and yanking a hand from his pocket, he ran it back through his hair. "You . . . uh . . ."

"I know." He replaced his yarmulke and headed for the door to post production. "You know where I am, just give me a call."

At least that's what Tony thought he'd said. The words had run together into one long, embarrassed sound. Fortunately, months on the ear jack had made him pretty skilled at working out the inaudible. "Hey, Zev?"

The music director paused, one foot over the threshold.

"That piece behind Mason at the window last ep? With all the strings? It really rocked."

"Thank you." His shadow slipped through the closing door at the last minute.

I'm losing my mind.

"He likes you."

"What?" Caught up in concerns about his own sanity, it took Tony a moment to figure out what Amy was talking about. "Who? Zev?"

"Duh. He's a nice guy. Oh, but wait, why would you notice a nice guy who likes you when there's . . ." She paused and smirked.

"What?" Tony demanded as the pause lengthened.

Behind him, the front door opened and a familiar velvet voice said, "Man, you would not believe the traffic out there! I almost had to take the bike up on the fucking sidewalk at one point."

Answering Amy's sarcastic kissy face with a single finger, Tony turned.

Lee Nicholas, aka James Taylor Grant, Raymond

Dark's junior partner and the vampire detective's eyes and ears in the light, was six foot one with short dark hair, green eyes, chiseled cheekbones and the kind of body that owed as much to lucky genetics as his personal trainer. Although the show kept him in preppy casual, he was currently wearing a black leather jacket, faded jeans, black leather chaps, motorcycle boots . . . When he unzipped the jacket to expose a tight black T-shirt, Tony felt his mouth go dry.

"Hey, Lee, how many cows were killed for that outfit?"

"Not a one." He grinned down at Amy, showing perfect teeth and a dimple one of the more poetic online fan sites had described as wicked. "They all lived long, fulfilled bovine lives and died happily of old age. How many migrant workers did you exploit for all that cotton?"

"I picked every blossom with my own lily white . . . CB Productions, can I help you? Left you on hold?" Mouthing *oops* she waved both Tony and Lee away from her desk.

"So, you're off the set." He handed Tony his helmet in full realization that it would be taken and carried for him. "Has Peter finished up early?"

"No. Uh, late. That is, he's going to be finishing late and he wanted me to tell you that you wouldn't be needed on the set until after, you know, lunch." Tony smiled weakly, fully realizing how he sounded. He'd been taking care of himself, one way or another, since he was fourteen. He'd seen things that redefined the word terrifying. He'd fought against the darkness—not metaphorically, *literally* fought against the darkness. Well, helped . . . He was twenty-four years old for Christ's sake! And yet he couldn't talk to Lee Nicholas without coming across like a babbling idiot. Idiot being a particularly apt description since the actor was straight with a well documented weakness for the kind of blondes he couldn't take home to Mother.

Lee's mother was a very nice woman. She'd been to the studio a couple of times.

Tony suddenly realized that Lee was waiting for him to reply to something he'd totally missed hearing. "What?"

"I said, thank you for carrying my helmet. I'll see you on set."

"Right. Yeah. Uh, you're welcome." And the dressing room door closed, the scuffed paint less than a centimeter from his nose.

Tony had no memory of leaving the production office.

He walked back to the sound stage; his shadow lingered outside Lee's door.

♠

"Hey, Tony, you up for some second unit work tonight?"

Marshmallow strawberry halfway to his mouth, Tony turned to see Amy approaching the craft services table waving a set of sides—the night's schedule reduced to pocket size. "Out on Lakefield?"

"That's the one. Arra's going to blow the beemer. You'll pick up a little overtime and get to watch a symbol of bourgeois excess take a hit. Hard to beat."

"Bourgeois excess?" He snorted and chewed. "Who talks like that?"

"Obviously, me. And if you're going to give me a hard time, I'll call in another PA to do it."

Tony waited. Picked a marshmallow banana out of the bowl.

"Okay, Pam asked for you and CB wouldn't let me call in even if she hadn't. Happy?" She shoved the cut sheets up against his chest. "Trucks are there at eleven, shoot by midnight, gone by one and if you believe that, I've got some waterfront land going cheap."

♠

"He led his city through the darkest night toward the dawn."

Heart slamming against his ribs, Tony jumped forward and spun around, managing to accomplish both movements more or less simultaneously and still stay on his feet. He scowled at the shadowy figure just barely visible at the edge of the streetlight's circle, knowing that every nuance of his expression could be clearly seen. "Fuck, Henry! You just don't sneak up on a guy and purr bad cutlines into his ear!"

"Sorry." Henry stepped into the light, red-gold hair gleaming, full lips curved up into a smile.

Tony knew that smile. It was the one that went along with *It's fun to be a vampire!* Which was not only a much better cutline than the one plastered all over the *Darkest Night* promo package, it was indicative of an almost playful mood—playful as it referred to an undead creature of the night. "Where did you park?"

"Don't worry; I'm well out of the way."

"Cops give you any hassle?"

The smile changed slightly and Henry shoved his hands into the pockets of his oiled-canvas trenchcoat. "Do they ever?"

Tony glanced down the road to where a pair of constables from the Burnaby RCMP detachment stood beside their cruiser. "You didn't, you know, vamp them?"

"Do I ever?"

"Sometimes."

"Not this time."

"Good. Because they're already a little jumpy." He nodded toward the trucks and, when Henry fell into step beside him, wet dry lips and added, "Everyone's a little jumpy."

"Why?"

"I don't know. Night shoot, moderately dangerous stunt, an explosion . . . pick one."

"You don't believe it's any of those reasons."

Tony glanced over at Henry. "You asking?"

"Not really, no."

Before he could continue, Tony waved a cautioning hand and continued the movement down to pull his walkie-talkie from the holster on his belt. "Yeah, Pam?" One finger pushed his ear jack in a little deeper. "Okay, I'm on it. I've got go see when Daniel's due out of makeup," he told Henry as he reholstered. "You okay here?"

Henry looked pointedly around. "I think I'll be safe enough."

"Just . . ."

"Stay out of the way. I know." Henry's smile changed yet again as he watched Tony hurry off toward the most distant of the studio's three trailers. In spite of the eyebrow piercing, he looked, for lack of a better word, competent. Like he knew exactly what he was doing. It was what Henry came to night shoots to see—Tony living the life he'd chosen and living it well. It made letting him go a little easier.

Not that he had actually *let go*.

Letting go was not something Henry did well. Or, if truth be told, at all.

But within this small piece of the night, they could both pretend that he was nothing more than the friend he appeared to be.

Pretend.

He made his living writing the kind of books that allowed women—and the occasional man—to pretend for 400-odd pages that they lived a life of romance and adventure, but this, these images captured and manipulated and then spoon-fed to the masses as art, this was pretense without imagination. He'd never had to actually blow up a BMW in order for his readers to imagine a car accident.

Television caused imagination to atrophy.

His upper lip pulled back off his teeth as he watched the director laying out the angles of the explosion for the camera operator.

Television substituted for culture.

The feel of watching eyes turned him to face a middle-aged woman standing beside the craft services table, a coffee clutched between both hands, her gaze locked on his face, her expression asking, *What are you?*

Henry pulled his masks back into place and only then, only when he presented a face that spoke of no danger at all, did he turn away. The woman had been curious, not afraid, and would easily convince herself that she'd been asking *who are you?* not *what.* No harm had been done, but he'd have to be more careful. Tony was right. *Everyone* was a little jumpy tonight.

His nostrils flared as he tested the air. He could smell nothing except . . .

"Hey, Henry!"

. . . a chemical fire retardant.

"This is Daniel. He's our stunt coordinator and he'll be crashing the car tonight."

Henry took the callused hand offered and found himself studying a man not significantly taller than his own five six. Given that Tony was five ten, the stunt coordinator could be no more than five eight. Not exactly what Henry had expected.

"Daniel also does all the stunt work for Mason and for Lee," Tony continued. "They almost never get blown up together."

"I'm pretty much the entire department," Daniel admitted, grinning as he brushed a bit of tangled wig back off his face. "We can't afford to blow them up together. Tony says you're a writer. Television?"

"Novels."

"No shit? My wife used to write porn, but with all the free stuff out on the web these days there's no money in it so she switched back to writing ad copy. Now, if you'll both excuse me, I've got to go make sure I'll survive tonight's pyrotechnics." He sketched a salute and trotted across the road to a parked BMW.

"Seems like a nice guy," Henry said quietly.

"He is."

"There's free porn on the web?"

Tony snorted, his elbow impacting lightly with Henry's side. "Stop it."

"So what's going to happen?"

"Daniel, playing the part of a car thief . . ."

Eyes narrowed, Henry stared across the road. "Whose head is being devoured by a distant relative of Cthulhu."

"Apparently that's what happens when you soak dreadlocks in fire retardant."

"And the size?"

"The wig's glued to a helmet."

"You're kidding me?"

"Yeah, that's what our hairdresser said." Tony's shrug suggested the hairdresser had been significantly more vocal. "Anyway, he's going to drive the beemer along this stretch of road until he swerves to miss an apparition of evil . . ."

"A what?"

"I don't think the writers have decided what it actually is yet, but don't worry, the guys in post always come through."

"I'm actually more concerned that this vampire detective of yours drives a BMW."

"Well, he won't after tonight, so that's okay. So Daniel swerves to miss this apparition and the car flips, rolls, and bang!"

"Cars don't blow up that easily." Henry's pale hand sketched a protest on the night as Daniel slid behind the wheel.

"Explosions make better television."

"It makes no logical sense."

"Now, you're getting it." Tony's face went blank for a moment, then he bent and picked up the fire extinguisher he'd set at his feet. "Looks like we're ready to go."

"And you're . . ."

"Not actually doing anything while we're shooting since we've got Mounties blocking the road, so I'm part of the safety crew. And as long as you're not planning on telling the union . . ."

"I'm not talking to your union as much as I used to."

He could feel Tony staring at him but he kept his gaze on the car.

"You're in a weird mood tonight. Is it . . . ?"

Henry shook his head, cutting off the question. He didn't know what it was.

He wasn't entirely certain it was anything at all.

Jumpy.

Everyone was jumpy.

The car backed up.

A young woman called scene and take, then smacked the top down on a piece of blackboard in front of the closer of the two cameras. About fifteen people, including Tony, yelled, "Rolling," for no reason Henry could immediately determine since the director's voice had carried clearly over the entire location.

The car began to speed up.

When they finished with it in editing, it would look as though it was racing down Lakefield Drive. Considering that Daniel was driving toward a certain crash, it was moving fast enough.

A squeal of brakes just before the outside tires swerved onto the ramp.

Grip tightening on the fire extinguisher, Tony braced for an impact even though he knew there was nothing there.

Nothing there.

Except . . .

Darkness lingered on the other side of the ramp.

An asinine observation given that it was the middle of the night and the darkness had nowhere else to go. Except . . . it seemed darker. Like the night had thickened just in that spot.

I must've inhaled more accelerant than I thought.

Up.

The darkness seemed to be half in the car although

logically, if the darkness existed at all, the car should have been halfway through it.

Over.

The impact of steel against asphalt as the car hit and rolled was always louder than expected. Tony jerked and winced as glass shattered and the BMW finally skidded to a stop on its roof.

Flame.

"Keep rolling!" That was Pam's voice. "Arra, what the hell's going on?"

There shouldn't be flames, not yet.

Daniel wasn't out of the car.

Couldn't get out of the car, Tony realized as he started to run.

He felt more than saw Henry speed by him and by the time he arrived by the driver's side door, the crumpled metal was screaming a surrender as the door opened. Dropping down to one knee, he allowed Daniel to grab onto his shoulder and, backing up, dragged him from the car and out through the billowing smoke.

The rest of the safety crew arrived as the stunt co-coordinator gained his feet, free hand waving away any additional help. He stared at the car for a long moment, brow furrowed under the masking dreadlocks then he visibly shook it off. "Goddamned fucking door jammed! Everyone back off and let it blow."

"Daniel . . ."

"Don't worry about it, Tony. I'm fine." Guiding the younger man away from the car, he raised his voice, "I said, let it blow!"

The explosion was, as all Arra's explosions were, perfect. A lot of flash, not much smoke, the car outlined within the fire.

For a heartbeat, the shadows held their ground against the flames. A heartbeat later, they fled.

And a heartbeat beyond that, Tony glanced away from the wreck to find Henry beside him, smelling of accelerant. "He was muttering about something touching him. Something cold."

"Daniel?"

The vampire nodded.

"Something touched him before you got there?"

Henry glanced down at his hands. "I didn't touch him. He didn't even know *I* was there."

The light from the fire painted the night orange and gold as far back as the director's monitors. It looked as though Daniel, helmet in his hands, sweat plastering his short hair to his head, was telling Pam what happened. Leaving Henry staring at the burning car, Tony headed for the craft services table—well within eavesdropping range.

". . . hardly see the end of the ramp, then I could hardly see at all. I thought it might be some kind of weird fog except it came with me when I rolled."

"I didn't see anything."

"I didn't exactly *see* anything either," Daniel pointed out acerbically. "That's kind of my point."

Tony waited for him to mention the touch. He didn't.

"It was probably just the fumes from the fire retardant affecting my eyes."

"Probably."

It sounded like a pact. An agreed-upon explanation.

Because what else could it have been?

As Daniel moved away, Arra came into view behind Pam's shoulder. She looked terrified.

Not for Daniel.

Not about the part of the stunt that had nearly gone wrong.

Given her expression, Tony'd be willing to bet serious money that she'd forgotten both Daniel and the stunt.

Tony found himself quietly murmuring, "Apparition of evil," as Pam finally yelled "Cut!" and Daniel's crew moved in with the fire extinguishers.

Two

"TONY?"

He glanced up from his sides to find a sprite-like figure with enormous blue eyes attempting to both stare at him and simultaneously watch everything going on inside the soundstage.

"Hi, I'm Veronica. I'm the new office PA. I just started. Amy sent me to tell you ... Oh, my God, that's Lee Nicholas, isn't it? He's my ... I mean he's just so ..."

And the sprite devolved into yet another new hire too starstruck to last—although Tony had to agree with the sentiment. Lee was sitting on the edge of Raymond Dark's desk, one foot on the floor, one foot swinging, khaki Dockers pulled tight across both thighs as he waited to do his reaction shots. Tony had been doing his best not to look. He'd discovered early on that he could watch Lee or he could do his job, but he couldn't do both.

Taking a deep, strengthening breath, he turned his back on the set. "Amy sent you to tell me ... ?"

"What?" Veronica's already wide eyes widened further as though they could encompass both the vision that was Lee Nicholas and the more mundane view of the person she was actually supposed to be dealing with. Tony could have told her it wouldn't work, but he doubted she'd listen. "Oh. Right. Mr. Bane wants to see you in his office ..."

Peter's voice cut her off. "Let's go right away, please! Can I have a bell!"

As the bell rang out, Tony took hold of Veronica's arm, his fingers nearly encircling her tiny bicep, and tugged her gently away from the set. "Mr. Bane wants to see me in his office . . . ?" he murmured.

"About last . . ."

"Quiet, please!"

All color blanched from Veronica's cheeks and Tony had to fight a snicker, as he and half a dozen others echoed the first half of Peter's injunction, their voices bouncing around the soundstage. First day on the job, he'd been afraid to breathe after the bell and had stood frozen like a particularly geeky statue until one of the sound crew had come up behind him and knocked his knees out.

Maintaining his grip, he tugged her across the terrace, as the assistant director yelled, "Let's settle, people!"

Two sets away from the action and still moving, he said, "Mr. Bane wants to see me about?"

"Last . . ."

"Rolling!"

". . . night."

Tony laid a finger against his mouth as the second assistant camera called the slate.

"Scene eight, take four."

Veronica jumped at the crack.

"Mark!"

And she jumped again as Peter snapped, "Action!"

Even the muttering in Tony's ear jack stopped. They were far enough from the actual set to allow quiet movement, so he continued pulling her across the concrete floor, past the back walls scribbled over with cryptic construction notes to the line of small dressing rooms for the auxiliary cast.

Most production companies with similar space limitations used a second location trailer parked close to an outside door. Chester Bane refused to pay for the power necessary to keep one running and had the construction crew throw up a row of cubbyholes against the back wall. Each unpainted "dressing room" was six by six, with a padded bench across the back, a full-length mirror, a row of hooks, and a shelf. The whole thing looked not unlike the "private rooms" in some of the sleazier bathhouses. The only thing missing: a dented condom dispenser.

Gesturing for Veronica to remain quiet, Tony scratched lightly on the door marked with *Catherine* scrawled across a strip of duct tape.

The door opened.

Darkness spilled out.

Tony leaped back and, heart pounding, found himself pinned under the questioning eyes of two confused women.

Catherine's shadow stretched from her feet to his.

Dredging up a smile, he flashed a fifteen minute sign, nodded as she did, and watched as she closed her shadow back in with her. Wondering if he should say something. Do something.

About what?

Shadows?

I've got to start getting more sleep. He waved Veronica in front of him, pulled her back as she nearly stepped on the edge of a new hardwood floor—where the hardwood was paint and the actual floor was plywood. The art director, faking slightly salacious delft tiles by the fireplace, turned and flashed him an emphatic thumbs-up.

Life had been a variation on that theme all morning.

By the time he'd hit the craft services truck at seven, the genny op had been embellishing the story of him pulling Daniel from the burning car for almost an hour. No one had made a huge fuss—well, no one except Everett although that was pretty much a given regardless—but most of the crew had taken a moment to say something.

"Jaysus, Tony, you couldn't of let the bugger fry? I'm after owing him fifty bucks."

Under other circumstances he wouldn't have minded being the center of attention, but he hadn't actually done much. Since he couldn't explain that Henry had yanked the car door open, all he could do was hope that something else provided a new focus for people with long stretches of too much time on their hands—and provide it sooner rather than later.

Just as they reached the exit, the red light went off and as he waved Veronica through, the voices started up in his ear again.

". . . redress, reload, redo . . . let's go, people, we haven't got all day."

Unhooking his radio's microphone from the neck of his T-shirt, he waited for a break in the tumbling current of voices. "Adam, it's Tony. CB wants to see me, but I gave Catherine her heads-up on the way. Over."

His head murmured *soon* at him.

Soon?

"Yeah, great." The first assistant director turned his head from the microphone and carried on a low-voiced conversation as Tony followed Veronica along the hall, envying the way she could move through the costumes without actually touching them. She was what? Ninety pounds soaking wet? *"Listen, Tony, while you're passing, tell Everett that Lee's got that cowlick thing happening again and we need him in here."*

"Roger, that." He holstered and peeled off into makeup to deliver his message, emerging to find Veronica waiting for him practically quivering.

"Amy said Mr. Bane wanted to see you right away!"

Tony frowned and shook his head. What was her damage? He'd been moving toward the office since she'd given him the message. "You're going to give yourself an ulcer if you don't calm down."

Wide eyes widened impossibly further. "It's my first day!"

"And all I'm saying is that you need to pace yourself."

As they emerged out into the pandemonium of the office, Amy stood, leaned out around Rachel, and beckoned them over to her desk without pausing her conversation. ". . . that's right, two hundred gallons of #556. Well, it might be battleship gray on your side of the border but ours are more a morning-after green. Yeah, great. Thanks. New supplier in Seattle," she said, hanging up. "Charlie knew someone who'd cut us a deal."

"Who's . . . ?" Veronica began.

"One of the construction crew." Her gaze switching to Tony, she added, "Hail the conquering hero! So, for an encore, do you think you could save Canadian television?"

"No."

"Way to stop and consider it. Fine. Veronica, you've got dry cleaning to pick up. Here's the slips." Amy shoved a sheaf of pink paper into the new PA's hand and closed her fingers around it. "And if Mr. Palimpter tries to make you pay, remind him that we're on monthly billing and if he wants to know where his payment is for last the two months, tell him you're just the messenger and he's not to shoot you."

"Is he likely to?"

"Probably not."

"Doesn't the dry cleaner deliver?" Tony asked, abandoning an attempt to read what looked like a legal document upside down.

Amy snorted. "Not for about two months now, funny thing. Oh, and while you're out grab two grande Caffe Americanos, a tall cinnamon-spiced mochaccino, and three tall, bold of the day unless they're Sulawesi, then get two of them and one decaf. Don't panic, I wrote it down." She snatched a ripped corner of paper clipped to a twenty up off her desk. "I had to print kind of small, but you should be able to read it."

"Unless they're Sulwhat's?"

"Sulawesi. Go! And smile, you're in show business! So . . ." As Veronica ran for the door, she sat back down and flipped a strand of fuchsia hair back off her face. "... Zev's still in with Mr. Bane, which gives you time to tell me all about last night."

Tony shrugged. "What's to tell? I'm just not as used to this stuff as Daniel's guys, so I panicked first." Four years with Henry had taught him the most believable way to lie usually involved the truth. "You think it's safe sending her for coffee? Isn't that how you lost the last one?" Deflecting attention he'd always been good at.

"Trial by fire. If she can handle Starbucks at lunchtime, she can handle ... CB Productions, can I help you? One moment please." Jabbing at the hold button, she leaned across her desk and yelled, "Barb, line three!"

A faint, "Thanks, sweetie," drifted out of the accounting office.

"Intercom busted again?"

"Still. Too bad it wasn't Lee in the car. You could have given him mouth to mouth."

"It was a car crash; he wasn't drowning."

Amy looked arch. "So?"

Before Tony could think of a suitable reply, the boss' door opened and Zev emerged carrying a stack of CDs.

"Well?" Amy asked.

"He wants Wagner."

"Under the stunt? Isn't that a little ... Wagnerian?"

Zev grinned. "Actually, yes." Spotting Tony, he flushed and nodded toward the office. "CB says you can go right in."

The static in Tony's radio seemed to be making patterns that were almost words.

"Tony?"

He flicked at his ear jack and shot Zev half a reassuring smile as he started toward the open door. "It's nothing."

"If you're sure ..."

"Oh, yeah." No. Maybe.

To give CB credit, he'd spent no more cash on his office than he had on anyone else's. The vertical blinds had come with the building, the rug that covered the industrial tile floor was the same cheap knockoff they used in Raymond Dark's study, and the furniture had been jazzed up by the set builders to look less like Wal-Mart and more like Ethan Allan. The tropical fish tank and the three surviving fish had been used as a prop in episode two.

Not that it mattered because at six six and close to three hundred pounds, Chester Bane dominated any room he was in.

As Tony stepped onto the rug, he lifted his head slowly.

Like a lion at feeding time . . .

If lions had significantly receding hairlines and noses that had been broken more than once while playing pro football.

"Tony Foster?"

"Yes, sir."

Lying flat on the desk, the huge hands covered a good portion of the available space. "You're the set PA?"

"Yes." Tony found himself staring at the manicured fingernails and had to force himself to look away. They'd met three or four times since he'd started working for *Darkest Night*—Tony couldn't decide if CB really had forgotten him or was just trying to screw with his head. If the latter, it was working.

"You did good work last night."

"Thank you."

"A man who thinks quickly and can get the job done can go far in this business. Are you planning on going far, Tony Foster?"

"Yes, sir."

"Think quickly and get the job done." The dark eyes narrowed slightly under scant brows. "And keep your tongue between your teeth; that's the trick."

A warning? Or was he being paranoid? *If I haven't said anything yet, I'm not likely to start talking now* seemed like an impolitic response. Tony settled for another, "Yes, sir."

"Good." One finger began to tap a slow rhythm against the desk.

Was he being dismissed?

"So. Get back to work."

Apparently.

"Yes, sir." Resisting the urge to back from the room, Tony turned and left; walking as fast as he could without making it seem like he was running away.

He stepped back into the production office as Arra emerged from the kitchen, a pale green mug cupped between both hands. Their eyes met.

And the voice in his ear breathed a name he didn't quite catch.

What the . . . ? Flicking a finger against his ear jack, Tony bent to adjust the volume on his radio, wondering where the hell the barely audible voice was coming from. He had to be picking up bleed through from someone else's frequency.

When he looked up again, Arra was gone.

"TONY? WHERE THE HELL IS CATHERINE?"

With Adam's unmistakable bellow echoing inside his skull, he cranked the volume back down. "I'm on my way back to the set, I'll get her."

Amy glanced up from the photocopier as he passed her desk. "What did the boss want?"

"Are you planning on going far, Tony Foster?"

"Honestly?" He shrugged. "I'm not really sure."

♣

Mason Reed, in full Raymond Dark, was standing just inside the soundstage door. He jumped as he saw Tony, turned the movement into an overly flamboyant gesture, and snapped, "The girl is not on the set."

"Adam told me. I'm going to get her now."

"I was looking for her."

Tony had no intention of arguing with him although it was obvious he'd been having a quick smoke—the gesture hadn't waved off all the evidence. Legally, he couldn't smoke on the soundstage, but the whole crew knew he did it whenever he had a break but not enough time to return to his dressing room. Stars didn't stand outside in the rain with the rest of the addicted.

Used to skirting Mason's ego for the sake of the shooting schedule, they ignored him for the most part, accepted his lame excuses at face value, and bitched about it behind his back.

Mason, who seemed to think no one knew, maintained a carefully crafted public image of an athletic nonsmoker making sure he was photographed on all the right ski hills and bike trails.

Actors, Tony snorted silently, as he walked back toward the auxiliary dressing rooms. *It's all "fool the eye. Don't look at the man behind the curtain."*

He rapped against the plywood door, knuckles impacting the strip of duct tape at about the middle of the Catherine.

No answer.

About to call out, he discovered he had no idea of what her actual name was. If he thought of her at all, she was just Catherine—her actual identity wiped out by the bit part she was playing. Unexpectedly bothered by this, he pulled the day's side from his pocket and stepped back into the light—nearly stepping on Mason who'd apparently followed him. "Sorry."

The actor's lip curled. "Why don't you just open the door?"

"Well, she could be . . ."

"Could be?" His tone was mocking and Tony realized with some dismay that the young actress was about to pay the price for Mason almost having been caught with a cancer stick on the soundstage. "I don't care what she could be; she *should* be on the set right now and I have no intention of waiting any longer." He curled his fingers around the cheap aluminum doorknob, twisted, twisted harder, and yanked.

With a rush of cool air, shadow spilled out onto the soundstage, pooling on the concrete, running into the cracks and dips in the floor.

A body followed.

She'd been pressed up against the door, her right arm tucked across the small of her back, her fingers clamped around the doorknob. They retained their hold as she fell backward. She dangled for a moment, then cheap nails pulled out of the chipboard and with a shriek of metal against wood, the door came off its hinges.

A small bounce as the back of her head impacted with concrete.

Enough of a bounce to rearrange her features into the *nobody's home* expression of death.

Enough to wipe away the expression the body had worn on its way to the floor.

Terror.

She looked as though she'd been scared to death.

Mason scowled down at his errant guest star. "Catherine? Get up!"

"She's dead." Tony shoved the sides back in his pocket and unhooked his microphone.

"What? Don't be ridiculous; she doesn't die until tomorrow afternoon."

"And her name was Nikki Waugh." It was the name he'd almost heard out in the office. He'd realized it the moment he'd read it on the cast list.

"Was?" Mason sounded like he was about to fall apart, like his hindbrain knew what the more civilized bits refused to acknowledge, so Tony let it go. Reality would bite him in the ass soon enough.

At least Nikki's shadow seemed to be staying where it belonged.

♣

"You seem remarkably calm about this, Mr. Foster."

RCMP Constable Elson said *Mr. Foster* the way Hugo Weaving said *Mr. Anderson* in *The Matrix*. Maybe it was subconscious, but Tony was willing to bet it was on purpose—a guy in a uniform with delusions of grandeur. He shrugged. "I spent a few years living on the streets in Toronto. I've seen dead bodies. Four or five poor fucks freeze every winter." No point in mentioning the baby soul-sucked by a dead Egyptian wizard.

"Living on the streets? You got a record?"

He didn't think they were legally allowed to ask him that, but they'd find out as soon as they ran him so what the hell. "Small stuff. You want to talk to someone in Toronto about it, call Detective-Sergeant Michael Celluci at violent crimes. We go back."

"Violent crimes isn't small stuff, Mr. Foster."

"I just said he knew me, Officer, not that he'd booked me."

"You being smart with us?"

There were a hundred answers to that. Unfortunately, most of them were *not* smart, so Tony settled for a sincere but not too sincere, "No."

The constable opened his mouth again, but his partner cut him off. "Let's just go over this one last time, shall we? Ms. Waugh was late coming onto the set. You went to get her, followed by Mr. Reed. He pulled open the door. Ms. Waugh fell out, still holding the handle. The door pulled off and she hit the floor. You told Adam Paelous, the first assistant director, who told Peter Hudson, the director, who called 911. Correct?"

"Yeah, that's right."

"And you didn't call because . . ."

"No one carries their phone on the soundstage."

Constable Danvers flipped her occurrence book closed and tapped the cover with the end of her pen. "I think that's everything, then." As Tony started to stand, she raised a hand. "Wait; one more thing."

He sighed and sat.

She leaned forward slightly, elbows braced on the edge of the ancient table the office staff had secured for their kitchen and said, "So, is Mason Reed always so full of himself? Because he's nothing like Raymond Dark."

Tony stared at her, hoping his reaction didn't show on his face. He'd never actually thought of cops as people who watched bad syndicated television and were just as into the whole celebrity thing as everyone else. Which, he supposed, was fairly stupid of him—a uniform and a gun didn't necessarily come with taste and cops, more than most, could use a few hours of escape into the tube.

Two guys in front of the camera, forty behind, and everyone wanted to know about the actors.

The short answer to Constable Danvers' question was: Yes.

Longer version: Most of the time, he's an egotistical pain in the ass.

The answer from someone who intended to go far in this business: "You know actors." He shrugged. "They're always acting."

"So we can take his observation that he knew instantly Ms. Waugh was dead with a grain of salt?" Elson growled with an impatient look at his partner. It seemed that Constable Elson was not a *Darkest Night* fan.

Tony shrugged again. "Don't know enough about him. I guess he could of known." He'd certainly recovered from his initial shock fast enough.

"You knew."

"I figured. Like I said, I seen . . . I've seen dead bodies before." Twenty minutes with the cops and street rhythms were creeping back into his voice. *Jesus, good thing Henry's not here.*

"At the risk of going all Professor Higgins on you, people judge you the moment they hear you speak. If you want to be taken seriously by the people in power, you use the words and inflections they use." Henry had stopped pacing and turned to stare down at Tony sprawled on the couch. *"Do you understand?"*

"Sure. 'Cept I don't know who this Higgins dude is."

A third RCMP constable stuck his head into the kitchen. "Body's bagged. Coroner's moving out." His gaze flicked down to Tony and back up to his fellow officers. "You done?"

"We're done." Elson stood, Danvers a second behind him. "If we need anything else, Mr. Foster, we'll be in touch."

"Sure." He stayed where he was until they'd cleared the kitchen, then he went to the door to watch them cross the office. He'd missed the first part of their conversation, but the end of it rose clearly over the chaos.

". . . and I got to talk to that Lee Nicholas guy you like."

"Bastard. Did you check for the nipple ring?"

"Why the hell would I do that?"

" 'Cause I've got twenty bucks riding on it."

And the door closed behind them.

Tony supposed it was mildly reassuring that certain members of the RCMP were as shallow as the world at large. Added benefit—should the need arise, he knew how to get on the good side of Constable Danvers. Provided that twenty bucks was pro nipple ring.

Amy mouthed *Get your ass over here!* at him and he obediently crossed to stand in front of her desk. There was half a grande Caffe Americano tucked between her monitor and the phone, so he assumed Veronica, although nowhere in sight, had made it back from the wilds of downtown Burnaby.

"That's great, thank you." She hung up, looked for a moment like she was going to take his hand, and settled instead for lacing silver-tipped fingers together. "You okay?"

Interesting question. "Why wouldn't I be?" he asked, honestly curious.

"Duh, I don't know. Maybe because you found a corpse?"

Oh, yeah. He shrugged. "Compared to the corpses we usually get around here, it was pretty anticlimactic."

"What do you mean, anticlimactic?"

"No chew marks, no demon slime, no attempting to shove twenty feet of intestines made of condoms stuffed with spaghetti sauce back into the body . . ."

"Eww." Amy tossed a crumpled piece of paper at his head. "This was real, fuckwad!"

"Yeah. It was." But, sadly, still anticlimactic.

A moment of silence

Amy rubbed her forehead, smudging ink across pale skin. "I never even talked to her, you know? I feel like I should have."

"Why?"

"I don't know."

There was nothing Tony could say to that although he sort of understood.

"Anyway . . ." More rubbing and the ink smudge moved down one side of her nose. ". . . Adam came in while you were with the cops and he wanted me to tell you that Peter's going to shoot reaction shots this afternoon. Lee first. Mason's all . . ." She sketched a remarkably sarcastic set of air quotes. ". . . 'I'm too stressed to work,' but he hates to think Lee's getting attention he's not getting so . . ." She shrugged. "Peter's hoping Liz'll have found a close enough match for Nikki by tomorrow that he can pick up today's schedule."

"We're not ditching the ep?"

"Can't afford to." Tone and cadence added *the show must go on* as clearly as if she'd spoken the cliché out loud. "Besides, Catherine's only in two more scenes and she dies horribly in one of them."

Tony pulled out his sides and flipped through to the script. "Today's pages were all about her exposition in the office. That's going to need a good match."

"So she'll be distraught. With enough runny mascara no one'll ever notice as long as the hair and clothes match."

"The original Catherine's still *in* the clothes."

"Oh, yeah." Amy looked intrigued by the macabre thought. "Bet you CB has them back by tomorrow."

Skin crawling, Tony shook his head. "No bet. But will the new Catherine be willing to wear them?"

"Hello? We went to Liz."

Liz Terr's agency wasn't called Starving Actors R Us, but it should have been.

"Good po . . . What are you looking at?"

"You've got an audience."

Tony turned in time to see one of the writers jerk back behind the shelter of their workroom door.

"He was staring at you like you're suddenly a resource."

"For what?"

"Dead bodies. Police interaction. How should I know?"

"Those guys need to get a life."

"If they had a life, would they be working here, fleshing out the boss' holy writ? Giving form and function to the dark thoughts of Chester Bane?"

Glancing over at the open door to CB's office, Tony wondered at the risk Amy had just taken. Rumor had it that CB didn't care what was said about his size, his temper, or his fish, but the very short leash he allowed the writing staff was never to be acknowledged. Impossible to blame disaster on the writers if it was. "Are *you* okay?"

"I'm fine. CB Productions, please hold." She rested the phone against her cheek and sighed. "It's just . . . one minute she was alive and then she wasn't; you know?"

"Yeah." Although Tony had a terrible feeling it hadn't happened that quickly. "You'd better get back to work before this whole place falls apart."

"You, too."

He turned his radio back on as he crossed the office, but all he could hear was the kind of quiet chatter that said nothing had started happening yet. Hand outstretched to open the door that led to the halls of costumes and ultimately the soundstage, he paused, his attention caught by his shadow. The banks of flickering fluorescent lights lit him up in such a way that it looked as though he was going one way and his shadow was going another, gray and barely visible fingers stretching out across scuffed paint to turn the handle of the basement door.

The basement.

Where the FX workrooms were.

Where Arra Pelindrake was. She'd been on location last night and he'd seen her today just before he found Nikki's body. He'd been looking right at her when that voice had murmured Nikki's name in his ear jack.

Maybe his shadow knew something he didn't.

♣

The big room at the bottom of the basement stairs was remarkably well lit. Between the fluorescent lights and the scattered fill lights, the illumination was essentially constant. Floor, walls, and ceiling had been painted a pale gray. Doors were set flush and the various tools of Arra's trade were arranged neatly on gray metal shelves in such a way that they . . .

. . . that they threw no shadows.

One hand still on the banister, Tony glanced down at the floor, twisted and looked over his right shoulder, examined the nearest walls. *No* shadows. He had the strangest feeling that if he turned around, he'd see his shadow waiting for him at the top of the stairs, unable to come any farther.

After a moment's reflection, he decided not to look.

Arra's desk was in the far left corner of the room. He couldn't see her behind the bank of multiple monitors, but he could hear the shuff-click of her mouse.

What was he doing down here again?

He couldn't remember even speaking to Arra during all the months he'd been with CB Productions. Even when called in to do second unit work, he did his job and she did hers and long conversations over the state of the industry or what gunpowder makes the prettiest boom never happened. Was he actually going to walk up to her and say, *"I think you know what's going on."*

Considering he was halfway across the room and still moving, it certainly seemed as though he was going to say *something*.

She didn't acknowledge him in any way as he came around the monitors although she had to know he was there. Right hand on her mouse, left hand on the keyboard, her eyes remained locked on the half-dozen screens of various sizes and resolutions—every one of them showing a different game of solitaire. Two were the original game, two spider solitaire single suit, one spider double suit and one the highest level, all four suits.

She lost that one as he watched.

Dragging her mouse hand up through short gray hair, Arra sighed without turning. "I've been expecting you."

Not good. In Tony's experience, when slightly scary people said they were expecting you, things were about to go south in a big freakin' way.

"You have seen things," she continued, quickly placing three cards. "You are not certain what you have seen, but neither are you willing to disregard the evidence of your own eyes merely because it does not fit with a contemporary worldview. This leads me to believe that you have seen things on other occasions."

And worse. It was *always* bad news when people started talking without using contractions. Since she seemed to be waiting for a reply, Tony pointed toward the far left monitor, an old VGA with a distinct flicker. "You can move that black jack."

"I know. I'm just not sure I want to." Kicking away from the desk, she swung her chair around and stared up at him. "So, Tony Foster, tell me what you've seen."

She knows my name!

And closely following that thought, *Of course she knows your name, you idiot, you work together. Sort of. More or less. In a way.*

He could still walk away. Shrug and lie and leave. Not

get mixed up in whatever the hell was going on. If he answered her question, which wasn't so much a question as an expectation of an answer, he'd pass the point of no return. Putting it into words would make the whole thing real.

Screw it. It can't get any more real for Nikki Waugh!

"I've seen shadows acting like shadows don't. Don't act," he added when Arra's brows rose. He'd never noticed before that her eyes and her hair were the exact same shade of gray. "And that's not all. I've heard a voice on my radio."

"Isn't that what it's for?"

"Yeah and that'd be funnier if someone wasn't dead."

"You're right. I apologize." She looked down at the front of her *Darkest Night* sweatshirt and brushed a bit of imaginary fluff off Raymond Dark's profile.

Tony waited. He knew how to wait.

Eventually, she looked up again. "Why have you come to me?"

"Because you've seen things, too."

"I saw your friend last night. On location. He walks in shadow."

"Different shadows."

"True."

"You know what's happening."

"I have my suspicions, yes."

"You know what killed Nikki."

"If you believe this, why not go to the police?"

One moment the baby was alive and the next moment it was dead.

"Some things, the cops can't deal with." Before she could speak again, he held up one hand. "Look, this dialogue is heavier than even the guys upstairs would write; can we just cut to the chase and leave this crap to those who get paid to say it?"

Arra blinked, snorted, and grinned. "Why not."

"Good." He wiped damp palms on the front of his thighs. "What the hell is going on around here?"

"Do you have time for a story?"

"Tony!" He jerked as Adam's voice jabbed into his left ear with all the finesse of an ice pick. *"Where the hell are you? The cops left fifteen minutes ago!"*

Apparently not. "I'm sorry. I have to go."

"Wait. Give me your radio." When he hesitated, she frowned. "I don't care what he wants you for. This is more important."

He unholstered the unit and passed it over, carefully stepping back out of her personal space.

Arra looked distastefully at the ear jack and left it lying on her shoulder as she raised the microphone to her mouth. "Peter, it's Arra. I've stolen your PA for a while."

The director's voice sounded tinny but unimpressed. *"What for?"*

"Do you care?"

"No. Fine. Whatever. I've only got a show to shoot here. Do you want a kidney, too?"

"No, thank you. Tony will do."

As she handed the radio back to him, he realized two things. He shouldn't have been able to hear Peter's reply—not from a meter and a half away—and she hadn't changed the frequency. She shouldn't have been able to reach Peter on that frequency.

"So, it seems you have time for a story after all."

It seemed he did.

Three

"IT'S A FAIRLY long story." Arra nodded toward an old wooden chair nearly buried under a stack of paper—mostly technical diagrams and the mathematical notations necessary for pyrotechnics. "You'd better sit down."

The time it took him to clear the chair gave her a bit of a breathing space, a chance to collect her thoughts.

Tony Foster had seen the shadows. More importantly, he had *seen* her.

He wanted to know what he had seen.

Fair enough.

Curiosity had been the driving force behind the rise—and fall—of innumerable civilizations. It prodded creation and destruction equally. And once let off the leash, there was no catching it again until it was satiated. This left Arra only one option.

Well, actually, two options; although the odds of her taking the second were so infinitesimally small she felt it could safely be ignored.

As he settled himself, she leaned back, crossed her legs, and steepled her fingers. When those pale blue eyes—eyes with the rare ability to see the world as it was without the usual filters of disbelief and denial—fastened on her face, she began. "I came to this world from another seven years ago."

Fingers stopped worrying at a faded patch of denim. "From another world?"

"Yes." She waited, but he only indicated she should continue, his expression suggesting he'd merely asked for clarification in case he'd misheard. "My people were about to lose a war they had been fighting for many years. The enemy was at the gate and the gate had fallen and hope was dead. As it happened, hope had been *dying* for days—the last battalions of the army had been destroyed and nothing remained of our defenses save terrified men and women fighting individual losing battles against the shadows. I stood on the city wall, I watched the darkness advance, and I realized it was over. Certain I was about to die, I retreated to my workroom. It would only be a matter of moments before the enemy found me. In desperation, I tried something believed impossible. I tried to open a gate between my world and . . . and any world. My order had long insisted that the number of worlds were as infinite as the possibilities, but all previous attempts to break the barriers between them had failed.

"I don't know why I succeeded that day. Perhaps because failure would not result in a scholar's footnote but rather a shallow grave. That kind of certainty tends to give one . . ." She could still feel the panic clawing at her; still taste the bile in the back of her throat. A drop of sweat rolled down her side, pebbling a line of flesh as she fought to keep her voice from trembling. ". . . encouragement. Perhaps I succeeded because for the first time a world—this world—was close enough to reach. I don't know. I'll probably never know. The gate opened up into an empty cardboard box factory just as Chester Bane was investigating its potential as a home for his production company."

"So CB knows about . . . ?" A disapproving flick of pale fingers served to indicate the general situation.

"Not all of it. He hasn't seen the shadows."

"Why haven't you told him?"

Easy to hear the subtext—*Why haven't you told him so he could've done something?*

"There's nothing CB can do." This was the absolute truth. If not all of it.

The boy seemed to consider that for a moment, brows drawn in, a fold of his lower lip caught up between his teeth, then: "So, in this other world, you were a scientist?"

"A what?" Arra hurriedly revisited everything she'd just said and snorted. "No, in this other world, I was a wizard." She waited, but the comment about robes and pointy hats and Harry Potter never came. Upon reflection, hardly surprising. She very much doubted that Tony's friend the Nightwalker slept in a crypt on a layer of his native earth. Their relationship—whatever it was and she was certainly in no position to judge—would have dealt speedily with cliché or it wouldn't have lasted long enough to develop the bonds so obvious between them. "Our enemy was also a wizard. Naturally powerful, he had . . . It's difficult to describe exactly what he had and what he did without indulging in excessively purple description."

"Yeah, well, too late." From the sudden flush, it was obvious the comment had slipped out accidentally. Arra decided to ignore it—and not only because she had a strong suspicion it was accurate. The story was difficult to tell without falling into the cadences of home.

"Wizards, like most people, are neither good nor evil, they merely are. This wizard, the enemy wizard, made a conscious decision in his search for ever more power to turn to the darkness and, in return for that power, accept its mantle."

"The mantle of darkness?"

"Yes. It sounds like the title of a bad fantasy novel, doesn't it?"

A sudden grin. "I didn't want to say . . ."

"He had a name once, but he came to be called the Shadowlord."

The grin disappeared. "He's found the gate and he's followed you through."

Arra blinked. *That* was unexpected. "Has anyone ever accused you of leaping to unwarranted conclusions?"

"Unwarranted?" Tony's eyes narrowed and Arra found herself surprised by the intensity of his emotion. She had expected astonishment, wonder, even, in spite of all he'd seen, disbelief. Perhaps fear when he finally realized what her story meant. But rage? No. She'd forgotten that anger was the first response of the young; the gods knew she'd seen the evidence of that often enough in the past. His left hand raised, one finger flicked up into the air. "You opened a gate from another world where . . ." A second finger. ". . . you were fighting an evil wizard called the Shadowlord and, hey . . ." A third and final finger. ". . . the shadows around here are suddenly Twilight Zoned!" All three fingers folded into a fist. Not threatening, but definitely challenging. "I'm right, aren't I?"

Was there any point in denying it? Maintaining a carefully neutral expression—her emotional responses were hers alone—she picked up a pad of drawing paper and pencil. "Not entirely, no. He hasn't *found* the gate. It only remained open for a brief time after I arrived. He's used the research I left behind to reopen it. And the Shadowlord himself hasn't dared to cross over. He's merely sent shadows—minions—through the gate to see what he might find on the other side."

"Merely? There's no merely!" Anger pulled him up off the chair. "Nikki Waugh is dead!"

"And there's nothing you can do about it. Rage will not return the dead to life." The pencil moved over the center of the page with enough pressure to indent the lines into the paper. "Neither will sorrow." The lead broke and Arra laid the pencil down, exerting all her will to keep her hand from shaking. When she finally looked up, it was to see Tony staring down at her. "Neither will guilt," she continued as though there'd been no pencil, no pause. "Trust me that I know this, Tony Foster."

"All right. Fine. You know." He whirled around, walked three steps away, whirled again, and walked two steps back, hands opening and closing by his sides. "What are you going to do to stop it from happening again?"

Ah, yes, the sixty-four thousand dollar question, unadjusted for inflation. "There's nothing I can do."

"Why the fuck not? You're a *wizard*!"

He said the word like it was an answer. Or a weapon. Stretching out an arm, she scooped a square art eraser up out of the clutter in her desk drawer. "Weren't you listening? We lost. The Shadowlord cannot be defeated. Now he has tasted this world. The next shadow he sends will have more purpose." The pattern she'd been doodling began to disappear. "It will find a host and use that host to gather specific information."

"A host? What does that mean?"

"Exactly what it sounds like. The shadows are his spies, his advance scouts. They're simple creations at first, but he uses the information they bring him to make each successive sending more complex. Nikki Waugh's death will allow him to tailor a very complex shadow indeed."

Tony's brow furrowed. "He can make a shadow that can take over a person?"

"Yes."

"A person here?"

"Yes. Here is where the gate is and these shadows—unlike the simpler versions—can't travel far."

"Close the gate permanently."

"Research seems to indicate that the gate can only be manipulated from the originating world."

"Research seems to indicate?" he repeated incredulously.

Fair enough, that *had* sounded a bit pompous. "It was

one of the few things my order discovered that they were certain of," she clarified.

"All right. Fine. If you can't close the gate, then stop the shadow!"

Arra sighed. She lifted her head, met his gaze squarely, and, although it would weaken what she hoped to accomplish here, lied. "I can't."

"You can't?"

"The Shadowlord was not affected by anything we threw at him." And back to the truth. Such a small lie, like a single dropped stitch, could hopefully be ignored. Not that hope was something she had in great supply of late. The important thing was that all of Tony Foster's questions be answered. That his curiosity be satisfied.

"I have to do something."

"I'm getting that impression." The pencil lines were gone and nothing remained on the paper but a little pile of eraser leavings, dark with lifted graphite.

"I'm *going* to do something!" Pivoting on one rubber heel, he stomped back toward the stairs—young, defiant, and dead sooner rather than later if he interfered.

At least that was the reason she gave herself as she carefully lifted the sketch pad toward her mouth. And paused.

There was always the chance that his friend, the Nightwalker, would notice her work. Although it was coming to an end, she liked the life she'd built for herself here in this new world and the last thing she wanted was to be noticed by those who lived in Mystery.

Well, actually not the *last* thing she wanted . . .

One step from the top of the basement stairs, as his hand reached out for the door handle, Arra murmured, "Forget," and blew the top sheet of paper clean.

◆

Tony stood by the basement door and realized he felt a lot better about things. The questions that had been gnawing at him seemed to have lost their teeth. Nikki

Waugh was still dead and that truly sucked, but there was nothing he could do to bring her back so maybe, just maybe, he should let her go.

"Hey!"

He let Amy's beckoning finger pull him across the office.

"What were you doing downstairs?"

"Downstairs?"

She rolled her eyes. "In the basement. The dungeon. The wizard's workshop."

"Wizard?" Something waved from the edge of memory; gone when he tried to work out exactly what it was.

"Duh. CB's own special effects wizard. Arra. Short old broad who blows things up." Artificially dark brows drew in. "You okay?"

"Yeah. Sure. I'm . . ."

The shrill demand of the phone cut him off. "Don't go anywhere," Amy ordered as she lifted the receiver. "We're not done. CB Productions." Her voice dropped nearly an octave. "Where the hell are you? It *does* matter, Gerald, because you were supposed to deliver that replacement coffin pillow today!"

Shaking his head, Tony propped a hip on her desk. Welcome to the macabre world of vampire television.

"Hey, Tony!"

He jumped as Adam's voice blared from his ear jack and bounced around his skull a couple of times. Cheeks flushed—he hadn't overreacted like that since his first week on the job—he reached for his radio muttering, "The volume control on this thing is totally fucked," just in case Amy or anyone else in the office had seen. Then, dropping his mouth to the microphone: "Go ahead, Adam."

"If Lee's up to it, we're ready for him on the set."

Tony glanced at his watch. Nikki's body had been out of the building for just over an hour. An hour? That seemed . . .

"Tony! Thumb out of your ass, man!"

"Yeah. Sorry. Uh, what if Lee's not up to it?"

The 1AD snorted. *"Peter says you're to get him up to it but I'm not touching that. Just do what you can to get him back out here. Losing a day won't bring Nikki back."*

"The show must go on?"

"Yeah, like I haven't heard that a hundred times in the last hour. Hustle up, we're burning money."

Death came, death went, and it was amazing how fast everything got back to normal. He waved a hand in front of Amy's face and pointed toward the exit.

She nodded. "No, we don't need it immediately, but that's not the point . . ."

Shadow following, Tony headed for the dressing rooms.

◆

For all his bulk, Chester Bane knew how to remain unnoticed. If being Chester Bane meant bluster, then a lack of bluster meant a lack of Chester Bane. He stood silently just inside his open door and watched the door leading out of the production office swing closed.

Tony Foster had been in the basement.

◆

The one good thing about finding a dead body was that the rest of the day, no matter how mired in suckage, could only get better. That was the theory anyway, but by quitting time, Tony figured no one could prove it by him. He had to talk to someone about this.

Someone.

Yeah. Right. There was only one person he *could* talk to about this.

Although he hadn't lived at the condo for almost eighteen months, he still had his keys. He'd tried to give them back, to cut the final tie but Henry, his eyes dark, had refused to take them.

"Many people have keys to their friends' apartments."

"Well, yeah, but you're . . ."

"Your friend. Whatever else I may have been, whatever else I am, I will always be your friend."

"That's uh . . ."

"Yeah, I know. Way over the top."

The place was a little neater without him, but nothing else had changed since he'd left. "Henry?"

"Bedroom."

Henry slept in the smallest of the three bedrooms, the easiest one to close off with painted plywood and heavy curtains against the day. He wasn't there now, so Tony continued down the hall. Henry *slept* in the smallest bedroom but he kept his clothes in the walk-in closet attached to the master suite. For a dead guy, Henry Fitzroy had a lot of clothes.

He paused in the doorway and watched the vampire preen in front of the mirror. Popular culture had gotten a few minor details wrong. Vampires had reflections and, if Henry was any indication, they spent a significant slice of eternity checking them out. "The pants are great, but strawberry blonds can't wear that shade of red. The shirt doesn't work."

"You're sure?"

"Trust me. I'm gay."

"You have a gold ring through your eyebrow."

"And it clashes with nothing."

"You're wearing plaid flannel."

"I'm getting in touch with my inner lesbian." Tony pointed toward the discarded clothing on the bed. "Try the blue."

Henry stripped off the shirt, yanked a cream-colored sweater off the pile, and dragged it over his head.

"Or not." Grinning, Tony backed away from the door so Henry could leave. Feeling better than he had in hours, he fell into step beside the shorter man. Feeling grounded. Which said something about the entertainment industry when he turned to a vampire for grounding. Or maybe it just said something about him.

"You sounded upset when you called."

And the ground disappeared again. Once the show had stopped going on, once he was on his way home from the studio, he hadn't been able to stop thinking about what had happened. He'd found himself thumbing in Henry's number before he came to a conscious decision to pull out his phone.

"Someone died at work today."

Henry paused at the end of the hall, turning to look at him. "The stuntman?"

What stuntman? It took Tony a moment to remember that Henry had been at the second unit shoot. "Daniel? No, those guys are hard to kill; knock them down and they just bounce back. Daniel's fine. It was the victim of the week. On the show," he added hurriedly as Henry's eyes widened. "There's always a body; I mean there has to be, right? The show's about a vampire detective. But this was a real body." He swallowed although his mouth had gone so dry it didn't help. "I sort of found it."

"Sort of?"

"Mason Reed was with me. He yanked open her dressing room door and she fell out." One hand dragged back through his hair. "Dead."

Cool fingers on his elbow, Henry steered him over to the green leather sofa and gently pushed him into a sitting position before dropping down next to him. "You okay?"

"Yeah . . ."

"But you don't think you should be."

"It's not that she's dead. That's bad, but it's not what's got me so . . . I don't know, freaked, I guess." Resting his forearms on his thighs, hands dangling, Tony laced and unlaced his fingers, not really seeing the patterns they made. Trying not to see Nikki's face. "Just for a moment, before her head hit the floor, she looked terrified. You've seen a lot of bodies, Henry. Why would she look terrified? Never mind, don't answer that. Obviously something frightened her. But she was alone in the dressing room. I mean, of course she was alone; those things are so small most actors can barely fit their egos in with them, but she was alone . . ."

"I've left a lot of people alone in locked rooms."

"Well, it wasn't you, so you're saying . . ." Twisting around, he raised a hand as Henry opened his mouth to reply. "Oh, don't give me that fucking 'more things in heaven and Earth' quote. You're saying it was something like you. Something not of this world . . ." Not of this world. Not *this* world. Fuck! He almost had it.

"Tony?"

"I feel like I've put down the last bit of toast and now I can't find it. I know I haven't eaten it, but it's gone and that unfinished feeling is driving me bugfuck!" Unable to remain still, he leaped to his feet and walked over to the window. He laid one hand against the glass and stared out at the lights of Vancouver. "She shouldn't be dead."

"People die, Tony. They die for a lot of reasons. Sometimes, it seems like they die for no reason at all."

The glass began to warm under his palm. "And I should just accept that?"

"Just accept death? I think you're asking the wrong person."

"I think I'm asking the only person I have a hope in hell of getting an actual answer from." When he turned, Henry was less than an arm's length away. He hadn't heard him move. "I don't need more platitudes, Henry."

"All right. What do you need?"

"I need . . . I need . . . Damnit!" He tried to turn again, but an unbreakable grip on his shoulder held him in place.

"What do you need, Tony?"

He fought for a moment against relinquishing control then surrendered and sank into the dark, familiar gaze. "I need to remember."

"Remember what?"

Impossible not to answer. His mouth moved. He wondered what he was going to say. "Remember what I've forgotten."

The dark eyes crinkled at the corners as Henry smiled. "Well, that's a place to start."

♦

In a business where twelve-hour days were the norm and seventeen not unheard of, Chester Bane often stayed late at the office. His third wife had divorced him because of it. He'd enjoyed her company, but he'd preferred to walk around the soundstage, around the world he'd created, without the distraction of actors and crew. Over the years, security and cleaning staff both had learned to avoid him.

Tonight, fish fed, he walked across the dark production office and stood outside the basement door. His set PA had been down in the basement the day after he'd distinguished himself at a second unit shoot.

The day after something had gone wrong at a second unit shoot.

The day a young actress had died, the body found by that same set PA.

Individually, the first was unusual, the second unexpected, and the third a tragedy. Together, they added up to something. CB didn't believe in coincidence.

In the seven years since buying the old box factory, he'd seldom gone down to the basement. He could have. Nothing stopped him. He just hadn't. Arra Pelindrake provided him with inexpensive special effects and he in turn provided her with a way to exist in this new world. They never spoke of how the air had torn above his head and she had dropped through the rent stinking of blood and smoke. They never spoke of flames that didn't burn and squibs that used no gunpowder. They never spoke of what she did or how she did it as long as his shows came in on budget. In under budget, even better.

That was the sum total of their relationship.

He neither knew nor cared if she spoke of him outside the studio although he expected she did. Everyone bitched about their boss.

He was unable to speak of her. His choice. He wasn't fool enough to believe that he'd never want to share so unbelievable a story and rather than lose her—and what she could do for him—he'd asked her to ensure his mouth stayed shut. He remembered everything and could put the necessary spin on her activities vis-à-vis the outside world but he was incapable of discussing what she was or where she'd come from.

At the time, it had seemed like the smart thing to do in order to protect his investment. All of a sudden, he wasn't so sure.

His hand closed around the door handle.

Something was going on. Something attempting to make an end run around his control.

The stairs made no noise as he descended into the gray on gray of the lower level. He noted models and masks as he crossed to the desk, adding them to the mental inventory he kept of his possessions. Although the computer had been powered down, the ready lights on both monitors and speakers glowed green. He barely resisted turning them off. Wasted power meant wasted money.

There were modern fetishes scattered all over the desk. Little plastic Teletubbies. An octopus with only six arms. A red cloth frog exuding cinnamon and dust about equally mixed.

He had no idea what he was looking for and suddenly felt ridiculous.

A startled squeak from the stairs spun him around and he glared silently at the cleaning lady standing frozen in place about a third of the way down. The CB in CB Productions stood for Chester Bane and he had every right to be where he was. When it became clear she was not going to move without his permission, he beckoned her forward and, as she stepped off the last tread, he growled, "Do your job and go."

Arms folded, he watched her scuttle across to the desk and scoop up the garbage pail. As she tipped it up into the green plastic bag she carried, he frowned.

"Hold it!"

She froze again; a tiny statue in a green duster.

He scooped half a dozen sheets of paper out of the trash one-handed. "These are not garbage. The writing staff can use the backs for notes."

She nodded although it was clear she had no idea what she was agreeing with.

"Carry on."

For her age, she moved remarkably quickly back up the stairs. CB followed considerably more slowly, the knees that ended his football career protesting painfully as they hauled his weight back up to the first floor. He flicked off the basement lights, recrossed the production office, and paused at the door to the bull pen. No. He'd give the paper to the writers in the morning. They'd likely need it explained.

Back in his own office he tossed the papers on the desk.

Paused.

Picked up the top sheet. Thick, slightly rough. Drawing paper. Blank on both sides. Wasteful. Perhaps it was time to have a word with . . .

Flicking on the desk lamp, he aimed the circle of light directly at the sheet of paper. Faint gray lines ghosted across the page. There. And then gone. Although under the caress of a fingertip, the imprint of a pattern remained.

Something was *definitely* going on.

♦

"It's no use." Henry sat back in his chair, allowing Tony to look away and break the contact between them. "There's definitely something blocking the memories."

"Shock?"

"Perhaps. I've seen shock block memories in the

past and for all your experience with the . . . unusual, you've never had the corpse of a friend drop at your feet before."

Tony sighed. "She wasn't exactly a friend."

"And you feel guilty about that now she's dead?"

"No. Maybe." He picked at the faded patch of denim on one thigh. "I don't know. Henry, what is it if it *isn't* shock?"

"I have no idea."

"Educated guess?"

Prince of Darkness safely tucked away, Henry smiled and stood, dragging his chair back to its usual place at the dining room table. "You must believe I had an interesting education, Tony."

"Well, yeah. Interesting experiences anyway."

"True enough. But, in this instance, none of them seem to apply."

Tony didn't entirely believe that, but since he had nothing to back up an accusation except that Henry was spending just a little too much time fiddling with the chair, he dropped his gaze to his watch before his face gave the whole thing away. The numbers took a moment to sink in, but when they did he stood. "Oh, crap. It's almost 3:00. No wonder I'm feeling so punchy. I've got to get going."

"Why not stay here?"

"Why *not?*"

Henry ignored him. "There's an extra bed and a change of clothes and we're not a lot farther from Burnaby than your apartment. What time do you have to be at work tomorrow?"

"Uh . . . unit call's at 9:30."

"An early enough call given that it's nearly 3:00."

What he could see of Henry's expression showed nothing more than an almost neutral concern. They were long over and he'd ended it. They were friends. Friends had the keys to friends' apartments. Friends offered crash space. "I guess it wouldn't hurt to stay."

"Good."

"Will you be . . ." Funny how a distance of eighteen months suddenly made what had once been a perfectly normal question sound like horror movie dialogue. ". . . going out to Hunt?"

"No." One hand rose to tug at the edge of the cream-colored sweater. "It's too late."

Suddenly the earlier indecision over which shirt to wear made sense. Tony felt his cheeks flush. Knew Henry was aware of the sudden rush of blood and that only made it worse. "You were on your way out."

"Yes."

"You were going to feed."

A graceful nod in acknowledgment. "I'll call her to-morrow and explain."

"I'm sorry . . ."

"Weighing a new acquaintance against the needs of an old friend was no choice at all, Tony."

"I'm not your responsibility."

One red-gold eyebrow rose. "I know."

"I feel bad about you not feeding."

"I can wait until tomorrow night."

You don't have to. He could feel the words waiting to be said and was fairly certain Henry could as well. And if not, he *knew* Henry could hear his pulse pounding. Trouble was, he couldn't think of a way to say them that wouldn't make him sound like a desperate hero-ine in a bad romance novel. Not that he read bad romance novels or anything. It was just something that he thought a desperate heroine would say because it had been eighteen months, for fuck's sake, and Henry saw him now as a person, an individual, and surely that meant they could—all right, *he* could—act like an adult and not fall back into need at the feel of teeth through skin.

The moment lengthened, stretched, and passed.

Henry smiled. "Good night, Tony."

"Yeah . . ."

◆

"It's a great piece of music, Zev, pretty damned near perfect, but you know CB won't pay much for it."

"Not a problem. It's a local band; they're desperate for publicity, and I can get the rights for little more than a screen credit." The music director glanced up and smiled as Tony came across the office. By the time he reached Amy's desk, Zev's smile had slipped slightly. "Are you all right? You look . . . tired."

"Just didn't get much sleep last night. All I have to do is hang on until lunch, then I can catch some zees on the couch in Raymond Dark's office."

"Catch some zees?" Amy snorted. She slid the headphones off and passed them back to Zev. "Do people actually say that?"

He shrugged. "Apparently."

Before Tony could get up enough energy to wave a finger at the two of them, the door to CB's office opened and Barb emerged looking pale.

"Your turn, babe," the company's financial officer muttered to Zev as she passed the desk. "Word of warning, if you want him to spend money, he's in a mood. Play this wrong and you'll end up humming the score yourself."

Amy raised a hand as Barb disappeared into her office. "I can help. I used to play the kazoo!"

"Everyone used to play the kazoo."

"In a marching band?"

"Okay, that's different."

"Sero!"

The three of them winced in unison.

"Our master's voice," Amy whispered dramatically. "Good luck. Vaya con dios."

"Tracht gut vet zain gut."

"What does that mean?"

"Think good and it will be good."

"SERO!"

"Yeah, you just keep thinkin', Butch. In this particular situation, I'd push the *free* in free band." Amy watched Zev until the door closed behind him then turned her attention to Tony. "He's right. You look like crap. Hot date?"

He sighed. "Weight of the world. Wasn't your hair pink yesterday?"

"Fuchsia. And that was then. What do you want?"

"Tina sent me in to see if they . . ." A nod toward the closed bull pen door. ". . . have spit out something like the final rewrite of next week's script."

"You're in luck." She lifted a file folder off the stack of assorted papers on the floor beside her desk and handed it over. "Hot off the press. I'd have sent it in with Veronica, but she's dropping a deposit for our next location shoot off at the city manager's office. And then getting coffee."

"What's wrong with the pot in the kitchen?"

"The writers emptied it again. What do you mean, 'weight of the world'?"

"Things on my mind."

"Like?"

"I don't remember."

"You need more B vitamins."

"I need . . ." He stopped, ran a hand up through his hair, and exhaled explosively. "I need to get back on set."

Her eyes narrowed. "Before something happens."

"What?"

"That's the part you didn't say. Before something happens. What's going to happen?"

"Answer the phone."

"It's not . . ." The ring cut her off. "How did you . . . ?"

Tony shrugged, turned, and headed out of the office, the familiar "CB Productions" sounding behind him. A no brainer on the phone ringing since it rang every thirty seconds eight to ten hours a day.

Before something happens.

He had no fucking idea what Amy was talking about. All that dye was obviously affecting higher brain functions.

The red light went off as he passed the women's washroom and the sound of flushing followed him out onto the soundstage. The living room set for the whatever-the-hell-they-decided-to-call-it estate looked incredible even though it was the same old furniture from Raymond Dark's living room, jazzed up with a couple of cushions, a blue-and-yellow sheet, and some duct tape. One of the electricians was already sound asleep on the couch. Had Peter called lunch? Tony checked his watch, the movement dumping papers out of the file and all over the floor.

"Son of a fucking bitch."

It had just been that kind of a day. Nothing had gone right from the moment he'd woken up in Henry's condo. Between the whole déjà vu of that and the forgotten toast problem with his memory, he hadn't been able to concentrate on anything. Fortunately, they were killing Catherine this morning and once Nikki's replacement had been safely delivered to the set, he didn't have a lot to do.

Dropping to his knees, he started gathering up the papers.

One of them had slid almost to the edge of the fake hardwood floor. He stretched out his hand and froze as a line of shadow crossed the piece of paper and was gone. His heart started beating again as he realized the sleeping electrician's boot had moved for a moment into the light. Boot shadow. That was all.

Given the variety of lights in play, the soundstage was filled with unexpected shadows.

Tony had no idea why the thought made him feel like running.

From the corner of one eye, he caught sight of another shadow moving past him, moving out toward the offices. He whirled around too fast for balance and nearly fell. The shadow was attached to a sound tech. Probably heading in to jiggle the toilet handle.

This is insane.

His fingers closed around the last piece of paper and he refused to turn as a second shadow slipped along the concrete heading for the door. A darker shadow. Its edges more defined.

Hurrying to catch up as the door whispered closed.

A quiet click as it latched.

There, and he hadn't looked.

Clutching the file, he stood, took half a dozen steps toward the set, and realized he'd only heard one set of footsteps go by. The sound tech.

The second shadow had been moving in total silence.

Something . . .

Peter's voice jerked him away from the thought. "That's it for now, people. Lunch!"

Thank God. He really needed to get some more sleep.

Four

THE BODY lay crumpled against the side of the building, a smear of blood against the bricks tracing its trajectory toward the ground. Shadows hid most of the details, but an outstretched arm placed one pale hand, like a crumpled flower, out into a spill of light.

"An inch more to your left."

The hand moved.

Tina consulted the photograph she'd taken before lunch, cocked her head to check the body from another angle, and finally straightened out of her crouch. "That's got it."

"Good." Adam took the picture from her as she passed and shoved it into the continuity file on his clipboard. "Let's freshen up the blood and I want a warm body in there to check Lee's light levels. Mouse . . ."

The camera operator looked down from his rig. "What?"

"You're six one, right?"

"Six two. And I'm twice his size horizontally. And I'm working."

"Fine. Dalal, hit Lee's marks beside the body."

Looking like he was wishing he'd stayed at his work-table, the prop man shook his head. "I'm five eleven."

"So think tall. You're not doing anything, get over there. Tony! Go get Lee!"

As Dalal reluctantly crossed the set, Tony headed off

the soundstage. Technically, the part of the warm body should have been played by a stand-in, and whether or not they had one on set was generally a fairly good indication of the company's current financial standing. Given the hurry-up-and-wait nature of shooting television, there were always people standing around with nothing to do until someone else did their job. Given the people CB tended to hire, no one was likely to report him for screwing with union rules. Those who might didn't last long.

So far, Tony had managed to stay on the move and out from under the lights. The thought of being in front of the camera, even without the camera actually being on, made him sweat.

"Lee?" He took a deep breath, reminded himself that geeky was not a good look, and rapped on the dressing room door. "They're ready for you."

The door opened almost before he moved his hand away. Frowning, Lee peered out at him as though he wasn't entirely certain he understood what he was seeing. "For me?"

"Yeah. Scene 22B." The room behind the actor seemed unusually dark. "You discover the body."

"The body?"

"Catherine's body." With the wig and the blood—and according to bar talk *Darkest Night* used more blood than any other program currently shooting in the Vancouver area— fans of the show would never know it wasn't Nikki.

Stepping back, Tony indicated that Lee should precede him down the hall. He'd learned early on that expecting actors to follow was like expecting cats to follow and after the whole "quickie in the broom closet" incident with Mason and the previous wardrobe assistant, he never let them out of his sight. When Lee continued to merely stand and stare, he stepped forward again, suddenly concerned. "Hey, are you all right?"

"I'm fine."

Tony wasn't so sure. "You look . . ."

"I'm fine." Lee gave himself a little shake and slowly moved out into the hall. It seemed that rather a lot of the shadows moved with him. The dressing room visibly lightened as he left.

And that's just wrong. Tony stood where he was for a moment, eyes narrowed. *Not to mention, well, wrong!* He'd have asked himself if he were imagining things except that he had no idea what he thought he might be imagining. Finally, when it became obvious that nothing was out of place, he hurried after Lee, careful not to step on the actor's shadow.

♥

"Oh, for Christ's sake, it's one goddamned line and I've already said it seventeen fucking times!"

The crew suddenly became very busy, looking anywhere but at Lee and Peter.

"It's not about your performance, Lee," the director said calmly, "it's a technical glitch. There's a shadow . . ."

"So get rid of it!"

"That's what we've been trying to do." Peter's genial voice picked up an edge. "We've been trying to do it all afternoon." As one, they turned toward the lighting crew clustered around the director of photography, who continued describing his latest concept in an exasperated mix of English and French.

Although over the course of the afternoon the lighting layout had practically been rebuilt, the shadow continued to reappear in take after take. Scene 22B, take one: it had covered Lee entirely as he'd leaned forward and flipped over the body. Scene 22B, take seventeen: it was a dark bar across his eyes.

Watching from the sidelines, Tony found himself wondering where the shadow was going. And then wondering when he'd started thinking in cheap horror clichés. Actually, he knew the answer to the second question: right after he'd met Henry.

"Get rid of it in post!" Lee snapped. "And why is it so fucking cold in here?" Usually someone who took the inevitable technical delays of television in stride, his temper had frayed a little more with every take. Hartley Skenski, the boom operator, had tried to make book on whether or not he'd stomp off the set before they were finished, but no one had taken him up on it.

"We'll do it just once more. I promise," Peter added as Lee's lip curled. "If it's still there, I'll let the guys in post deal with it." He opened his mouth and closed it again, clearly deciding to leave the temperature question unanswered.

Green eyes glittered during a long pause. "One more."

While another five hundred milliliters of blood were applied to the latex gash in the actress' throat, Lee dropped back onto one knee.

Tony moved quietly around behind the video village and checked out the monitor showing the close-up of the actor's face. The bar of shadow was still in place. He stepped hurriedly out of the DP's way and winced as Sorge began to swear.

The shadow quivered.

And disappeared.

The torrent of French profanity stopped between one word and the next. "Go now."

Peter dropped into his chair and jammed on his headphones. "Quiet!"

No need for anyone to repeat. The soundstage was so quiet, Tony reminded himself to breathe as he crossed his fingers.

"Roll cameras! Slate!"

"Scene 22B, take 18!"

Lee didn't wait for *action*. Reaching down, he grabbed the corpse's shoulder, flipped her over onto her back, and snarled, "Well, it looks like Raymond's secret is safe."

"Cut! Print."

"It looked good," Sorge murmured.

"It sounded like shit," Peter snapped. "But we can fix that in post. Tina, I want the sound from take one."

"Sound from one, got it." As she noted it on her lined script, everyone else turned to watch Lee stomp off the set.

Peter pulled off his headphones as the corpse sat up and rubbed her shoulder. The crew moved about their usual post-print routine strangely subdued, as though they weren't entirely certain how to react. "I don't need a second prima donna around here," the director sighed as the distant sound of a slamming door marked Lee's passage from the soundstage.

"Maybe he's still upset about the body. The *real* body," Tony elaborated as everyone now turned to look at him. "You know . . ." He added a shrug to the explanation. ". . . Nikki."

After a long moment, during which Tony mentally rewrote his résumé, Peter sighed again and gestured wearily in Lee's wake. "Go make sure he's all right."

"I told CB we should have taken at least one day off," he added as Tony hurried away.

Sorge snorted, the sound remarkably French. "And CB said the show must go on?"

"No, he told me to get the fuck out of his office."

♥

Lee's dressing room door was open when Tony reached it. He paused, wiped sweaty hands against his thighs, and leaned forward just enough to see inside. Still in costume, Lee stood in the center of the room, slowly turning in place. It looked almost as though he was seeing the room for the first time.

"Uh, Lee?"

He continued turning until he faced the door, then stopped and frowned.

Tony had no idea why he was suddenly thinking of Arnold Schwarzenegger in *The Terminator*. "Are you okay?"

"Yes."

And *The Terminator* thing fell into place. Lee was staring just slightly beyond him, like he was accessing an internal filing system. "Can I, uh, get you anything?"

Focus snapped onto his face and a long finger beckoned Tony forward. "Come in and close the door."

"The door?"

He'd never seen Lee smile like that before. It was almost . . . mocking. "Yes. The door. Come into the room and close it behind you."

Unable to think of a reason why he shouldn't, and not sure he wanted to, Tony did as he was told.

"Turn off your radio."

"But . . ."

"Do it. I don't want to be interrupted."

While you're doing what? Tony wondered as his left hand dropped to the holster on his belt. But Peter had sent him. He was supposed to be here.

"I want you to tell me things." The actor's voice stroked over him like wet velvet. "In return, I will give you what you desire." The requisite vampire-show leather coat slipped off broad shoulders and hit the floor. The burgundy shirt followed a heartbeat later.

Half a dozen heartbeats actually, given how quickly Tony's heart had started beating. The total weirdness of the situation helped him keep a partial lid on his physical reaction although he was definitely reacting. A dead man would react to a half naked Lee Nicholas and—given a specific dead man—Tony knew *that* for a fact.

As Lee reached for him, he astounded himself by stepping back.

This was rapidly becoming everything he'd ever dreamed of and a bad soap opera scenario pretty much simultaneously.

No! Another step and his shoulder blades were against the door. This was wrong! It was . . .

It was . . .

He slammed his head back against the door, almost had it, and swore as the memory slipped away.

♥

CB stared down at the sheet of drawing paper on his desk. The lines pressed into the surface had gone gray again, just for an instant. He frowned. He didn't like mysteries and he had already wasted far too much time on this one.

Still frowning, he opened his desk drawer and pulled out a pencil.

♥

Palm flat against the cool skin of Lee's chest, Tony struggled to ignore the little voice in his head trying to convince him to shut the fuck up and enjoy the ride. "Lee, this is, uh . . ."

"What you want. I give you what you want; you give me what I want. There are other ways I could gain the information, but since you're here . . ." His voice trailed off as his hand connected with Tony's crotch.

"No, you don't WANT to be doing THIS . . . Fuck! Stop doING that!"

"No."

"Look, I don't want to hurt you." The words emerged kind of jumbled together, but he managed to sound like he meant the threat.

Again, a smile that didn't look like it belonged on Lee's face. "Try."

Damn. Four years on the streets, four years with Henry; he could take care of himself if he had to. A little more difficult when he really didn't want to hurt the guy feeling him up, but still . . . Tony tensed, and froze. There was something wrong with Lee's shadow. There was something wrong with shadows in general.

"*. . . nothing remained of our defenses save terrified men and women fighting individual losing battles against the shadows.*"

♥

CB worked carefully, methodically, quickly; stroking a line of graphite along the imprinted pattern.

♥

"The Shadowlord cannot be defeated. Now he has tasted this world. The next shadow he sends will have more purpose."

Tony jerked back against the door, partially because of the sudden rush of memory. Partially because of what Lee was doing. Wondering how a guy got selected for sainthood, he twisted away and gasped, "You're a minion of the Shadowlord!"

Which sounded so incredibly stupid, he regretted the words the moment they left his mouth.

Lee stared at him for a long moment, blinked once, and started to laugh. "I'm a what?"

Oh, crap. Now he was going to have to repeat it because there really wasn't any variation on this particular theme. "You're a minion of the Shadowlord."

"That's what I thought you said." Scooping his shirt up off the floor, Lee shrugged into it, still chuckling. "You know, you're a very weird guy."

Tony merely pointed.

Lee's shadow appeared to be investigating a pile of shadow magazines.

It was a cheesy effect on screen and unexpectedly terrifying in real life.

The actor sighed, reached out, and slapped Tony lightly on one cheek. "Who's going to believe you? You're nobody. I'm a star."

Tony cleared his throat. "You're a costar."

The second slap was considerably harder and almost seemed to have more of Lee in it than shadow. "Fuck you."

"You're not leaving this room."

"Is this supposed to be where I strike a dramatic pose and tell you that you can't stop me?" Lee leaned closer, his position a parody of his earlier seduction. "Guess what? You can't."

And he couldn't.

The shadow dropped the magazine and swept across the room, holding him against the wall. Tony couldn't move, he couldn't speak, and most importantly, he couldn't breathe. It was like being trapped under a pliable sheet of cold charcoal-gray rubber that covered him from head to foot like a second skin, curving to fit up each nostril and into his mouth. Obscenely intimate.

As the door closed behind the thing controlling Lee's body, the shadow flexed, flopped away from him, and slipped through the final millimeter of open space.

Bent over, sucking his lungs full of stale, makeup redolent, slightly moldy, but glorious air, Tony spent a moment or two concentrating on breathing before straightening and staggering toward the door.

He had to stop Lee before he left the building.

He should never have let him leave the dressing room.

He should never have gone *into* the dressing room.

I should have figured something was up when the straight guy started coming on to me.

And hard on the heels of that thought, came a second.

If that thing's in Lee's head, then Lee knows how I ... what I ... want.

And a third.

This just keeps getting better ...

♥

Completely redrawn, the pattern appeared to be a random squiggle. A pointless collection of curves. Nothing had happened when the final line had been retraced. The pencil set aside, a hand laid flat on each side of the paper, CB stared down at the nondesign and wondered exactly what he thought *would* happen.

How could he recognize the answers when he didn't know the questions?

"CB?" Rachel's voice over the intercom broke into

his fruitless speculation. "Mark Asquith from the network is here."

He swept the paper into the trash. "Send him in."

♥

Tony pounded out into the middle of the production office and realized his quarry was nowhere in sight. Had he guessed wrong? Had the thing gone through the soundstage instead? He took the half-dozen extra steps to Amy's desk. "Have you seen Lee?"

"Yeah. He's gone."

"What do you mean gone?"

"I mean, gone. As in not here." She snorted derisively. "As in was an ass to Zev and strutted out. As in Elvis has left the building. As in . . ."

"I get it." Gone. But maybe not too far gone. "He didn't take his helmet."

Amy shrugged. " 'Cause he didn't go for a ride on his motorcycle. He walked out the front door and grabbed the network guy's cab."

"Oh that's just fucking great." That thing had Lee's wallet, Lee's credit cards; if it got to the airport, it could go anywhere in the world.

"You got a message for him from Peter?" Amy picked up the phone before he could answer. "No problem. I'll just call his cell."

"That's not . . ." He frowned. "Do you hear a phone ringing?"

She glanced down at the flashing light and back up at Tony as the office line rang again. "Duh."

"No, in the distance." He turned slowly, trying to make it out. "It's in the dressing room." The sound could have been coming from any one of half a dozen small rooms behind the thin interior walls, but Lee's phone had been in the charger on the coffee table. "He didn't take it with him."

"An actor without a phone." Heavily penciled eyebrows rose dramatically. "Isn't that against some kind of . . ."

"Amy!" Rachel's bellow cut her off. "Would you answer that damned thing, I'm on another line!"

As the familiar "CB Productions" sounded behind him, Tony ran for the basement stairs. Arra. The wizard. She'd know how to stop him. It. How to stop the shadow and get Lee back.

Except that Arra wasn't in the basement.

Tony stared at the empty chair, at the bank of monitors, and fought a sudden urge to smash something. The bitch had screwed with his memories. Made him forget. Made him forget the shadows, and the Shadowlord, and the danger they were all in.

He'd told her he was going to do something and she'd stopped him.

Maybe even stopped him from protecting Lee.

Heart pounding, he took the stairs back up to the production office three at a time, slamming the door behind him hard enough to pull curious glances from the surrounding smaller offices. Even Zev reemerged from post, a set of headphones slung around his neck like a stethoscope.

♥

"If you'll excuse me a moment." As his visitor nodded a confused assent, CB surged to his feet and walked over to his open door. He considered himself to be a lenient employer, but petty displays of unnecessary noise were among the few things he refused to put up with. If it was one of the writers overreacting to script changes again, he would not be pleased.

He reached the doorway in time to see Tony Foster race across the production office.

♥

"Where's Arra?"

Amy slammed a staple through a set of sides and frowned up at him. "What?"

"Arra!"

"I'm not deaf, dipwad. She's with Daniel, checking out cliffs for a new car-blows-up-in-midair-releases-a-fire-demon-into-the-world shot."

"Where?"

"Somewhere along the coast, I guess. She said she was heading home after; that just because we're running obscenely late, there was no point in her hauling ass all the way back out here." The frown became more questioning than accusatory. "Why?"

Tony shook his head. "Where does she live?"

"I'd have to look it up."

"A co-op on Nelson," Zev put in unexpectedly, crossing to the desk. "Downtown Vancouver, across from the Coast Plaza Hotel. What's the problem?"

Already turning, Tony paused. *An evil wizard is about to come through a gate between worlds and kick ass.* No. Not a good idea. That just wasn't the kind of news that most people took well. "Let's just say it's none of your business." It came out sharper than he'd intended and he regretted the sudden hurt on the music director's face, but he didn't have time to regret it for long. He had to find Lee.

"Man, you're two for two on assholes today," he heard Amy murmur as he ran for the door.

♥

Returning to his desk, CB bent down and plucked the piece of drawing paper out of the trash. He slipped it under the edge of his desk blotter and settled back into the large leather chair, smiling across at his network visitor. "You were saying?"

♥

He needed wheels. Riding transit, no matter how environmentally sound, was just not going to cut it. Fortunately, he knew where there were wheels to be had.

Lee's helmet was in the dressing room. So was his biker jacket. He'd left wearing his costume; gone out into the world as James Taylor Grant. And the only good thing about that was, given their latest numbers, the odds were high no one would recognize him.

Bike keys were in the jacket pocket.

One hand gripping the smooth leather, Tony had a sudden flashback to the feel of smooth skin.

It wasn't really Lee, he reminded himself, shrugging into the jacket. *It doesn't count.*

♥

He hadn't been on a bike in years and never one so powerful. As he guided the big machine into the city, Tony prayed that the cops were busy busting more deserving heads. If he got pulled over, he was totally screwed.

He'd never had a license.

But he had to get to Arra and this was the fastest way. He had to force her to help him. Help him find Lee. Help him free Lee. Then they'd talk about the whole forgetting thing.

Except . . .

She could just make him forget again

She was a wizard.

And she blew things up for a living.

He was just a PA for a third rate production company. How could he stop her?

Roaring past a late '70s pickup, he squinted into the red and gold of a brilliant sunset over the distant towers of the downtown core and smiled.

♥

Tony's message had been short and to the point. *"I've remembered. I need you to meet me at the Coast Plaza Hotel or she'll make me forget again."*

So Henry had canceled his plans for the second night in a row. Just like Tony had known he would. He couldn't quite decide if he was pleased that the young man not only needed his help but acknowledged his right to give it or if he was annoyed at being so predictable it was unnecessary to even *ask* for his help, secure in the knowledge that he wouldn't refuse. A bit of both, he decided as he parked the car.

And there was, of course, the curiosity factor. What had Tony forgotten? Who had made him forget and how had she done it?

After four hundred and fifty years, the unexpected was almost as great a motivation as concern for a friend or plain possessiveness. Impossible to separate the latter two anyway.

He spotted Tony pacing in front of the hotel, caught his eye, waved, and walked over to him.

Tony had phoned the moment he'd parked the bike behind the wizard's building. Specifically, the moment his hands had stopped shaking enough for him to actually hit the right numbers. Adrenaline had started letting him down about the time he reached the city and the last bit of the ride in rush hour traffic had been less than fun. Waiting for Henry to arrive, he'd worked through his reaction and emerged ready to be freaked about wizards and shadows and Lee once again. "Hey. Thanks for coming."

"You knew I would; in spite of how remarkably cryptic you were."

"Sorry. I didn't have time for *War and Peace*." He turned and started across the wide sidewalk toward the road.

Assuming he was to follow, his concern deepening toward worry as tension rolled off the younger man like smoke, Henry caught up at the edge of the asphalt.

Traffic held them in place.

"There's an evil wizard sending shadow minions through from another world." Tony tried to sound matter-of-fact about it; hoping his tone of voice would make the whole thing more believable. Unfortunately, he had a bad feeling that his matter-of-fact sounded more like about-to-totally-lose-it. "One of the shadows has taken over Lee. From the show. Lee plays, um . . . he plays . . ." Oh, just fucking great, now he couldn't remember *that*.

"I know who he plays," Henry said gently.

"Right. We need to find him and free him." He slipped into a break after a parade of SUVs and hurried across to the center line. Henry's hand on his arm kept him from moving on although he continued to shift his weight back and forth from foot to foot as traffic roared by inches away both in front of and behind them. "Arra, the woman who does special effects for the show, she's a wizard from the same world as the shadows. I'd seen some stuff and I told her and she told me what was going on, and then she made me forget."

Henry maintained his grip as they crossed the final lane. Just in case.

"Anyway, this is where she lives." Tony nodded up at the six-story, peach-colored building. "I checked the mailboxes before you got here; she's on the fourth floor in one of the front apartments. I have to make her tell me how to save Lee, and I need you to stop her from making me forget again."

"All right."

For the first time since Henry'd arrived, Tony was still. Pale eyes locked on Henry's face, he murmured, "You believe me? Just like that?"

"Why wouldn't I?"

"Wizards, shadow minions . . ."

"Vampires, werewolves, demons, mummies, ghosts." Henry smiled reassuringly. "And besides, why would you lie about something like that?"

"I guess." He shrugged, more because he needed to move than because he needed to add a physical emphasis to his words. "I mean, it's just that between Lee and the memories and the motorcycle . . ."

"I understand." Well, not about the motorcycle, but under the circumstances, it seemed unimportant. Henry frowned at the building. It had gone up during the '80s real estate boom and was definitely not traditional architecture. Personally, he found the multiple angles aesthetically unpleasant but had to admit he was probably biased about the number of additional windows the design allowed. Large sunny apartments were not to his taste. "Are you sure she's home?"

"Someone's home. The lights are on and I saw a shadow moving behind the blind. A real shadow. Not the invading kind."

"Are you sure she hasn't seen you?"

"Please." This time the shrug was pure disdain. "From her angle I'm just another guy, and there's no shortage of *guys* around this neighborhood. The gym on the second floor of the hotel is one of the best cruising spots in the city. She's not going to expect us; she thinks I'm still completely fucking clueless."

"Good. I imagine that a wizard on her own ground with a chance to prepare a welcome can be very, very dangerous."

"You imagine?"

"This is my first wizard, too, Tony. They're not something you run into every day."

"But you can handle her, right?"

"I don't know."

"She knows you walk in shadow. I didn't tell her; she saw you at the night shoot and she just knew."

"Probably because she's a wizard."

"You think?"

"Best that one of us does." Tony rolled his eyes and, Henry was pleased to see, looked as though the verbal sparring had helped him regain control of his emotions. For Tony's sake then, he was glad he'd managed to keep the edge from his voice. If this wizard had seen him at the night shoot, seen him with Tony, knew what he was, and still used her power on one of his . . . he'd do what Tony needed him to but the whole slightly ludicrous situation had just become personal.

They slipped into the building as one of the tenants

left, a tan Chihuahua cradled in the crook of his arm. The tenant took one look at Henry's face and higher brain functions dealing with self-preservation in the twenty-first century kicked in, assuring him he had not seen what he thought he'd seen. That he had, in fact, seen nothing at all. The dog curled her lip and, in spite of the relative size differences, informed the invading predator he could just get the hell out of her building.

"I just don't get the whole gay men and Chihuahua thing," Tony muttered as they headed for the elevators. The shrill, indignant yapping could still be heard fading into the distance.

"How do you know he was gay?"

"You means *besides* the Chihuahua?"

Three elderly women watched them pass from the safety of the laundry room. Before they could decide whether or not to raise the alarm, the elevator door closed and made the decision for them.

Tony jabbed at the button for the fourth floor, then bounced heel to toe as they slowly rose. "The stairs would be quicker."

"I doubt it."

"It's just Lee's out there, with that thing in him . . ."

"You saw this happen?"

"Yeah. I've been seeing lots of weird shit with shadows, Henry. That's what Arra made me forget. But she said the next shadow would take over someone in the studio to get information about this world and I saw it take over Lee."

"And that made you remember?"

"Maybe. No. I don't know. I just did."

Hard to keep his lips down over his teeth. "Well, we'll speak to her about that, too."

"She's going to help him!"

"Yes. She will."

"What are you smelling?" Henry's nostrils had flared.

"Besides you? Cleansers."

Tony jerked as the elevator chimed and barely managed to stop himself from forcing his fingers between the doors and yanking them open faster. The moment the opening was large enough, he slipped through and raced down the hall, his Doc Martens thudding against the carpet. Although he'd neither seen nor heard him move, Henry was beside him when he reached Arra's door.

"Now what?"

Henry reached past him and knocked.

"Yeah, okay, I suppose that'll work."

He waited, thought he heard movement, and had raised his hand to knock again when Henry's fingers closed around his wrist.

"She heard it the first time. She's standing just inside the door." The words didn't so much get louder as more definite, more penetrating, as though they were being thrust through the painted wood. "I can hear her heart beating. It sped up the moment she saw us and it's beating so quickly now that I have a strong suspicion she knows exactly why we've come. And she knows that if she doesn't open the door, I will break it down, and even if there's an alarm or she's called for help, she'll be dead before security even knows there's a problem."

Tony punctuated the threat by punching the air. He only just barely resisted the urge to sneer, *I've got a vampire by my side and I'm not afraid to use him!*

The door opened.

"Do I have to invite you in, Nightwalker?"

"No."

Arra nodded and stepped back out of the way. "There was always a risk you'd realize his memories had been tampered with."

"*He's* right here!" Tony snapped, pushing into the apartment. "And Henry's not here because you screwed with my memories. Not *only* because you screwed with my memories," he amended as her brows rose. "There's a piece of shadow in Lee Nicholas!"

"What?"

He turned to face her, his hands curled into fists. "You heard me. There's a piece of shadow in Lee Nicholas! It came through and it took him over just like you said it would."

"Are you sure?"

"Yeah, I'm sure. I saw it happen!"

"So you're sure." The sound of the door closing was almost the sound of a door slamming. "What do you want me to do about it?"

"Fix it!"

"I can't."

This time, Tony heard the lie. "You can."

She stared at him for a long moment, then brushed a bit of cat hair off her sleeve. "All right, then; I won't. And at the risk of sounding childish, you can't make me."

"I got that covered. I can't make you, but Henry . . ."

"Can what?" she asked wearily, walking into the living room and dropping onto the end of the couch. "You can kill me, Nightwalker, but you can't force me to have anything to do with the shadows."

Henry swept his gaze slowly around the apartment. Arra had turned out to be the middle-aged woman with the coffee who'd seen behind the masks that night on the street. He wasn't exactly surprised. He could smell two cats in the bedroom, judged by their heart rate that they were asleep. "All right."

"All right what?" she snapped.

"As I'm sure you're aware, my kind are very territorial. Tony is mine."

About to protest, Tony bit back the words. This was, after all, why he'd wanted Henry with him. To lean on the wizard. To act as metaphysical muscle. The whole *Tony is mine* thing was just a lever. At least he hoped it was because they'd settled that when he left.

"You put your mark on him and I can't have that." He was at her side between one heartbeat and the next. Tony was almost used to the way Henry could move when he had to; Arra had no frame of reference and she paled.

"If you kill me, I can't help you with the shadow."

"You've already said you won't help."

Her nostrils flared. "You could try and convince me."

His hands cupped her head in an almost loverlike fashion. "I don't want to."

Tony couldn't see Henry's face, but he could see the sudden realization on Arra's that this was Death standing in her apartment. Not an abstract death sometime in the future, but a flesh and blood and immediate death. Even knowing that Henry would no more follow through on this particular threat than he would feed on fear, Tony's skin crawled.

Lee had been out in the city, ridden by shadow, for over two hours. They didn't have time to be subtle.

"All right! I'll do what I can."

Death lingered.

"Henry."

Henry turned slowly, the Hunger still very close to the surface. He hadn't fed the night before and having allowed so much of the Hunter to rise, he would have to feed tonight. He fought for focus as Tony stepped forward, understanding in his eyes, and murmured, "The moment Lee's free of shadow." No need to be more specific, his blood spoke for him.

"Why wait? Go now. Eat, drink . . . or rather just drink and be merry." Arra looked from the Nightwalker to Tony and sagged back against the cushions in defeat. "Or not. Just a suggestion."

Five

"SO, TONY . . ." Arra settled back into the couch
cushions and crossed her legs, her posture suggesting that while Henry may have shaken her confidence he had by no means destroyed it. ". . . just what is
it you and your friend . . ." Her eyes flickered left to
where Henry stood; the motion involuntary. ". . . expect
me to do?"

Tony couldn't believe she was asking. "Find Lee and
get that thing out of him!"

"You know, you're really overreacting," she sighed.

"I'm overreacting?" He wanted to grab her and shake
her until she admitted that Lee was in danger. Until she
agreed to do something about it. "There's a dark wizard
from another world sending shadows through some
kind of gate to gather information. Yesterday, one of
those shadows killed someone, and today one of them
took over Lee Nicholas and sent him off into the city
acting way out of character. And I'm *over*reacting?"

"Well, I'd have to say you're underreacting about the
wizard, but given your friends . . ." Another corner-of-
the-eye glance at Henry ". . . that's hardly surprising.
You're *over*reacting . . ." She matched his emphasis.
". . . about Mr. Nicholas. You don't need to go looking
for him—and I certainly don't—because the shadow
will return to the gate approximately twelve hours after
it came through."

"What?" Tony froze in place and stared down at her, searching for another lie. "It'll bring Lee back to the gate and just leave him?"

"Essentially."

"So all we need do is make our way to the soundstage and wait?" Henry asked.

Arra nodded. "Be there at 11:15, it's as simple as that. Research also indicated . . ." She glanced over at Tony, who curled his lip. ". . . that the mirror image of the gate equations would also work. On this world, that means there's the potential for a gate every twelve hours. The Shadowlord will want to retrieve his spy and the information it carries as quickly as possible—he won't wait until tomorrow."

"Wait a minute!" Tony took two quick steps closer to the couch. "What the hell does essentially mean?"

"It means that it's unlikely to be as simple as Ms. Pelindrake is indicating. It never is," Henry continued when Tony spun around to face him. He returned his attention to the wizard. "Is it?"

She shrugged. "It could be. The gate will open, the shadow will leave; any complications will be completely separate from that."

"Lee?" When she didn't answer immediately, Tony knew he was right. "Any complications will involve Lee, won't they?"

"It's possible he may have been damaged by the shadow's possession."

"Possible?"

"Some are; some aren't. Those who are . . ." She looked inward, toward memory, and obviously didn't like what she saw. "Some of them shake it off, some are damaged beyond repair; it depends on the individual and there's no way of knowing until the shadow's gone."

"So what do we do?" Tony demanded.

"To prevent the damage? Once the shadow is in control, there's nothing you can do. After . . ." Another inward look, then she shook herself free of the past. "There was a potion we had some success with in the early days, but the ingredients are a world away."

"Can you substitute?"

An emphatic snort made her opinion of Henry's question clear. "And what would you suggest I substitute for glinderan root, Nightwalker?"

"That would depend on what its properties were."

"You're serious?" When his expression made it obvious that he was, she snorted. "What do you care? Lee Nicholas isn't yours."

"No, but Tony is and Tony cares."

"So you're here, threatening me, because your exboyfriend . . ." She jerked her head in Tony's direction. His lip curled. ". . . has a crush on an actor?"

"I'm here, threatening you, because an evil wizard is attempting to gain a foothold in this world, my world. And the fact that I can make so ludicrous sounding a statement with a straight face should give you some indication of how serious I am." Henry's eyes darkened as he allowed the Hunger to rise, capturing the wizard's gaze and holding it. "I will not sit by and allow that to happen and neither will you."

When he finally released her, Arra shivered. "Fine. If you put it like that, I guess I don't have much choice."

"Astute of you to notice."

"Thank you." She heaved herself up off the couch, pushing past Tony without really acknowledging him, and walked into the dining room alcove where two computers were set up on a long table. Both screens showed partially completed spider solitaire games. "I'm blocked here by the queen of spades." Arra waved toward the laptop. "Caution and an older woman. Now that you two have arrived, it's easy enough to interpret the problem as my refusal to become involved." She reached down and closed off the game. "Not really relevant now that my choices have narrowed a bit. This one, though . . ." The big seventeen inch monitor showed a game with almost all the cards in play. ". . . here I'm blocked by red twos. Hearts for love, diamonds for outside influences, twos for those unable to make a decision." She turned that game off as well. "Signs are hazy; ask again later."

"You use computer games for divination?" Henry sounded fascinated by the concept.

"Why not? Three or four games puts me into a trance state anyway. I might as well make use of it." Dropping into a chair, she reached for her mouse. "I'll find an herbal encyclopedia on-line, then you two will have to go out and do some shopping."

"Lee . . ." Tony began.

"Will return to the soundstage in . . ." Arra glanced at the lower right corner of the screen. ". . . a little more than four hours."

"Yeah, but right now he's out in the city controlled by shadow and acting weird! You're a wizard; can't you do a locator spell or something?"

"I could or I could create a potion that will hopefully keep him from spending the rest of his life eating soft foods while wearing an adult diaper. I can't do both. Your choice."

He looked at Henry who was clearly waiting for him to make the decision. *Oh, that's just fucking great; one minute I'm his and the next minute I'm in charge.* That whole on and off again, "I'm over four hundred and fifty years old and a prince and a vampire so I know best," possessive attitude had been one of the main reasons he'd walked. There were times, and this was one of them, when he just wanted to punch Henry Fitzroy right in the fangs. *Not that I'm ever going to. And right now, I need to stop reacting and start thinking.*

They didn't know where Lee was now.

They knew where he was going to be in four hours.

They *didn't* know what condition he'd be in when the shadow left.

"Fine. Make the stupid potion."

Wonderful. He sounded like he was twelve and a petulant twelve at that.

Fortunately, Lee was an actor; acting weird was part of the off duty persona and, in an area overpopulated by actors, most people had stopped noticing.

♠

"All right, I got the stuff." Tony kicked the apartment door closed behind him causing both of the wizard's cats to glare up at him like he was some kind of big, scary door-slamming army. "Can we get started now?"

"Elecampane will the spirits sustain," Arra muttered, taking the bag. "At least according to www.teagardens.com. And the vodka?"

He handed over the bottle. "What's this for?"

"Screwdrivers." She walked past Henry and into the kitchen. "After you two leave, I'm going to need a drink." As they crowded into the tiny space after her, she glanced up at them and shook her head. "No sense of humor, either of you." Cracking the seal, she poured the vodka into a Pyrex pot. "The alcohol will lower his inhibitions and open him up to the possibilities inherent in the potion." She dumped in four tablespoons of the powdered elecampane root then: "Lemon balm to dispel melancholy. Bay leaves to protect the user from witchcraft—used sparingly because of narcotic properties which may, however, also come in handy. Interesting that even the worst stews in the world always have a bay leaf tossed in. Maybe we're supposed to hallucinate better-tasting food. Catnip used to treat hysteria and boredom." She tossed a handful on the floor where the black and white cat and the orange and white cat began drooling all over it. "And a little valerian because, well—why not; your herbalists call it heal-all and we can use the insurance."

Tony leaned toward the pot and then back again, nose wrinkling. "It stinks."

"It always does."

"It doesn't look like wizardry either. It looks like . . ."

"Like something my mother used to do," Henry finished. "Ignoring the vodka, of course."

"Oh, don't ignore the vodka." Arra tipped the bottle back and took a drink.

"I get the feeling you're not taking this seriously," Tony snarled.

She nodded toward Henry. "Ask him if I'm not taking this seriously."

"You're taking *him* seriously, but the whole shadow thing . . ."

"Is something I've been through before and if I was taking it as seriously as you think I should be, I'd be sitting in the closet with a blanket over my head unable to function. I watched a good green land destroyed and the people right along with it. So, to put it in a way you might understand, to put it, in fact, in the vernacular of this world, if you don't think I'm taking this seriously, you can kiss my wrinkled ass!"

The rhythmic thrum of two cats purring, the buzz from the fluorescent light over the sink, the shuff of clothes rearranging as Tony shifted his weight—but mostly silence. He felt he should apologize, had a strong suspicion Henry was waiting for him to apologize, but he wasn't going to do it. He wasn't sorry—he was right. Arra had messed with his memory, let Lee be taken over by shadow, and, in spite of knowing that the evil wizard was spying on them, had no intention of doing anything but playing computer games. If he hadn't gotten his memories back, if he hadn't brought Henry with him, she'd still be *sitting* on her wrinkled ass.

And the silence continued.

Henry could wait, predator patient, for as long as he had to. Apparently, so could Arra.

Tony squared his shoulders, lifted his chin, and said softly, "You'd think, having seen one world conquered, that you'd be working a little harder to keep the same thing from happening here."

The wizard turned from the stove and stared at him for a long moment. Stared until Tony began to run over recent memories just to make sure they were still there. "I said destroyed, not conquered," she pointed out at last.

He shrugged. "Same thing, aren't they?"

"Not always." Her brows drew in and he felt like he did when Henry turned that kind of intensity on him. Like she was looking inside his skin. "In this case, yes." Still frowning, she bent and picked a clean jam jar out of the recycling container beside the fridge. "Find the lid for me."

What did your last slave die of? He'd have asked the question out loud except that he was half afraid she'd have an answer. The lid had slipped down to the bottom of the bin, under a dozen or so washed and crushed cat food tins. Tony brushed it off against his jeans as Arra laid a strainer over the top of the jar and decanted the hot, greenish-brown vodka into it. When she held out her hand, he placed the lid in it, asking, "Shouldn't that cool down a bit before you close it?"

"Expert on potions, are we?"

"No, but . . ."

"Then be quiet, I'm concentrating." Cupping the jam jar in both hands, she took a deep breath and, exhaling, sang a string of words that seemed to be made up mostly of vowels held together with a couple of els. Henry stepped back. The cats roused themselves from their catnip stupor and raced for the bedroom. The liquid began to glow. Placing the jar carefully on the counter, she took her hands away. Multiple lines of tiny lights swirled through the potion.

Okay, *that* looked like wizardry.

From the glance she shot him, Tony was momentarily afraid he'd actually spoken.

"You'd better hurry if you want to get to the soundstage on time," she said, moving over to the sink and running cold water over her hands. "Get that down him before the last light goes out and he should be fine."

"Should?"

"You won't know until you try. He might be fine without it. He might not be fine with it."

"Oh, that's helpful."

"Maybe. Maybe not. You have my number; you can let me know how it turns out."

"I thought you were coming with us."

"No. I made the potion. I'm done."

Catching sight of Henry's expression, Tony remembered that the vampire almost always had his own agenda. "The shadow within Lee Nicholas cannot be allowed to take the information it carries back to its master."

"What kind of information is an actor going to pick up?" Arra snorted, drying her hands on a blue-checked dishcloth. "Apple martinis are in. Nicotine is a memory aid, not a poison that'll take years off your life. And if you can't manage a vacant expression 24/7, botox will take care of those embarrassing facial lines."

As much as Tony hated to admit it, at least where Lee was concerned . . . "She's got a point, Henry. You don't have to come either," he added as Henry's attention switched over to him. "I appreciate your help, I really do, but you've got me what I need; I'll take care of Lee, then meet you at the condo."

"The condo?"

"Yeah, you know. I don't want you to think I've forgotten about . . . uh . . ." He tapped the inside of his left wrist with the first two fingers of his right hand.

Arra rolled her eyes. "He . . ." She nodded toward Tony. ". . . hasn't forgotten the offer he made you . . ." An identical nod in Henry's direction. ". . . earlier. You feed. He bleeds. As long as I'm not on the menu, feel free to discuss it. I'm not squeamish."

"No, you're terrified." Henry was using his Prince of Man voice, as commanding of attention as his Prince of Darkness although in a different way. Slightly different.

Death wasn't quite so imminent. "You hide it well, but I saw it on your face two nights ago when the stunt went wrong, and I can smell it on you now. It clings like the smoke from a crematorium."

Nice image. Tony leaned a little forward and sniffed.

They both ignored him.

"We're all going out to the soundstage," Henry continued, "because any information that shadow takes back is too much. We have no defenses here against wizardry and, unless we want to see this land destroyed, he can't know that. Evil is never content with what it has. It has to keep moving, keep acquiring. That shadow must be stopped before the Shadowlord is convinced we're ripe for conquering."

"Too late." Her smile held no humor. "Not the first shadow, remember?"

"But one of the first. Perhaps it took time for us to muster our defenses; he can still be convinced."

"We're not defenseless," Tony broke in. He jabbed a finger toward Arra. "She can defend us."

"She is the cat's mother."

"What?"

Arra draped the cloth over the oven door handle, carefully spreading it flat. "Just something my gran used to say. If you know a person's name, use it."

"Fine. *You* can defend us." Another jab for emphasis. "If you destroy the shadow, he'll know we're not helpless."

"If I destroy that shadow, he'll send more." Her lip curled as she straightened and turned. Under lowered brows, her pale eyes were hard. "Do you think we didn't destroy them the last time? That we sat around with our thumbs up our collective asses? We fought back. And we lost."

Tony could hear that loss in her voice. The anger. The pain. The screaming.

"Then close the gate. You opened it originally," Henry reminded her. "Surely you can close it."

"I've been over this with him." She jerked her head at Tony, who muttered, *"He is the cat's father."* Wizard and vampire ignored him. "I can't affect the gate from this side. Only from the world of origin."

"Then, when it opens, go through it and *affect* it."

"If I go through it, I die, Nightwalker, and we've agreed—you and I—that I'm not yet ready to die."

"So basically," Tony said as Henry considered that last bit of information, "what you're saying is, now that he knows about us, about this world, we have no hope."

The smile she turned on him was so bleak it closed around his chest and squeezed. "Now, you've got it. Still, look at the bright side." Lifting the jam jar off the counter, she placed it in his hands. "You might get Lee back in one piece." A quick glance at the clock on the microwave. "If you hurry."

She followed them to the door, all but pushing them from the apartment.

Once in the hall, Tony headed straight for the elevator but Henry paused, turned, and said, "The spell you put on Tony, the one that took away his memory?"

"Yes," she answered warily, unsure of where the question was.

"It only lasted one night. I'm just wondering if maybe it failed because you didn't want it to last."

"You think I wanted to be threatened in my own home?"

"I think that, deep down, you wanted other people to know what was going on."

Her brows rose. "So you're a psychiatrist now? You have no idea what I want, Nightwalker!"

And the door slammed shut.

♠

Tony parked Lee's motorcycle in its usual spot, pulled off the helmet, and stared at the cinder-block building that housed CB Productions. It was dark, deserted looking, but since the greater portion of it was windowless, that was hardly surprising. The exterior security lights around the office windows made it hard to tell for certain if anyone remained in the building.

At only 10:50, it was highly likely that the geeks in post were still at their consoles and entirely possible that at least some of the writing staff were hanging around the bull pen—although Tony wasn't entirely clear about what the latter might be doing at that hour besides drinking CB's coffee.

Chester Bane, the man himself, might be a problem. Rumor had it that he wandered the sets at night, in the dark.

"Blocking out new shows?" Tony asked.

The writer shook her head, bloodshot eyes flicking from side to side. "His last divorce really wiped him out; we think he lives in Raymond Dark's apartment."

"There's no bed. Raymond sleeps in a coffin."

"Your point?"

Not entirely believable, considering the source, but CB on set, for whatever reason, would be a problem.

One they'd have no choice but to deal with, Tony acknowledged as Henry parked his BMW in Mason Reed's reserved spot. Still, if worse came to worst, Henry could always do the vampire mind whammy on him.

"There's a door in the back," he said quietly as Henry came up beside him holding the jar of potion in both hands. "It's got one of those electronic security locks on it, but I know the code." Catching sight of Henry's expression, his face illuminated by the light coming off the liquid, Tony smiled tightly. "No, I'm *not* supposed to have the code, but I watched the key grip open up one morning and it kind of stuck in my head."

"Useful."

"Yeah. That's what I thought at the time."

Tony steered clear of the shadows as they hurried toward the back of the building. He told himself that skulking through them would scream "people up to no good" should a cop car or the private security hired by the industrial park happen to pass by. Two guys walking to the back door, well, that was obviously two guys who were there for legitimate reasons. That's what he told himself, and it was an accurate enough observation. But it *wasn't* why he was staying out of the shadows.

"Don't codes get changed on occasion, to prevent this very thing?" Henry asked as they reached the door.

Tony flipped up the cover on the keypad. "Yes."

"And if they have?"

"Then we're screwed. Unless you can climb up onto the roof, go down a ventilation shaft, and open the door from the inside."

Henry looked at his watch. "In less than twenty minutes? I'd rather not."

"Then I guess it's a good thing they haven't changed the code." He pulled the door open, slowly and carefully, and only far enough for them to slip inside.

"Does Lee Nicholas know the code?"

Frowning, Tony paused, the door almost shut. "I doubt it."

"Then you'd better leave it unlocked. He's going to have to get into the building and it would be better for all concerned if he did it quietly."

Arra hadn't been entirely certain where the gate would open.

"It was a big empty room when I arrived and I wasn't in the best condition. It was closer to the offices than the back wall, but that's all I can remember. I suggest you wait until Lee arrives and follow him. The shadow will know exactly where the gate is."

"Who knows what gates lurk within the heart of CB Productions. The sha . . ." Tony broke off as both Arra and Henry turned to stare. "You were thinking it, too," he grumbled.

The jar of potion shed enough light for Tony to find an alcove that would hold them both, giving them a clear line of sight to the door and along the closest thing to a central aisle the soundstage had. Once inside, pressed shoulder to shoulder, Henry tucked the jar in under his coat.

The darkness was nearly absolute, the dim red of the exit sign barely enough for Tony to orient himself. "He'd better make some noise," he murmured, "or we'll never see him arrive."

"I will."

"Oh . . . yeah." The darkness was nearly absolute to *human* eyes.

Tony tried not to fidget, but he'd never been much good at waiting. "Henry? Are you still going to try and stop that shadow?"

It took so long for the vampire to answer, Tony began to think he hadn't been heard. Which was stupid because Henry could hear his heart beating. Although, at the moment, it wasn't so much beating as pounding.

"Yes."

"How?"

"I don't know. The wizard may be right; now that the Shadowlord has found this world we have no chance, no hope, but I choose to think differently."

"Because no one messes with what's yours?"

He could feel Henry's smile in the darkness. Knew how it would look, sharp and cold like a knife.

"Something like that."

A sudden line of gray below the exit sign warned them that the door was opening. For barely an instant, a body stood silhouetted against the night, then an arm reached in and around to the right. Way up above the heavy steel grids where the grips hung the heavy kliegs, banks of low-level fluorescents came on.

It made sense. Shadows needed light to survive.

Tony shrank back into the alcove as Lee hurried by. He looked like he had when he left that afternoon and that was a good thing. Probably. It meant the shadow was still there, but it also meant it had done no visible damage. He let Henry slip out first, knowing the vampire could stay close without being spotted—standard operating procedure for Raymond Dark and *his* side-kick. When Lee and Henry disappeared around one of the walls defining Raymond Dark's office, he followed, eventually catching up to Henry by the video village on the edge of the new living room set.

Lee stood near the couch, looking up toward the ceil-ing and trembling.

There was—although had Tony not known what he knew, it would have been easy enough to convince him-self he wasn't seeing it—an arc of shadow rising up above the actor's head.

"The shadow's separating," Henry murmured, mouth close to Tony's ear. "But it seems to be taking some time."

"Yeah, it took some time getting in. Henry!" He'd set the potion on the seat of Peter's canvas chair and was walking across the set. "Where are you going?"

Henry stopped an arm's length from Lee and leaned forward, nostrils flaring. The possessed actor didn't move, didn't twitch, didn't acknowledge his presence in any way. "The separation seems to be keeping all senses occupied."

"It wasn't like that going in. Except . . ." Tony frowned, remembering. "Except that going in took most of the afternoon."

Henry glanced up. "If the gate's about to open, it doesn't have that kind of time. Nor, when leaving, does it need to fit itself into a complex template."

"Yeah, whatever." Tony glanced up as well. He swept his gaze across and back, up and down, over and out but couldn't see anything resembling a gate. He *could* see . . . "Henry. What destroys shadow?"

"Light."

He pointed.

"Arra's people would have tried something like that."

"Maybe." His lips pulled off his teeth in a pseudo smile, a smile he'd learned from Henry as it happened.

"But they didn't have one of those babies." Not really caring if Henry thought it would work, he ran for the light board.

Sorge, the gaffer, and the key grip had completed a rough setup for the next day's shoot. The script called for a meeting in this living room on a bright, sunny afternoon. Bright sunny afternoons in the middle of box warehouses required a lot of light. Most shows would use a couple of 10-K lamps, but at some point CB had acquired a high intensity 6,000 watt carbon arc lamp—speculation among the crew was that he'd won a bet—and the gaffer liked to use it for high contrast between daylight shots and the creature-of-the-night lighting they usually used. The actors hated it since it cranked up the temperature on the set. Lee had been heard to say, "To hell with Raymond Dark, *I'm* about to burst into fucking flames." But it had been a major contributor to the "look" of *Darkest Night*.

Critics were split on whether or not that was a good thing.

As it was far too powerful for the enclosed space, the gaffer had rigged it with its own dimmer; planning on starting low and then cranking it up until Sorge stopped him. His hands sweating so badly that he left damp prints on the plastic, Tony spun the dimmer around as far to the left as he could then hooked one finger behind the switch.

Turning, he could see only the outside wall of the living room. Crap. "Henry, let me know the instant the shadow's out of Lee."

"I'm not sure . . ."

"I am. And you'd better get under cover."

"That had occurred to me."

It wasn't sunlight, but Henry's eyes were sensitive and . . . "What was that?" It felt as though his fillings were vibrating loose.

"I can't see anything, but I suspect it's the gate opening."

"The shadow?"

"Not quite free. Almost."

Needing to act or scream, Tony started counting the pulse pounding in his temples. *One-two. Three-four. Five-six. Seven* . . .

"Now!"

He didn't so much flip the switch as bring it along with him when Henry's voice jerked him forward.

Without fill lamps to soften its edges, the light slammed through the set like a battering ram. Even behind the beam, Tony's eyes watered.

Then the soundstage plunged into total darkness.

For a moment, Tony was afraid he'd gone blind. A moment later he realized it was only a tripped breaker and began stumbling back toward the set. Once he cleared the wall—not hard to find after slamming face first into it—the light from Arra's potion guided him to the two men in the center of the fake hardwood floor.

"Get his shoulders up," Henry instructed as Tony dropped to his knees. "We've got to get this down him."

Tony slipped an arm behind leather-clad shoulders and lifted. Lee was heavier than he thought he should be, as though some of the shadow lingered, weighing him down. *Don't be such a dumb ass. He's a big guy, that's all.* He looked like hell, but that was probably the fault of the light source. Tony didn't need Everett to tell him that green and glowing complimented no one's complexion. Case in point: pouring the potion down Lee's throat, Henry looked demonic.

"Did it work? Did it destroy the shadow?"

"I don't know." Continuing to pour, the vampire managed a shallow shrug. "I wasn't looking into the light."

"Oh. Right."

"It was a good idea, though, something Vicki might have tried."

"Yeah?" Tony felt his ears grow hot and shifted his grip on Lee's shoulders to hide his pleasure. From the first time she'd hauled his fourteen-year-old ass in off the streets, Vicki Nelson had been his hero, a cop who honestly wanted to serve and protect, a friend when he needed one, his entry into Henry's life. He wasn't sure she knew about that first part, the hero bit. He wasn't sure he wanted anyone to know.

Lee coughed and tried to shove the jar away, jerking Tony's wandering attention back to the matter at hand. The jar was about half full. "Does he have to drink it all? I mean, that's one fuck of a lot of vodka."

"Arra was nonspecific, but I think we should try to get as much as possible into him." Henry's thumb stroked Lee's throat, coaxing him to swallow. "Good thing he's semiconscious or we'd have a fight on our hands. Vodka has no real flavor and this sort of herbal mix traditionally tastes as foul as it smells."

"He's getting a little more active!" Which was interesting considering the amount of alcohol they were pouring into him. "You don't think he's going to hurl, do you?"

"Hurl what?"

"Puke."

"Let's hope not."

It was taking all of Tony's strength just to hold the actor in place. A line of sparkling liquid ran down his chin, the tiny lights dancing over a hint of dark stubble. He spent a moment wondering what they were going to do in about thirty seconds when the last of the liquid disappeared, taking the light with it—Henry would have to find the panel—then a leather clad elbow caught him hard in the ribs.

"Perhaps we'd better change places."

"Good idea," Tony gasped. "Let the guy with super vampire strength take the . . . Henry?" He twisted around, following the line of Henry's narrowed gaze, to see a circle of light sweep the set behind him. From behind the light came the deep bellow of a familiar voice.

"What's going on in here?"

Chester Bane.

Wonder-fucking-ful. The rent-a-cop he might have been able to bullshit. *Looks like it's vampire whammy ti . . .* Strong fingers grabbed his arm, hauled him to his feet, and threw him into the only available hiding place—the triangle of space between the couch and the far wall.

"But Lee . . ." He protested against Henry's ear as the vampire landed beside him.

"We've done all we can for him."

"What if the potion didn't work?"

"The potion was all we had."

"But CB . . ."

"Needs Lee Nicholas, doesn't need you."

Unpleasant, but true. Production assistant was an entry level position and a lot of people were banging on the door to get in. Lee, on the other hand, had a vocal and growing fan base. As much as Tony hated abandoning him, he'd hate to be fired a lot more.

Jamming his shoulder and head under the back edge of the couch, he reached out and lifted the front edge of the slipcover a centimeter off the floor in time to see the circle of light return to illuminate the figure lying in the center of the floor.

♠

Although not entirely certain of what he *had* expected to see, finding Lee Nicholas flat on his back was not it. When the power had suddenly gone off throughout the building, CB had spent long moments finding his flashlight then—followed by the anguished screams of a writer whose creative genius had swept her right past the concept of saving her prose—he'd made his way to the soundstage.

Security had joined him by the women's washroom and left him again when the sound of voices had drawn him away from his search for the panel.

"Mr. Nicholas."

The actor moaned and drew one knee up.

He closed the distance between them and glared down at the sprawled body. Drunk, definitely. Hopefully, only drunk. Before he could speak, the beam from a 6,000 watt carbon arc lamp burned the words away.

And left a few new ones as the soundstage plunged into darkness again.

"Go to the light board, Mr. Khouri! Turn the largest dimmer all the way to the right, then try the main breaker again!"

The security guard's disembodied voice drifted down out of the darkness. "Yes, sir, CB."

By the time the dancing blobs of color had cleared from his vision, Lee Nicholas was sitting up in his own personal spot-light, rubbing his eyes.

"Oh, man, my head!" He peered beyond the flashlight beam. "CB? Is that you?"

"It is."

"What are you doing here?" A tentative swing from left to right of a precariously balanced head. "Forget that, what am *I* doing here?"

"I was about to ask you the same thing."

"I just . . . that is, I don't . . ." Brows drew in. "I have no idea."

As the younger man rose unsteadily to his feet, Chester Bane's eyes narrowed. "You're in costume."

"I'm in what?" From the panicked look on his face, it was clear he was not expecting to see the conservative clothing of James Taylor Grant, vampire associate. Embarrassment quickly followed relief. "I'm shonny . . . shoory . . . sorry, CB."

"Good." It was a reaction that would have piqued the producer's curiosity at any other time but not right now. "Change. Then come to my office; we'll talk."

"Yeah. Sure. Talk."

He swept the flashlight beam around the set, then fell into step beside the actor—fully aware of how intimidating his size had to be. "It must have been some party."

"I don't remember a party." Lee staggered, fell against CB's large and unyielding surface, and hurriedly hauled himself erect.

"I expect tomorrow's tabloids will tell us everything we need to know."

"Oh, God."

"Prayer is always an option."

The dribble of liquid running down Lee Nicholas' chin had held a line of moving sparkles. One by one, the tiny lights had dimmed and disappeared. CB had a strong suspicion the tabloids would have even less of a handle on the truth than usual.

Six

TONY WAITED for the Translink bus to pull away and then, squinting a little in the early morning sunshine, stared diagonally across the intersection at the studio. It looked like it had on a hundred previous mornings—or at least like it had on the thirty of those hundred mornings when it hadn't been raining. There were no mystical messages indicating that he'd fried the shadow, discouraged the Shadowlord, and stopped an invasion. There were no declarations of surrender. No proffered treaties. Not even a simple, "You win. I quit."

He glanced down at his watch. 7:20. He had about four hours to wait before the gate was scheduled to re-open. Four hours before he found out if the gate was even going to reopen.

And if it did?

What then?

He took another look at the studio. Nothing about it gave any indication of what might or might not happen in only four short hours.

Which was too bad, really, because if it had looked different, if physical evidence of either the gate or the Shadowlord had marked the building, he'd be able to take what he knew to the proper authorities. It was the twenty-first century after all; surely *someone* had plans for dealing with an off-world invasion. Someone, that is, besides people who ran web sites called theyarecoming.com or prob_me.org and who clearly had way too much free time. He made a mental note to scrub that prob_me.org cookie or he'd be getting porn spam for the rest of his life.

Unfortunately, the only evidence he had supporting an invasion was an invisible gate that made his teeth hurt, a wizard who'd deny everything, and an actor who hadn't remembered being possessed—although one of the tabloids did have a slightly blurry, page 17 shot of him coming out of the main branch of the public library which would certainly strengthen the possession story. Not much in the way of support. Fox Mulder couldn't have made a case out of it.

The light changed and Tony headed across the street, absently rubbing his right thumb across the nearly healed puncture in his left wrist. Spending two nights in a row at Henry's condo hadn't been smart. And that was the problem. He wasn't smart around Henry, he was . . . dependent. Sure, running to Henry for help the moment things got weird made a kind of sense—friends with specialized knowledge and all that—but allowing it to go further, supporting that whole vampire *everyone I make a connection with is mine* attitude—his wrist throbbed—what had he been thinking? Other body parts made a couple of suggestions. He ignored them.

There was no chance of leaving Henry out of things now; if the gate reopened, he'd have to be told. But the next time . . .

Oh, yeah, Tony snorted, stepping up on the curb. *Because this sort of thing is likely to happen again.*

And anyway, since Arra seemed pretty damned sure they wouldn't survive this time, speculation seemed a bit moot.

Arra.

Tony'd called from Henry's to fill her in and ended up leaving a message on her machine. He knew she was standing beside the phone, listening, and refusing to become further involved. Too bad. If that gate reopened, he wasn't going to give her a choice.

He wondered if blackmail would work. *You help stop the Shadowlord and I won't tell everyone what you really are.*

Yeah, that'd work. Tony snorted again. If it came down to his word against Arra's, his story against Arra's, well, he'd put money on people believing the part that didn't involve wizards and dark shadow invasions.

Maybe he'd try guilt. *Never mind, you've been through enough. You just stay home with your cats while the rest of us die.* He had to try something because without Arra, it was up to him, and unless it turned out that a 6,000 watt carbon arc lamp was all it took, the world was fucking doomed.

As he retraced last night's steps to the back door, he glanced over at Lee's bike. Given the amount of vodka they'd poured into him, he'd probably taken a cab home. Lee had told CB he didn't remember anything and that was good. Tony knew his memory of what had happened in the dressing room was going to make it hard enough to face Lee—the last thing he needed added in was Lee's reaction. In his experience, a straight guy with a morning-after memory of copping a feel off a gay guy was more likely to blame the gay guy and get freaked and angry than think, *Oops, my hand must've slipped.* It was just human nature and Tony was usually fine with that, but it wasn't something he wanted to find out about Lee.

For the first time since he'd started working on *Darkest Night*, he wasn't looking forward to seeing the actor on set.

The problem was, the whole dark wizard, gate, shadow, invasion thing was just a little too big to really get a hold of.

The thing with Lee; *that* he had a hold of just fine.

Oh, that's just fucking great. Like I don't have enough going on without mental innuendo.

As usual, most of the early crew stood gathered

around the craft services truck nursing coffees and muffins. Carpenters talking with electricians, talking with drivers, talking with the props guy, talking with camera operators; the craft services truck was the studio's Switzerland. Neutral ground. By unspoken agreement, arguments were left on the soundstage and a certain level of good manners was carefully maintained—people who regularly worked a seventeen-hour day were willing to do what it took to help facilitate the smooth delivery of carbs and caffeine.

Tony grabbed a coffee and headed inside to pick up his sides. He'd gone chasing off after Lee in such a hurry yesterday afternoon that he hadn't . . .

"Mr. Foster. A word."

Wondering what he'd done, Tony crossed over to where Peter was standing with Sorge and the gaffer by the light board. As he closed the distance, he told himself that the positioning had to be coincidence. Unless he'd dusted for fingerprints, there was no way the director could tell he'd been at the board the night before.

Eyebrows raised high enough that they seemed to be following his receding hairline back up over his skull, Peter held out a set of sides. "I believe these are yours."

He'd gone chasing off after Lee in such a hurry yesterday afternoon, Tony's brain reminded him.

Chasing off after Lee before Peter had called a wrap.

Without even considering what he was doing, he'd just left work.

Crap.

"I can explain."

"Good."

"Remember how you sent me in to check on Lee? To see if he was all right because he was acting so strangely on the set? Well, he just left, in one hell of a hurry, and so I went after him because I didn't know if he was all right." He flashed the smile he'd perfected on Toronto street corners staring up at uniformed cops and had kept around to grease his way through slightly more legal problems with authority. "See?"

"You ran out after Lee because I told you to go check on him?"

"Yes."

"You were so worried about him, you forgot you were still wearing your radio. Remembered to turn it off, but forgot you were wearing it."

Tony glanced down at the holster riding his hip. "Yeah. I was worried."

"And how was he?"

Controlled by a minion of the Shadowlord.

Flat on his ass under a gate leading to another world.

Sloshing with vodka . . .

None of the above.

"I . . . uh, I never actually caught up to him."

"So you're saying you left early and still didn't do what I asked you to?"

"Uh, yeah. Sorry."

Peter stared at him for a long moment, then snorted softly. "You just used up all your saved-the-stuntman goodwill, Tony. Next time you run off like that, you can return the radio and keep on going."

"Right. Sorry."

"Tell Alan Wu I need him on set to run over his blocking the moment he's done then hit the office and see if those dialogue changes are ready. And," he raised his voice, "I'd like to get started on time for a change, people! Why aren't those cameras set?"

As Tony hurried for the exit, he heard the soundstage begin to rev up behind him. And the good news, he still had a job. And the bad news, that job was still at ground zero for a Shadowlord invasion.

Unless it wasn't.

Seven fifty-one.

Three and a half hours.

He hated waiting.

Alan Wu, who played Detective Emanuel Chan, *Darkest Night's* recurring police presence, guaranteed at least one day's work a week, was still in the chair when Tony reached the makeup room.

"Look at this hair, Tony." Everett waved a thick strand of black hair in Tony's general direction without much regard for the head it was attached to. "Don't quote me on this, but is this not beautiful hair?"

"It's the same hair he had last week, Everett." Tony grinned as he moved around so Alan could see him in the mirror. Everett's fascination with Alan's hair and the crew's awareness of it left the actor alternately flattered and embarrassed. "As soon as you're done here, Peter would like to see you on set so that he . . ."

". . . can run over my blocking. Same old. Same old."

Detective Chan liked to move when he talked, his constant motion in direct and deliberate contrast to Raymond Dark's brooding stillness. It made his scenes harder to shoot, as a stationary actor was easier for both light and sound but, since CB himself had been responsible for that bit of character development, no one argued too loudly against it; they just scheduled extra time and counted on Alan to hit his marks.

Fortunately, twenty years in the business made Alan the closest thing to a sure bet on the set.

The late Catherine's less than loving mom and dad were in the other two chairs being worked on by Everett's assistant—who worked part-time for CB Productions and part-time at a local funeral parlor. She'd told Tony once that thanks to *Six Feet Under,* people saw her second job as the more exotic. "But for me—you know, corpses, actors—meat's meat. At least the dead dudes don't complain that natural beige foundation makes them look fat."

Lee was in the same scene, but he wasn't due on set until 8:30. Two hours and forty-five minutes before the gate. Tony paused outside his dressing room door, imagined he could hear the rustle of fabric, actually could hear muffled profanity, raised his hand to knock, changed his mind, and ran.

Terrified he'd hear Lee's door open before he was out of sight.

Jesus. What are you afraid of? He's a guy; it's not like he's going to want to talk about it.

He hit the production office just as Amy, hair and fingernails a matching burgundy, was shrugging out of her jacket. Crossing toward her, he lifted a hand in greeting. "Hey."

"Hey yourself, Kemosabe. You still work here?"

It appeared that yesterday's early departure was common knowledge. Great. The last thing he needed was a reputation as a slacker. Well, maybe not the last thing; he supposed he needed homicidal shadows less, but still . . . "All has been forgiven," he told her, pushing the staple remover around her desk with the tip of one finger, "but apparently I'm going to have to rescue another stuntman before I do it again."

Amy glanced around the office. "Don't see anyone in need of rescue."

"Too bad. Did you know that clock is two hours off?"

She turned to look and snorted. "We reset it to Hawaiian time."

"That's not . . ."

"Did you come in here to criticize, or are you actually hanging around for a reason?"

"I need today's dialogue changes."

The changes weren't on Amy's desk. Just to be on the safe side, she quickly checked Rachel's desk, the top of both filing cabinets, and the gray metal shelving unit.

Together, they turned toward the bull pen.

"I went in last time," Amy told him, crossing her arms over her UBC sweatshirt.

"I'm the *set* PA," he reminded her. "The bull pen's way outside my job description."

"You want to get anywhere in this business, Tony, you have to show initiative."

"I'd rather wrestle Richard Simmons."

"You wish."

"Hey, guys, what's up?"

Together, they turned toward the office PA.

Veronica's eyes widened at the sight of their smiles and she took a step back. "What?"

"I need you to pick up some dialogue changes from the writers for this morning's shoot," Amy told her while Tony tried to keep the word "sucker" from showing on his face in any way.

She looked a little confused but nodded. "Sure, no problem."

They watched her stride purposefully into the bull pen and exit considerably faster a few moments later clutching four sheets of paper to her chest.

"What is that smell?"

"No one knows." Amy pried the pages from Veronica's white-knuckled fingers and headed for the photocopier. "What're we up to? Blue?"

Tony checked his sides for the latest script revision color. "Yeah, blue."

"Why blue?" Veronica asked.

Tony shrugged. "Because the camera breakdowns are on green."

"That's not a reason for blue."

Amy patted her on the shoulder as she handed Tony the photocopies. "One of the first things you've got to learn in this business, kid, is that a lot of stuff happens just because."

"But why do . . . ?"

"Because."

"Yes, but . . ."

"Just because." Dropping into her chair, Amy reached for the ringing phone. "And while we're on the topic, can you try and find another ream of blue paper in that stack of office supplies in the kitchen. CB Productions. How can I help?"

When Veronica continued to look confused, Tony

turned her toward the kitchen and gave her a little shove. He'd taken two steps toward the soundstage when the front doors opened and Zev came in, one hand beating time to the rhythm in his headphones. Tony waited until he was sure the musical director could see him, then he smiled and waved.

Zev's return salutation was distinctly frosty and he continued straight through to post without stopping to talk.

By the time Tony had turned to ask Amy what was up, she already had her hand over the mouthpiece of the phone.

"Because you were a shit to him yesterday."

"You could at least wait until I asked."

"Time is money, buckaroo. Go apologize."

He waved the dialogue changes in answer as she turned her attention back to the phone and headed for the soundstage. Apologize? A suggestion that proved Amy didn't understand guys. Guys didn't apologize; the other guy, the guy not being apologized to, got even. *Fucking great. If Lee thinks what happened yesterday was my fault, I'm going to have to pull CB himself out of a burning car if I want to keep my . . .*

"Shit. Sorry." He sidestepped the body heading for the makeup room, realized who it was an instant later, and kept walking. Maybe a little faster. Places to go. Things to do. Dialogue changes to deliver.

"Hey, Tony!"

Crap.

Half hidden behind a not very convincing fake bearskin hat, he turned and tried to look as though he wasn't remembering the feel of bare skin under his hands. "Yeah?"

"Yesterday, after I left, Brenda says you took off on my bike."

And crap again. The wardrobe department's windows looked out into the parking lot and Brenda had been trying to get into Lee's pants in more than a professional way for months. Over half the crew believed she already had.

Not surprisingly, Lee sounded pretty pissed off.

"Uh, yeah. Don't you remember?" Because if Lee'd gotten his memory back overnight, Tony needed to know now.

"Remember what?"

Good. Anger turning to suspicion and uneasiness. Well, not exactly *good* but definitely better than it could be. Tony dredged up a smile and proceeded to lie through his teeth. He'd been told more than once it was one of his most marketable skills. "You told me to take it to your condo for you, but you never showed and I couldn't get into the garage so I brought it back here."

"I told you to take it to my condo?"

"Yeah."

"Why?"

Tony shrugged and flipped a bit of off-color fur back and forth. "Beats the hell out of me. You said you had a killer headache, asked if I could ride, I said I could and . . ." He shrugged again and played the only hand he had. "That must've been one hell of a headache if you can't remember. You okay?"

"Uh . . ." Lee's brow furrowed and Tony flinched to see the flash of panic in his eyes. Sure, anyone might panic at losing so large a chunk of time, but for an actor to suddenly feel he couldn't rely on his memory . . . After a long moment, Lee decided to grab the line Tony'd thrown him. "It was a killer headache, totally killer—still not entirely gone, I'm afraid. Listen, thanks, man."

"No problem." He waved the blue sheets again, like cerulean semaphore for *I've got to haul ass*, and hauled ass for the soundstage. *And the Oscar goes to . . .* Except this was television not movies and syndicated television besides but an Oscar caliber performance regardless. He just wished he didn't feel like such a shit.

I should tell him. I should tell him that it has noth-ing to do with him. That the shadow minions of a dark wizard took over his body and that's why he can't re-member. Tony snorted as he shoved through the last of the costumes. *Oh, yeah, I'm sure it'd comfort him to think that while he was losing his memory, I was los-ing my mind.*

Better the comfort of a lie than the absurdity of the truth.

And ain't that a proverb for the millennium.

At the monitors, he handed Peter the changes. The di-rector glanced over them then passed all but two sets to Tina. Those two sets, he passed back to Tony. "Give these to Mum and Dad. Tell them I need them out here in . . . Sorge!"

The DP glanced up from sketching Alan's path across the living room in the air with long sweeping move-ments of both arms.

"How long?"

"Vingt." Unaware he was standing directly under an interdimensional gate, Sorge shrugged. *"Vingt-cinq."*

"Make it twenty." Peter turned his attention back to Tony. "Tell them I need them out here in twenty min-utes. Suggest that they actually know the new lines."

"Really?" That last bit sounded suspect.

"Be diplomatic."

"Uh, sure." Apparently not.

"And get them back here on time."

"Right."

He could be diplomatic. He checked his watch against the time code running across the bottom of the tech monitor and headed back toward the dressing rooms. Odds were good they were both out of makeup by now and anyway, the dressing rooms were on the way.

Memory making his heart pound, just for that mo-ment envying Lee's memory loss, Tony reminded him-self that *that* shadow was gone. That the shadow following it had been destroyed. *He'd* destroyed it.

The door to Catherine's—Nikki's—dressing room remained off its hinges and Mom and Dad—he didn't bother checking their actual names, if the morning went well, they'd be gone by lunch—were in the two farthest away. Fortunately, both doors were open. *Fortunately*, because Tony was suddenly afraid that if he had to knock, he wouldn't be able to. Dad was reading the paper. Mom had her laptop out.

Their shadows were muted and gray.

He cleared his throat and held up the pages. "Dialogue changes, guys. The director needs you on the set in twenty minutes with the changes down."

"In twenty minutes?" Mom looked appalled.

Tony glanced at the top page. "I think most of the changes are Alan's. Detective Chan's. He usually gets the exposition and that's what the writers keep changing, so it's probably changed a couple of your reactions." He smiled reassuringly as they took the pages. "Nothing big."

"I mean, I know my lines."

The newspaper was abruptly folded down. "Are you implying I don't?"

"I wasn't talking about you. Jesus, Frank. Get over yourself." She flipped through the pages and frowned, the makeup on her forehead creasing. "We're doing all four pages today?"

"Hopefully, we're doing all four pages by 11:00," he told her, glancing at his sides. Her name was Laura. He couldn't know one and not the other, it just didn't seem fair. "Then three more before lunch and we're doing seven this afternoon—touch wood." Reaching out, he pressed a finger against a two by four. "We're a bit behind."

Both actors turned to look at the far dressing room.

"Because of . . . her?" Frank asked.

"Nikki Waugh."

"Right." He stepped far enough away from the dressing rooms to get a better look. "That's where it happened, isn't it?"

Shadow spilled out onto the soundstage, pooling on the concrete, running into the cracks and dips in the floor.

"Yes."

"She didn't die of anything catching, did she?"

A small bounce as the back of her head impacted with concrete.

"No. Nothing catching."

"I heard she was all twisted up." Laura moved out to stand beside her temporary matrimonial partner. "Heart attack, my ass."

"I heard it was drugs."

Tony checked his watch. Fifteen minutes until he had to get them to the set. No way he could take fifteen minutes of lurid speculation. Not when he knew. Hell, not even if he hadn't known. "Excuse me. I have an errand I have to run; I'll be back for you."

"Don't worry about it, Tommy . . ."

"Tony."

"Of course." Laura cocked her head toward the sound of Sorge's voice, his unmistakable hybrid of French and English loud enough to echo against the distant ceiling. "I think we can find our way."

"It's all part of the service." He found a smile from somewhere and managed to keep it in place as he hurried for the exit. Behind him, Mom and Dad—Laura and Frank—settled down for a good gossip, script changes forgotten in their need to visit rumor and innuendo.

Nothing like human nature to make incoming Shadowlords look good. Keeping an eye out for Lee, he pushed his way back through the costumes, out into the production office, and down to the basement when Amy's back was turned.

He didn't want to go down to the basement.

There was no reason for him to go down to the basement.

If he needed to talk to Arra, it would be a lot more

efficient if he just called her and had her come up to the soundstage.

Tony stopped about halfway down the stairs. He turned, raised his foot to start back up again, and stopped.

He *did* want to go down to the basement.

And he had a damned good reason for going.

Two steps farther down and he began to feel slightly nauseous.

Who knew what chemicals she was using down there. Half of them would probably blow up if looked at the wrong way and the other half were likely toxic. Better he just go back upstairs and call her.

He was three steps up before he stopped himself.

Bite me, old woman!

Four steps from the bottom, the hair lifting off the back of his neck, sweat running down his sides, he said a silent, *Screw it!* and jumped.

He felt better the moment he landed.

Wiping his palms against his jeans, he came out from behind a set of shelves and face-to-face with a rotting corpse standing and swaying in the middle of the room.

Sagging gray flesh had ripped open under its own weight and well-fed maggots squirmed out of the rents. A hand with bones protruding through three fingertips reached out for him while white rheumy eyes tried to focus on his face. Dark, withered lips parted and a voice said, "It takes a lot to discourage you, doesn't it? All right, fine. As long as you're here, you can tell me if the maggots are too much."

"Th . . . th . . . th . . ." It felt as though all connections between his mouth and his brain had been severed.

"The maggots, Tony. Are they over the top? I think they give a corpse a nice lived-in look, but they're not for everyone."

"Arra?"

The corpse sighed and was suddenly the much

shorter, older wizard—the maggots nowhere in sight. "It's just a glamour," she said, checking her fingertips. "Raymond Dark'll be stopping the villain du jour from raising the dead in a couple of weeks and I need to work out the details. It's not as easy as it looks maintaining three separate glamours over moving actors. Good thing CB's too cheap to hire more than three corpses. So . . ." An eyebrow rose. ". . . what can I do for you?"

"That was . . ." He waved a hand. "Fuck. I mean . . ."

"Thank you. Always nice to have an appreciative audience. I take it Mr. Nicholas is functional this morning?"

"Uh, yeah."

"Good." She waited, then folded her arms and sighed again. "Since you managed to get down here in spite of wards set to prevent that very thing, I assume you want something. What?"

"Right." Tony glanced down at his watch. Seven minutes before he had to get Laura and Frank to the set. "The gate. We're shooting right under it."

"So?"

"I don't think we'll be done by 11:15."

"I repeat, so?"

"You have to be there. You should be there. Just in case."

"As I believe I mentioned last night, there's no just in case."

"But I . . ."

"Yes. I got your message. You used a really bright light on the shadow leaving Mr. Nicholas and you think you destroyed it, but you're not one hundred percent positive." She folded her arms. Tony had read somewhere that people folded their arms as a protective gesture. Arra didn't so much look like she was protecting herself as putting up battlements, raising the moat bridge, and hanging out no trespassing signs. "The shadow could have returned unaffected," she continued, "and therefore the shadows that would have been sent today still will be sent. It could have been injured but not destroyed in which case shadows will come through to find and remove the threat. It could have been destroyed and so nothing went back through the gate at all in which case shadows will come through to find out why.

"The Shadowlord will continue to send his shadows through. You might as well just live your life while you can because there's nothing you can do about it."

"Hey, I have access to a 6,000 watt carbon arc lamp!"

"*If* the lamp destroyed the shadow, can you shine it on the gate every time it opens?"

"No, but you can . . ."

"I can what?"

"I don't know!" Everything he knew about wizards came from the movies and none of it was particularly helpful. "You could help!"

"I helped last night and unless my memory is faulty, which it isn't, I told you that I'm not going after the shadows. As you might say, been there, done that, got the scars." Her arms still crossed, her right hand gripped her left sleeve with white-knuckled force.

"You fought before!"

"Older and wiser now. Didn't you have somewhere you need to be?"

He looked at his watch. Shit! "This isn't over."

Arra shrugged—although a certain twist to her mouth made the motion look more fatalistic than nonchalant. "That's what I keep telling you."

♣

"All right, let's get Mom's reaction shots." Finding himself at the end of his tether, Peter yanked off his headphones and tossed them back to Tina before walking out onto the set. "Lee, if you don't mind . . . ?"

Cracking open a bottle of water, Lee indicated that he didn't.

There were stars, Mason Reed among them, who saw no reason they should have to reread their lines so that the cameras could catch the reactions of the secondary characters. On more than one occasion, Tony, as the least essential member of the crew, had found himself holding a script and trying not to sound like a complete idiot while reading Raymond Dark's dialogue. Given Raymond Dark's dialogue, that wasn't exactly a job for an amateur.

Unless Lee had another commitment, he always stayed. Tony felt this gave his scenes a depth that Mason's didn't have and that it could be at least part of the reason for the amount of fan mail Lee had started to receive—although he didn't kid himself that the larger reason involved the eyes, the smile, and the ass. It had taken *him* a couple of months to actually notice Lee's acting ability and he was a trained professional.

Under normal circumstances, Tony was all in favor of Lee's presence on the set. Today, he'd have been happier had Lee been out of the building. Hell, out of the country. If Arra was right and the next opening of the gate would release more shadows into the world, Lee needed to be as far from the gate as possible—not standing underneath it chatting to the boom operator while Peter went over the reactions he wanted with Laura.

If Arra was wrong . . . well, Tony would still have been happier with Lee anywhere but unavoidably in sight. He couldn't stop thinking about what had happened between them—between him and Lee's body at any rate—and it was distracting.

"TONY!"

He jerked his head toward the microphone so quickly he nearly gave himself whiplash. "Yeah, Adam?"

"Find Everett and get him out here. Frank's comb over needs to be touched up before his shots."

And faintly from the background. *"It's not a comb over!"*

Everett was in makeup with Mason Reed in the chair. Startled, Tony checked his sides. "Uh, Mr. Reed, you're not . . ."

"Promo shots," the actor snapped. "For *The Georgia Straight*. Yet another article about my personal life—rich and single in Canada's hippest city." His sigh was deep enough to waft a cotton ball off the counter. "They should be concentrating on my art; I don't know why they're so fascinated by what I do in my minimal amount of spare time."

They're not fascinated, they're inundated—you won't shut up about it. Flashing Mason the "sorry I'm interrupting but I'm carrying a message from someone much more important than me" smile he'd perfected after three days on the job, Tony turned to the other man, currently wiping lotion off his fingers. "Everett, you're needed on set."

"He's not finished with me."

"It's not a problem, Mason. We need a moment for that bronz . . . moisturizer," Everett corrected quickly as Mason glared at him, "to set."

"*Georgia Straight* interview my ass," the makeup artist muttered a moment later as they made their way back to the soundstage. "They've never shot him in anything but black and white. I'm betting he has a hot date with one of his parasailing, snowboarding bimbos. Hard bodies young enough to be your daughter are seldom impressed by vampire pallor. Don't quote me on that, though."

Tony winced. "Harsh."

"I call them as I see them, kid. And I knew Frank's combover wouldn't be up to the overacting he was going to put it through. What happened to subtlety?" he demanded as they waited at the soundstage door for the red light to go off.

"It's a show about a vampire detective," Tony reminded him, opening the door and motioning him through. "Subtle isn't exactly the selling point."

♣

". . . which is when the police arrived."

"Keep rolling," Peter called as Laura allowed her

shocked expression to fade. "Let's try it again with more sorrow less indignation. Lee . . ."

"Unfortunately, Mr. and Mrs. Mackay, that was when Raymond Dark found your daughter. It was too late for him to do anything, too late for anyone to do anything, which is when the midget basketball team arrived."

"Keep rolling. Do it again. A little *less* sorrow this time although the tear was terrific if you can work up another one. Lee, stop trying to make her laugh. We've got nine pages to get through today and you know how CB feels about overtime."

Laura smiled across the set. "That's all right Peter; I don't find midget basketball funny."

"Yak herders? Operatic mutes? The Vancouver Canucks?" Lee grinned at the older woman. "You've got to be able to laugh at the Canucks or you'll die of a broken heart."

"That's a fiver for the hockey jar, Lee." The hockey jar was a direct result of differing opinions during the previous season's playoffs; differing opinions that had resulted in a black eye, two broken fingers, and an assault with a blueberry muffin. "And line . . ."

"Unfortunately, Mr. and Mrs. Mackay . . ."

As he delivered the line once again, Lee seemed fine. He was a little hyper, but his energy levels were always high while the camera was rolling. Had Tony not been specifically looking for the effects of yesterday's adventure, he would have missed the pinched looked around the actor's eyes or the way his usual fluid gestures had picked up a slight staccato movement—like a physical stutter. It could have been a lot worse—he'd expected it to be a lot worse—and it could, in fact, be nothing more than a perfectly normal reaction to being force-fed half a bottle of warm, catnip-flavored vodka.

The shadow appeared to have caused no actual damage.

Tony glanced at his watch. 11:10.

That shadow appeared to have caused no actual damage. And as much as he wanted to believe it was over, lessons learned from a thousand movies and a hundred television shows were telling him it couldn't possibly be that easy.

A thousand movies, a hundred television shows, and one real downer of a wizard

♣

Arra had every intention of staying away from the set—from the set, from the gate, from the whole inevitable disaster. At 11:11, according to the clock on the tech monitor, she was standing behind the video village wondering just what, exactly, she thought she was doing.

Gathering information?

Yes. That sounded safe enough.

She needed information in order to plan, in order to survive, which meant that vested self-interest had brought her out of her workshop—not curiosity nor, heaven forbid, an inexplicable desire to become involved. Once was enough. More than.

The big carbon arc lamp was on, maintaining ambient light for the close-ups. It was throwing an uncomfortable amount of heat, and was clearly the reason her T-shirt was now sticking to a line of sweat dribbling down her spine. As long as it stayed on, she couldn't see a shadow making it through.

Peter sat back and pushed his headphones down around his neck. "That's got it."

And the light shut off.

Cue dramatic irony.

♣

"No!"

As all eyes turned toward him, Tony suddenly realized he'd spoken aloud.

Yelled actually.

Peter leaned around the edge of the monitor to fix him with an interrogative gaze. "Problem, Mr. Foster?"

Mister? He was so screwed. He could feel the vibration beginning, the gate opening. What difference did it make if he looked like an ass? He had to say something! Arra! Arra was there. Behind Peter. She'd back him up. *Right. Who the fuck am I kidding.* "Sorry. I uh . . . thought I saw one of the lights shift."

Everyone looked up. Everyone but him.

He looked at Arra. Who was looking up. But *not* at the lights.

Her face had paled and she was panting; even from ten feet away, he could see her chest rise and fall. He could almost see the terror oozing off her like . . . like the maggots oozing out of the corpse. *Oh, yeah, I really needed that image.*

The vibrations grew stronger.

"Can anyone else feel that?"

Together, Tony and Arra stared at Lee.

"Feel what?" Laura asked cautiously.

Frowning, the actor rubbed his jaw. "It's like there's a . . . I don't know, like a bee trapped in my head."

Tony would have said dentist's drill, but bee was close enough. No one else seemed to be noticing. *Because of the shadow in him?* he mouthed at Arra.

She shrugged—he had no idea if the gesture was an answer or because she couldn't lip-read.

"All right people, if we give it some gas, we can get Dad's reactions in the can before lunch. B-camera, you ready?"

"Good to go, Boss."

"Lee?"

A shadow brushed across Lee's face. He stiffened and screamed.

Seven

TONY JUMPED forward as Lee's knees began to buckle and managed to slide an arm under his head just before bone impacted with concrete.

A small bounce as the back of her head impacted with concrete.

He'd reacted as much for his own benefit as Lee's; he didn't think he could bear hearing that particular sound again. A line of cold air brushed feather light against his cheek, and he turned his head in time to see a shadow pour off his shoulder. And another slide across the floor.

When Lee screamed again, Tony turned back toward him so quickly he courted whiplash, saw a tendril of shadow pool in the hollow of the actor's throat, saw it dribble down to join the shadow cast by solid flesh, saw it separate and disappear behind the camera mount.

"What the hell is going on?"

"Shadows."

Arra's whisper pulled Tony's gaze past Peter to where the wizard stood, visibly trembling.

"Shadows?" The director looked as well, and when no answer was forthcoming, directed his next question out at the floor. "What the hell does that mean?"

Multiple shoulders lifted and fell.

No one else had seen them. Or, possibly, no one else was willing to admit that such a thing could exist. It was a defense mechanism Tony'd seen a hundred times.

Henry and his kind survived because of it. And Henry'd made it pretty much impossible for him to use it.

He pulled a word from the air. "Seizure?"

Someone dropped down at Lee's other side. A hand moved his arm away gently and placed a pad of fabric between concrete and skull. Tony looked up to see Laura on her knees, her sweater off and her fingers against the pulse point in Lee's throat.

"I don't know about a seizure," she said briskly, "but his heart's racing, his temperature is up, and there's a certain rigidity in his muscles that I don't like." The silence that followed held so many questions, she looked up and frowned. "I've been a nurse for twenty years. You can't honestly think I can make a living doing the occasional character role on Canadian television?"

The murmur of agreement from cast and crew held distinct overtones of relief; *someone* knew what they were doing.

"We're heavily syndicated in the American market," Peter muttered under his breath.

"Not my point." Laura sat back on her sensible heels as Lee opened his eyes.

The clear jade green looked murky. Flawed. *Or I could be overreacting just a bit*, Tony admitted, his own heart working in quick time.

"Lee, are you back with us? How are you feeling?"

His eyes locked on Laura's face with a desperate need to know. "Is it over?"

"It seems to be."

Question and answer held no subject in common, but Tony was just as glad he hadn't had to answer the question actually asked. No. It wasn't over. Including the original shadow that had set Lee off, he'd counted four, but with his focus so narrowed, he couldn't swear there hadn't been a dozen more.

Adam stood at Lee's feet, pencil tapping against the edge of his clipboard, eyes narrowed as though he was working out the logistics in his head. "Should we call a doctor?"

Suddenly aware he was flat on the floor and the center of attention—and *not* the kind of attention actors required—Lee struggled to sit up. "I'm fine."

Tony inched back, aware he had no right to be inside the other man's personal space but unwilling to surrender his position entirely.

"Screaming and collapsing doesn't generally indicate fine," Laura told him, helping him sit up. Her tone was so matter-of-fact it cut the ground out from under rising panic.

Drawing in a deep breath, Lee managed a wobbly smile. "That was then, this is now."

"Can you tell me what happened?"

The smile wobbled a little more. "No. I was cold then . . ."

"He should see a doctor."

"Hey, I'm good." He sounded fine. But then three weeks ago he'd sounded like a fifteenth-century Italian nobleman by way of a Canadian screenwriter, so Tony wasn't putting much stock in the pronouncement.

Neither was Laura. "Something caused that reaction. It would be wise to see a doctor."

He stood as Lee did, fairly certain the other man had no idea whose shoulder he was using and, considering their interaction over the past two days, just as happy. The last thing he wanted was to be tied in Lee's mind to personal disaster. Although given the whole memory-loss, screaming-and-falling-over thing, it might already be too late.

Lee glanced around at his audience. "We're behind already."

Heads nodded. Someone had died and the show had gone on. Falling over and screaming was fairly far down the list in comparison.

"We'll be farther behind if this continues," Laura

pointed out reasonably. "It could be something serious. It might be nothing. But you should know."

Heads nodded again. The same heads.

Hands spread, Lee smiled; the wobbles under control, the only indication that anything had happened a certain tightness around his eyes. He was a better actor than most people gave him credit for. "I'm fine."

"Obviously, you're not." The deep voice pulled everyone's attention around. CB, who never came out on the soundstage while they were shooting, stood at the edge of the set. It looked significantly smaller than it had. He waited until the murmurs of surprise died down—waited with an attitude that clearly said they'd better die down damned fast—and then continued. "You are too valuable to me and to this show to allow what might be a potentially serious situation to continue. Do you have a doctor in the area, Mr. Nicholas?"

"No, I . . ."

"Then you will see mine. I will take you myself. Now."

"But the scene . . ."

"Reaction shots can be done without you."

Tony wondered how CB knew they were on reaction shots. Direct video feed to his office? Psychic powers? Lucky guess?

"Mr. Wu . . ."

Alan jumped at the sound of his name.

". . . can read your lines to Ms. Harding and Mr. Polintripolous. Mr. Polintripolous can read your lines to Ms. Harding and Mr. Wu. While I appreciate your willingness to do the job, at this exact moment I would rather you tend to your health. Mr. Foster."

Tony's turn to jump.

"Accompany Mr. Nicholas to his dressing room and then, once he has washed up and changed into his own clothing, to my office." As Lee began to protest, he raised a hand. "If whatever happened just now happens again, I want someone near enough to you to help."

So much for not being associated in Lee's mind with personal disaster.

A lesser man would have extended his scene by sweeping those assembled with an imperious glare; CB merely turned on one heel and left, his force of personality such that Tony almost expected to see the swirl of an Imperial cape and hear the studded sandals of his Praetorian guard slap against the floor.

No one moved until they heard the door to the soundstage close.

"All right, people, let's reset for Laura's reactions. Alan, you're reading Lee's lines."

As Peter moved back behind the monitors, Adam gently took hold of Lee's shoulder and shoved him toward the exit. "You'd better go; he's waiting."

"I don't need to see a doctor." He sounded annoyed. It wasn't quite enough to cover the fear.

"CB thinks you do, so . . ." Adam shrugged. "What can it hurt? It's probably nothing."

"Probably," Lee repeated, but from the look on his face he was thinking of some of the things it *probably* wasn't.

Tony wanted to tell him that it was none of those. It wasn't MS, it wasn't ADSS; it wasn't any of a dozen neurological disorders that would destroy his career then finally take his life. Unfortunately, it was something worse. Worse numerically anyhow, since an invasion by the Shadowlord would also destroy his career and take his life—along with countless other lives.

"Tony."

About to fall into step beside the actor, he glanced over at Adam.

"The moment Lee's in CB's office, you head right back."

He felt his cheeks flush. "Sure." Skip out early once and never hear the end of it.

Lee was half a dozen steps in front of him now, the set of his shoulders announcing that he neither needed nor wanted company. Too bad. As Tony hurried to catch up, he checked out the spot where Arra had been standing and wasn't surprised to find her gone. He hadn't actually expected her to stay around and do something useful. Something wizardly.

The red light came on seconds after they closed the door.

The show going on.

Stepping into the cleared area in front of the washroom, for the first time walking side by side, a shadow skittered across their path. They jerked back. Lee caught a kind of moan in his throat and held it there.

"Just this coat," Tony said, grabbing a fistful of fabric and yanking the coat still. "It sort of moved out in front of the light."

Lee had shoved his way through the costumes with enough force to set the racks swaying and, in turn, the costumes. He looked at the coat, then turned just far enough to stare at Tony; kept staring long enough so Tony was sure he was going to demand an explanation.

"You know what's happening around here, Foster. Spill it."

Or perhaps a little more twenty-first Century. *"What the hell is up with these shadows?"*

Lee's eyes narrowed. Then, without a word, he stomped the last three meters to his dressing room, entered, and slammed the door.

"Yeah." Tony leaned on the scuffed drywall between Lee's dressing room and makeup. "I'll just wait out here."

◆

". . . go through thousands of bottles of water every week and so crushing them before they go into the recycling bin is crucial or they're just not going to fit." Amy speared a piece of spiral pasta and frowned into its pattern. "Not to mention that whole wind catching them when they're dumped and bouncing them over hell's half acre thing." Looking up, her frown deepened. "Tony? Are you even listening to me?"

He tore his gaze away from a patch of shadow climbing the soundstage wall. "Yeah. Crushing plastic water bottles. I heard you. Amy, can I tell you something a little . . . weird?"

"About Lee?"

Lee was the principal topic of a hundred lunch discussions. "Sort of."

"Good thing Mason wasn't on the set," she snorted, picking through her chicken fettuccini. "He hates it when Lee gets more attention than he does." The office staff had their own kitchen and their own caterer, but every one of them believed that the food on the soundstage was better. When the show was shooting on set, they ran a lottery to see who'd get to eat with the cast and crew. Amy won fairly often and when the inevitable protests arose, she reminded her coworkers that eventually someone would complain and the odds were good she'd be the one catching the shit. So far, no one had. Since there was always enough food for a dozen extra people and Mason usually ate in his dressing room, it was unlikely anyone ever would. She looked up, caught sight of Tony's face, and stilled. "This is serious." When he nodded, she put down her fork. "Go ahead."

Where to start? "There's a gate to another world, like a metaphysical gate, in the soundstage."

When he paused, unsure, she nodded. "Go on."

"Shadows come through it controlled by an evil wizard they call Shadowlord."

"He controls the gate or the shadows?"

"Both."

"And the shadows call him Shadowlord?"

"No. The people of that world." He slipped his hands under the table and wiped sweaty palms against his thighs. This was going better than he'd hoped. "The other world."

"Right."

"These shadows are like his spies and they're coming through to find out about this world so that he can invade and conquer it."

"Why?"

"Why what?"

"Why invade and conquer? What's his motivation?"

"I don't know; invading and conquering, I guess. What difference does it make?"

"You have to know his motivation, Tony."

"It doesn't matter!" As heads turned he lowered his voice. "The point is; these shadows can kill, have already killed, and now there's at least four more."

"So how do you stop them?"

"I don't know."

"You need a hero."

"Tell me about it. Although I'm not sure a hero would solve the problem. Arra's a wizard . . ."

"So she's working on this, too?"

"Not really. She doesn't want to get involved. I think she's afraid."

"Of what, bad writing?" Amy snorted. "Because if she is, she's working on the wrong show."

"Of the Shadowlord!"

"Well, he doesn't sound very scary. But let me take a look at the script; you never know."

"Script?"

"Yeah, for your show about the Shadowlord." Her brows drew in as she reached for her butter tart. "Or was it an episode of *this* show? You weren't exactly clear on that."

"It's not a script! It's . . ." About to say it was real, Tony paused, looked, really looked into Amy's face, and realized he'd never convince her. She had nothing to anchor this kind of a situation on. She'd never faced the possibility of a demon's name written in blood across her city, never seen an ancient Egyptian wizard kill with a glance, never felt sharp teeth bite through the skin of her wrist, never heard the soft sounds of her lover feeding. Well, maybe the latter, but . . . never mind. The point was; if he tried to convince her, she'd think he was either yanking her chain or losing his mind. "It's not a script," he repeated. "It's just an idea." He shoved back his chair and stood. "I need to go talk to Arra."

"Can I have your Nanaimo bar?"

He found a smile from somewhere, probably the same place Lee'd found his earlier. "Sure."

"Work on the hero. The whole thing falls apart without one."

♦

The magic on the basement stairs tried once again to turn him back. Tony gritted his teeth and ignored it. It wasn't real. Or it wasn't any more real than anything thing else she did for *Darkest Night*. It was all smoke and mirrors. Or maybe smoke and shadows . . .

Arra was at her desk, back toward him as he crossed the shadowless room. All but one of her monitors showed solitaire games. On the final monitor she seemed to be combining a graphics program with data entry. Equations scrolled up around a complex spiral made up of strange symbols rather than a solid line. As Tony closed the final distance, the last equation reached the center and disappeared. Arra right clicked her mouse and the spiral flared . . . he had no idea what color that was although watering eyes insisted purple came closest. The light lasted for less than a second, then vanished, and the monitor screen was blank.

About to ask her what she was doing, Tony suddenly realized he didn't have to.

"You're going to gate out. That was a computer mock-up of a new gate!"

"A computer mock-up of a metaphysical construct?" Arra spun around to face him, eyes rolling. "You know that's impossible, right?"

"There are more or less sentient shadows falling

through a hole in the air and killing people!" He was shouting. He didn't care. The situation certainly called for shouting and he had no idea how he'd resisted to this point. "I think you'll find that the bar for impossible has been set pretty damned high!"

"Don't you mean low?"

"I have no fucking idea!"

"You tried to tell someone, didn't you?"

"What?"

She jerked her head back toward the solitaire games. "Sixes blocked on all of them. A romantic idea of responsibility and justice; you tried to warn people, to raise the alarm." Her tone softened slightly as she met his eyes again. "The trouble is no one will believe you. You're talking about things that ninety-nine percent of the people of this world refuse to see."

"Yeah. I get that." He'd dialed down the volume, but the anger was still very much there. "They'd believe you."

"Me?"

"You could make them believe you. You could prove that it's real."

"How? With magic? I should show them walking corpses or turn a sofa into a flock of geese? Tony, I do that every day and all they see is a special effect. They've seen wizards fly and petrify their friends and strike down their enemies from across the room. They *know* it's a trick. Nothing I can do will convince the ninety and nine otherwise."

"Fine! What about the one percent?"

"Well . . ." Arra sighed and spread her hands. ". . . that would be you."

"You can't make this whole thing my responsibility!"

"I'm not."

She sounded so calm and matter-of-fact, it drove the volume right back up again. He wanted to wrap his hands around her throat and shake her until she took him seriously; until she agreed to help; until she destroyed the shadows—unfortunately, he could only shout. "You can't just fucking run away from this!"

"Yes, I can."

"But it's *your* fault! You opened the gate to this world! You gave him a way to get here!" A small voice in the back of Tony's head seemed to be suggesting that pissing off a wizard was less than smart. Tony ignored it. "If you run, eventually he'll find that gate, too and he'll think, 'oh good idea, another world to conquer' and you'll have to run again. And again. You're thinking of no one but yourself!"

Her lip curled. "And who do you suggest I take through the gate with me? Who chooses who lives and who dies? Do I take you and leave the rest?"

"That's not what I fucking meant! How many worlds are you going to leave in ruins behind you?"

"Do you think I wanted it to turn out this way?" She surged up out of the chair with enough force to slam it back against the desk and shake the monitors.

"I think you don't care that it has."

"Caring means *nothing*!" Loud enough to echo, the word circled around them for a moment. When it faded, she took a deep breath and continued, back in control. "It didn't then, it won't now. It won't ever! If I could have saved my world, I would have! If I could save this world, I would. But I couldn't and I can't, and if all I can save is myself, then I'm not going to sit around here and die! Tell the world if you want to. Give a news conference. Maybe someone in that one percent is a person in power and, convinced, will face the Shadowlord with soldiers and weapons. It still won't matter. It didn't and it won't. He can't be stopped. And if you need to hear it, I'm sorry. But that doesn't matter either. He's barely begun and the end is already in the can. You can't stop it."

"I have to try."

Her snort spoke volumes. "If you go down fighting, you're just as dead as if you lived out your final days happily ignoring the inevitable. I can make you forget again."

"And that worked so well last time," he sneered. "In fact, now that I think of it, your previous work was not exactly inspiring. We don't even know if your potion did anything but drop Lee drunk on his ass. You said that sometimes the shadows have no effect. This could have been one of those times. So you know what? I'm going to take out those four new shadows my . . ."

"Seven."

"What?"

"I counted seven shadows."

"Fine. Whatever. Seven. I'll take them out myself." He spun on his heel, the rubber screaming against the floor, and headed for the stairs. "I don't need you."

"Good. Because I have no intention of watching another world die."

Anger carried him to the top of the stairs, then, hand on the latch, he paused. And turned. He couldn't see the desk, couldn't tell if Arra was still standing where he'd left her but, to borrow a phrase he'd heard too damned many times in the last few minutes, it didn't matter. She could hear him. "What about your cats?"

"What?"

"Your cats. They'll die, too."

"Grow up, Tony. They're cats."

"And you took responsibility for their lives."

As he closed the basement door behind him, he thought he heard her say, "What's two more?" but the words were so quiet and weighted with sorrow, he couldn't be sure.

◆

'Tony, what the hell are you doing?"

It wasn't quite a scream. The complicated patterns of light and darkness that came with television lighting had been scraping at his nerves. Shadows that were nothing more than patches of blocked light kept mov-

ing, changing shape, and disappearing. Crawling out
from under the worktable, Tony switched off the beam
of the strongest flashlight he'd been able to find and
twisted around until he could stare up at Adam. "I
thought I saw . . ." A quick glance to either side, an obvious check for eavesdroppers, and a lowering of his
voice. ". . . a rat."

"Jesus."

"Yeah, well I thought that while I wasn't needed for
other stuff, I should have a look and see if I could find
droppings and shit."

"Droppings are shit."

"Right."

The 1AD waited a moment then sighed. "And?"

"And what?"

"And did you find any?"

"Not yet, but this place has a billion nooks and
crannies."

"Yeah, it's a regular English muffin."

"What?"

"Nothing. Forget it. And keep looking. The last thing
we need is to be part of *another* remake of *Willard*."

Official sanction—of a sort—didn't help. By the end
of the afternoon, he'd found a dozen pens, a radio, three
scripts for two different shows, a rather disturbing number of condom wrappers, and some rodent droppings,
but no minions of the Shadowlord.

Seven shadows.

Twenty to thirty people on the soundstage. But not him,
or Lee, or Arra. And why not Lee? Because he'd already
been taken over and therefore pumped dry of all relevant
information? Why not; that theory made as much sense as
any of this did. So say, twenty-five minimum. Unless . . . was
that why Arra was leaving? Because she was controlled by
shadow? Possible, but not likely. After yesterday's adventure in Lee's dressing room, he was about 99% certain that
he'd be able to spot the shadow-controlled; so, no easy excuses for the wizard. She was leaving because she was a . . .

"Tony."

Still not quite a scream but getting closer.

Peter frowned. "Are you all right?"

Any one of the twenty-five could have been taken over by shadow. Peter's looked to be attached to his heels, but they were sneaky. Tricky. "Just a little jumpy."

"Well, don't be. I get enough overemoting from the actors." His smile suggested a shared joke. Tony tried to respond and didn't quite manage. "Anyway, good job on the rat thing. Those little bastards can do more damage than a touring fan club. Which reminds me; there'll be one through on Monday. One of Mason's, I think. So, on your way out, tell someone in the office to order some poison."

"For the fans?"

"Don't tempt me."

◆

"Not poison. The rats eat poison, then they die in the walls or under a piece of equipment and the whole place stinks more than it usually does. We need traps. And not the sticky traps either because then you've just got a scared, pissed-off rat with his feet stuck to a giant roach motel, I mean it's got to be embarrassing for them. We need the kind of traps that . . ." Amy brought the side of her right hand down on the palm of her left.

Tony jumped.

"Are you all right? Because you're looking a little spooked."

"Rat traps. You know, things dying," he continued when she frowned. Amy had been in the soundstage for lunch. He leaned around her desk trying to get a look at her shadow.

"What the hell are you doing?"

"I just . . . nothing. I thought I saw something fall. Off your desk."

Eyes rolled between dark green lashes. "It had better not be the damned highlighter again. I spend half my life crawling around after it." Holding a fall of cranberry hair back with one hand, she shoved her chair out from the desk and bent down. Her shadow went with her.

Not Amy, then.

Not unless this lot was cleverer than yesterday's and were lying low until they got away from the people who might identify them. The person. Him. How was he supposed to follow twenty-five people. *No, stupid, you don't need to. You just need to be back here at 11:15 tonight to take them out. One zap of the lamp. A bright idea that'll shed a little light on the matter. Ha! Take that, Shadowlord. We laugh at your darkness!*

"Yo! Earth to Tony! Is there like a laser site aimed at my forehead or something because you've been staring at that same spot for a truly uncomfortable amount of time?"

"What?" He blinked and focused on Amy's face. "Sorry. I was thinking."

"It looked painful."

"You'd be surprised." *Oh, man, I'm going to need gallons of that potion.*

"What about?"

He dragged his focus back into the production office and away from the thought of trying to get half a liter of warm, green, sparkly vodka down the throats of seven semiconscious people. Next thing to impossible even with Henry's help. "What was I thinking about?"

Amy snorted. "Duh. Are you dehydrated or something because ..." She spun her chair around and glared at Veronica, seated at the office's third desk, receiver under her ear and an expression of near panic on her pale face. "Are you going to get that?"

The office PA's eyes widened and "near panic" inched closer to losing the word "near." "I'm already talking to three people, well one person and two on hold, and Barbara wanted me to go through last week's files to find an invoice from Everett and Ruth wants the phone bills entered and filed and . . ."

"Never mind." She turned back to her desk, mouthed *wuss* at Tony, and picked up the phone. "CB Productions . . ."

Allowing the familiar sound to wash over him, Tony turned away from the desk just as Zev emerged from post. Zev! Zev hadn't been on the soundstage in days. There was no way he could be a minion. Although he *was* clearly a little confused by the way Tony was smiling at him considering how things had been left between them earlier.

Time to fix that. Tony needed to be with someone he knew wasn't possessed and work a little of the twitchy out. Get himself grounded so he could plan. Fill at least some of the time between now and 11:15. Amy would be likely to ask him about his "script" and besides it was Friday night. She probably had a date. Arra—well, he'd had a bellyful of her for one day and he still had to approach her about the potion. Given the cooperation he'd got from her this afternoon, he was definitely going to need Henry for that and Henry wouldn't be awake for another three hours. But Zev! Zev was . . . starting to look just a little nervous.

Ratcheting down the smile, Tony crossed to where the music director was standing. *Hang on. Maybe he has a date, it being Friday night and all.* A little late to worry about that now. "Hey. Sorry I was such an ass yesterday. Can I make it up to you?"

"By not being an ass?"

"Well, yeah. That, too, but I was thinking maybe we could go out for coffee or a beer or you know, something."

Zev's brows rose—arched innuendo.

"No, not that kind of something. I mean, I just thought . . ." He sputtered to a halt and was relieved to see Zev smile.

"Coffee or a beer would be fine. When?"

"Now. Well, as soon as I finish up which should be no

more than half an hour. With Lee gone, we're stopping early."

Zev glanced down at his watch. "I've got to be parked by sunset so that might be cutting it a little close."

"Sunset's not for *three* hours," Tony pointed out then added, as Zev's brows rose again. "They list it in the paper. I just happened to remember." After all those years with Henry, he couldn't stop remembering—no need to mention that.

"Friday night traffic can be a problem, even heading into the city, but I guess half an hour won't make that much difference. It had better be coffee, though. There's a place that carries kosher about four blocks from my apartment; it'd make it a little easier for me if you don't mind."

"I don't mind."

They agreed to meet back in the office and as Zev disappeared back into post, Tony turned to see Amy giving him two thumbs up. Fucking great. Now everyone would assume he and Zev were out on a date. And, except for in Amy's tiny little mind, it wasn't a date. He liked Zev and all, but the music director just wasn't . . .

. . . Lee Nicholas.
God. I really am an ass.

♦

The clientele in the coffee shop/bakery was mostly the same Gen-X group that hung around in coffee shops all over the city; the main difference being that most of the men wore yarmulkes and the bakery sold hamantaschen, the triangular Purim cookies.

"Oh, man, I love these things," Tony enthused as the counter staff put two on a paper plate.

"So do a lot of people," Zev sighed as he moved his tray toward the cash register. "That's why they bake them all year now."

"Is that a problem?"

He shrugged and smiled a little sheepishly. "No, I just think it makes them less . . ."

"Special?"

"Yeah."

"Just part of the whole strawberries in February thing. I have a friend who thinks the world went to hell when we started being able to get strawberries in February," he elaborated as Zev looked confused. "He says we've lost touch with the circle of life."

"I'll pass on the singing warthogs if it's all the same to you."

"Okay, I'm paraphrasing a bit. He doesn't actually quote Disney." Although the thought of Henry facing off against the Mouse was pretty funny. Reaching for his wallet with one hand, he grabbed Zev's arm with the other. "I'll get it. I asked."

"I made you come all the way to South Granville, I'll get it."

"You drove and I'm a lot closer to home than I was."

"I make considerably more than you do."

"Okay." Grinning broadly, Tony stepped back and motioned him forward. "That's convincing."

Although they'd said very little during the drive into the city and had barely spoken during the short walk after parking the car, the silence when they sat down was suddenly weighted. Watching Zev take a swallow of coffee, Tony tried to come up with something they could talk about besides work. Talking about work would just remind him of shadows. Seven shadows. Seven shadows possessing. Seven shadows spying . . .

"Tony?"

"Sorry." He took a bite of apricot hamantasch, chewed, swallowed, and said, "So, what do you do when you're not working?"

It was a good thing they *weren't* dating. He sounded like a major spaz.

"Um . . . you know. The usual stuff. Laundry. Television. Scrabble."

"What?"

His cheeks slightly flushed, Zev stared into his mug. "I play competitive Scrabble."

"Really? I mean, I don't doubt you or anything," Tony hastened to add, "it's just that's so cool. I had a cheap Scrabble CD-ROM I got attached to a box of cereal and the computer kicked my ass, even at the idiot level. And you play competitively?"

"Yes."

"Wow."

"Sometimes I play in Hebrew."

"Now, you're bragging."

"A little."

They shared a smile and all of a sudden it wasn't so hard to find things to talk about.

Zev was an ardent Libertarian, slightly unusual in Socialist-leaning British Columbia. Tony, who'd picked up most of his political beliefs from the bastard son of Henry VIII, had to admit that a number of Zev's points made a lot of sense. Someday, when he thought life was getting dull, he'd mention them to Henry. Fortunately, before Zev could wonder just what he was smiling about, a fan of the show spotted their production jackets, enthused for a few minutes, and reminded Tony that he'd wanted to ask a question about the *Darkest Night* theme.

"That creepy bit under the title; what instrument is that?"

"The piece under the title is all voice. A trio, two women, one man—Leslie, Ingrid, and Joey are their names—I think, it's been a while—but they go by FKO."

"Okay, I get the KO; that's Knockout, but what's the F stand for."

Grinning, Zev raised both hands. "I didn't want to ask."

Eventually, they segued into a discussion of the Olympic highway extension up to Whistler—an obligatory topic when two or more Vancouverites got together.

Away from work, CB Productions' musical director

let loose a sardonic sense of humor and was actually a pretty funny guy. And it *wasn't* a date or anything, but Tony was having a good time. Starting to relax. No longer jumping at shadows. Much.

"Is that the time?" Zev shoved his chair out from the table and stood. "I've got to get going."

Tony checked his watch as he got to his feet. 7:25. A little more than half an hour until sunset. Still plenty of time to get Henry and have him convince Arra to prepare more sparkly green vodka.

"I hadn't realized it was so late," Zev continued as he hooked the strap of his laptop case up over one shoulder. "I'm sorry, but I can't drive you home."

"It's okay, I didn't expect you to."

"Do you even know how to get home from here?"

Smiling, Tony fell into step beside him as he headed for the door. "There's a transit stop about ten meters up Oak, Zev. I think I can manage."

"Up Oak along Broadway . . ."

"I've got it."

"It's raining . . ."

"It's Vancouver."

"Good point." Another awkward silence. "I'll, uh, see you at work on Monday."

"Sure." Unless the world ended over the weekend; and a 6,000 watt carbon arc lamp aside, Tony wasn't ruling that out. They stood in the rain for a moment, then Zev shrugged, waved, and headed west along Fifty-first.

There was one other person in the transit shelter, a big guy staring at the city map Plexiglas-ed into one wall. Shifting his backpack onto one shoulder, Tony projected the *I'm not worth bothering vibe* he'd perfected living on the street as he dug around in his backpack for his phone. Past time to call Henry.

Then the big guy looked up.

"Mouse? Jeez, I didn't recognize you."

The cameraman blinked at him, headlights from a passing car throwing shadows across his face.

Except that when the car was gone, the shadows remained.

Crap.

Minion of the Shadowlord front and center.

Big minion.

Really wishing he'd gotten that whole hero thing worked out, Tony stepped back until his shoulders hit Plexiglas and back was no longer an option.

Eight

THE LEADING edge of the shadow army was less than a day's march away. Standing on the city walls, mirror raised to catch the late afternoon light, Arra could see past the pockets of battle, past the men and women struggling to defeat an enemy their superior in both strength and numbers, past the black tents well warded against magical attack, and into the swath of destruction that stretched back to the border.

Crops had been burned in the field and the ground salted. She could see the remains of livestock slaughtered and devoured by the invaders. After his victory, the Shadowlord would feed those who abased themselves before him; those who forgot pride and honor and crawled on their bellies to his feet.

Every building still standing after the front line passed by had been put to the torch. When winter came, only the abject would survive.

Above the camps of the captured were stakes that held the bodies of those who had tried to escape, those who had tried to stand up to the random cruelty of their guards, those who hadn't quite given up hope. Some of the bodies were moving, but they were still bodies for all that. The living were prisoners now, slaves when the conquest was complete.

Arra looked away from her mirror and out at the empty landscape between the city and the army. She could see shadows lying where shadows should not be. Moving in ways shadows did not move. The vanguard of the Shadowlord—his eyes and ears.

Magic kept them from the city—hers and the two remaining members of her order. Three. All that was left. Four had died in battle, unable to stand against dark magics fueled by a seemingly endless supply of pain and blood. Two had been killed when they returned to the city controlled by shadow—but not before the shadows had used their power to do great damage. The eldest had died finishing the wards that protected the walls, wards fraying under the constant onslaught of power, wards that would fail, by her calculations, just about the same time the invading army reached the gates.

The last three wizards would walk out together to face the Shadowlord.

In spite of all they had done, in spite of all they had made ready, in spite of all they hoped, their linked power would not be enough.

Arra had looked into the crystal. She knew how this would end.

They would die, then the wards would fail, the gates would fall, and the city, filled to overflowing with those who had thought it a refuge, would be destroyed.

She turned, the heavy rubber soles of her sneakers squealing against the dressed stone. The city stretched out before her now, both the large icons like Stanley Park, Lions Gate Bridge, and Science World as well as the smaller, more personal ones like the Sun-Yat-Sen Garden, The Boathouse, and Café Bergman. All these would fall to shadow, the people into slavery.

No more walking down to the coffee shop on the corner for the *Saturday Globe and Mail* and a double mocha latte.

She looked deep into the cardboard cup she held between both hands and breathed in the steam rising off the foam, enjoying for maybe the last time the scent of . . .

... tuna?

That wasn't right. The cup filled with shadow. She fought to draw in breath against the weight on her chest. A point of pain on her chin. And then another ...

Arra opened her eyes to find Zazu perched on her sternum, one paw half raised, the claws still extended. Freeing her hand from the tangle of the afghan, she rubbed between the black ears.

"We asked for help from those countries we traded with across the sea. And do you know what they said?"

Zazu blinked amber eyes.

"They said, 'This is no concern of ours. *We* are not under attack.' " Arra sighed and waved on the lights. She hated falling asleep on the couch. Sinking into the overstuffed cushions eventually folded her spine into serpentine shapes and the less than comfortable position always brought on dreams. Memories. "Those who conquer for the sake of conquering," she continued, lifting the cat off of her chest and onto the coffee table, "will not let so small a thing as an ocean stand in their way. Do you think the Shadowlord is a concern of theirs now or does he search through the gate for an easier conquest?"

Zazu's answer concerned an empty food dish. Whitby, always the less vocal of the two, knocked a stack of CDs off the table.

"You're right." She grabbed the back curve of the couch, and hauled herself into a sitting position. "This is no concern of yours."

Standing, she watched both cats run for the kitchen and sighed. "Yet."

Tony should never have brought them into this.

♥

Henry had been to Tony's newest apartment, the compromise apartment halfway between downtown Vancouver and Burnaby, only once officially—the week Tony had moved in. Twice if he counted the time he'd caught Tony's scent at a club, followed it out to an alley, then later followed Tony home—wanting to ask just what the hell the younger man thought he was doing but unable to find a way that wouldn't make it seem as though he'd been stalking him like some clichéd horror movie creature of the night. He'd sat in his car, in the rain, watching a shadow move behind curtained windows and reminding himself that Tony was not his responsibility. That he hadn't been for some time. That it was possible to have a friend—to be a friend—and not control the relationship. He wasn't certain which aspect he was trying to convince: vampire or prince. Or if, in this instance, there was any difference between the two.

It was raining again on this, his third, visit although he was there for a better reason. Tony should have called right after sunset to let him know what had happened at the studio when the gate had opened. What fallout, if any, had there been from their adventure last night. What reaction, if any, from the Shadowlord at the loss of his minion.

Tony hadn't called. Not right after sunset. Not since.

Perhaps he was busy.

The television industry worked obscene hours. It didn't seem to make any difference to the end product, most of which seemed created for hormonally challenged adolescents, but he knew that twelve- or thirteen-hour days were the standard. Tony could easily still be at work although it was unlikely that he'd consider a bad forty-three minute syndicated program more important than the possible end of life as he knew it.

Perhaps he was in trouble.

It was possible that the Shadowlord had reacted aggressively and that Tony had borne the brunt of whatever had come through the gate.

Neither possibility could be confirmed by breaking into Tony's apartment, but it was a place to start. And, as it was almost exactly halfway between his condo and the studio, it only made sense to check it first. The answering machine had picked up when he'd called; the recorded voice no answer at all. But then, if CB Productions *had* fallen under the thrall of a dark wizard, it was unlikely anyone would be manning the phones.

Henry'd also called the wizard—who worked with Tony, who'd theoretically also been there when the gate had opened at 11:15 AM. If she was home, she'd invoked the modern magic of call screening.

Tony's building, a three-story brick cube built like a thousand others in the late seventies, had no security. The door leading into the stairwell from the small vestibule holding the mailboxes had been locked while open so that the steel tongue slammed against the frame preventing it from closing. Handy if the residents had friends coming over. Not so handy if they had anything worth stealing. Given the condition of the halls, Henry suspected the latter was unlikely.

The building superintendent was in apartment six. Moments after he answered the door to Henry's knock, Henry was in Tony's apartment and the superintendent had forgotten he'd ever moved away from his recliner.

Tony's sofa bed was unmade, his breakfast dishes still in the sink, and the clothes he'd worn yesterday in a pile on the bathroom floor. The fridge held mostly packets of condiments from various fast food establishments as well as eight eggs, a loaf of bread, a half-empty jar of peanut butter, and a bottle of generic cola. It took Henry a few minutes to find the television remote— although upon reflection the top of the toilet tank was an almost logical place. Disk one of the extended *Two Towers* was in the DVD player and last week's episode of *Federation,* the new *Star Trek* series, was in the ancient VCR. Tony'd mentioned he was saving for a TiVo, but apparently he hadn't managed it yet.

Henry tossed the remote back onto the tangle of blankets. He was no farther ahead than he had been. Although Tony's scent permeated the apartment, he clearly hadn't been there for some hours. He'd gone to work. He hadn't returned.

There were only two possible scenarios. He was still working. He'd been taken by the Shadowlord. Either way, he was still at the studio.

About to open the door, Henry paused. He could feel a life in the hallway; he'd wait until the way was clear. If Tony was all right, if it turned out he was only working late, the fewer people who saw him here the better. Less embarrassing for them both.

Then the life paused outside the door.

And knocked.

Lee Nicholas' familiar face filled the peephole. The distortion made it difficult to read his expression.

As Henry understood it, Tony and the actor were barely considered coworkers given their respective positions on *Darkest Night*. While they might be friendly, they were certainly not friends, and no matter how much Tony might want it to be otherwise, it was highly unlikely that anything more than friendship would ever develop between them.

So, what was Lee Nicholas doing at Tony's door on a Friday night?

Henry smiled. He opened the door, the Hunger held carefully in check. There was always the chance that the actor was controlled by shadow once again and he had no intention of giving away more than he had to.

"Yes?"

The flash of a photogenic smile. "I was looking for Tony Foster." He was nervous. He hid it well, but Henry could smell it. That, and expensive cologne, was all he could smell—there was no taint of another world.

"Tony's not home from work yet."

"That's strange." One hand swept up through dark hair. "I heard they quit early today."

"Early?" Not good.

"Yeah."

"How early?"

"About . . ." The green eyes narrowed slightly as he looked past Henry's shoulder. "Who are you?"

And Henry realized that he'd never bothered to turn on the apartment lights. About to explain that he was on his way out, he watched Lee's gaze track back to the damp patches on the shoulders of his trench coat and decided the truth would serve better than a lie. "I'm looking for him, too." He held up his own key ring. "I have a key." Well, most of the truth.

"Oh." And a visible jump to the wrong conclusion. "Right."

"Did you want to leave a message?"

"What? No, that's okay. I, uh . . . I have to . . . um . . . I left my *date* waiting in the car. I'll see Tony at the studio on Monday."

Interesting emphasis; although the *date* in the car meant this next part had to be quick. He allowed the Hunger to rise to the border of terrifying where coercion waited then caught Lee's gaze with his and held it. "What do you remember of your time under the control of shadow?"

"I don't know what you're talking about!"

Not a lie. Tempted to turn the question to a command, Henry reluctantly acknowledged that the hallway of an apartment building where neither of them lived, with a *date* waiting, with no idea of how the actor would react to the memories, was probably not the best place. So he settled for, "What did you want to speak to Tony about?"

"He was there, this morning, when I . . ." Terror surfaced from the depths of the green. Terror Henry wasn't evoking. ". . . collapsed. I just wanted to know if he . . . If there was anything . . ." Hands rose to waist level, opening and closing as though trying to hang onto the thought. "I just . . ."

This was a man perilously close to the edge. Half tempted to push him over to see where he'd land, Henry allowed his better nature to rule and backed the

Hunger down, releasing the actor's eyes. "I'll tell him you stopped by."

"No, that's … yeah, sure." Barely holding it together, he turned away then turned back again, dark brows drawn in. "Do I know you? I mean, have we met before?"

Interesting. As far as Henry could remember, they'd never actually met before last night. "Perhaps you've seen me with Tony."

"Yeah. Sure. That must be it." Squared shoulders and a crisp nod, but Henry could see the tremors mortal eyes would miss.

He waited in the hall until he heard the door to the building clang not-quite-closed then hurried down to the landing to look out the window. Shoulders hunched against the rain, Lee Nicholas trotted across the street to where a busty blonde waited in his classic Mercedes. As he got into the car, he said something to make the blonde laugh, his body language suggesting that nothing worse than bad hair had happened to him in the last forty-eight hours.

The man was definitely a better actor than most people gave him credit for.

Tony was with him when he collapsed. Something had happened when the gate reopened. What? And where was Tony?

On cue, his cell phone rang.

"Tony? Where the hell have you been?"

"Close but no cigar, Nightwalker. I assume he's not with you?"

"No."

"He's not answering his phone."

Henry glanced up the stairs toward the apartment before he realized which phone the wizard was referring to. "He can't turn it on in the studio."

"He's not at the studio. They finished early today."

"Sometimes he forgets to turn it on when he leaves." He was grasping at straws and he knew it.

"Seven shadows came through the gate this morning,

Nightwalker. Seven. He would have called and told you about that were he able. And then the two of you would have appeared at my door demanding more of my time. More of the potion."

Were he able. "Yes."

"Where are you?"

"At Tony's apartment."

"I assume there's no sign of him?"

"None."

"Wait there. I'll make a couple of calls and get right back to you."

"I had thought, wizard, that you were unwilling to become involved in this fight."

"Did I say anything about fighting?"

He stood there holding his silent phone and admitted that, no, she hadn't. Enough for now that she was willing to help find Tony—who, it seemed, had, one way or another, been taken by shadow.

♥

"You see me."

"Jesus, Mouse, you're a big guy." Tony tried for a sardonic snort and didn't quite make it. "How could I miss you?"

The cameraman's callused hand closed around the back of Tony's neck. "You see me," he repeated. "The voice of the light did not see me. But you see me."

"Yeah, well, seeing a little too much of you right now." Mouse's face loomed so close over his that Tony could see every broken capillary, every enlarged pore, and he was getting a really good look at the scar from where Mouse's ex-wife had jabbed a nail file through his nose. He placed both hands flat against the barrellike chest and shoved. It worked about as well as he'd expected it to. "You want to back off a bit?"

"No. You and I are going to have a . . ." He fell silent, eyes squinted nearly shut as a set of high beams swept through the bus shelter.

Out of the direct line of light, Tony could see the police car approaching. Could see it slowing down. *Yes! Let's hear it for law and order. Little guy's getting manhandled by big guy, and the police . . .*

Mouse's mouth closing over his cut off the thought. And pretty much every other thought besides: *What is it with shadows in straight boys coming on to me?*

By the time Mouse lifted his head, the police car was gone.

Just fucking great, Tony thought, wiping his mouth on his sleeve. *We couldn't be in Toronto, where the cops'll bust your ass for PDAs. Oh, no, we have to be in fucking officially-tolerant-of-alternative-lifestyles Vancouver.*

"Don't do that again," he snarled.

"Or you'll what?"

"Tell Mouse's old lady."

A flash of fear. Either Mouse was in there listening or the shadows took on more than the physical form of the bodies they wore. Tony had a feeling that was important, but he didn't have time to work out why as Mouse's hand tightened to the point of pain and he was propelled out of the bus shelter and into the rain. "Hey! Where are we going?"

"Somewhere . . . quiet."

That didn't sound good. Tony went along without struggling, being no threat, no problem, giving Mouse no reason to think he might make a run for it. When they stopped beside Mouse's 1963 cherry-red, Mustang convertible, when Mouse—or rather the thing in Mouse's body—started digging for his keys, Tony dropped straight down to his knees, spun around, surged back up onto his feet, took two running steps away, and crashed face first into the wet sidewalk. His teeth went into the edge of his lip and his mouth filled with blood. He spat and twisted around. Within the circle of the light from the streetlamp, Mouse's shadow tangled with his.

The shadows in the bodies controlled the shadows of

the bodies—he should have remembered that—and those shadows could mess with the shadows of people—like him—who weren't being controlled. And that made so little real world sense it sounded like one of the less than brilliant ideas the bull pen horked up after a night of generic beer and cheese pizza.

Mouse smiled broadly enough for a pair of gold crowns to glitter. "Get in the car."

Tony spat again. He was through making it easy. "Make me."

One huge hand grabbed the waistband of his jeans, the other both straps of his backpack. A moment later he was in the passenger seat. He spared half a thought for the total shit-fit Mouse was going to have when he was back in control of his body and saw his upholstery and then tried to fling himself out the door.

Mouse's shadow flowed up and over his face.

Oh, crap . . .

Clawing at it didn't work. It gave under his fingers and then seeped back into the gouges. He already knew he couldn't breathe through it . . .

♥

Phone cradled between ear and shoulder, Arra tossed another handful of lemon balm into the vodka. "You might want to write this down, Nightwalker. He's at the Four Corners Bakery and Coffee Shop on Oak by Fifty-first—in South Granville. It's right by Schara Tzedeck, the Orthodox synagogue."

"You did a locator spell."

"No, I called Amy, his friend from work." A sniff of the steam and a bit more elecampane root. "She overheard Tony and Zev talking as they were heading for the parking lot."

"Tony and Zev?"

"Uh-huh." She pushed Zazu away from the stove with the side of her foot and wondered if she shouldn't have waited until the last minute to add the catnip.

"He had a *date?*"

"He's young, he's single, and it's Friday night." Arra grinned as the Nightwalker sputtered. "Jealous?"

"No. I am *not* jealous! I am . . ." The pause lasted long enough for her to get the cap off the jar of bay leaves. ". . . *appalled*. How can he consider dating, knowing what he knows about the Shadowlord."

"Knowing what he knows, he's wise to enjoy himself while he can." She could feel the grin slipping away. "I'll have potion enough for seven ready before the gate opens again."

He started to say something, but she shrugged the phone down into her hand and hit the disconnect. If he wanted to find Tony and if the two of them wanted to shine bright lights on the Shadowlord's spies, that was their business. Eventually, one of two things would happen; they'd realize they were whistling into the wind or they'd die fighting.

Since they'd already forced her involvement, she'd continue to make sure the taken had a chance to recover. Having done it once, balking at doing it again seemed foolish. And it put her in no more danger than any other person on this world.

This world.

Just another place she couldn't save.

There were people in the building who'd take the cats when she left.

♥

"I saw you this morning."

"Yeah? So?" Tony had pressed himself back as far into the bucket seat as he could, trying and failing to get away from Mouse's shadow as it pooled in his lap like a big, black . . . really creepy thing! It moved continually, like liquid but not, and in a futile attempt to get out from under its cool weight, his balls had climbed up so high they were practically sitting on his shoulder.

"You ran to Lee's side."

"Because he fell!"

"No." Mouse glanced over at him and then turned his attention back to Friday night traffic on the Granville Bridge. "You moved before he fell. You know something."

"I don't know anything! I just did what anyone would do."

"No one did."

"Did what?"

"What you did."

Tony rolled his eyes. Mouse had always been one of those guys who saw no point in using five words if three would almost do the job. "I was already there, so no one else had to do anything, did they?"

The cameraman/minion of the Shadowlord shrugged; a minimalist move of one burly shoulder that was all Mouse. As was the two-wheeled turn onto Hastings Street and the speed he was using to maneuver the Mustang around lesser vehicles. Tony thought the driver of a dark green Chevy Impala flipped them off as they passed, but they were by too quickly for him to be sure. *Oh, sure, if he drove like this across the border in the US, some guy with a Bud tucked in his crotch'd get so pissed off he'd haul out the shotgun and pop a few off which would get the cops into the act and we'd end up on the next episode of FOX TV's* High Speed Chases *heading for a dramatic finish where minion-guy here rolls the Mustang and I get rescued!*

Unfortunately, they were in Canada and the worst that could happen would be having the license plate recorded by the occupants of a police car who weren't allowed to participate in a high speed chase lest someone get hurt. There were times, and this was one of them, when that whole peace, order, and good government thing totally sucked.

And if Mouse allowed himself to be pulled over? A massive fine, six points off his license, and no chance in hell any cop would believe Tony's story. Amy hadn't believed him and Amy was his friend. Of course, years of experience with cops meant he'd have no trouble coming up with the kind of commentary that'd get his ass hauled out of the car. Police brutality, use it wisely. Then Henry'd come bail him out and he'd be safe. His moment of hope faded when he realized Mouse—or rather the minion riding in Mouse—would never allow himself to be pulled over.

A sudden lane change—closer to a lateral movement than should have been possible in a thirty-year-old Ford—nearly threw the shadow off Tony's lap. Without thinking, he caught it and scooped it back into place. It sloshed a bit and then settled, cool and weighted, against him.

His hand felt . . . soiled. He scrubbed it against the side of the seat.

"Stop that."

"But . . ."

"Now."

No mistaking the threat in Mouse's low growl, but it almost wasn't enough. Tony'd never wanted his hands clean quite so badly. And, once, way back, he'd held vomit. Someone else's vomit. Sitting there, suddenly terrified, he understood why people took wire brushes to their own skin.

♥

A little surprised that a kosher bakery hadn't closed for the Sabbath—although there was no actual reason *all* the staff had to be Orthodox or even Jewish for that matter—Henry picked up Tony's scent on the door. He wasn't inside, he wasn't anywhere in sight, and it was still almost raining in that ubiquitous West Coast more-than-a-mist not-quite-actual-drops way. It wouldn't be easy to track him.

On the bright side, in this neighborhood at this time on a Friday, there weren't a lot of people on the street.

Maybe he'd gone home with Zev.

And if he has . . . The growl sounded low in his throat before Henry could prevent it. An elderly man sitting at one of the bakery's small tables glanced up and, feeling a little foolish, Henry turned back toward the street. He should just call the wizard for Zev's address. The music director was a nice guy, attractive, smart—Tony could do worse. Perhaps a little of Arra's end-of-the-world pessimism had rubbed off and Tony was taking advantage of an opportunity to do what any young man would do in the same circumstances. Perhaps he'd decided to celebrate their victory over the shadow that had possessed Lee Nicholas. Perhaps whatever had happened with Lee Nicholas at the studio that morning had driven him into the arms of another.

Henry shook his head to clear that last thought. *Perhaps I've been writing romances for far too long.*

There were any number of valid reasons Tony hadn't called him.

But the wizard's phrase "were he able" kept sounding over and over again in Henry's head.

If Tony hadn't gone home with Zev, he'd have taken the bus north up Oak. A three-meter walk to the transit shelter would settle it once and for all. If Tony's scent wasn't in the shelter, he'd call the wizard for Zev's address. If it was . . .

It was.

The damp air had kept the scent from dissipating. Scent of Tony. Scent of fear. Scent of another world.

Seven shadows had come through that morning.

One of them seemed to have been studying the city map on the side of the shelter.

A mix of the two—one dragged by the other against the outside wall.

Away from the shelter, the rain had washed most of the Tony scent away but had had little effect on the other. Even the weather seemed to be avoiding it. It was easy enough to follow, though.

Henry snarled as the Hunger surged up at the scent of blood; faint, diffused, but unmistakable. Unmistakably Tony's.

On the sidewalk, caught in cracked concrete.

Again at the edge of the road, a drop against the side of the curb barely above the water running past in the gutter.

The obvious explanation: Tony had been flung, injured, into a car. The shadow-held had followed.

And the car had then been driven away.

He could be anywhere.

♥

They were heading for the studio. There was no other reason for them to be in Burnaby. Well, actually, according to the Burnaby Chamber of Commerce there were any number of reasons, but in this specific instance Tony had a feeling that only the studio and its gate to another world was actually relevant. "I won't tell you anything."

Mouse merely swung out around an SUV, muttered, "Fucking Albertans," and kept driving.

"I don't *know* anything!"

"You see me."

"Total fluke, I swear. I had a few years there where I did a lot of drugs. Probably melted the 'I don't see you' parts of my brain." He was babbling. He knew it, but he couldn't seem to stop the flow of words spilling out of his mouth. "I've seen a lot of things, you know. Things you wouldn't believe. That's probably why I see you. That's all."

Racing the end of an amber light, Mouse turned his head, eyes narrowed. "What have you seen?"

Shit.

"Nothing like you!"

The shadow pooled in Tony's lap began to slosh slowly back and forth, its movement independent of the movement of the car.

"Like what?"

A truck roared by in the other direction, horn blaring.

"Like watch the fucking road, man!" Heart slamming against his ribs, half convinced that the puddle in his lap was significantly warmer than it had been, Tony fought to bring his breathing under control as Mouse calmly swerved back into the eastbound lane. What would happen to the shadow if its host was jam under an eighteen wheeler? *And since I'll be jam right alongside him; do I really want to know?*

♥

Arra had no intention of getting into the Night-walker's car. She'd bring the two thermoses of potion down to the curb, pass them over, and wish him god-speed. Pick a god. If Tony had been taken by one of the shadow-held— Well, it was a shame, but it wasn't her concern.

"But it's your fault! You opened the gate to this world! You gave him a way to get here!"

"I did not." She shrugged into a bright yellow rain-coat and pulled her umbrella out of the painted milk can by the door. "All right, technically, I opened the gate, but it closed behind me. I went through it and it closed, and that's where my part in this ended."

Zazu rubbed up against her ankles and she pushed her away from the door. "Don't even think about it." A thermos tucked neatly into each of the huge yellow pockets. "I'll be back in . . ." Whitby raced down the hall chasing invisible invaders. Fur up, tail to one side, he slid to an undignified heap under the coffee table. Arra sighed. "Well, I'll be back."

"You're thinking of no one but yourself!"

Locking the door to her apartment, she headed for the elevator, ignoring with the ease of long practice the voice shouting accusations in her head.

"Caring means nothing!"

Her own voice had taken up the litany. That was new.

"If you're expecting me to argue that, think again," she muttered as the elevator doors opened.

Julian Rogers, her neighbor from across the hall, shifted his chihuahua to his other arm and sniffed disdainfully as he pushed past her. "Talking to yourself again, Arra?"

"I find it's the only way to have an intelligent conversation around here. And your dog is fat," she added with the doors safely closed.

The Nightwalker's car pulled up to the curb seconds after she arrived. If he'd taken a little longer, given her more time to think . . . but he hadn't, and when he reached across the front seat and opened the passenger door, she folded her umbrella, shook it once, and climbed in. She wouldn't waste either her time or her strength fighting the Shadowlord, but if the Nightwalker intended to rescue Tony, she had information that might help.

Might.

Might not.

Of course the whole thing would be moot if she died in a fiery car crash before she even got her seat belt done up. Thrown left and then right as the Nightwalker roared back onto the street and then around the corner onto Denman. The thermoses were making it impossible to do up her seat belt, so she pulled them out and set them at her feet—under her feet after a particularly angular lane change cracked one against her ankle.

"What makes you think the shadow-held is taking Tony to the studio?" she asked, finally managing to buckle up.

"He's being taken somewhere and the only somewhere these things have is the gate."

"That's logical enough, I suppose."

"You suppose? If you have a better idea . . ."

"No. And watch the road!" As he turned his gaze back to traffic, Arra tugged at a plastic fold in her lap. "I won't face it. I won't get that close to the shadow-held. Not again."

"Then why are you here?"

"We used to say, in my world, in my order, that knowledge is power."

"We say that here as well."

"Duh."

A muscle jumped in the Nightwalker's jaw. "You have knowledge I can use."

She shrugged, the plastic over her shoulders crinkling. "I have knowledge; whether or not you can use it, that's up to you. What I know is theory, extrapolated from past experience and the little I've observed since this . . . invasion began. The first shadows were scouts with no independence. It was as though the Shadowlord swept dark sponges through the gate and then squeezed out what they'd picked up. A second-generation scout followed us away from the studio on that location shoot and then returned with us. Then he sent through a shadow specifically seeking to know if there were lives here he could use . . . and Nikki Waugh died. He examined her life and decided that, yes, these were lives he could control."

"How do you know what he decided?"

"The people here are very like my people were—a little more technologically advanced but otherwise not so different." The streetlights divided the night into flickering shadow. Arra stared at the dashboard. "And that was what he decided the last time; when his shadow brought him one of *our* lives. Now, he sends spies to gather information to ease his conquest. The shadow in Lee Nicholas was what we called a rider, designed to live his life for a time and then return to be—reusing the sponge analogy—squeezed dry. On my world, the first riders stayed no more than a couple of hours. Then days. The last two we destroyed had been within their hosts for just over a week, making over those hosts into dark shadows of themselves."

Two members of her order died screaming, darkness pouring from them.

Arra shook herself free of the memory. "If one of the shadow-held has grabbed Tony . . ."

"One has." The two words were a low growl.

". . . then they're showing a greater degree of independence than he granted them in the past."

"He's had some years to work on refining them. In the time since you left, he could have created a whole new kind of shadow with, as you say, a greater degree of independence."

"So you're saying my information is out of date? Useless to you?"

Eyes locked on the road, he ignored her question. "I think he's sent these shadows through to discover what destroyed the shadow that was in Lee Nicholas. I think he sent them through looking for the light."

"It was a carbon arc lamp . . ."

"The metaphorical light."

The metaphorical light? Arra repeated silently. Then asked aloud, "And what makes you think that?"

"I've done some detective work in the past . . ."

"A vampire detective? Well, that's . . . original."

The steering wheel creaked under the Nightwalker's tightened grip. Probably not wise to poke at him—all right, definitely not wise—but impossible to resist. "The . . . shadow-held as you call it, grabbed Tony less than two blocks away from the largest, oldest Orthodox synagogue in Vancouver."

"And you think?"

"That Tony was coincidence. He was grabbed because he was there and knew the shadow for what it was. That the other six shadows are checking out churches and mosques. This world has no wizards, but it *has* light."

Temples fell, bodies seeking sanctuary were crushed under burning rubble.

"Not the kind that will help."

He glanced over at her, his eyes dark. "It causes you pain."

"What does?" she asked suspiciously.

"Talking about the shadows."

"Yeah. Well . . ." Arra grabbed for the dashboard as he accelerated through the end of an amber light and the beginning of a red. Horns blasted out a protest from two different directions. ". . . it's a welcome distraction from your driving!"

♥

It was Mouse and it wasn't Mouse, Tony decided by the time they reached the industrial park. The shadows were a separate personality—it had referred to itself as *me* so it had to be self-aware—but obviously they used parts of the personalities of their hosts. *Unless that other world comes with muscle cars and Vin Diesel wanna-bes.* Tony closed his eyes as the Mustang slithered between two trucks and opened them again as they turned into the studio parking lot.

Unfortunately, symbolism—not to mention the whole minion of an evil wizard thing—suggested the shadows used the darker parts of their hosts. These days, Mouse was a quiet guy who worked hard and seldom partied, but Tony'd heard some stories about Mouse's past, stories that came with interesting scars, stories that always finished with, "You should see the other guy."

He really didn't want to be the other guy.

He didn't think he'd be strong enough not to spill his guts. He wrapped a hand around his stomach, just above the line of shadow. He'd talk. He'd tell them how much he'd seen since the beginning. He'd tell them how he destroyed the shadow as it left Lee.

Lee . . .

Had it been the shadow or the darker parts of Lee putting the moves on him?

And this was *so* not the time to be thinking about that.

Nine

WAY PAST time to change that code, Tony thought muzzily as Mouse worked the keypad one-handed. The shadow covered his mouth and lapped at the edge of his nose, sending the occasional tendril up into his nostrils—playfully or threateningly, Tony wasn't sure. His stomach heaved, but puking wasn't an option with his mouth already full.

The moment the car had stopped, he'd thrown open the door and flung himself out into the parking lot, mouth open to scream for help. They'd crossed the too-macho-to-scream line way back on Oak Street. Cool weight around his ankles had slammed him to the ground. The double pain of gravel cutting into his palms had been lost in the feel of shadow wrapping around him and cutting off all sound by slithering into his mouth.

Mouse had taken the time to lock the car, then had hauled him onto his feet and half carried, half walked him to the studio's back door. Struggling had resulted in the remaining airflow being cut off until he calmed. One short visit to suffocation land had been enough to convince Tony that struggling was a very bad idea.

The door opened. A large hand between his shoulder blades shoved him into the dark soundstage. Stumbling forward, he missed the sound of the door closing behind him, but as he found his balance, he clearly heard the

snap of the lock reengaging. It was the first sound in a
while to drown out the pounding of his heart. So much
for rescue.

Tony strained to see as Mouse dragged him off to the
left, moving unerringly around bits of set and equipment, the ambient light from the exit signs and various
scattered power indicators obviously enough for him to
maneuver. Unlike Lee last night, he didn't bother turning on the overhead lights. Hang on . . .

Shadows required a minimum amount of light for . . .
well, definition was probably the closest word. A
shadow without definition would be fuzzy. Fuzzy meant
a weaker shadow, right? Not the shadow in Mouse but
Mouse's shadow. The shadow actually holding him.

He took a tentative breath through his mouth.

Found he could breathe.

Ripping free of Mouse's loose grip on the back of his
neck, Tony ran for the far end of the soundstage and the
door to the production offices. *It can't be much after
9:00. 9:30 tops. Maybe quarter to ten. Ow! Son of a bitch!*
He stumbled around whatever he'd run into—a light
pole from the crash as it hit the floor—bounced off a
wall, got his bearings, and lengthened his stride. No way
the geeks in post were gone so early. It wasn't like they
had somewhere to go on a Friday night. All he had to do
was get to the . . .

The rounded edge of Raymond Dark's leather wing
chair caught him across the stomach. Gasping for breath,
he fell forward, rolled across the seat on his shoulders,
and hit the floor. He was still fighting to untangle his feet
from the coffee table when the lights came on. Definitely
a good news/bad news situation. He could see—he
kicked himself free and scrambled to his feet—but the
moment Mouse caught up to him, he'd be . . .

The fake Persian rug spread over the concrete floor
did nothing to cushion the impact. He rolled sideways,
slammed up against Mouse's legs, and was hauled to his
feet.

"You done?"

The knee in the crotch took the big man completely by surprise. More than willing to fight dirty—the definition of someone who fought fair against a guy twice his size was *loser*—Tony put everything he had in it and hit the ground running. Fingers closed around a handful of his jacket. He squirmed free.

And then he was back on the floor, the rug grinding into his cheek, a massive knee grinding into the center of his back.

Oh, yeah, I'm done.

No more messing around with shadows, Mouse had taken that last blow personally. Not much point in defending himself either although Tony did what he could. When Mouse finally hauled him back onto his feet— *Third time lucky, big guy?*—he dangled. Heels dragging, he watched the ceiling go by as Mouse hauled him out of the office, across a concrete corridor, and into the empty space that had been the living room set. Monday morning it was due to be set up as a Victorian dining room for a dinner party flashback.

He couldn't quite keep his head from bouncing as he hit the floor. Once the bells had stopped ringing, he realized he was in the exact spot, and pretty much the exact position, Lee had been in last night. Under other circumstances, he'd have appreciated that more.

The gate wouldn't open for hours—hour . . . a while . . . he'd kind of lost track of time—so what the hell were they doing here? Mouse couldn't take him home and whale on him, not without having to do some explaining to the old lady, but surely there were better places for the kind of question and answer session about to happen. Unless ET's shadow was about to call home.

Humor hurt.

So did a number of other things.

Tony didn't think his ribs were broken. *Broken* ribs would have hurt a lot more when Mouse squatted beside him, grabbed the front of his T-shirt, and yanked him into a sitting position. He was working on passive resistance now. And apologies to Mr. Gandhi, but it didn't seem to be any more successful than the active kind.

About the only part of him unpummeled was his face; it seemed black eyes and broken noses would be making up the big finale. Looking at the bright side, at least he had a head start on passing out.

As he sagged forward, he caught sight of Mouse's shadow flowing up over his feet. So they were going back to suffocation land. *Been there, done that. Hurts less. Yay.*

Except Mouse's shadow was also stretched out behind him; across the floor, up the side of a chair, behaving its two-dimensional self.

Two shadows?

Seven shadows had come through the gate.

Oh, fuck.

♠

"I'm not getting out of the car, Nightwalker." Arra locked both hands around the shoulder strap of the seat belt. "If I get too close, the shadow-held will know me."

"Then why . . ." When she turned to face him, Henry realized there was no point in finishing the question. He knew terror when he saw it, knew what it could do, how it could hold a person. The wizard's reasons for accompanying him this far were moot—she wasn't going any farther. "Fine. How do I fight it?"

Her grip relaxed slightly and he wondered if she'd honestly thought she'd be strong enough to prevent him from dragging her out of the car had that been his decision. "I'd use the same light you used last night."

"Will that work while the shadow's still in a host?"

"I doubt it." Her gaze turned inward for a moment; when she focused on him again, her expression was bleak. "Kill the host and the shadow will leave."

"Kill the host?"

"Don't even try to tell me you have a problem with that, Nightwalker."

"And you have never killed to survive?"

"Yes, but . . ."

"Killed for power?"

"Not the innocent."

"And who declared them guilty?"

Another night, questions from another wizard. The similarity was . . . ultimately unimportant.

"I don't kill the innocent."

This wizard shrugged. "Suit yourself, Nightwalker. But it's the only way."

The other wizard had also called him Nightwalker; used it as this one did, as a definition. He turned into the production company's parking lot. "Call me Henry."

"It doesn't matter what I call you, I know what you . . . Mouse."

"What?"

She nodded toward the red Mustang as Henry pulled into the parking place beside it. "That's Mouse Gilbert's car. He's one of the cameramen. He's big. Strong. If he's shadow-held, you might have a little trouble."

Henry stopped the car, slammed it into neutral, and turned off the engine. "No. I won't."

He was at the back door before the sound of the engine died.

And then back at the car again.

Arra jumped as his face appeared outside her window, a pale oval suspended in the night. A pale *pissed* oval. She rolled down the window.

"It's locked. Do you know the code?"

"Why would I?" she snorted. "I never go in through the soundstage; I have a key for the front door . . . oh. Right."

♠

The front door lock was stiff. After a moment wasted, Henry reamed the key around hard enough to twist half of it off in the hole—fortunately, *after* the tumblers had turned. He slipped inside, leaving the ruined key where it was.

There were people in the small offices to both his right and his left. Two right, three left; five hearts beating out an espresso rhythm. They were noted in a heartbeat of his own and ignored. He moved on. Farther in.

The doors on the far wall were labeled, black letters on sheets of white office paper, the contrast so great that in spite of the darkness even mortal eyes would have been able to read them. WARDROBE. POST. SPECIAL EFFECTS. KEEP THIS DOOR CLOSED.

Henry opened the last door and found himself pushing through racks of clothing. He couldn't hear Tony. He should have been able to hear Tony. If Tony's heart was still beating. If it wasn't, a second death became a lot more likely. Easy enough to race along scent trails to another door and another sign: DO NOT ENTER WHEN RED LIGHT IS ON.

The soundstage.

Soundproof.

As he pushed open the door, the terrified pounding of Tony's heart rushed out to fill all available spaces. Snarling, Henry ran toward the source, following it unerringly through the maze of walls and cables and equipment. There was light, but he didn't need it. Tony's terror acted as both guide and goad.

He found Tony on the floor under the gate, half-sitting, cradled in a parody of affection against the body of a large man. His heels drumming on the floor, Tony clawed at both meaty arms wrapped around his chest.

Henry came one running step closer.

And saw the band of shadow across Tony's eyes.

Two steps.

The shadow disappeared.

Three steps.

Tony stopped struggling. His heart slowed between one beat and the next to just below normal speed.

The man—Mouse—let go. Head cocked to one side, Tony folded his legs and sat cross-legged on the concrete. Then he looked up and met Henry's eyes.

"I see you, Nightwalker."

Henry snarled to a stop inches from Tony's folded legs.

"Just so you know, I'm not going to let you stop this," the thing that wasn't Tony added as Mouse rose slowly to his feet.

In his own time, Henry had not been tall. In this century, he was short. Mouse—the thing that was Mouse—towered over him.

"You have no power over us, Nightwalker."

Henry glanced down at Tony, back up at Mouse, smiled and swung, not particularly caring about the crack of bone. From the look of him, the cameraman had probably been in hundreds of fights. This one ended before he had a chance to join in. His head snapped back, his eyes rolled up until only the whites showed, and he crumpled to the concrete.

His shadow hit the concrete with him and no metaphysical shadows appeared. It seemed that an unconscious body produced an inoperative shadow. That was definitely something to remember.

"He'll be pissed when he wakes up." The Tony-thing sounded almost cheerful as he stood. "Even think of slamming me like that and before I go, I'll fry the kid's wetware."

Henry forced his fists back down by his side and growled, "Get out of him!"

"No problem. The moment the gate opens, I'm gone. I know what he knows and he knows what the boss wants to know."

"He doesn't know anything."

"And I'd believe that, too, except I'm in his head and you aren't, dude."

"Dude?"

"Hey, that's in here."

Perhaps, but it wasn't a designation Tony would ever use for him. The impersonation was off by just a few degrees. Something else to remember.

"And so's the info on what destroyed the earlier minion," he continued. "Not as much about this world's tech as the boss'll want, but the other stuff he knows, that'll so make up for it. This guy . . ." An exaggerated tap to one temple. ". . . knows where that pesky wizard ended up. Who'd have thought she'd be stupid enough to stay so close to the gate?" The thing rolled Tony's eyes. "Wizards, eh? Too stupid to keep running, too fucking freaked to save the world. Boss'll be overjoyed to have found her after all this time. Unfinished business, you know how it is."

Henry let the words wash over him as he circled around, looking for an opening. Although an opening to what, he wasn't certain. Tony's body turned with him, pivoting around on one heel.

"You're making me dizzy. I'm going to hurl hamantaschen." It glanced down at Tony's watch. "10:02. A little more than an hour. What are we going to do with ourselves, Henry? You hungry?" Familiar fingers pulled the collar of the T-shirt down off Tony's throat, exposing bruises rising along the ridge of his collarbone.

The sight of blood pooling under Tony's skin, the knowledge of exactly what had to have been done to mark him so, pushed Henry back to the edge. He stopped circling. His lips pulled back off his teeth. He let the Hunger rise. Scavengers would not have what was his until he was done with it.

"Tony. Is. Mine."

"I recognize your power, Nightwalker." Tony's cadences were gone. "But you cannot move me from this body until I am ready to leave."

The thing's words were drowned out under the song of Tony's blood.

He felt a warm weight wrap around his legs and he ignored it. All that mattered was the life he had claimed, not once but countless times. "Mine."

"Not right now, dude."

"MINE!"

Sudden recognition flared behind the shadows in Tony's eyes. Followed by a fear so primal all else fled before it. His heart began to pound. Faster. Faster.

Then his eyes rolled back and he doubled forward, retching.

Shadow poured from his mouth and nose, pooled on the concrete, moved toward Henry. He retained barely enough hold on self to realize this was not something he could fight and in the face of it, the Hunger began to fade. One step back. Two. He had no idea how to control the light they'd used the night before or even if it was still in place. Tony, who knew, was on his knees, arms wrapped around his body like he was trying to hold disparate pieces of flesh together.

♠

Arra pulled the front door open, paused, and looked down at the broken lock. Maybe she should just stay here and fix it. Maybe she should have just stayed in the car. Actually, no *maybe* about it . . .

She stepped into the office.

What the hell am I doing?

The thermoses were comforting weights in her pocket. Their contents would be useless as long as the shadow remained in Mouse, but they were a clear indication of what her role was in this . . . this ridiculous attempt to save a world already lost.

She glanced toward CB's office and almost wished he was there. Almost wanted to walk through his door, walk past the fish tank, almost wanted to stand in front of his desk and confess all. Fortunately, he was in Whistler with two of his kids from his first marriage. She had no idea what they were doing in Whistler at this time of the year, but whatever it was, it was keeping her from making an ass of herself in front of the one person in this world likely to ask the right questions.

The costumes rustled as she passed as though they whispered among themselves; a choir boy's cassock asking a slightly shiny tux what was happening.

Good question.

It was curiosity; that was all, the same thing that had prodded her out of the basement and up onto the soundstage in time for the morning opening of the gate. Wizards were like cats. Curious. Sometimes, it got them killed.

Not me. I know when to run.

She pushed open the door and heard retching. In the silence of the soundstage, it could have been coming from anywhere.

Yeah, right. Who am I kidding ...

Tony was on his knees under the inactive gate, looking like crap, the last bit of shadow dribbling from his nose. Mouse was stretched out behind him. Maybe dead. Fully separate now from its last host, the shadow slithered across the floor toward Henry.

He was fast. It was faster.

Did it know what he was? Would it be able to control him? From the look of things, it was going to have a damned good try at it. If it succeeded, a shadow-held Nightwalker would be able to destroy this small resistance.

As darkness swarmed up Henry's body, Arra reacted. The questions and the commentary shut off and her hands rose. She'd cast the incantation countless times in the last futile attempt, it wasn't one she was ever likely to forget.

The shadow froze, twisted in on itself, and vanished with a soft *sputz*.

Moving quickly, before the questions had a chance to start up again, she jogged across the empty set to Mouse's side, the rubber soles of her sneakers squealing against the floor. She dropped to her knees, and, grabbing two handfuls of his jacket, heaved him over onto his back. As his head bounced once against the floor, his eyes opened.

"You!"

"Me," she agreed and drove her hand wrist-deep into his chest. Only the element of surprise gave the maneuver any chance at all, and for a moment she was afraid surprise wouldn't be enough. Then her searching fingers closed. Leaning back on her heels, she hauled the shadow clear, flinging it free and destroying it in the same movement.

If asked, she'd have had to say that final *sputz* was one of the most satisfying sounds she'd heard in the last seven years.

Except that no one was asking.

When she turned, it was to see Henry crouched in front of Tony, one pale hand extended. To her surprise, Tony flinched back from his touch.

"Not yours," he said hoarsely. "My own!"

The Nightwalker nodded. "I know."

And then they both pretended to believe it.

Holding in the hurt, Tony remembered. Lee hadn't remembered—maybe because the shadow had left him, not been puked out—but Tony did. Remembered how it felt to be trapped in the back of his own head, able to feel his body, to know it was his, but to have no control over it. He felt it move, heard it speak, and could do nothing to prevent either. It threw him back to his worst times on the street, when he was young and new and too stupid to run. He couldn't win if he fought and screaming made no difference because no one would hear him. He'd learned to hide, to just let things happen.

Maybe that was why he remembered; because he'd been there before.

Christ, he hurt. Ribs, back, arms, legs, brain . . .

When Henry stood, he almost laughed. Henry standing. Him on his knees. That final "MINE!" still sounded with every beat of his heart and resounded at every pulse point. The barely healed bite on his wrist throbbed.

It didn't help that Henry's Prince of Darkness face was essentially the same face he wore for everyday. Nothing changed; no bumpy foreheads, no road map of veins, just a thin veneer of civilization over a primal Hunger. A Hunger that seduced even as it devoured.

"MINE."

The seduction frightened Tony more than the Hunger. Even shadow-held, he'd responded. Death had called in its marker and his answer had been to evict the current possessor, acknowledging the earlier claim. He was alive because Henry wanted him alive. He'd die when Henry decided it was time. Sure, that applied to pretty much everyone who shared a vampire's territory, but he *knew* it. Personally. Hell, Biblically. He bit his lip to keep from laughing. If he started, he doubted he'd be able to stop.

Henry would never let him go.

As unpleasant as the implications were, bottom line, it had saved him.

Right on cue, Henry held out a hand.

Tony forced himself not to flinch back again.

"Tony?"

He understood the question Henry was asking. Were they okay? He supposed it depended on the definition of okay. Henry's mask was back in place so, honestly, had anything changed? Same mask as he'd been wearing, covering the same power. And the shadow was gone. And it wasn't like that whole possessive thing should be a surprise. *And fuck, Tony, stop fucking thinking so goddamned much!*

It all came down to trust, really, and if he trusted Henry enough to let him open a vein and drink, then he might as well keep trusting him to not abuse the power that gave him.

Not to abuse it much, anyway.

Unwrapping his right arm from around his stomach, he gripped Henry's cold fingers and allowed the vampire to pull him to his feet. "We're cool." He turned to Arra before Henry could respond. Further conversation on the topic was way more than he wanted to face. "How's Mouse?"

She looked up, liquid continuing to dribble from a thermos cap down between Mouse's lips. "Well, I'm no doctor, but I think his jaw's broken."

"Broken?"

"Interesting purple knot coming up on one side, too." Her lip curled slightly. "You don't know your own strength, Nightwalker."

Tony had no need to turn to know that Henry's lip had curled in answer.

"Yes," he said. "I do."

Arra's gaze flickered between the two men, settled on Tony, and she made a speculative noise that could have referred to anything. Setting the plastic cap on the broad shelf of Mouse's chest, she reached down into her pocket and pulled out a second thermos. "Here, get some of this down you."

She tossed it in a slow, underhanded lob, but Tony couldn't seem to get his arms to move away from his body. An inch from impact, Henry bent and scooped it from the air.

"You'd make a hell of a shortstop."

Henry grinned as he placed the thermos in Tony's hands. "Only for night games."

"Well, yeah." As long as they could play the denial game, they were maintaining a version of same old/same old. Same old/same old was doable. He looked dubiously at the thermos. "Is this . . . ?"

Arra snorted. "Yes."

"I'm fine."

"Drink some anyway."

"But I was only a minion for like a really short time and . . ." A sudden memory of being trapped and helpless, of being used. He came back to himself as Henry wrapped his fingers securely around slick curves of orange plastic. He didn't think he reacted, but Henry backed away.

Giving him space. And a thermos top filled with magic potion. It smelled exactly like he remembered.

It tasted pretty much like it smelled, like a cocktail for alcoholic cats. He'd had worse but not recently and he was out of practice.

"It doesn't do any good coming back up your nose," Arra snapped as he choked and coughed. "You have to swallow it."

He flipped her off with his free hand—at this point he honestly didn't give a crap about being rude—and took another mouthful. It didn't taste any better, but after the fourth mouthful the vodka started numbing things out. A little. "How much . . . ?"

"Drain the cup."

"All of it?"

"Isn't that what drain means?"

"Give me a break," he muttered, wondering if the tip of his nose was supposed to be tingling, "I've had a rough night."

"And it's not over."

"Fucking great."

Hands shoved in the pockets of his coat, Henry took a step closer to the wizard. "So, you're involved now."

"I'm . . ."

"The shadow in Tony said you were unfinished business. That his master would be thrilled to know where you were after all this time. And the one in . . ." His gesture took in the fallen cameraman. ". . . knew you."

"Would be thrilled," Arra repeated, screwing the cap back onto the thermos and sitting back on her heels. "*Knew* me, past tense. Both shadows have been destroyed, so no information's going back through the gate. No one's going to be thrilled on my account."

"But it seemed to know you'd be here."

"Well, of course, it knew. As Tony pointed out," she added wearily, "I'm the one who opened the original gate. The son of bitch found this world by using my research."

"It said you were unfinished business."

She shrugged. "Who likes loose ends?"

"Your hand was in his chest."

The non sequitur seemed to throw her for a moment, then she snorted. "You saw that, did you?"

As far as Tony could see, Mouse's chest looked pretty much like it had all night. Okay, the horizontal part was new, but other than that, big and plaid pretty much covered it. "You had your hand in his chest?"

"I had the essence of my hand in the essence of his chest. I reached into the place where the shadows have substance and we don't."

"How . . . ?"

"Clean living." Raincoat crinkling, she got slowly to her feet, her opinion of the question clear.

"Look, magic might be the obvious answer where you come from, but it isn't here." Tony swallowed the last of the potion and belched. A spray of tiny green sparkles danced in front of his face. "Not usually, anyhow." The world tilted slightly sideways. "I think I need to sit down." The floor seemed like the best option. It was close and he'd already proved that he could hit it. His legs folded. Another belch. More tiny sparkles.

"Is it the shadow?" Henry's face swam in and out of focus.

Tony stretched out a finger and poked him in the cheek. "The objects in your mirror may be closer than they appear."

"What?"

"I'm guessing it's the eight ounces of warm vodka." He poked him again. "I'm fine."

Henry straightened. All he could do at this point was believe him. "Will there be others tonight?" he asked the wizard.

"Other shadows returning?" She glanced toward the

ceiling and although Henry heard her heart speed up, there was no outward manifestation of her fear. "Could be, but I doubt it. These seem to be the extended wear version, good for a few days. And if you're right and they've been sent purposefully to look for the . . ." She sketched a set of air quotes. ". . . light, then they'll stay as long as they can."

"What was the waiting one waiting for?" When both wizard and vampire turned to look down at him, Tony waved. "There was one in Mouse and one waiting here by the gate."

Arra frowned. "I'd guess it was guarding the gate— the gate was open when you destroyed the shadow last night. The Shadowlord probably felt it die and wanted to make sure that wouldn't happen again."

Tony's eyes widened as sudden realization dawned. His mouth opened and closed a couple of times and then he said, "I killed . . ."

"No, you didn't." Arra cut him off. "They're pieces of the Shadowlord, of the evil he has become. They have no life, no sense of self, until they imprint with a host. You destroyed a tool. A weapon. A thing, not a person."

"Oh." He rubbed his fingertips along the painted floor. "That's okay, then."

Pulling Henry to one side, Arra leaned close to his ear and murmured, "Look, you stay here with him and deal with whatever shows up, and I'll take Mouse to a hospital. He smells like a vodka-catnip cocktail and he's clearly been fighting, so there shouldn't be any questions I can't deal with."

"Given your ability to banish the shadows; shouldn't you be the one who stays?"

"First, I'm obviously not the one who hit him. They might not believe that so easily of you. Second, you haul that light stand around and you can banish them just as easily. You already have. Third, there's no point in chancing me so close to the gate. If the Shadowlord knows I'm here . . ."

About to ask, *He'll what?* Henry changed his mind at her expression. Or rather her lack of expression; in all his long life, he'd never seen anyone so desperate to hide her true feelings. There would be a time of reckoning between them but not now, not with innocents needing their attention. "You can drive?"

"I can ride the heart of the whirlwind secured in place with a rope braided from the dreams of trees."

"That's not what I asked."

She rolled her eyes. "How hard can it be?" A raised hand cut off Henry's reply. "Kidding. Of course I can drive. I live in downtown Vancouver and I work in Burnaby—only the young have the kind of stamina commuting by transit requires." A glance down at Tony and then over to Mouse. "Carry him out to the car for me, Henry, time's wasting."

Still on the floor, Tony watched Henry follow Arra out of the soundstage, Mouse's large body cradled ludicrously against his. *He says he's coming back,* he reminded himself. *Don't get rid of a vampire that easily.*

Don't get rid of a vampire at all.

His head felt like the city was doing road repairs across his cerebral cortex. Jackhammers, hot tar, the whole nine yards. As far as he could tell, it was the potion's only effect. Even the alcohol seemed to be wearing off. If he poked at the right place, he remembered how it felt as the shadow shoved him to the back of his own mind . . .

Not going there.

A deep breath and he got to his feet, just as glad he was doing it out from under Henry's watchful gaze. He couldn't have really indulged in the wincing and the groaning with Henry there.

He was unlocking the wheels of the carbon arc's stand when Henry returned. "This thing's worth a fortune," he said, motioning Henry around to the other side. "The security around here sucks."

"That thought had crossed my mind, not the price of the lamp but definitely the sucking."

Tony pointed and Henry rolled the heavy lamp back where it had been on the edge of the set.

"When you were asking Arra . . ." He stopped and started again. "Do you think the Shadowlord is looking for Arra, specifically?"

"I don't know. If he knew he was opening the same gate she did, he had to know she'd be here somewhere. But I got the impression he didn't expect her to stay around the gate."

"Maybe you should ask her why she did?"

Red-gold brows rose. "Me?"

"Why not you?"

"I don't think she likes me much."

"Vampire, remember?" He dragged the sleeve of his jacket across the glass lens. "You could make her like you."

"You know it doesn't work like that."

Tony discarded half a dozen responses. Some of them were even true. Finally, he sighed and nodded. "Yeah. I know." Bending to resecure the brakes, he had to catch himself on a cross brace, sucking air in through his teeth.

Henry didn't say anything until he straightened.

"You're hurt."

"It's just bruises."

"There's blood."

Right. Tony picked at the bits of gravel embedded in his other hand. "I'll heal."

I always have.

When he looked up, he knew that Henry'd heard the subtext. Another night, he might have said something. Tonight, he was allowing the illusion of boundaries.

The lighting crew had merely moved the lamp out of the way without unhooking it from the board. Since this wasn't going to end tonight, since another night they might not be so lucky, he studied the setup, noting where everything was plugged in.

Which reminded him . . .

"Henry, when the gate opens, you should go stand by the circuit board. It blew last night, remember?"

"Yes."

An interesting tone to that single syllable. Tony sighed and turned, not quite meeting dark eyes. "What?"

"You seem very calm." The long pause echoed with a shouted *MINE*. "All things considered."

"Hey, have I ever done the hysteria thing? I mean baby-eating ancient Egyptian wizards and ghosts screaming for vengeance aside?"

After a heartbeat, Henry smiled. "No, you haven't."

"Well, then." He folded his arms, trying to move as though muscles weren't shrieking at him, carefully missing what bruises he could. "I was thinking—we have to wait until the gate opens and the shadow separates before the light works, right?"

"Yes."

"So the Shadowlord'll still be able to sense that his guys are continuing to die on his doorstep."

Henry glanced up toward the ceiling. "Yes."

"What do you think he'll do?"

"I think," Henry said slowly, "at some point, he'll send something through that can't be killed by light. Something physical."

"You sound upsettingly happy about that."

The mask slipped. "If it has flesh and blood, I can deal with it."

Tony's blood agreed.

Ten

SATURDAY morning found Tony standing in the fourth floor hall outside Arra's apartment. She opened the door before he knocked. Standing there, one hand raised, he had a strong suspicion he looked like he'd just seen Siegfried and/or Roy get up close and magical with a white tiger. Arra's expression confirmed it.

Shaking her head, she stepped back out of the way. "It's a front apartment, Tony. I was removing Zazu from the dieffenbachia and saw you coming up the walk. Even Raymond Dark—hampered as he is by writers with but a single brain cell between them—could have figured that one out. Wipe your feet and hang your jacket to drip over the mat."

He did as he was told, then followed her into the kitchen, nearly tripping over the orange and white cat.

"That's Whitby. Ignore him, he's eaten."

"Does that mean don't feed him or don't worry, he won't go for my throat?"

"Bit of both." The wizard studied him for a long moment while he pretended he was paying attention to the cat. "You look like shit," she said at last. Turning, she took a big blue mug from the cupboard and filled it from an opaque thermal carafe. "This should help."

"What is it?" His tongue was still fuzzy from the after-effects of the potion and his sense of smell was dicey at best. The frozen spring roll he'd heated up for breakfast had smelled strongly of acrylic paint—which, granted, might have been the spring roll since it was a month or two past its best-before date.

"It's coffee; organic, free-traded Mexican, picked by barefoot, sloe-eyed virgins."

"Really?"

"I couldn't swear to the virgins. There's cream in the fridge and sugar in that bunny bowl on the counter." She shoved Whitby out of the way with the side of her foot and headed out of the kitchen.

Tony hurriedly splashed some cream in his coffee—wondered briefly about a bloody plate of liver a little too *interestingly* arranged to be food—and followed. He found the wizard at her computers, both screens showing games of spider solitaire.

"Mouse is fine," she told him, laying a jack of hearts on its queen. "Where fine means he has a broken jaw and an extraordinarily pissed-off wife. I told the hospital I found him wandering around disoriented and he passed out once I got him into the car." She shuffled two columns, finished the run of hearts, and moved to the other game as the cards flipped down to the bottom of the screen. "They bought it." Eight of clubs on a nine of spades, six of diamonds on the seven of spades, and the eight of clubs moved again to the proper nine now uncovered. "How are you?"

His lip hurt, both palms were scabby, his torso was coloring up nicely, but he wasn't pissing blood so, all good. "I'm fine."

"All right. What happened at the gate?"

"Nothing."

"Where nothing means . . . ?"

Tony forced his attention away from the hypnotic movement of the cards. "Nothing . . ."

♣

"It's about to open."

Tony glanced over at Henry and wished he hadn't.

The vampire's eyes were dark and his lips were pulled back off his teeth. Nothing he hadn't seen a hundred times before, but tonight the knowledge of his place in the Hunter/hunted scheme of things was just a little too close to the surface. Then he started to feel the buzz and Henry became of secondary importance.

As the vibrations grew stronger, he had a pretty good idea why Lee had reacted the way he had.

The last gate opening had been no more annoying than having a wasp caught in his skull. The potential for disaster was there, sure, but the actuality was pretty much all sound and fury. Tonight it was like having teeth drilled just as the Novocaine was wearing off. Not screaming pain, not yet, but every muscle tensed against the rising vibrations, anticipating the moment when the soft tissue would be hit.

"There's no one here. None of the other shadow-held have returned," Henry clarified as Tony stared at him blankly.

"So what do we do?"

"Stop anything that comes through from the other side."

♣

"And did anything?"

"No." Tony took a long swallow of coffee. "The gate stayed open for a couple of minutes and then it closed."

"A couple of minutes?"

"Or less. Or more. When you're thinking about evil wizards and brain-sucking shadows, you don't really have a grip on time passing."

"Next time check your watch. The interval might be important later."

"What do you care? I thought you weren't helping."

"And yet you keep showing up at my door."

He wasn't sure that twice merited "keep showing up." Setting his backpack on the floor, he sat down and almost instantly had a black and white cat on his lap.

"That's Zazu." Brows drawn into a deep vee over her

nose, Arra didn't look happy. Tony slowly moved both hands away from the cat. "She doesn't ever do that."

"Do what?"

"Sit on strangers."

"She's not exactly . . . OW . . . sitting."

"She's just making your lap more comfortable."

The cat's claws went once more through denim and into skin. "For who?" Tony yelped.

Arra's expression suggested the question was too stupid to answer. She went back to her games and Tony tried to hold perfectly still. God only knew what the cat would stick a claw into if she thought she was in danger of falling.

"I could feel it more this time," he said after a moment when no further blood loss seemed imminent. "The gate, I mean."

"It's because you were shadow-held."

"Yeah, I figured. But it was more of a shadow-grab than a hold. I mean, shouldn't there be a time limit on *held*?"

Hand poised over the laptop's touch pad, Arra turned to face him, brows up. "Does humor help?"

He risked a shrug. Zazu rolled over on her back in the crease between his tightly clamped legs, all four feet in the air, her stomach a blaze of white. The fur looked soft. He tentatively reached out a finger.

"I wouldn't."

And he snatched the finger back. The cat looked disappointed.

Arra snorted and turned back to the games. "So, as much as I'm thrilled to have the company, why are you here?"

"I brought back the thermoses." About to bend over and open his backpack, he caught sight of the expression on Zazu's face and reconsidered. "We didn't use any more of the potion, but I wasn't sure how long it would last. You know; the sparkly part of it."

"The potion part will last indefinitely but I will need

to reactivate it before it'll do any good magically." She turned up a king, moved queen to ace over, and waited while the line collapsed. "Now why are you really here?"

"The potion . . ."

"See that?"

He leaned forward. "The game?"

"Stalled on that seven. I had no way of knowing what was under the king, but it was my only option." Swiveling her chair around, she lifted a limp Zazu off his lap. "Look beyond the obvious. Examine the truth behind your motives. Buy low, sell high."

"What?"

She sighed as the cat leaped back onto Tony's lap. "Why are you really here?"

"I was thinking . . ." He paused, waiting for a smart-ass remark that didn't come. ". . . the construction crews are going to be in today building new sets. I might be able to hang around, but I'm not going to be able to move the lamp back into place and I sure as hell won't be able to turn it on."

"Your point?"

His point seemed obvious but she was going to make him say it. "You have to be there."

"No. I won't go near the gate while it's open."

"You don't have to. You don't even have to leave the basement. You're my cover story—just send me upstairs with a light meter or something to take some readings."

"The carpenters will still be working . . ."

"Yeah." He snorted. "Like it's hard to get them to take a break."

"They'll still be there, though. If one of the shadow-held does show up, how will you explain it?"

Greatly daring, he stroked the top of the cat's head. "I have no idea. Which is why I think we need to get the addresses of everyone who was on set yesterday. We need to find where the rest of the shadows are and take them out before they get back to the soundstage."

"Take them out?"

He mimed shoving his hand in someone's chest. Zazu stretched out one paw and embedded the claws in his leg.

Ignoring his whimpers, Arra snorted. "So this whole 'I'm your cover story' on the soundstage is just a . . . cover story? You want *me* to take the shadows out."

"Two part plan!" Tony protested. "First the sound-stage because we don't have time to get them all before the gate opens, and then we go after whoever doesn't show up away from the gate."

"Fine. You still haven't told me how you'll explain the shadow-held to the carpenters then."

"I thought you . . ."

"What part of I'm not getting involved in this do you not understand?"

"I'm not asking you to do any more than you've already done." Even to his own ears that sounded sulky. "Look, we're trying to stop an invasion and save the world without a lot of options, so we need to make the Shadowlord wonder a bit. Confuse him. Throw him off-balance. Not, why are my shadows being destroyed at the gate but why aren't they coming back to the gate at all? Maybe that'll convince him there's something here he doesn't want to tangle with."

Arra set up a new game on the laptop. "Have you spoken to the vampire about this?"

"Yeah. Sort of . . ."

♣

"Tony . . ."

"I'm fine."

"I don't doubt it, but I'd appreciate it if you could move just a little faster; I've got to feed."

Still struggling with his seat belt, Tony froze. *I can't.*

Something of the thought must have shown on his face because Henry sighed. "Not on you. I don't think that would be safe for either of us tonight."

"Good call." The buckle jammed. Working the release with one hand, he yanked on the strap with the other. It didn't help. In fact . . . "Uh, Henry. I think I've really fucked this up."

Cool fingers shoved his out of the way. "It's stuck."

"No shit."

Henry glanced up at him, his eyes darkening, the masks slipping. Vampires didn't screw around with seat belts. The strap separated from the buckle. Vampires ripped their victims free.

Adrenaline lent Tony's bruised body speed and he all but threw himself out onto the sidewalk. Then, in an attempt to reclaim a little dignity, he braced himself between the door and the roof and leaned back into the car. "I was thinking that maybe we should try dealing with these things before they get back to the studio."

"Fine." The dashboard lights painted eerie highlights in Henry's eyes which were . . .

Oh, fuck. And the worst of it was; Tony wanted to climb back into the car. To offer his wrist or his throat. To offer his life. No. That wasn't the worst. It was much worse that Henry knew it, too. Leaping back, he slammed the door closed and muttered, "Why don't I just leave a message on your machine," at the BMW's ass end as it disappeared down the street.

♣

"Yes, I'd say that fits the definition of *sort of.* His kind are not unknown on my world; I'm amazed you've managed to retain as much self-determination as you have. A man cannot serve two masters after all."

Tony's lip curled. "That's not how it is."

"And I believe you where thousands of others wouldn't." Arra closed down the laptop and stood. "Let's go."

"Go?" The cat on his lap showed no indication that it planned to move any time soon.

"Studio, gate, shadows . . ." The wizard sighed as he

continued to sit awkwardly in place, not daring to stand. "Just dump her on the floor, she won't break."

Figuring he had enough mayhem in his life at the moment, Tony tucked his hands in Zazu's armpits—front leg pits?—and carefully lifted her down to the floor. She snorted, sounding remarkably like Arra, sat down, and licked her butt. Never having spent much time with cats, Tony'd never realized they were so good at making their opinions known. "I thought I didn't understand about you not getting involved?"

"What?"

"You *said* you weren't going to get involved." He stepped carefully around Whitby who was now winding between his feet, determined to be punted across the apartment.

"I'm still not going near the gate when it's open, but I suppose I can bullshit you past a few carpenters."

"What changed your mind?"

She paused, yellow raincoat up over one arm, and stared for a long moment at a framed *Darkest Night* promotion poster. "The cats like you," she said at last.

♣

"Arra!"

She jabbed at the elevator call button a couple more times as though hoping it would realize she was in a hurry and arrive.

"Arra!"

"I don't think he's going to go away," Tony murmured.

Smiling tightly, she turned. "Julian."

He shifted the Chihuahua in the crook of his left arm and, eyes narrowed suspiciously, stared around her at Tony. "It's your turn to dust and vacuum the party room."

"I don't even live here," Tony protested.

"Not you. Her."

Except he was still staring at Tony—who'd have

found it creepy had his creep level not risen over the last few days. It was, however, becoming more than a little annoying.

"The party room's done."

That snapped an equally suspicious gaze back to Arra. "It wasn't *done* a moment ago."

"Well, it's *done* now. And look, here's our elevator." Her hand closed tightly around Tony's arm just above the elbow, she propelled him inside, following right on his heels.

"Ow!"

"Sorry." Arra turned and waved jauntily at Julian through the last six inches of open space.

Shoving his foot back into his shoe, Tony waited until the door was fully closed before asking if the wizard had magicked the room clean. He hadn't seen any incantations or a wand or even an ambiguous gesture but then, what did he know about wizards?

She leaned against the back wall and folded her arms. "No. I lied."

"You lied?" Wizards lied. All things considered, it was something to remember.

"Prevaricated, even. Julian's an ac-tor, you know. He got up my nose before he became president of the co-op board; now he's unbearable."

Even on such short acquaintance, Tony could see where *unbearable* might be a justified definition. "And his dog is fat."

"Tell me about it."

♣

"What if we shot flamethrowers through the gate?"

Arra finished merging her mid-'80s hatchback with traffic and glanced over at her passenger. "Flamethrowers?"

"Yeah. We just sit under the gate and when it opens . . ." He mimed shooting toward the ceiling. ". . . whoosh."

"Where would we get flamethrowers?"

Tony shrugged, shuffling his feet into a more comfortable position among the discarded coffee cups that littered the floor. "Same place we get them for the show; the weapons warehouse."

"They aren't . . ." Her voice trailed off and Arra scowled out at the road, her frown deepening slightly at each slap of the windshield wipers.

When she didn't say anything more for about five kilometers, Tony figured that was it. The suggestion of flamethrowers had clearly brought up some bad memories. Beginning to doze off—even with all the lights on, it hadn't been a particularly restful night—he jerked awake as she started talking again.

"I think he'd take it as a challenge. He's never been stopped, so at this point he has to believe he never can be."

"We've stopped some of his shadows."

"Minor players. They are to his power as UPN is to network TV. He wouldn't for a moment assume that because you've defeated them you could defeat him." She snorted. "Evil wizards who style themselves the Shadowlord and go on to conquer vast amounts of territory seldom have a problem with self-esteem."

"Do you think he's conquered your whole world?"

"He's headed for this one; does it matter?"

"I guess not."

Another three kilometers passed. Tony wondered what was happening during the silences. Finally, she shrugged. "It's only been seven years; I doubt it."

"Then why is he coming here?"

He was looking at her when she turned toward him, but it wouldn't have mattered if he hadn't been, the force of her expression would have dragged his head around. Pain and anger and other emotions less easily defined chased themselves across her face.

"You're right," he told her soothingly. "It doesn't matter why he's coming here, only that he is. Now, could you do me a favor and get your eyes back on the road!"

♣

As the old analog clock on Arra's workshop wall ticked around toward 11:00, Tony moved restlessly from shelf to shelf picking up and putting down the heads and hands and other accumulated body parts. "I thought your special effects were all, you know . . ." He waggled his fingers in the air.

"Piano playing?"

"Magic."

"Some of them are. Most of them are a combination. A glamour works better than an illusion and a glamour has to be cast on something. Even computer-generated effects work better with some kind of reference point. Sometimes it's manipulating pixels, sometimes it's squibs and corn syrup, and sometimes it's magic."

He manipulated the snarl on a stuffed badger and frowned; he'd been with the show since the first episode and he couldn't remember them ever needing badgers. There'd been an episode with wolves once and an inadvertent raccoon on a night shoot but never badgers. It smelled funny, too—although that might have been the jar of rubber eyeballs propping it up. "It never looks this fake on the screen."

"It's television, Tony. You've been in the business long enough to know that nothing is what is seems, it's all smoke and mirrors."

"It *was* all smoke and mirrors," he muttered, walking over to her desk. "Now it's smoke and shadows."

"Very profound if a little obvious." As he stopped behind her, Arra placed a six of diamonds on a seven of clubs. Four of the monitors showed games in progress.

"Don't you ever get tired of that?"

She shrugged. "When it happens, I switch to a mahjongg for a while."

"Don't you ever work?"

A snarl cut off her response and he whirled around to see the badger charge toward him—the force of its leap having knocked over the jar of eyeballs which hit the floor and shattered. Dodging away from tooth and claw, Tony's foot came down on something round that popped wetly. When he glanced at the floor, an eyeball rolled to face him, pupil dilating in the midst of familiar blue. Then he felt claws catch the back of his jeans . . .

"Yes."

Badger and jar were back on the shelf. He supposed they'd never actually left it. Heart pounding, he clutched at the back of Arra's chair. "Yes, what?"

"Yes, on occasion, I work."

"Right." Straightening, he forced his voice back down to its usual register. "That wasn't funny."

"It wasn't supposed to be." She spun her chair around to face him, her expression serious. "If you're going to fight the Shadowlord, you'll have to know what's real."

"You took me by surprise."

"And he won't be e-mailing you his intentions. Your ability to see has cost him the element of surprise. It is your greatest weapon." Gray brows drew in. "It's pretty much your only weapon," she added thoughtfully.

"Great."

"Probably not." Reaching into her desk drawer, she pulled out a light meter and tossed it to him. "Here, gird yourself with this and get going or you'll miss the gate."

"Right." He bent and pulled a set of sides out of his backpack. "These are from yesterday. They'll have most of the names we need, you'll just have to pull the addresses out of the files."

Arra snorted as her fingers closed around the papers. "Who put you in charge?"

Tony's snort answered hers. "You did."

♣

"Any particular reason she can't keep her knees together until we go to lunch?"

"She didn't give me one, Les." Tony rolled the carbon

lamp into position and picked up the coil of cable. "She just said she wants it done now."

The head carpenter scratched at an armpit and sighed. "Whatever. You going to be long enough for me to do a little research?"

"I doubt it." He flipped the cover off the light board. "How's the dissertation going?"

"Not good. 'Pastoral Imagery in Late Eighteenth Century Amateur Poetics' just isn't enthralling me like it used to."

"Hard to imagine."

"Yeah. And the thought of teaching freshman English gives me hives."

"You could always commit to a career in show business."

Les snorted. "At the rates CB pays, it's not a career, it's a job. So, Sorge know you're using the board?"

"I have no idea." Tony checked that the big lamp was the only thing plugged in, then stepped away, casting a critical eye over his work. With only one connection to get right there were limits on how badly he could screw it up. On the other hand, if he did screw up, he'd not only blow all the power to the building and destroy a very expensive piece of equipment he shouldn't be touching, not to mention an equally expensive light—resulting in him being unemployed at the very least—but also grant the Shadowlord unopposed use of the gate. *So, no pressure.* Without a clear line of sight, he squatted to peer under the loops of cable to check that the board was plugged into the grid and that this particular junction was live. When he straightened, Les was still standing there, clearly waiting for him to expand on his answer. "Look, if Sorge has a problem, he can talk to Arra. I'm just doing what I'm told; it's safer that way."

"You getting paid for this?"

"No." 11:07. Eight minutes, give or take, until the gate opened. *Les, go the fuck away!* "Just a little free on the job training. You know, learning the business."

Les rolled his eyes. "Because some day you want to be a director."

That pulled Tony's gaze up off his watch. "How did you know that?" He didn't think he'd ever mentioned it.

"Jesus, Tony, I'm hardly psychic; everyone from the meat on up wants to be a director. I got three guys in my crew working on scripts as a means to that end. Although one of them isn't looking past being a writer, God knows why."

"Says the guy working on 'Pastoral Imagery in Late Eighteenth Century Amateur Poetics.' "

"Yeah, well . . ."

Les' voice got lost amid the rising vibrations in Tony's head. A dribble of sweat ran cold down his side. As his muscles began to tense, he reached out and, with his hand poised over the switch, paused. If something happened and Les saw it, there'd be another voice to cry warning. Enough voices and people would have to listen!

But if something happened and he didn't stop it, what then?

Could he risk another Nikki, another death, on the off chance that Les would see what a vampire, a wizard, and he had seen? No. *And why me?* he demanded as the vibrations pushed past the point of pain. He flipped the switch blasting the half demolished set with light. *I'm nothing special. I'm nothing supernatural. And I'm no fucking hero.*

"Ah, Tony?" Les' grip on his arm dragged his attention out of his head. "Didn't Arra want you to take readings?"

Right. The flaw in the plan. In order to take any kind of believable reading, he'd have to get a lot closer to the gate. A lot closer to the source of vibrations ripping great jagged holes in his brain.

Memo to self; next time come up with a less painful cover story.

Unsure if he was holding the light meter believably, and not really caring, Tony followed the cable to the back of the lamp, took a deep breath and, with his eyes squinted nearly shut, stepped forward.

Step out into the light.

Hang on, isn't that what they say to dead guys?

Oh, yeah, just what he needed; portents of doom from inside his own head.

Either the light levels were making his eyes water or his eyeballs had burst and the fluid was now dribbling down his cheeks. Either option seemed equally possible. His vision had gone not so much blurry as fizzy.

Tony thumbed the control to capture and hold the reading, turned, and realized he was directly under the gate. Not at the board, not crouched by Lee's side—directly under the gate. Every hair on his body lifted—not a pleasant feeling—and, unable to stop himself, he looked up. Light. And barely visible through the light, the ceiling. Beyond that, or beside it—there weren't really words to describe how the gate both was and wasn't there—distance. And at the end of that distance, something waiting . . . trying to see . . . trying to decide. Something cold. Calculating. Terrifying.

Then the lamp shut off and a heartbeat later the gate closed.

"Are you trying to blind yourself?" Les' voice boomed out somewhere behind him. "Even pointed up at the ceiling this big bastard's putting out enough lumen to do some damage."

Tony swiped at the moisture on one cheek, realized his eyeballs were intact, saw that Les was waiting for him to say . . . something. "Uh, I got the reading."

"Good on you. Now put this fucking thing back where it belongs and get the hell off my set. I got work to do." The tone of voice suggested a deeper concern than the words.

"Right. Sorry."

"Dumb ass."

As Les called his crew back to the job, Tony rolled the

lamp back along the path of its cable. With his stomach tying itself in knots, he quickly separated it from the board, secured the wires, and made sure everything was exactly the way he'd found it. Somehow, he managed to keep his hands from shaking too badly.

Outside of his conscious control, his shadow flickered around the edges.

♣

Arra was just hanging up the phone as Tony walked down the stairs into the basement. She turned as he tossed the light meter onto her desk, looking him up and down. Her brows drew in as she completed the inspection. "You okay?"

He wondered what he looked like. Wondered if she could see the fear that had his guts in knots and stuck his shirt to the sweat on his back. "I'm fine."

"Uh-huh."

It sounded like she didn't believe him. Tough. He was fine. "No one showed up. Nothing came through. He's sitting up there considering things."

"He?"

"The Shadowlord."

Her frown deepened. "You felt that?"

"Not the sitting." Dragging the second chair out into the middle of the room, out where the arrangement of the overhead fluorescents banished shadow, he dropped onto it. "But the considering, yeah." He'd never seen anyone's eyebrows actually touch before. "What?"

"You felt the considering."

"Yeah. I guess." The noise she made was in no way reassuring. "What?"

"Nothing."

"Something!" he snapped.

"I'm just impressed by your sensitivity."

She sounded sincere and even if she wasn't, he suspected he didn't want to know the actual answer.

Slouching deeper in the chair, he shoved both hands in the pockets of his jeans. "Yeah, well, I'm gay."

"So I've heard." Twisting around, she plucked a piece of paper off her desk. "I made a few calls while you were gone."

"On the phone?"

"There's an alternative I haven't discovered in the last seven years?"

"I just wondered why you don't do a locator spell or something."

"Because if I locate them using wizardry and we don't stop them and they get back through the gate ..."

"He'll know you're here," Tony interjected into the pause. "Does it matter? There's only one of you here and you said that back in the day he wiped out the rest of your order." Her expression didn't change, but her cheeks paled and Tony realized he might have put his foot in it. "I mean, it's not like he's going to be afraid of you being here."

The presence he'd felt on the other side of the gate caused fear, it didn't feel it.

After a long moment, when it was quite obvious that Arra was seeing neither him nor the basement workroom, she sighed, blinked, and focused. "No. He won't be." She held the piece of paper out toward him. "The names underlined in red are the possibles."

Okay. If that's how she wanted to play it. Tony was just as glad to move on; a little more sitting around wallowing in the terror and he might start joining Arra's chant of *this is it; we're all going to die.* Good thing she'd gone into television because she sucked as a motivational speaker.

Thirteen names on the much longer list were underlined. He tried not to see significance in the number. "What about Alan Wu?" The actor's name wasn't only underlined, it had been circled.

Arra shrugged. "His wife says he didn't come home last night."

"There could be a hundred reasons for that."

"He was on the soundstage, on the set; practically under the gate and his wife gave me the impression that this was very unusual behavior."

"Yeah, Alan's pretty dependable." He stood, folded the paper in quarters, and shoved it in his pocket. "So let's go get him back." Two steps toward the stairs, he paused, and turned to see Arra sitting where he'd left her. "Are you coming?"

"You do realize that in the long run it won't matter. The moment the actual invasion begins . . ."

". . . you're out of here. I know, you've said." Over and over and over. "But if you go home now, Julian's just going to ride your ass about cleaning the party room."

She looked startled, then, to Tony's surprise, she smiled. "True enough. So we find them one shadow at a time and we make sure that one doesn't get back to the gate."

We. She'd used it twice. Tony figured he'd better not point that out. "It's a big city."

"But they're searching for the light."

"Henry told me his theory."

She shrugged and stood. "It seems sound." Opening the middle drawer on her desk, she pulled out the Greater Vancouver Yellow Pages. Turning, she jerked her head to one side, indicating that Tony should move out of the center of the room. The instant he was clear, she heaved the massive book up into the air and shouted two words that seemed made up mostly of consonants.

In the midst of a shower of pale ash, a single box ad fluttered down to the floor.

Tony grinned. "Cool."

♣

The Royal Oak Community Church was a large, fake Tudor building on Royal Oak just down from Watling Street. The multiple additions gave it a comfortable, welcoming appearance only slightly offset by the disturbing presence of a pair of trees so severely pruned they looked like giant gumdrops on sticks.

Tony leaned forward and peered through the streaks of rain on the windshield. "You figure he's inside?"

"That would be where they keep the light."

"Yeah, but they don't usually keep the doors unlocked."

"That wouldn't stop a shadow."

"No, but it would stop the guy they're riding. Unless these things come with break and enter already downloaded."

Arra pulled in behind a battered station wagon and turned off the car. "I expect Alan Wu called the minister and asked for a meeting."

"It can do that?"

"It knows everything Alan knows. I imagine Alan knows how to use a phone."

Since that level of sarcasm seldom required an answer, Tony got out of the car. The sky was still overcast and threatening although the rain had stopped. He waited until the wizard joined him—not entirely positive she was going to until she was standing beside him—then started up the three steps to the concrete walk. "Everything Alan knows?" he asked after a moment.

"That's right."

."So, that'd include pages and pages of really crappy dialogue."

"Probably."

"You know, it'd almost serve the Shadowlord right if we let this one back through."

"No, it wouldn't."

"That was a joke," he pointed out, glancing over at Arra's profile.

"It wasn't funny."

Okay.

The front door of the church was locked. The side

door was open. Even though it was just past noon, so little sun shone through the many windows that the lights were on. A lone figure stood at the front of the sanctuary staring up at the altar. Even at this distance there was no mistaking Alan Wu's great hair. Or the fact that his shadow was facing in another direction entirely.

Arra closed her hand around Tony's arm and when he turned toward her, she laid a finger against her lips.

Momentarily distracted by the depths to which the wizard chewed her nails, he jumped when she pinched him. Since he hadn't planned on bellowing a challenge as he charged forward, he nodded, rubbed his arm, and together they started up the aisle. Twenty feet. Fifteen. Ten . . .

Alan Wu's body turned. His eyes widened. "You!"

Then they widened further as the shadow surged free in one long whiplike motion, clearly trying to escape.

No. Not escape. Attack. It was heading straight for . . .

He dove into a pew as Arra lifted her hands and shouted out the incantation. This time, the third time he'd heard them, the words almost made sense. Might have made sense had they not been immediately followed by a scream from Alan Wu. Tony lifted his head over the barricade of polished wood just in time to see the actor hit the floor in convulsions.

Scrambling back out into the aisle, he raced forward, dropped to his knees, and ripped off his backpack. He had one hand inside, fumbling for a thermos when Alan's back arched, his shoulders and heels the only body parts touching the floor. Then he collapsed, apparently boneless.

"Fuck!"

Throwing the backpack to one side, Tony pressed his fingers into the cold and clammy skin of Alan Wu's throat searching for a pulse.

"What is going on here?"

No pulse.

"I said . . ."

"I heard you!" Tony glanced up at the astonished minister as he started CPR. "Call 911!"

♣

"Tony Foster." RCMP Constable Elson stepped out of the path of the paramedics as they wheeled Alan Wu out of the church, but his gaze never left Tony's face. "Another body and here you are again. It's a small world, isn't it?"

Tony nodded. He wasn't going to argue the point, not when explanations were going to be . . . complicated. Two deaths connected with *Darkest Night* and he'd found both bodies; a guy didn't have to be on the crew of *DaVinci's Inquest* to know that wasn't good.

Interesting to note that not only was Arra nowhere in sight, her car was gone.

Yeah, well, she's good at running, isn't she.

More interesting to realize that he had no idea if the shadow had been destroyed or if it had found another ride.

Where *interesting* had a number of meanings, each darker than the last.

Eleven

"ALL RIGHT, let's go over it one more time. Just to be sure."

Tony fought the urge to roll his eyes and nearly lost. A messy desk away from a cop who clearly didn't much like him was not the time for street kid attitude to reemerge. Squaring his shoulders, he took a deep breath—hoped it sounded like impatience and not the start of a practiced speech—and stared down into his empty coffee cup. "I was driving along Royal Oak with a friend . . ."

"Arra Pelindrake. The special effects . . ." Constable Elson checked his notes. ". . . supervisor at CB Productions."

"Yeah." And now possibly the shadow-held wizard. Tony wet his lips and tried not to think about that. "Like I said, I was doing a little on the job training with her; learning a different bit of the business. She was working on this new thing and she says she thinks better when she drives, so she was driving. I was just along for the ride. Anyway, I saw Alan Wu go into the church and I remembered I needed to tell him that he hadn't filled out the ACTRA sheet on Friday . . ." A safe lie because Alan never remembered to do his paperwork. ". . . so I got Arra to stop and I went into the church and he fell over. I couldn't find a pulse. I started CPR. You guys showed up. Well . . ." He picked up the cardboard cup and turned it around in his hand. ". . . the paramedics showed up first."

"And Arra Pelindrake is where?"

Looking the RCMP officer in the eye, Tony shrugged. "I have no idea. I guess she kept driving after she let me out."

"What is it about her that makes you nervous?"

"What?"

Constable Elson's eyes narrowed, but he didn't repeat the question.

Oh, crap. He's not as dumb as he looks. Unfortunately, *I'm afraid she might be a minion of the Shadowlord* wouldn't go over well.

"The Shadowlord? Is this some kind of a gang thing?"

"No, it's an evil wizard setting up to invade thing."

"Funny guy, eh? You know what we do to funny guys around here?"

Make them listen to bad tough cop dialogue. Make them piss in a cup. Make them miss the next gate so that a shadow gets back through with the information needed to destroy the world.

And Constable Elson was still waiting for an answer.

Tony shrugged again. "She blows stuff up. And there was this thing with maggots . . ." The shudder was legit. Yeah, not very butch of him, but so what.

"So you being there in the church when Alan Wu dropped dead, that was coincidence? Bad luck on your part?"

"Worse luck for Alan."

"I guess it was. Bad luck for Nikki Waugh, too."

"Yeah, well, if I am killing them, I wish you'd find out how they died because I'd really like it to stop!" He rubbed a hand over his mouth, gave some serious thought to puking—just, well, because—and looked up to find Constable Elson watching him, wearing what was almost a sympathetic expression. Or the closest he'd come to it all afternoon.

"No one's accusing you of killing anyone."

"I know. It's just I was there and you were there and . . . fuck it." He sagged back in the chair, confused by the outburst. It was either spontaneous method acting or he was more screwed up about all the shit going down than he thought. "Any chance of another coffee?"

"No."

So much for that growing camaraderie. "Are you almost done with me?"

"Why? Do you have someplace to go?" Pale blue eyes flicked over to Tony's backpack sitting open on a corner of the desk. "That's right. The party you were bringing your vodka-catnip cocktails to."

He could have said no when they asked if they could go through his backpack. He could have. But he wasn't that stupid. "Hey, there's nothing illegal about vodka or catnip!"

"Are you two still on about that disgusting combination?" Constable Danvers asked coming back into the squad room. "And it *is* illegal to carry open containers of alcohol."

"They were closed." Fortunately, not sparkling. *Wouldn't that have been fun to explain.*

"Unsealed containers," she amended, tossing the backpack into his lap and propping one thigh in its place on the scuffed wood. "Contents did wonders for our drains. I called your friend in Toronto, Detective-Sergeant Celluci—just as an unofficial character reference."

This time, he let his eyes roll. "Yeah? He must've been thrilled."

"Not really."

"Let me guess. You mentioned the name Tony Foster and he said, 'What's the little fuck got himself into now?' "

She grinned. "Word for word. Then he expressed some concern and allowed that you were a good kid . . ."

"Christ, I'm twenty-four."

One shoulder lifted and fell as the grin broadened.

"Kid's a relative term. Then he said you should call and that Vicki wanted him to ask if you've forgotten how to use a phone."

Elson snorted. "Vicki is?"

His vampire. "His partner."

"On the force?" Danvers asked, looking interested.

"She was, but she had to quit. Long story."

"Skip it," Elson growled.

Tony wondered if they were playing good cop/bad cop or if Constable Elson really suspected something was going on. The last thing he needed was to be on the wrong side of a cop playing a hunch. Hell, at this place and this time it was the last thing the world needed. But if a hunch had already done the priming, maybe he could tell him what was going on. Get some reinforcements with weapons. Back in the day, if he'd gone to Vicki with this, she'd have . . . assumed he was shooting up again and hustled his ass off to detox.

Never mind.

"So, where are you going now?"

"Now?" Confused, he glanced from constable to constable.

"Looks like you were just in the wrong place at the wrong time."

"Twice," Elson interjected.

His partner ignored him. "We've got your statement. You're free to go."

"Okay." He stood, swung his backpack over one shoulder, found himself caught by two pairs of eyes, and realized that last question was still hanging there, waiting for an answer. "I guess I'll go back to the studio, see if Arra's there." *See if she's still Arra. And if not, well, I'll probably die.*

Fucking great. I think I'm getting used to the possibility.

"She's not answering her phone."

Good news or bad? He had no idea. "Then I guess I'll go home."

Elson's lip curled. "Not to your party?"

"Not at 3:20 in the afternoon, no." It had been a long day. Tony figured he was entitled to the attitude. Fine upstanding members of the community would be screaming for their lawyers by now. Only people who had history with the cops played nice.

Both RCMP officers knew it, too.

"Thank you for your cooperation, Mr. Foster. If we need you, we'll be in touch."

"Yeah. Well, you're welcome."

He was almost at the door when Elson growled, "Don't leave town."

"Oh, for Christ's sake, Jack, get off his case. He's a witness—not a suspect."

Since Constable Danvers seemed to have his defense well in hand, Tony just kept walking. Out the door. Into the hall. It was weird that squad rooms all smelled the same. Past the front desk. He ignored the speculative stares. Tried not to care that another three cops could pick him out of a lineup. Out the front doors.

It was raining again.

Nikki Waugh was dead. Alan Wu was dead. Arra was . . . who the fuck knew.

He was in way, way over his head.

Man, this place had better be on a fucking bus route.

♦

Arra wasn't at the studio. She wasn't at her condo. She wasn't in either of the two churches he'd gone to just because he had to go somewhere.

The sunset over English Bay was a brilliant display of reds and oranges that made it look as though sea and sky were on fire. With any luck, it wasn't an omen.

Although, given the way his luck had been running . . .

Bouncing the keys to Henry's condo in the palm of one hand, he admitted he didn't have a hope in hell of finding her without help.

◆

"It's like she's totally disappeared!"

Henry nodded thoughtfully. "She's good at running."

"Yeah, I thought that, too, except that if the shadow took her, she's not running—she's investigating. Checking out the light. Or not." Unable to remain still, Tony paced back and forth in front of the wall of windows in Henry's living room. "Maybe she'd just hang around out of sight, waiting to go back through the gate. The one that was in me, it said that the important news was that she was alive, so a shadow in her, well, it's going to want to get that information back to the boss. Right? So all we have to do is destroy the shadow in her just like we destroyed Lee's shadow."

"I doubt it will be that easy. Obviously, these things can protect themselves and with the wizard's knowledge it'll be able to set up protections we won't be able to break."

"So we get there early and when she arrives, we sneak up behind her and hit her over the head." He punched his right fist into his left palm.

"And then we're stuck with an unconscious wizard and no way to remove the shadow in order to destroy it—the shadow can't separate from an unconscious host or the one in Mouse would have gone for me last night."

Last night. Tony slid past the memory. "Fine, then while she's unconscious, we tie her up and we gag her. When she wakes up, we stick her under the gate, let it suck the shadow out, and then we hit it with the light."

"Again, I doubt it will be that easy."

"That sounds *easy* to you?" He turned and laid his forehead against the cool glass and wondered if the lights across False Creek looked like the campfires of an advancing army. Probably not; too much neon. "She'd better have been grabbed by that shadow. She ditched me, man. Just tossed me to the cops."

"Perhaps she thought you'd do better on your own and she didn't want to cramp your style."

Tony snorted, his breath misting the window. "Yeah. *Perhaps* you were right when you said she was good at running."

"*Perhaps* I was right?"

He pivoted his head around just far enough to grin at Henry. Realized he was doing it when it pulled on the swollen edge of his lip. Stopped. Watched Henry's expression change. He'd walked in and started talking—about finding Alan Wu, about the cops, about Arra. Until now, there hadn't been a big enough opening for an awkward silence to slip through. *Oh, fuck; here it comes.*

"Tony, about last night . . ."

"Hey, you were hungry, I understand. You had to feed. No big."

"What?" Realization dawned before Tony had to explain. "No, not when we parted. Earlier, when . . ."

"When you called and I came running? Like I said; no big. I've found my happy place with it, Henry. I'm living with it, just like I have been since we met. And you know what else? I'm bored with it. You own my ass—it's old news. I have a life because you allow it? Well, thanks. Let's move on. We don't need to keep revisiting the . . ." He sketched the most sarcastic set of air quotes he could manage, knowing full well that Henry could hear the pounding of his heart. ". . . underpinnings of our . . ." And a second set, air quotes Amy would have been proud to display. ". . . relationship. This isn't one of your romance novels, this is real life and no one talks about this kind of thing in real life. Okay?"

Now *he* could hear the pounding of his heart—mostly because it was the only noise in the room.

Finally, after what felt like a year or two, Henry sighed. "Never underestimate the North American male's capacity for denial."

Tony's lip curled. "Bite me."

Red-gold brows rose.

One of the two dozen or so tiny lights in the chandelier over the dining room table flickered. The refrigerator compressor kicked on, the noise spilling out of the kitchen. A gust of wind off False Creek blew rain against the window, the drops hitting the glass in a sudden staccato rhythm.

Henry snorted.

Snickered.

Started to laugh.

Tony blinked, stared, and actually felt his jaw drop. Had he ever seen Henry totally lose it like that? The vampire had collapsed back into the couch cushions. Was, in fact, bouncing himself against the padded green leather, eyes closed, arms wrapped around his stomach. Just as he started to calm, the hazel eyes opened, he looked up at Tony, and lost it again.

"Hey, it wasn't that funny!"

Henry managed a fairly coherent, "Bite me?"

And then again, maybe it was.

It took a while before they stopped setting each other off. His ribs were aching as they walked together to the elevator.

"You have no idea how worried I was that you would . . ."

He bumped his shoulder against Henry's. "Hate you?"

"At the very least."

"Nah, we're good." Motioning Henry in first, Tony stepped over the threshold and hit the button for the lobby. "Although I am feeling a rousing chorus of 'You and Me Against the World' coming on."

"You're twenty-four; how do you even know that song?"

"The woman who runs the craft services truck is a big Helen Reddy fan. Plays the greatest hits tape over and over and over."

Henry winced. "I'm fairly sure the Geneva Convention doesn't cover evil wizards; if you could get your hands on it, we could toss it through the gate."

"And that really bad cover of 'Big Yellow Taxi.' "

"And polyester bell-bottoms. I went through the seventies once and I don't think I should have to do it again. Platform shoes, big clunky gold chains, hair spray . . ."

Leaning against the elevator wall, Tony listened to Henry listing the flotsam and jetsam of modern life he could do without and felt something he thought he'd lost. Hope. And annoyance. Because now he couldn't get that damned song out of his head.

◆

"Has Arra ever said that the gates are one way only?"

Tony ran back over every conversation he'd had with the wizard and shook his head.

"Then it seems to me that a shadow controlling her could take more than mere information back."

That was a possibility he hadn't considered. "You think it'll take her? I mean, physically?"

"It depends on how independent these shadows are. If they're operating on very narrow parameters, like say . . ." Henry's voice dropped into a doom and gloom octave. ". . . find the light that is capable of destroying the others, then . . ." His voice lifted back into normal ranges on the last word. ". . . no. But if they've been given more autonomy and since they obviously know their master wants the wizard that got away, then I think it's something we need to consider."

"Yeah, that's . . ."

"That's what?" Henry asked after the pause lengthened to the point where prodding seemed necessary.

"I was just thinking of something Amy asked me. About . . . Turn left! Now!"

Henry deftly slid between an SUV and an approaching classic VW Beetle and turned left onto Dunsmuir Street.

"That was Tina's van. She's the script supervisor. She

was on set when the shadows came through, and if she's heading this way, then she could be heading toward Holy Rosary Cathedral."

"That's a lot of qualifiers. Are you sure it was her van?"

"Yeah, we all chipped in and got her vanity plates for Christmas. There!"

"OURSTAR?"

"Because everything in that place revolves around her," Tony explained as Henry tucked his BMW in behind the van. "Cast, crew—if there's a problem, Tina deals with it. If Peter thinks Dalal—that's the prop guy—isn't taking what he wants seriously, he complains to Tina who talks to him. If Dalal thinks Peter's being unreasonable because he never said *how* he wanted the potted plant wrapped . . ."

"Not a random example?"

"Like I'd make that kind of thing up . . . Anyway, Dalal will whiffle to Tina in turn and she'll work the whole thing out without damaging any delicate egos in the process."

"The prop guy has a delicate ego?"

"It's show business, Henry. It's all about ego."

"Good thing you're immune."

"Isn't it. She's parking."

"Good for her." As in any major city, finding parking in downtown Vancouver depended as much on luck as anything. Henry drove another block past the van—slowing to get a good look at Tina as he passed—before he found an empty spot almost at the cathedral.

"I'm not sure this spot's legal," Tony pointed out as he parked. "In fact, given that we're under a no parking sign, I'm pretty sure it's not."

"We won't be here long. I'll go back and meet her, find out if she's shadow-held." He tossed Tony the keys. "Here. Move the car if there's a problem."

"Right. Hey, what are you going to do if there is

shadow?" The car door slammed and he was sitting alone in the front seat. "Never mind."

◆

Over short distances, Henry could move too fast to be seen if he had to. Tina was barely three meters from the van when he caught up to her, slipping into a triangle of darkness made by the corner of a building before she was aware of his presence. Caution was called for. The world through the gate knew his kind and he had no doubt that he would, like the wizard, be returned to the Shadowlord as a prize were he to be taken.

And that would be the good news.

The damage a shadow could do while in control of his body didn't bear thinking about.

As Tina passed him—her stride purposeful, her gaze fixed on the middle distance—he sifted the night air for an otherworldly taint. She was flesh and blood and as much in control of herself as anyone in this day and age.

Flesh and blood. He felt his lips draw up off his teeth. The Hunger flared. It was always harder to put the genie back in the box. "Tina."

She turned at the sound of her name, curiosity taking care of the very little choice Henry's voice had left her. "Yes? Hello?"

Stepping out into the circle of illumination cast by the streetlight, he smiled and caught her gaze with his. "Just a moment of your time."

When he stretched out his hand, she frowned slightly, not fighting the compulsion but very nearly questioning it. When he called her name a second time, she cocked her head, considered, then smiled and laid her fingers across his palm.

Two steps back and they were both shielded by the darkness. He lifted the hand he held to his mouth, turned it, and touched his lips to the soft skin of her wrist. Her eyes, still locked on his, widened then, as she sighed, half closed. For a change, the emotional component of feeding was more on his side than hers. A chance to stroke the Hunger—a gentle acknowledgment that left it easier to control.

To the casual observer they were now more than just friends. Anyone looking closer would refuse to see what was actually happening.

◆

"Fuck, Henry; you fed off her?"

Half into the driver's seat, Henry paused. "How . . . ?"

"It's all over your face."

Startled, he leaned toward the rearview mirror.

"Not blood," Tony snorted. "It's this whole preternatural calm thing you've got going just after you feed."

"Preternatural?"

"Don't change the subject. You fed off Tina."

"There was no shadow." He held out his hand for the keys.

"So very much not the point," Tony told him, dropping them on his palm.

"It was, in one way, for her own protection."

"Against what? High blood pressure?"

"Against the shadow."

Tony waited for the rest of the explanation as Henry started the car and put it in gear.

"You were able to disgorge the shadow when I called on the link we share," Henry continued calmly, pulling into traffic. "While I can't protect the whole city, it is possible that should it come to it, Tina will be able to do the same."

"Disgorge the shadow?"

"Yes."

"After one quick snack? Don't you think highly of yourself."

"Tony . . ."

He slouched as far as the seat belt allowed, picking at

one of the scabs on his palm. "And she's old enough to be my mother!"

Although not a good judge of human aging—it went by too fast as far as he was concerned—Henry guessed the script supervisor was in her mid to late fifties. "I'm significantly older than that."

"Yeah, but you don't look it. You and Tina, well, there's this whole creepy *Harold and Maude* thing going on."

"Who?"

"*Harold and Maude.* A Hal Ashby movie from 1971. Bud Cort and Ruth Gordon; it was brilliant, a cult classic, and you need to watch more movies without subtitles but again, not the point." Tony ran his less scabby hand back through his hair and sighed. "You don't just do that whole crunch, munch, thanks a bunch thing with people like Tina."

"She won't remember it."

"Good."

Henry turned onto Hastings and sped up to make the next light. "You were about to make an observation; back before we spotted the van?"

"Was I? Well, it's totally gone now."

"Let's hope it wasn't important."

"Yeah, let's."

♦

There were half a dozen cars in the studio parking lot when Henry turned off Boundary Road; Arra's hatchback conspicuously not among them.

Henry parked where he had the night before, hoping that passing security would consider it to be his spot and not question his presence. He'd long ago learned that life was simpler if it was arranged in his favor rather than adjusted after the fact. "Do you know who these cars belong to?"

"No." Tony popped his seat belt and opened the car

door. "I think the old Impala belongs to one of the writers."

"I used to have a car just like that," Henry noted as they started for the back of the building.

"Well, you know what they say, there's a dark green Chevy Impala in everyone's past."

"Who says that?"

"Them."

"And who are they?"

Tony snorted softly as he stopped in front of the keypad. "The same guys who say you don't put the bite on women old enough to be my mother."

"You don't think that attitude's a little ageist?" Henry asked, leaning against the wall.

"No." The lock released and Tony carefully pulled the door open. "I think . . ." He stiffened as Henry raised a quieting hand and decided not to get pissed off about it when he saw the vampire's eyes were fixed on the line of black that was the soundstage. Henry'd put on his hunting face. There was something in there. Someone . . .

One of the shadow-held or one of the crew?

The lights were off.

It could be one of the crew sleeping it off before heading home after a few too many drinks at the bar down the road.

Or it could be security patrolling on the other side of the soundstage, flashlight beam blocked by the permanent sets. Okay, probably not that. According to one of the writers, if CB wasn't in the building, the rent-a-cop spent most of his time in the office kitchen working on his screenplay.

It *could* be one of the shadow-held. Lee had turned on the lights, but Mouse hadn't. If it wanted the body it wore to remain unseen, then darkness was better—better for hiding even if it meant it lost the ability to use its cast shadow as a weapon. It wouldn't need a weapon if it wasn't seen.

Maybe it had other weapons. Maybe it had a gun.

Maybe I've been watching too much American television.

Hang on: it could be *all* of the remaining shadowheld. Unless there were rules he didn't know, nothing said they had to show up one at a time.

A quick glance down at his watch. 10:43.

Half an hour early for the gate.

He stepped back as Henry stepped forward. No point in speculating, when all he had to do was ask. "How many?" he whispered.

"I hear a single heartbeat."

"Arra?"

"I don't know."

"Shadow-held."

A flash of teeth. "I'll let you know. Give me thirty seconds."

"And then?"

"Make your way to the gate and start setting up the big light."

"In the dark?"

"Use the flashlight. Remember that the darkness handicaps them. They can't use the shadows the body casts in the dark."

"Duh, Henry. My intel, remember?"

Henry's brow creased in annoyance. "Then why did you ask?" he demanded and slipped into the soundstage.

♦

The darkness in the soundstage was not absolute, but then in this day and age, darkness seldom was. Exit lights and LEDs on equipment left running gave Henry illumination enough to see by. Not clearly, but sufficiently.

The taint of the otherworld seeping through twice a day prevented him from scenting and identifying the life he could hear, and the reek of fresh paint permeating the soundstage like a mist didn't help. No matter. The heart rate told him his quarry was awake and humans seldom sat awake in darkness. Shadow-held, then. Waiting for the gate.

He slipped around a false wall and paused, close enough now to scent his quarry as female. The wizard? Still too many other, stronger scents masking subtleties.

It was standing just under the gate, wrapped in the ubiquitous plastic raincoat.

◆

". . . twenty-eight Raymond Dark, twenty-nine Raymond Dark, thirty." Tony dried damp palms against his thighs and squared his shoulders. "Ready or not, here I come." He hoped a thirty-second lead was enough time for Henry to take care of things—not that it mattered if it wasn't. The big lamp had to be in place and ready to go when the gate opened.

He thumbed on the flashlight, pointed it at the floor, and headed for the light board.

◆

Not the wizard. A girl, Tony's age. She had the raincoat shoved back and her hands deep in the front pockets of a pair of bib overalls. As Henry stopped at the edge of the open set—she was standing where they needed her to be, he had no need to go any farther—she shifted her weight back and forth from one red high-top to the other. Impatience, not anticipation. She couldn't know he was . . .

When the lights came on, the last thing Henry saw before being flung to the floor was her smile.

◆

Lights?

Tony blinked toward the spill of lights from the dining room set.

Why would Henry turn on the lights?

Answer: Henry wouldn't.

He started to run.

◆

Henry struggled against the shadow that wrapped around him from wrist to cheekbones; his arms held to his sides, his mouth and nose covered. It bulged but held.

When the girl squatted beside him, the shadow squirmed off his ears.

"We left a guard on the gate," she said conversationally. "It wasn't here, so someone had to have destroyed it. If someone knew how to do that, then that same someone knew way, way too much and would likely be back. Hello, someone. I was waiting for you. You should've checked for traps." Her smile broadened as she held up the remote switch she'd used to turn on the lights. "You'll be unconscious soon, and then you'll be dead."

Not soon. Definitely not before the gate opened. Although Henry needed to breathe, the air in his lungs would last him long enough. He could hear cables hitting the floor, the lamp's wheeled platform moving. All he had to do was lie here, listen to the shadow-held gloat, and wait for the gate to open. The shadow would attempt to leave, Tony would hit it with the light, and he'd be released. A slightly less dignified scenario, granted, but it would get the job done. And a good thing, too, since the tensile strength of shadow meant he wouldn't be doing the superman-breaking-his-bonds thing any time soon.

Her smile slipped and her eyes narrowed. "You're different."

He fought to keep the Hunger from showing, but it was still too close to the surface. Tina had helped but not enough.

"Nightwalker." One finger flipped a strand of his hair back and forth. "This one doesn't believe in you, but I wouldn't be too upset about that since she doesn't believe in me either. It's all metaphors and symbolism in here." The plastic raincoat crinkled as she leaned forward, one hand going to the floor beside his head to keep from overbalancing. "What's it like in there, I wonder? I imagine you've got a better grip on what's real. Shall we find out? Besides, it's always smartest to take over the strong. Makes it harder for the weak to stop you."

From the corner of one eye, Henry noticed a patch of darkness under the huge rectory table. Dark enough? Only one way to find out. Rolling seemed to be his only option.

"Oh, no, you . . ."

He was under the table before she finished her protest. He felt the binding ease—apparently it was *just* dark enough—and he ripped his way free; aware he was snarling as he got to his feet but not really caring.

Her lip curled in answer. "A creature of darkness fighting for the light? That's not how it works where I come from."

"It's how it works here."

She flashed him a cheeky smile and turned to run; *Chase me, chase me!* so strongly implied she might as well have shouted it aloud. Henry held the hunter in check, dodged the cast shadow she was attempting to distract him from, and stood in front of her before she could turn again. "Apparently my kind move slower where you come from."

She stiffened in his grip, her eyes staring at nothing as the shadow within her began to rip free.

Vibration in blood and bone announced the opening of the gate.

"Henry! Close your eyes!"

Even through closed lids the world turned a brilliant white. Tears streaming down his cheeks, Henry threw the girl forward, dropped to his knees and buried his face in his arms.

After a long moment, the light turned off.

"It's okay. You can look up now." Figuring Henry

could take care of himself, Tony ran across the set toward Kate Anderson's crumpled body. She was Mouse's focus puller and that was the only thing Tony knew about her. Muttering, "Not again!" over and over like a mantra against a worst-case scenario, he dropped to his knees, rolled her onto her back, and felt for a heartbeat. Lost it in the screaming pain still vibrating his skull. Found it again.

"She's alive."

"Yeah." Tugging the raincoat back into place, he looked up at Henry. "Why did you throw her?"

"I hoped that being right under the gate would activate the shadow's primary function—to return home with information—and keep it from remembering that it was heading for me. Seems to have . . ."

"Not real. Not real. Not real!" One hand clamped around Tony's arm, the other grabbed for the collar of his shirt. Kate's pupils had contracted down to black pinpricks and her eyes were opened painfully wide. "Not real!"

"Sorry." Tony wasn't sure why he was apologizing; it just seemed the thing to do. Then he remembered. "Henry, we don't have any potion, the cops dumped it. We didn't even stop to buy vodka!" Dropping his ass to the floor, he dragged her up onto his lap. "You're going to have to vamp her!"

Kate's heels began to drum as Henry dropped down by her other side. "To what?"

"You know, touch the primal terror. Convince her you're real and that'll help her deal with the rest!"

His mouth slightly open, Henry stared at him, his expression caught halfway between astonishment and amazement. "And if she can't deal with me?" he asked after a long moment.

"Jesus, Henry, she's twenty-three years old and you're . . . you. Just crank up the sex appeal!"

Shaking his head, Henry took hold of the girl's jaw. "Do you have any idea of what you're talking about?"

"Hell, no! I'm making it up as I go along. Do you have a better idea?" he asked as Henry stared down into Kate's face. "Or *any* other idea?"

"No."

"Then what can we lose? Damn it, Henry, there's already two people dead!"

Henry looked up at him then, his eyes dark, and, after a moment, he said, "What's her name?"

"Kate." Tony grunted as a plastic clad elbow drove into one of the bruises Mouse had pounded into him.

"Catherine?"

"Could be."

"Kate, then." Henry bent his head toward hers and called her name.

Tony stiffened. Literally stiffened. He knew the whole Prince of Darkness thing was going to affect him, no way it couldn't, not after last night, but this he hadn't expected. His whole body longed to answer the call. Blood was rushing south fast enough to leave him light-headed and he had an erection he could pound nails with pressed up against Kate's back. *Deal. You're the one who told him to crank up the sex appeal.*

The good news was, it seemed to be working on Kate, too. She'd transferred her grip from his collar to Henry's and stopped thrashing.

And thank God for that. Friction, even friction of the spine-encased-in-raincoat variety was not helping.

Teeth gritted, he fought to maintain his hold as Henry's voice caressed them both. It didn't seem to matter that it wasn't meant for him. Kate gasped as teeth met through the skin of her wrist. Tony gasped with her. She moved languidly on his lap. He closed his eyes and barely kept from . . .

. . . didn't quite keep from . . .

Then she was a limp weight against him and cool fingers touched his cheek.

"Tony? Are you all right?"

"Fine. Just a little sticky." He opened his eyes to see

Henry, only Henry, staring into his face. The relief would have left him limp had that not already been taken care of. "You're not all carried away?"

"I've fed twice tonight. The Hunger is replete."

"I thought too much blood got it going."

"I didn't take too much. Hardly any from young Kate."

"Is she?"

"She's asleep."

"Doesn't like to cuddle, then."

Henry paused, about to lift Kate into his arms. "What?"

"Never mind." Tony adjusted his jeans as her weight went off him, saw Henry's nostrils' flare and silently dared him to comment. "I've got to put the lamp back. Why don't you put her in the car and see if she's got her address written in her raincoat or something."

"Or something," Henry agreed. He straightened, Kate's head lolling against his shoulder. "You know, eventually we're going to miss one. Or they'll get smarter and all hit the gate at once."

"Yeah, I thought of that," Tony said as he got to his feet. Then he frowned. "They could get smarter?"

"The longer they ride their hosts, the more information they absorb."

"Oh, that's just fucking great."

They walked together to the lamp.

"On the bright side," Henry murmured as he turned toward the exit, "that's three down and only four to go."

Tony bent and began coiling cable. "Unless one's in Arra, in which case we're just generally screwed."

"So much for the bright side."

"Yeah." He sighed as Henry began walking and said softly as he heard the door open, knowing Henry would hear him even at that distance. "I'm thinking there's got to be a better way."

◆

Arra watched the Nightwalker leave with the girl, watched Tony clear away all signs that anyone had been in the soundstage after hours. Although the pull of the gate had been nearly overwhelming, she'd needed to be there as they dealt with the shadow, keeping just enough of her consciousness present to see and hear and not enough to alert the vampire.

It wasn't enough to know what they did, she had to know how.

And, knowing, what should she do with that knowledge?

Twelve

AT FIRST he thought he was in the east end. The buildings on both sides of the street were long abandoned, their dark windows staring down at him accusingly. There were no people, no traffic. The only sign of life was a small flock of pigeons strutting about the nearest intersection searching for food in the cracks between slabs of buckled asphalt.

Tony walked slowly down the center of the street, flanked on either side by the burned-out remains of cars and trucks and minivans. A glance into one of the cars gave him a pretty good idea of where the people had gone.

Then he nearly tripped over a charred a-frame advertising Italian ice cream and he realized he wasn't in the east end at all. He was on Robson Street. The abandoned buildings had once been rows of trendy boutiques and high-priced restaurants. He stepped from the street into Robson Square to find the trees dead and a body facedown in the six inches of dirty water filling the skating rink.

He was walking through the establishing shot of every post-apocalyptic move ever made. Could it get any more clichéd?

Behind him, a sign creaked ominously in the breeze and the light began to fade.

Apparently, it could.

Then the hair rose on the back of his neck. Off the

back of his neck? Well, it was standing, like it knew something he didn't and he didn't like that feeling at all.

There was something behind him.

Of course there was.

Screw it. He'd just keep walking and not give in to it. He wouldn't turn, he wouldn't look, he wouldn't play the game. Two steps, three—on four he felt himself begin to pivot. He hadn't intended to turn, but he wasn't driving anymore.

Oh, crap.

He'd just become a passenger in his own body.

Been there. Done that. Didn't want to do it again.

Robson became Boundary and the thing in his body walked him through the front door of the studio. Amy came toward him, asking him a question through lips the exact same fuchsia as her hair. He could see her lips move, but he couldn't hear her. He couldn't hear anything but the pounding of his own heart. And the hard/soft melon on concrete crack of her head hitting the floor as he shoved her out of his way.

Lee and Mouse were waiting on the soundstage under the gate. They moved in on either side of him and his world dissolved into hands and mouths and flesh that felt like clammy rubber and wouldn't let him breathe. When the gate opened, they separated and it drew them up one at a time; first Lee, then Mouse, then him. Through light, through pain, into a room with blackboards covered in patterns that might have been words that might have been illustrations, that might have been mathematical notion; it was impossible to tell because two of the three boards had a body crucified against it and the third had clearly been prepared for a body of its own.

Their eyes were open and their expressions suggested they'd been alive for a very long time after they'd been nailed to the walls.

There was a man—he *knew* there was a man, was as certain of it as he'd ever been of anything in his life—

but he could only see a formless shadow stretching out dark and horrible along the floor. He felt his body move toward it, as unable to stop itself as he was to stop it. His heart raced. If he touched the shadow, he'd be absorbed the way Lee and Mouse had been absorbed. He'd lose the self he'd found. Become nothing more than a part of the darkness. He couldn't let that happen. Not again.

But the compulsion was everything.

Greater than terror.

Greater than the need to be.

Darkness.

The room through different eyes. An instant of being himself *and* someone else. An instant of cold cruelty. Arrogance. Impatience. Why was such a simple task taking so long?

And a voice. A loud, obnoxious, unignorable voice. "It's 8:30 on a beautiful Sunday morning and you're listening to CFUN and another forty-five minutes of commercial free music. Let's start things off with a little Av . . ."

Tony was out of bed, across the room, and slapping off the radio before he was truly awake—a total aversion to so-called soft rock and Amy's suggestion of putting the radio where he couldn't reach it from the bed was the only thing he'd ever found guaranteed to get him up. Eyes squinted nearly shut, he wondered for a moment why it was so bright in the apartment and then remembered that for the second night in a row, he'd gone to sleep with all the lights on.

Not that it had helped much.

His skin prickled under a fine sheen of sweat as the terror returned and a glimpse of his shadow lying on the grubby carpet drove him two stumbling steps back into the wall.

"A dream. It was just a dream." And fuck but his subconscious was anything but subtle. He swallowed, suddenly felt trapped in the enclosed space of the apartment and staggered around the pull-out couch to the window where he threw back the curtains and squinted up at an overcast sky. It was threatening rain.

And that was normal enough that he managed to get his breathing under control.

A walk to the bathroom to empty his bladder helped and by the time he'd flushed and washed his hands, he walked to the refrigerator feeling almost normal. Well, as normal as he ever felt first thing in the morning.

Opening the fridge, he leaned in, grabbed the bomb bottle of cola off the top shelf, and twisted off the cap. A quick taste determined it was flat but not totally undrinkable. Besides, neither the caffeine nor the sugar was in the bubbles.

Bottle tipped back, feeling more human with every swallow, Tony closed the fridge door and screamed. Unfortunately, that resulted in rather a lot of flat cola going back up his nose. Once he'd finished with the coughing and the choking, he stared across the room with various liquids dripping from every facial orifice.

Arra was still sitting on his only chair.

Suddenly remembering he was naked, he rather belatedly moved the bottle in front of his crotch. "What the fuck are you doing here?"

She stared at him blankly and he realized she was wearing the exact same clothing she'd had on the day before. Not good. Not good at all.

"I don't know."

It took him a moment to figure out that she was answering his question. "You don't know why you're here?" he asked shuffling forward until he could squat down and grab a pair of jeans off the floor.

"I don't know why I didn't just keep going."

"Right." Personal modesty had already gone to hell so Tony set the bottle on the counter and shrugged into his jeans, turning around to tuck himself inside. A careful closure—because getting caught in the zipper would make the morning even more special—and he felt a little better prepared to face his uninvited guest.

"So . . ." He faced her again with studied nonchalance. "Am I talking to the wizard or the shadow operating the wizard?"

That elicited a bleak smile. "If I was shadow-held, would I tell you?"

"Yeah, well, so far, shadows . . ." The edge of the counter pressed into his back and his right hand closed around the handle of the silverware drawer. He was pretty sure not *everything* in it was plastic. ". . . big on the bwahaha."

"On the what?"

"They gloat."

"Ah. Yes, they do. They didn't used to." She closed her eyes for a moment. When she opened them again, her expression was strangely familiar. "They used to stay hidden, doing as much damage as they could for as long as they remained undiscovered."

"Maybe that was because they knew they had something to stay hidden from."

"Maybe."

"And it's been all television people this time; big egos to deal with."

"True."

Releasing the drawer handle, he took two steps forward. He'd known almost immediately that Mouse was shadow-held—one look at his face and he'd seen it wasn't the cameraman at the controls. He didn't like to look at Arra's face because he'd realized why her expression seemed familiar. The last time Tony'd seen it the body it belonged to had been spiked to a blackboard. Bodies, actually. "Arra, what happened yesterday in the church?"

"I destroyed the shadow."

"Good." Another step.

"But Alan Wu was dead and I could do nothing more."

"So you ditched me."

"I knew there would be authorities to deal with and this is your world."

"You're living in it. On it."

Plastic crinkled as she shrugged. "My history only goes back seven years."

"So you were afraid the cops would find out you've got no past?"

"No past *here*."

"Okay." Sounded reasonable, but reasonable didn't explain why she'd disappeared, why she was still wearing yesterday's clothes, and why she was in his apartment. "What else happened?"

The snort was a pale imitation of her usual explosive exhalation. "What makes you think something else happened?"

"I don't think you've been home."

"Adults don't stay out all night on this world?"

Tony sighed. "Who fed your cats?"

Her eyes widened and the nailed-to-a-blackboard expression was replaced by the dawning realization that the world hadn't actually ended—even though it might be better for some concerned if it had. "Oh, shit."

He grabbed her arm as she tried to rush by him. "Wait. I'm coming with you."

♥

Her car had been parked a couple of blocks away. After he'd thrown on some clothes, they'd all but run to it. Arra'd burned rubber out of the parking spot before Tony'd barely got his door closed.

Finally buckled in, he sank down in the seat and wondered where he should begin.

"How did you get into my apartment?" The door had been locked, the chain still on when they left.

"I'm a wizard. I have powers."

Well, duh. "You teleported?"

"I got a demon to carry me through . . . GREEN!" The light obediently changed. ". . . the Netherhells and emerge in your apartment."

Fucking great. He'd done the demon thing. It was

how he'd met Henry—ripped up by said demon and in desperate need of blood. "Seriously?"

"No. I suppose you could call it teleporting. The senior among us could move ourselves from point to point over short distances. It's what made us start thinking about other worlds."

"Why?"

"We had to be moving through something, didn't we?"

"I guess." He closed his eyes as she inserted the hatchback into a space maybe an inch larger than the car. When he opened them again—after the g-forces had returned to normal—he noticed something on the dash. "Is it magic that keeps this car going without gas?"

"What?" Her gaze dipped to follow his line of sight. "No. The gauge is broken, so I fill up based on mi . . . Get out of the damned way! I am in no mood to take prisoners!"

Silently urging the SUV in front of them to give it some gas, Tony frowned. "You were a senior?"

The pause lasted long enough he knew the answer had to be important. Or the SUV was about to be moved over a short distance.

"I was."

He breathed a sigh of relief when the sport vehicle turned. "Like Dumbledore or Gandalf?"

"Less hairy."

His frown deepened. Arra wasn't young, but he wouldn't have said she was old. Kind of in that in-between who-the-hell-can-tell age. If he'd had to guess, he'd have looked at the gray and the lines around her eyes and mouth and said mid-fifties but mostly because it seemed like a safe number—after a certain age it was always safer to guess low. But no matter what she looked like, Arra wasn't human. Not from this world at all and who knew how they aged where she came from. *And* she was a wizard—they probably aged differently. "Were you *the* senior? The head wizard?"

Both of her fists came down on the steering wheel.

"These lanes are wide enough for transports and you're in a fucking GEO! Pick a lane and stay in it!"

The Geo swerved to the right so abruptly it looked as though a giant hand had come down and shoved it to one side. Tony couldn't be absolutely sure one hadn't.

"No."

"No?" One hand clutched at the dash, the other at the side of his seat, his fingers almost a joint deep in the cheap vinyl, and he was still being flung about within the loose confines of the seat belt.

"No, I wasn't *the* senior."

Her emphasis was slightly different than his. Almost bitter. Had she thought she should be? Tony added that new question to the bottom of the list and returned to the top. "Why were you in my apartment?"

"Honestly, I'm not sure. You and your Nightwalker are the only people on this world who know me and the sun was up . . ."

What there was of an answer sounded like truth, so he let it go. "Where did you go yesterday?"

Her sigh was deep enough to lightly mist the inside of the windshield. "Whistler. I had a foolish idea of finding CB and telling him everything."

Again an interesting emphasis. Everything? He had a suspicion Arra's everything included a few somethings he didn't yet know about, but before he could ask, she continued.

"I saw him with his daughters and I realized that a man who has no idea he's being played by an eight year old and an eleven year old couldn't help me."

"Harsh."

"Perhaps. There's always the chance I just chickened out at the last minute and ran."

Given her history, Tony found the latter more likely. "Uh, you know that if the police stop you, you'll be a lot later getting home."

"The police don't see this car."

"Damn."

"I move from world to world and this is what impresses you?"

"*This*, I understand. And . . ." Another light changed after only a moment of red. ". . . I was also impressed by the maggots."

The corner of her mouth he could see twisted up into a close approximation of a smile. "Fair enough. What happened to the girl?"

"What girl?"

"Kate."

"You know about Kate?"

"I was there. I saw. I needed to see." Her tone lengthened the list of questions even further—although the new ones hadn't quite acquired actual words.

"Henry took her home." At least he assumed Henry took her home. He'd been dropped off first and although Kate was sprawled across pristine upholstery in the back seat of the BMW still totally out of it, she was smiling. He'd reminded himself he trusted Henry, had stripped and fallen into bed. Sleep hadn't been long in coming and he really wished he hadn't thought about sleeping. Images from the dream played out like a slide show in his head.

Arra's voice disrupted the show. "You found a way without me."

"It's easier with you."

"Not always."

Okay. Enough was enough. "Stop doing that!"

"Doing what?"

"Adding another layer. Talking to you is like opening one of those nested doll things. You open one and there's another. I get that you're thinking things through, working out old shit—really I do get that—but every time you open your mouth, you're saying six or seven things besides the stuff you're saying out loud, but you're leaving me to figure out what those things are! How come I have to be the hero *and* figure all this shit out?" Whoa. Where had that come from? He didn't even feel better having said it.

"Maybe I should just drive."

"Yeah. Maybe you should."

♥

Arra screeched into her parking place at the co-op, turned off the car, tossed Tony her keys, and disappeared. Damp air rushed in through the open window to fill the empty space.

He swallowed as his ears popped. "Guess I'm taking the scenic route."

It took him a while to lock up the car and figure out which key went where. By the time he got to the apartment, Whitby had his head buried in a bowl of food, but Zazu was nowhere in sight. Dropping his backpack by the door, Tony followed Arra's voice into the living room to find her with her butt in the air and *her* head nearly under the couch. Wincing, he looked away.

"Look, I said I was sorry. What more do you want?" The wizard was sounding increasingly desperate with every word.

"Is everything okay?"

"She's making me pay."

"Pay?"

"For abandoning her." Shuffling backward on her knees, Arra straightened. "No one does guilt like a cat."

"And you were only gone one night."

From the way Arra narrowed her eyes she'd picked up the subtext. *Just think of how she'll feel if you abandon her for good.* But all she said was, "Grab that catnip lizard out of the basket. It's her favorite toy."

Tony grabbed the stuffed animal that looked the most like a lizard and tossed it across the room.

"This isn't a lizard, it's a platypus!"

Say what? "Who the hell makes catnip platypuses?"

"Platy*pi*. I get them at a local craft fair." She ducked back under the couch. "Zazu, sweetie, see what I've got for you."

"It's almost quarter to ten. We don't have time for this."

Arra shuffled backward again. "Don't tell me, tell her."

Tony snagged the platypus out of the air as she tossed it back to him. As Arra stood and headed for the kitchen, he suddenly realized she expected him to coax the cat out from under the couch. "I don't know anything about cats!"

"Good. Maybe a fresh approach will work."

He thought about refusing, decided there was no percentage in it, and took up the position. Zazu glared at him from what was clearly just out of reach. Wait a minute. Just out of Arra's reach . . . He wasn't tall but he had a good four inches on her.

Grabbing the cat by a foreleg he started to slide her across the hardwood floor and nearly lost his hand at the wrist.

Ow! God damn it! Bad idea!

Except that it seemed to have worked. Whether she was satisfied now that she'd drawn blood or whether she was so mortally insulted she wasn't staying under the couch for another moment, Tony couldn't tell—nor, he supposed, did it matter. Point was, as he nursed his injuries, Zazu swaggered toward the kitchen, tail in the air.

Tony followed with a little less swagger, sucking his wrist.

"That Nightwalker of yours teaching you bad habits?"

"What? Oh." A final lick and he let his arm fall to his side. "No. And he's not mine."

She tested the temperature of the alcohol in the pot and began adding herbs. "Does he come when you call?"

"Well, yeah, but . . ."

"That's more than you can say about cats and most people would tell you that these two are mine."

"Most people?"

"Some people know better. Pass me the bay leaves."

As he handed them over, Tony wondered just how dis-

turbed he should be about finding the smell of warm
vodka and catnip comforting. A sharp pain in his right
calf drew his attention down to an imperious black and
white face. "What!"

Arra snickered and, stirring with her right hand, tossed
him the paper bag of catnip with her left. "Try this. Why
so jumpy when I showed up at your place this morning?"
she continued as he tossed a handful of the dried leaves
on the kitchen floor.

"Why was I so jumpy?" He stared at her in disbelief.
"I don't know, maybe because I'm in the middle of
breakfast and this wizard who might have been taken
over by shadow—based on the whole ditching and disappearing thing—suddenly appears in my apartment!
Not to mention being caught with my dick waving
around."

"Ah, I see."

At first he thought she was laughing at him, but what
he could see of her expression looked serious.

"Still have my thermoses?"

"In my backpack."

"Get them."

If anyone had *reason* to be jumpy . . . He set the pair
of thermoses on the counter by the stove. "You know,
I've got to say, this morning, even after I knew you
weren't shadow-held, I was concerned about you."

"Why?"

"You looked bummed."

"Bummed?" The first soup ladle of potion splashed
into the first thermos with a hollow sound. "I suppose
that's as good a word as any." The sound grew higher
pitched and less hollow as the thermos filled. "The
shadow from Alan Wu touched me before I destroyed
it. Only for an instant, but in that instant I knew what
the shadow knew." She set the first thermos to one side
and began filling the second. "It is one thing to extrap-
olate the probable fate of your home; it's another entirely to see it."

"I'm sorry."

"About what?"

He shrugged, made uncomfortable by the question. "I'm not sure. It's a Canadian thing."

Her snort sounded more like the Arra he'd started to know. Setting down the ladle, she wrapped her hand around each thermos in turn, singing out the vowels she'd used to make the first potion sparkle. After the whole beam-me-up-Scotty, now-you-see-me-now-you-don't it seemed unnecessarily . . . twee. She snorted again when he mentioned it.

"All magic involves the manipulation of energy. Lesser magics like this are, as you say, unnecessarily twee because lesser wizards need their cue cards to get the desired result. Doing it their way is, therefore, easier."

Tony didn't see the "therefore." "So what's the cost?"

"Cost?" She paused, the second lid half tightened.

"Yeah, there's *always* a cost."

"You're really a very remarkable young man."

Pointing out that flattery didn't answer the question seemed rude, so he waited. He was still waiting when she screwed the cup back on over the lid and passed the first thermos back to him. He was good at waiting. By the time the second thermos was ready, Arra'd realized that.

She sighed. "The more energy manipulated, the more it takes of the wizard's personal strength."

Tony nodded. That sounded reasonable. As he tucked the potion into his backpack, he decided not to make the obvious "you're so strong" declaration. In the last twenty-four hours, Arra had destroyed a shadow, driven to Whistler and back, snuck onto the soundstage to watch him and Henry deal with the gate, spent the night away from home wrestling with personal demons—probably not literally, but he wasn't ruling it out—popped into Tony's apartment, shielded her speeding car from the cops, popped into her own apartment, and zapped two liters of potion. Energy manipulation levels: high. Wizard's personal strength . . .

"Give me a minute to change."

"Change?"

"Clothes." She tossed the word over her shoulder on the way to the bedroom, adding, just before she closed the door behind her: "You won't make it out to the studio by 11:15 unless I drive, and I reek."

She was right. Not about the reeking—not by guy standards anyway although he had no idea how women her age defined reek—but about the driving. Sunday transit schedules sucked as far as hitting the burbs in a hurry.

So, wizard's personal strength: energizer bunny levels.

In fact, ever since he'd reminded her about the cats it had been like he'd pulled a plug and the momentum of that initial "oh, my God" was keeping her moving. The faster she moved, the more she did, the less she had to deal with the crap the shadow had called up when it touched her.

Memo to self. Prepare for the crash and burn.

And hope it didn't happen at 80K.

♥

Or at 120K, for that matter . . .

Both hands white-knuckled around the shoulder strap, Tony couldn't decide whether he preferred eyes open or eyes closed. Eyes open, he could see his imminent death in a fiery car crash approaching and prepare. Eyes closed, he could pretend he wasn't in a hatchback whipping diagonally through westbound traffic and occasionally, when things were tight, into the oncoming lane.

He liked taunting death as much as the next guy, but since the next guy was a middle-aged and possibly old wizard from another world and there were still four shadows unaccounted for, all bets were off. She was worse than Henry and Mouse combined.

"So do you always drive like this?"

"Scared?"

"No."

"Lying?"

Like he'd tell her. "No."

"Good. To answer your question, almost never. But we're in a hurry."

There were high spots of color on her cheeks—technically cheek since he could only see one. On the bright side: at this speed they'd be there soon. On the other side, the less bright side: any idiot knew that the more energy burned, the faster it ran out.

He had to distract her or at least slow her down. "The other reason I was so jumpy . . ."

"Jumpy?"

"When you played pop goes the weasel . . ."

"Wizard."

"Whatever. . . . in my apartment was that I'd just had a dream."

The eyebrow he could see, waggled.

"Not that kind of a dream. A bad dream. I dreamed that the shadow was back in control and it took me through the gate."

"To Oz?"

"To a room. It looked like a schoolroom or maybe a lab. There were books and blackboards with, I don't know, equations covering . . ." When Arra hit the brakes, he realized distraction was relative. He tightened his grip as the car fishtailed across the wet asphalt and into a Timmy's parking lot.

When the squealing stopped—and he was 99% sure the squealing had come from the tires—when the only sound was the rain on the roof and the swish/click of the windshield wipers, Arra turned to face him and said, "Were there more than equations on the blackboards?"

Their eyes were open and their expressions suggested they'd been alive for a very long time after they'd been nailed to the walls.

"Yeah."

"People?" The steering wheel creaked under her hands.

Tony nodded.

She closed her eyes for a moment and when she opened them again, he knew he wouldn't have to describe what he'd seen. She'd seen it, too. "You weren't dreaming. Those were images the shadow left behind. While it controlled you, you touched its memory."

"I touched?"

"Yes. It explains why the shadow-stain is stronger on you than the others."

Shadow-stain. Fucking great. *Excuse me while I go home and soak my soul in cold water.* And then he realized . . . "So that . . . what I saw, it was real?"

"Yes."

"Who were they?"

"The last two members of my order who stood to face the Shadowlord."

"I'm sorry."

"Why? You didn't do anything."

"That was . . ." He sighed and sank back against the seat. "Forget it."

A light touch on his arm drew his attention back to the other side of the car. "*I'm* sorry."

"Hey." He shrugged. "They were your friends."

"Yes." A simple acknowledgment carrying an emotional payload that filled the car like smoke.

Because he couldn't look at her and because he had to do *something,* he checked his watch. Crap. 10:40. He'd just wanted to distract her, slow her down, not bring her back to a complete stop. "Arra, we have to get going or we won't get to the gate in time."

"Right." She fumbled the car into reverse and nearly backed over an elderly man carrying three medium coffees on a cardboard tray.

"Did you want me to drive?"

"Don't be ridiculous."

A skateboarder flipped her the finger as she cut him off.

"I'm just saying . . ."

"Well, don't!"

♥

They got to the studio at 11:02, only to find that the code on the soundstage keypad had been changed. Three sets of wrong numbers would set off the alarms. Tony remembered with one number to go and snatched his hand away from the pad. Alarms would bring police and with his luck Constable Elson would ride back into his life.

"Can you do something about this?"

"No."

"Can you pop inside and open it?" He knew the answer before she opened her mouth. Reaction had finally kicked in and her cheeks had turned an alarming shade of gray. "Are you all right?"

"I'll manage."

"This thing's been the same since I got here." The pad was off limits so he kicked the concrete foundation blocks. "Why are they fucking changing it now?"

"They had to change the front door lock. It probably reminded them about the back."

"Fucking great. Hang on; you have a key for the . . . *old* front door lock. Never mind." 11:07. This was going to be close. Actually, if he didn't come up with something, it wasn't going to be at all. "The carpenter's door!"

"The what?"

"The big door they use for deliveries of lumber and building crap. Three of them smoke and they won't want to keep locking and unlocking the door every time they want a butt." He started to run and stopped when he realized Arra wasn't beside him.

"Keep going," she snapped. "I don't sprint!"

"You'll catch up?"

"If you don't move your ass, I'll run you over."

Kicking up gravel, Tony raced around the corner and up the west side of the building. As long as she didn't ditch him again . . .

The carpenter's door looked like a corrugated section of the wall. Because the tracks were hidden and the latch had been painted with the same dark brown antirust paint as the door, it was hard to find without knowing where to look. Deliberately so.

And it looked like it weighed a fucking ton.

Fortunately, it was already open about an inch. Tony hooked his fingers around the edge and threw all his weight against it. It flew open so fast it dropped him on his ass, the big door sliding soundlessly along its tracks until his dangling weight stopped it.

Plus ten for maintenance. Minus several thousand for not warning a guy!

He scrambled to his feet, stepped over the lower track, and left the door open for Arra as he ran toward the gate. At least two hammers were pounding out a staccato rhythm back behind the permanent sets that made up Raymond Dark's office, but the dining room was finished and deserted. His back teeth beginning to vibrate and his hands sweating so heavily he could barely maintain his grip, he yanked the big lamp into position, threw a cable out of the box, and bent to make the connection.

"And what the hell do you think you are playing at?"

Shit! Sorge—no mistaking the DP's accent. *He's probably here to work out the lighting for tomorrow morning.* Unfortunately, knowing that was no help at all.

"I am waiting."

Teeth gritted in an effort to keep his skull from blowing apart, Tony finished making the connection and straightened. The gate was about to open. All he had to do was turn the lamp on; he could lie about what he was playing at just as easily with the gate blocked. Easier. More easily? Bottom line, he could

concentrate on the lie if he knew the shadows—
incoming, outgoing, pogo-ing—had been stopped. But
Sorge was between him and the lighting board and it
didn't look as if he was going to move.

Tackle him?

And get fired; losing access to the gate and any
chance to stop the Shadowlord.

Reason with him?

Given how pissed off he looked, that seemed even
less likely to succeed.

The sudden brilliant light took them both by surprise.

"Tony's doing some work for me, Sorge." Arra released the switch and came out from behind the light
board. "I need a number of readings off this lamp." She
tossed Tony the light meter. "Go."

He trotted toward the set, allowing Sorge's protests
and Arra's answering argument to wash over him. In another couple of minutes, it wouldn't matter. The gate
would close and Arra could even let the DP think he'd
won. In the meantime, Tony maintained the charade,
holding what looking like a light meter but felt like a
battery from one of the radios up in the light. He was as
far from the actual opening as he could get and still
make it look real but it wasn't far enough to escape the
feeling of being examined.

Yeah, and me wearing a big fucking shadow-stain.

Then the gate closed and the lamp switched off a
heartbeat later.

"Oh, don't be so Gallic!" Arra snapped. "Your lamp
is fine and I have all the readings I need. Tony!"

"Yeah." He tossed her back the alleged light meter.

She nearly fumbled the catch and just for an instant it
looked like a battery.

Sorge frowned and Tony prepared to assure him that
he hadn't seen what he'd thought he'd seen.

"You are not well?"

Okay, *that* he had seen.

"I'm just a little tired."

"You look like shit. You should not be here. Go home."

Blunt, but accurate.

Apparently Arra thought so, too. "I think I will." Rummaging in the pocket of her raincoat, she pulled out her car keys. "Tony, you're driving."

"Sure." He ignored Sorge's dramatically raised eyebrow and obvious assumption—*Hello, gay! And she's old enough to be my grandmother so eww*—and fell into step beside the wizard. Her fingers closed around his arm. He bent it up and a step later was holding about half her weight. As soon as they were far enough away so they wouldn't be overheard, he bent toward her and murmured, "Are you okay?"

"Maintaining that glamour took about all I had left."

Tony paused as she staggered and walked on a little more slowly.

"It's been too long since I've been what I am. Too long since I shaped a world's energy to my personal use. I shouldn't have wasted all that power this morning."

He shrugged, carefully so as not to dislodge her. "Everyone has shouldn'ts. You drag them around with you, they just weigh you down."

They were at the back door. She patted his arm as she released him. "You're a good kid."

"I'm twenty-four."

Her turn to shrug. "I'm a hundred and thirty-seven."

"No shit?"

"If you're asking about my bowel movements, that's none of your damned business." She reached up and tore a taped piece of paper off the wall. "Here, you'll need this tonight."

It was the new code numbers for the lock.

"You know, I was thinking . . ."

Arra snorted. "Well, it's a start."

". . . if one of the shadow-held showed up to use the gate, they wouldn't be able to get in. You know—new code . . ." He waved the paper and shoved it in his back pocket. "New front door lock. And if they didn't know about the carpenter's door . . ." *Fuck.* "Except it was open."

"I closed it behind me."

"Okay, then. They couldn't get in, so they could still be out in the parking lot." He threw open the door. The sun had come out, puddles sparkled, and a pair of pigeons stared up at him with vapid avian indifference. "Or not."

"Or they could be returning to their car," Arra allowed. "You'd better run and check. I'll follow as fast as I can."

"Yeah, but . . ."

"I'll be fine. I'll be better if I can kick shadow ass."

"But you look . . ."

"Go!"

So he went. The pigeons took flight, their shadows trailing earthbound behind them.

There were half a dozen vehicles in the parking lot and an unshaven man in damp, rumpled clothes about to get into one of them.

"Hartley!"

The boom operator didn't even look up. Fortunately, the car locks seemed to be giving him a little trouble.

"Hartley! Wait up, man. I got to tell you about the really weird thing that just happened inside!"

That got his attention. He glanced up just as the locks thunked down. "Weird thing?"

All the hair lifted off the back of Tony's neck. *Oh, yeah, definitely shadow-held.* He jogged to a stop beside the car, let his backpack slide off his shoulder, and forced a smile. "Buzzy shit and then it got dark and then there was music. Bad eighties power rock." He dropped the pack by the back tire, played a couple of air guitar riffs and decided, as Hartley's eyes narrowed, that maybe the music was a bit over the top.

"You see me."

Or maybe it wasn't the music at all.

"Of course I see you. Duh. You're standing right there."

Actually, he didn't blame shadow-Hartley for growling and grabbing. That line hadn't worked the first time and this time, even he didn't believe it. This time, however, he was ready for the grab. As Hartley's fingers closed around his jacket, he threw himself backward. They hit the ground together and Tony rolled the older man to the bottom.

"You cannot hold me."

He tightened his grip on skinny wrists. "Bet?"

The shadow began to separate.

"Arra!" She had to be in the parking lot by now, but he couldn't see her. The car was in the way.

The shadow was now a distinct shape, rising up out of Hartley toward him. If he let go, it would suck back in and make a break for it. If he didn't . . .

If I bash his head against the ground, could I knock him out? Unlikely. And he'd have to let go to do it.

"Arra!"

Six inches. Four. He wasn't . . . He couldn't . . . If it touched him . . . Releasing his grip, he scrabbled backward on his hands and knees, down the length of Hartley's legs until he slammed up against the open car door.

Only a short strand of darkness connected the shadow to the boom operator.

It surged against that last restraint. Snapped it. Slid along Hartley's prone body. Flowed down over his legs. Connected Hartley's shadow to Tony's as Tony flung himself up and into the car.

As Tony crawled as fast as he could across the bench seat, reaching for the handle on the passenger side, he could feel it still moving along his shadow, using it as a safe path through the midday sun. Then cold air caressed his ankle and he bit back a scream.

They could move faster than this. They could move faster than Henry. It was toying with him.

♥

Arra could taste blood in the back of her mouth as she forced herself over the last few meters to the car. What the hell had she been thinking this morning? Right. She hadn't been thinking. She'd been reacting. She'd been stupid. Careless.

She tripped over a groaning body, glanced down to see the boom operator as she slammed against the trunk of the car, and saw the shadow slip off his lower legs. No time to recover. One hand bracing herself against the warm metal, she sucked air in and breathed out the incantation. Sucked in air. Breathed out incantation. Her pulse was pounding so hard in her temples she couldn't even hear her own voice, but it didn't matter. She could say this particular incantation in her sleep. Had.

Sucked in air. Staggered forward. Finished incantation.

Dropped to her knees, looked up to see Tony staring down at her from the front seat of the car. She blinked and managed to focus. Recoiled a little as the taint rolled over her strong and dark. Relaxed as that was all she felt.

"Arra?"

"I'm fine. You?"

"Fine."

He looked terrified, but considering the alternative, that was close enough to fine. She dropped to her knees beside Hartley's writhing body as Tony got out of the car, and worked a thermos out of the backpack. "You need to get some of this down him."

When he reached for the thermos, she clutched it close and glared. "Get your own, this one's mine."

The vodka helped.

"Get as much of it into him as you can, then get him

into his car and get the bottle out of the glove compartment and put it in his lap."

"How do you know he has a bottle in the glove compartment?"

She took another long comforting drink and shrugged, the warm car against the back almost making up for the gravel digging into her butt. "People talk. Next person out will find him, assume he went on a bender, and deal."

"I never knew."

"The one thing alcoholics excel at is hiding; hiding what they are, what they do, what it's doing to them."

"But right now he's okay?"

About to snap out something rude, Arra took a closer look at Tony's face and reconsidered. He honestly cared. "Probably." It was the closest to reassurance she could manage, but it seemed to be enough. She watched as Tony handed the last cup of potion to Hartley and let him drink it himself, watched him help the boom operator into the front seat, watched him lean in, and saw him emerge a moment later with a set of car keys that he dropped and kicked under the car. She winced as he slammed the door. Everything had gone a little fuzzy and she was beginning to get remarkably cold.

The vodka was good, though.

Tony's shadow stopped about a quarter inch from her leg. She looked up to see Tony looking down at her.

"We should go."

She snorted as he took her thermos and screwed the cap back on, his shadow waiting impassively for him to finish. "I should have gone a long time ago."

♥

Arra wasn't exactly a dead weight as Tony helped her into the passenger seat of her car, but she wasn't light either. Not muscular, but solid. Heavier than she looked. He thought about making a "weight of the world" crack, but the smell of vodka combined with the distinctly lighter thermos decided him against it.

Besides, if anyone was holding the weight of the world, it was him.

Like she keeps saying . . . He fastened her seat belt, closed the door, and walked around to the driver's side. *. . . it's not even her world.*

If not those exact words, something like that.

As he pulled out of the parking lot, she unscrewed the thermos and took another drink. He thought about protesting, but figured the alcohol was more legal in her than in an unsealed container—just in case.

Traffic was light heading back into the city. He could feel her watching him, but he kept his eyes on the road. Still, the watching reminded him of something.

"Arra? You said you were there last night, watching in the soundstage, because you needed to know. What did you need to know?"

He started to think she'd fallen asleep by the time she answered. "I needed to know if you'd fight without me."

"Oh."

He fought the urge to speed up as another car pulled out to pass and then slowed to let it back into the lane. *Easy enough to fight without you,* he said silently. *You're not fighting!* Then he frowned and remembered how she'd looked at the back door, and how she'd made it to the parking lot and, running on empty, had still vanquished the shadow.

Maybe there was more than one fight going on.

Thirteen

L AID OUT fully clothed on her bed under a fuzzy blanket stamped with a Hilton Hotel imprint, Arra muttered an incoherent protest and immediately went to sleep. Both cats made wide circles around Tony, then leaped up onto the bed and settled on either side of the wizard, matching glares and lashing tails making it quite clear they thought he had no business being there.

Which, he supposed, he didn't.

On the other hand, he had a strong feeling he had to stay hidden. Remembering the feeling of being watched as he stood under the gate, he could only hope that the whole shadow-stained thing wasn't equivalent to a big neon sign—*In case of invasion break this guy*. And there were still three shadows on the loose. Arra's apartment felt safe.

His stomach growled.

Ears saddled, Zazu growled an answer.

Because he didn't feel right about raiding Arra's fridge, he slipped her keys into his pocket and headed out looking for food. The hall was empty. He moved quickly and quietly toward the elevator. The general paranoia might be undefined, but *this*, this was specific. The last person he wanted to explain himself to was Julian-from-across-the-hall as he had a strong suspicion that Julian would consider three visits grounds for assigning chores.

The elevator gave him a few bad moments, the word "weak" repeating itself over and over in his head. *Weak? Trapped, I could understand.* He squinted around the tiny, brightly lit space made even more claustrophobic by all the highly polished surfaces. Still, given the way *eau de disinfectant* seemed to be replacing a good part of the oxygen, maybe weak wasn't that surprising.

Crossing the co-op's lobby gave him no problems.

He paused on the threshold, strangely unwilling to step outside.

Three mountain bikers rode by closely followed by a skateboarder and two preteens on in-line skates. It was the kind of early spring day that made Vancouverites, who conveniently forgot the 250 days of rain a year, unbearably smug about their weather—winds off the ocean had blown away clouds and pollutants and the sun shone brilliantly down through a crystal clear sky. Micas in the concrete sparkled and the city gleamed.

No shadows, at least none that weren't the result of a solid object blocking the sun, and no Shadowlord. *There's nothing out there waiting for me except lunch.*

Heart pounding, he took a fast step, almost a hop, over the threshold.

Nothing happened, but the feeling of being watched remained.

Fine. He'd grab food and he'd head right back to Arra's apartment. Sighing at his interior drama queen, he glanced back at his shadow, still lying predominantly in the co-op lobby, and muttered, "Come on, then!"

All things considered, he was relieved when it followed.

♠

A thousand voices cried, "Save us! Save us! You are our only hope!" Hands clutched at her, desperate fingers shredding clothing and the skin beneath it. She was drowning in their need. They were pulling her under. How could she save them when she couldn't save herself *from* them?

♠

The cats were still on Arra's bed when he returned and they stayed there while he ate, watched some golf—the one thing on television he was sure wouldn't wake the wizard—and worked his way through five days of the *Vancouver Sun*. He didn't usually read newspapers, he just didn't have the time and from the pristine folds, he guessed Arra's time had been a bit short lately, too. *Wouldn't want to cut into all that spider solitaire . . .*

It seemed to be business as usual in the lower mainland.

While he hadn't been expecting to see SHADOWS STALK CITY in banner headlines, it was weird to think he was one of only three people who knew of the danger and if he told anyone what he knew, told them that two people were dead because of shadows slipping through from another world, they wouldn't believe him. Not without having seen the things he'd seen. Done the things he'd done. Known the people he knew.

Eyes rolling, Tony tossed the last paper aside. Right. The people he knew . . .

A vampire, a wizard, and a production assistant go into a bar . . .

Fortunately, a snort from the bedroom saved him from having to come up with a punch line.

Cats winding around her feet, Arra stumbled out into the living room, glowered at him for a long moment from under lowered brows, and finally snapped, "Make coffee!" before turning on one heel, going back into the bedroom, and slamming the door.

Tony did as he was told.

♠

"There's three shadows left and we have seven hours until the gate reopens. You've been very lucky so far, but there's nothing to say all three of them won't show up together and I can think of any number of ways that they can stop you."

So could Tony.

"Finding them and stopping them individually before they get to the gate was a smart plan. Is still a smart plan. We need to pursue it."

"Are you strong enough?" There were still dark circles under her eyes and the skin on the backs of her hands looked thin and translucent.

"In spite of the morning's evidence, I know how to marshal my power." Sitting at the tiny kitchen table, Arra held out her mug. "I will find them, I will destroy the shadow, and you will do everything else," she announced as Tony refilled it.

"Uh . . . You'll need to make more potion."

"Fine! *And* I'll make more potion." She nodded toward the living room. "Bring me my Yellow Pages. But first put a bagel in the toaster oven."

Apparently *everything else* meant everything else.

♠

One of the shadows was at Richmond Nanak Sar Gursikh Temple on Westminster Highway.

Holding the phone book entry in one hand, Arra sifted through the ashes with the other and sighed. "We need to find another phone book."

"No shit."

"No time to waste," the wizard added pointedly.

Which was when Tony realized *he* had to find another phone book.

"There should be one up in the party room. Sixth floor."

Even better. "You want me to steal the Yellow Pages out of your co-op's party room so that you can destroy them?"

"So that I can use them to discover the location of a shadow-held." She dusted the ash off her fingers. "A shadow-held that might be held by *the* shadow-spy that takes the information back through the gate that convinces the Shadowlord to invade and destroy your world. Yes."

"Yeah. All right. Perspective; I get it." Wondering when they'd started calling them shadow-spies—*Like shadows alone aren't enough?*—he headed for the door, dancing sideways as Zazu hissed at him.

"What did you do to my cat?"

It had to be the attempted drag out from under the couch. Clearly, Zazu was holding a grudge. "Nothing."

He heard Arra snort as the door closed behind him. She was the wizard; if she wanted to know, she could ask the cat. Stepping out of Arra's apartment didn't seem to have the same emotional effect as it had earlier. He felt . . .

Tony frowned. Actually, the feeling of safety had vanished about the time Arra woke up, and he'd felt antsy ever since. Doing her wizardship's bidding had masked it, but now that he had nothing to occupy his mind, it was hard to ignore. The empty hall felt crowded with indefinable dangers and during the short walk to the elevator, he kept spinning around, certain someone or something was walking behind him, treading on his shadow.

There was never anything there *but* his shadow, clinging to his heels as if it, too, was sensitive to whatever the hell was going on. The elevator was just as distressing as it had been earlier. Squinting, Tony pressed the button for the sixth floor and hoped the shadow-stain wasn't somehow making him sensitive to light.

Or Henry . . .

"That Nightwalker of yours teaching you bad habits?"

Henry had been feeding from him off and on for the last five years. More off than on lately, but still . . . Were there cumulative effects? He ran his tongue over his teeth. They didn't feel any sharper. Mythically—and Tony'd made a point of checking out the myths way back when—it didn't work that way, but Henry'd always insisted that the myths were flawed. Insisted without specifying exactly what the flaws were.

Was he changing?

Oh, get the fuck over yourself, he snarled silently as the elevator doors opened. *There isn't enough shit going on, you have to come up with new crap?*

At just past five on a sunny Sunday afternoon, the party room was empty. He could hear two people talking out on the deck, but a row of trees in pots blocked the view through the window and the phone books were stacked in a pale bookcase by the door—the perfect setup to grab and go without being seen. Yellow Pages for Vancouver and the lower mainland in hand, Tony wasted a moment checking out the room. About 99% certain Arra still hadn't cleaned it, he figured someone else must have because it looked spotless. Blue—carpet, walls, upholstery—but spotless.

If anything, he was feeling even more freaky riding down in the elevator. Maybe it was guilt although, given his life prior to Henry, he somehow doubted it. Lifting a set of Yellow Pages would easily be among the least of his crimes.

Massive tome tucked under one arm in an effort to be as inconspicuous as possible, he stepped out through the elevator's opening door and into a barrage of sound.

"Hush, Moira! Quiet, girl!"

Although still safely tethered in Julian's arms, the Chihuahua was making it perfectly clear that if Tony wanted to get any farther into the hall, he'd have to pass her. Ears ringing, Tony gave some serious thought to doggie-flavored chalupas and stepped sideways.

Julian stepped with him, the dog continuing to yap hysterically. "You're that friend of Arra's."

"Yeah. So?"

"So tell her that common room isn't going to clean itself!"

"Sure." Tony suspected that if Arra wanted it to, the

common room wouldn't only clean itself, it'd take itself out for dinner and a movie.

"And tell her . . ." He pushed his voice through Moira's continuing protest. ". . . that I *will* bring this up with the Borg!"

The Borg? That put a whole new slant on co-op management.

"And I guarantee the board will have something to say to her!"

Oh. The board. Not nearly as interesting. Holding the phone book like he had every right to it, Tony put his back to the wall and managed to slide past. Twisting in Julian's arms, Moira's eyes never left him although the high-pitched barking was mercifully replaced by a low growl, the vibration causing her substantial jowls to quiver. It seemed she had better phone book sense than her owner.

Julian's high forehead started to crease.

Or maybe not.

He clearly knew something was wrong and it would only be a matter of moments before he figured out what. Time for a major distraction.

"You're an actor, aren't you? I can tell by the way you use your voice." Smiling insincerely, Tony cranked the bullshit up to full power. Two syllable ac-tors were the most susceptible to unsubstantiated hope. "I work out at CB Productions, in Burnaby—we do *Darkest Night*, the highest rated syndicated vampire detective show in North America—and we're always looking for new faces. You know, people who haven't already cropped up in every show shooting out here? You should stop by sometime. Talk to Peter—he does most of the casting."

"I'm theater mostly . . . Moira, quiet!"

"Sure, but there's no harm in making some solid cash to help support the arts, right?" His reaching fingers touched Arra's door. Just another few inches . . .

"Well, I was critically acclaimed for my Mustardseed

at Vanier Park last year when Bard in the Park did—Moira, shut up!—*Midsummer Night's Dream.*"

"Great. Experience." Three fingers hooked around the doorknob. "Peter loves Shakespeare. Hope to see you out there!" He was inside before Julian could reply, a final volley of yipping sounding through the door.

"What was that all about?" Arra called from the kitchen.

"Moira objected to me stealing the phone book."

"Fortunately, Moira's small enough to punt down the hall, but how did you keep Julian from calling the police?"

"He never noticed. He had his dick in a knot about you blowing off the party room and then I . . ." Tony flushed as Arra turned from stirring the potion and raised a speculative brow. "Nothing like that. I just told him he should stop by the studio sometime and talk to Peter, him being an ac-tor and all."

"Oh, Peter's going to love that."

"Two people are dead. If these shadows get back through the gate, more people will die." The phone book slammed down on the counter. "Besides, you keep saying the Shadowlord can't be stopped. With any luck, we'll be ass-deep in Armageddon before he gets there."

She looked at him strangely for a long moment.

"What?"

"Nothing."

It was obviously something, but Tony didn't bother pushing. Arra's explanations never actually explained anything and he had enough unanswered questions already on his plate.

The second shadow was at the South Delta Baptist Church.

"They're widening their search."

"Yeah." Tony stared at the scrap of yellow paper. "Where the hell is Tsawassen?"

"About half an hour south of the city, very nearly at the US border. Now, we'll need one more phone book."

"No." He shook his head, addresses laid out on the table. "This first one, the temple? It's in Richmond. That's south of the city. Then this one is farther south. What's to say that when you did this first one that's where the shadow *was* and now it's here, at this one? It moved while I was finding the book."

"It doesn't work that way."

"Yeah, but . . ."

"That's not the way the spell works. I ask where I can find the shadow and this . . . these . . . are the answers."

"I get that; but time has passed. So, logically . . ."

Arra snorted. "And how long have *you* been doing this?"

"What?"

"Because I've been doing it for a while now and I know what the hell I'm talking about." She handed him the pair of thermoses. "Put these away and let's go."

But he noticed she didn't ask again for a third phone book.

♠

Children raced around the small groups of adults standing outside the Nanak Sar Gursikh Temple—something family oriented had obviously just finished. Tony parked carefully, then reached over and shook Arra awake.

"The Light of Yeramathia!"

"Okay."

She blinked up at him, the edges of her eyes pink and swollen. "What did I say?"

He told her, then asked what it meant.

Arra snorted as she straightened and unbuckled her seat belt. "It means nothing. It was hope that became a lie."

Since this was about as clear as her explanations usually got, Tony merely shrugged and stepped out onto the sidewalk looking for someone he knew. Someone who'd been on Arra's short list of the potential shadow-held.

He looked for Dalal first, figuring that since the prop man was Sikh, this would logically be one of the places where he'd look for the light.

Yeah, like logic has anything to do with my world . . .

Barking drew his attention to the temple parking lot where an elderly man, who was definitely not Sikh and had probably just been out for an early evening walk, was attempting to control his dog. Breeds didn't mean a lot to Tony; dogs came either large enough to avoid or small enough to ignore and this was one of the former. And then he noticed who the dog was barking at.

Ben Ward, one of the lighting crew.

Also not Sikh and looking like he hadn't been home in nearly forty-eight hours.

"Arra?"

"I see him. Let's go."

He glanced over at her. "Let's go? You make it sound like we're in an episode of *Law and Order: Magic and Mayhem*."

"Don't laugh." She started across the grass. "They pitched it."

Actually, Tony wasn't laughing. "What exactly are we about to do?"

"I get close enough to haul the shadow out of him, then I destroy it."

"That's what *you're* about to do."

"While you make with the potion and come up with a plausible story."

"Story?"

"For the three dozen or so witnesses."

"Right."

It looked like Ben had been heading across the parking lot away from the temple when he'd crossed paths with the dog. He was staring at it like he'd never seen one before. Maybe he hadn't. For all Tony knew, Arra's world didn't have dogs. Or, he amended, remembering his dream, dogs just hadn't been a part of the shadow's short life.

Too much to hope for that, even distracted by the dog, Ben wouldn't see them approach. They were still more than ten feet away when he turned, stared at Tony in confusion, then at Arra in fear. "You!"

Tony half expected to see the shadow surge out of him like it had out of Alan Wu but shadow-Ben smiled, winked, and ran toward an extended family piling kids into a minivan. He careened through them like an out of control billiard ball. A child screamed. Men and women yelled in two languages. Strong fingers grabbed the stranger and threw him away from the van.

Leaping out at the end of her leash, the dog kept barking.

Ben hit the ground and stayed there.

"It's left him!" Arra announced, panting a little as they quickened their pace.

"And gone where?"

In answer, one of the preteen boys raced away from his family and charged into a clump of older kids. More shouting. And a moment later, another body on the ground. The remaining teenagers scattered.

Men and older boys were running toward the parking lot.

Tony stopped at the edge of the asphalt. "Is that kid . . . ?"

"Dead?" Fingers closed around his arm as Arra leaned on him, catching her breath. "No, but if that shadow keeps moving through this crowd, I guarantee it's going to hit someone who can't handle it."

"Like Alan?"

"Exactly like."

"Where is it now?"

"I don't know!"

Someone did.

Twisting free, Tony sprinted toward the old man with the dog, tripped over the leash, and ripped it free of a tiring grip.

The dog took off across the parking lot.

"Shania!"

"I'll get her!" Tony leaped to his feet and followed, ignoring the deserved string of expletives flung after him. *Sorry about your dog, mister. Trying to save the world here!*

It seemed the shadow was still in one of the teenage boys. Great. They'd had a chance of pulling this off as long as it was in Ben, but the Sikh community was very protective of their own and Tony could only see this ending badly.

Still barking wildly, the dog slammed into a running teenager, flinging the boy into the outstretched arms of a middle-aged woman. She screamed as he sank into her embrace. He jerked, then stiffened and slid bonelessly to the ground.

Shania sailed over the boy and landed on the woman, making contact with all four paws. Ringed fingers stopped snapping teeth an inch from flesh.

This time Tony saw the shadow move.

Shania yelped once. Woman and dog collapsed together to the ground.

Tony got to the dog before the first boot could impact with her ribs. He took the blow on his thigh, gathered the trembling body up in both arms and rolled away yelling, "You don't understand; she wasn't attacking. This dog's a hero! We're from the health department," he continued, not giving anyone else a chance to talk. "The first man who fell was contaminated by some stupid kid with a new designer drug. It's a dust that works on contact with skin, he passed it on to that boy who passed it on to that boy," he jerked his head toward the two teenagers, now standing and being fussed over by family. "Who passed it on to this woman. The dog could smell it. This dog has kept everyone else from being contaminated."

"You're touching the dog!" But the voice held as much confusion as anger and Tony realized they actually had a chance of pulling this off. Witnesses were still too spread out for mob mentality to have taken over.

"I'm immune to the drug, that's why we were sent."

In the face of the inexplicable, people looked for explanations, something to make sense of what hadn't made sense. The explanation didn't have to make sense; it only had to sound like it did.

"And you're from the health department?"

"We are." Tony relaxed slightly as Arra pushed through the crowd holding up what looked like official documentation.

"Get out of my way," she snapped, "and let me make sure it ends at this dog."

"We should call 911," someone muttered.

They should, Tony agreed silently, but given cultural politics they probably wouldn't. *Lucky break for our side.*

Dropping heavily to her knees, Arra pressed a hand against the dog's heaving ribs. Only Tony saw that the hand had slipped through fur and flesh and emerged holding a writhing shadow. Murmuring the incantation under her breath, she forced her hands together as the shadow struggled to survive, finally squashing it into nothing.

Shania whined, wriggled, and bit Tony on the hand. Hard. As he jerked back, she squirmed free and ran into the arms of her owner.

"Good," Arra announced in a tone that brooked no argument. "The dog has neutralized the drug. Ought to get a medal. Now then, move aside and let me look at this woman. Thermos!"

It took Tony a moment to realize the last word had been directed at him and then he shrugged out of his backpack and pulled a thermos free.

"Eww." A girl in the crowd wrinkled her nose. "It smells like that stuff in the back of Uncle Virn's garden."

"Be quiet, Kira."

"No," another voice said thoughtfully. "It does."

"Catnip is a medicinal relaxant," Tony said with as much authority as he could muster. "Let's get those others over here, we'll need to have the . . . m looked at, too." He'd been about to identify Arra as a nurse and changed his mind at the last minute. With his luck there'd be a nurse in the group and he didn't want them suddenly thinking they should get involved.

Arra helped her middle-aged patient sit up. "How are you feeling?"

"What happened?"

The wizard rocked back on her heels, and nodded toward the surrounding people. "Explain it to her." She started for the teenagers as half a dozen voices began half a dozen different versions of the story. The younger teenager was protesting he was fine, the other, to Tony's critical eye, seemed to be milking his collapse for all it was worth.

Snagging Tony's arm as he tried to follow, she muttered, "I'll deal with the kids, you get as much out of the other thermos into Ben as you can, then get him into the car. If we give them time to think, we're . . ."

"Screwed?"

"Well put."

Fortunately, Ben wasn't much bigger than Tony, and they were essentially being ignored. By the time he had the electrician in the car, Arra was crossing the lawn toward him. "Final words," she murmured as she slid into the passenger seat.

"Thank you for your cooperation. If you have any questions, call health services." About to remind them that the dog was a hero, he noticed the dog and her owner were nowhere around and decided not to bring it up. *Out of sight, out of mind,* he told the world silently as he started the car. *Do* not *let any of this come back on Shania.* Shifting out of park, he pulled into traffic and headed away from the temple faster than could strictly be considered safe. But safe, experience had taught him, was a relative term. "Where are we going now?"

Arra waved the second piece of the Yellow Pages at him.

"With Ben?"

"We don't have time to take him home. We'll do it after."

"Man, the wife's going to kill me!" Ben slurred from the backseat.

"Let's hope not," Arra snapped. "Go to sleep."

There was a muffled thud as Ben's head hit the rear window.

"Health services?"

Tony shrugged as he slowed for a yellow light. "It worked."

"Yes. It did."

Safely stopped he turned to look at her. She was frowning speculatively. "What?"

"Nothing."

"The trick is to keep talking so no one has time to ask questions and then, you know, you showed up with the paperwork. Official documents carry a lot of weight. The whole Canadian peace, order, and good government thing."

"I'm sure. But there will be questions."

"Not our problem, now they'll call health services."

"And they are—specifically?"

"Good question. You okay? I mean you did some power stuff there."

"Very little. I'm fine." She sounded tired, but he wasn't going to argue. Tony didn't know how it worked on the wizard's world, but on this one *I'm fine* meant any injuries short of decapitation weren't to be discussed. "You?"

"I got bit," he said as the light changed.

"No surprise. It wasn't a fun experience for poor Shania. Or the shadow. It must have thought the dog was a perfect host; four legs against two, we'd never catch it. But the dog didn't have quite enough sense of self to sustain it."

"I was going to ask."

"I know."

"And," he added, his leg throbbing as he remembered, "I got kicked."

"Why?"

"They were aiming at the dog. Where are we going again?"

"Tsawassen. Near the border."

"Right." He headed up the ramp off Westminster and onto 99 South. "So the people are going to be okay? I mean, the shadow wasn't in any of them for very long."

"The one boy may not recover."

"What?" Tony fought the car back onto pavement as his jerk toward the wizard put the right wheels on the shoulder.

"The second boy, the older boy, was twisted—his pattern wasn't compatible. I doubt the potion will be enough."

"Can't you do something?"

"Like what?"

His fingers tightened around the steering wheel. "I don't know; untwist him."

"No."

"Fuck."

"This isn't all bright lights and vodka, Tony." He would have protested he knew that, but the memories weighing down her voice kept him silent. "Stopping the Shadowlord is about stopping death and destruction. Only two dead and one injured; we've been very lucky so far."

He supposed that was hard to argue with. They were twelve kilometers down the highway before he tried. "If we'd waited for Ben to come to the gate, this never would have happened."

"But if he'd gotten through the gate, if he'd given the Shadowlord the information he needs to invade, it would start happening with a soul-destroying frequency." After a long moment she sighed and said, "All the easy answers get lost in the shadows."

♠

They reached the South Delta Baptist Church at 8:10. Tony parked in the nearly empty lot, twisted around, and dragged his backpack out from between Ben's legs. "It's past sunset," he told the wizard, nodding west to where the sky had turned a thousand shades of orange and yellow and pink. "I need to call Henry."

"The Nightwalker cannot help us now."

Oh, great. Serious lackage of contractions. What's up her nose? The larger part of the drive south had been accomplished while listening to *The Best of Queen, Vol. 1* because it was the only tape in the car. Arra's eyes had been closed, so Tony'd assumed she'd been napping. Maybe she had. Given her history, the odds were good she hadn't been dreaming about Mel Gibson.

"Henry's helped in the past," Tony pointed out, punching in the number one-handed. "And he'll be helping later, so if it's all the same to you, I think I'll keep him in . . . Henry!" Henry could do both Prince of Darkness and Prince of Man over the phone, but tonight he sounded like neither. *Talk about locking the garage after the car's been stolen* . . . After making arrangements to meet at Arra's at 9:30, Tony hung up to find the wizard staring out the window at the collection of red brick buildings.

"That's a large facility," she said before he could speak. "It won't be easy finding the shadow."

"We'll split up . . ."

"Oh, yes, that always works so well." Her hands closed around her seat belt strap though she made no move to release it. "It won't always be so easy."

"Easy?" He waved the dog bite, now purple and swollen, in front of her. "*And* I've been grabbed, pummeled, kicked, shadowed . . ." Words seemed less than capable of describing what had happened with Henry, so he skipped it. "Two people are dead, one's twisted, Mouse has a broken jaw, Lee thinks he's going bugfuck, we have an enchanted electrician in the backseat, I've been living most of the last few days in a state of high terror, and you say it's been easy?"

"Yes. So far, it's been easy." She turned to face him. "Even on you. Realize that it's going to get a lot worse. The longer the shadow remains in a body, the more of the host's characteristics it absorbs—it stops acting and starts becoming. Humanity didn't become the dominant species on this world by playing nice. The shadow in Alan Wu chose to attack. His shadow . . ." She jerked her head toward the backseat. ". . . chose to run." Her voice roughened. "There are other more terrible options."

Tony stared at her for a long moment then pulled out the thermos holding the lesser amount of potion. "Drink?"

"Why the hell not." There was just enough remaining to fill the cup. She drained it in one long swallow. Tony's eyes watered in sympathy.

"Feeling better?"

"No. Now I've got to piss."

♠

Too early for air-conditioning, too warm for heat, the air inside the church still had a filtered feel in the back of Tony's throat. It smelled of cleansers—although not as overwhelmingly as Arra's co-op—and faintly of after-shave and perfume. "I don't like leaving Ben in the car."

"He won't wake up until I tell him to."

"So remember to save enough power to play alarm clock."

"I know what I'm doing, Tony."

"I'm just saying . . ."

"I know what you're saying. Stop it."

He shrugged and stepped away from the women's washroom. Right inside the west doors, it hadn't been hard to find. "I'll wait here."

"Fine." One hand against the wall, Arra disappeared from view.

It was obvious she still hadn't recovered from her reckless use of power. No, not reckless, Tony amended, leaning against the wall. Thoughtless. As in, she didn't think about it. Her reaction to being touched by the shadow had been essentially hysterical. Run and react; no thought for the consequences. And physical exhaustion often led to emotional exhaustion—thus the doom and gloom announcement in the car.

It all made sense.

They were winning. They had to be winning.

He tensed as voices sounded in the distance, but they headed in another direction and he relaxed again. And then he frowned. Was Arra taking longer than she should? Definitely longer than a guy would. How long did women take? He couldn't shake the feeling that she might have done a bunk and climbed out the window. Be halfway to Seattle and a new identity by now.

With a glance around the hall to make sure he wasn't observed, he pushed the door open a crack and heard, "You!" followed by a familiar string of nonsense syllables, and a soft *sputz*.

"Arra?"

"Better get in here with that potion."

He took two steps farther into the washroom and peered around a cinder-block corner. Women's washrooms definitely smelled better than men's. Arra was at a line of stainless steel sinks washing her hands. Lying stretched out on the floor was one of the girls from the catering company.

"Shadow-held?"

Arra snorted. "Not anymore."

"We forgot about the caterers when we made the list." Dropping to the floor, he lifted her head up against his leg. "They must've been setting up for lunch."

"Lunch." Red-rimmed eyes snapped open. "Do we always have to have lasagna? I am so tired of making lasagna!"

"Hey, it's okay." The potion sparkled as it dribbled between her lips.

She swallowed, looked up at him and said, "Three kinds of cookies are quite enough. There's cake." Another half a dozen small swallows. "Fifteen hundred bottles of water a month."

"That's a lot of water."

Her brows drew in as she finished the last of the potion in the cup. "Who the hell are you?"

Before Tony could tell her, Arra muttered, "Sleep." And her eyes closed.

"Why did you do that?"

"Easier than explanations. Also . . ." Stepping away from the sink, she indicated that Tony should pick the snoring young woman up. ". . . easier transport."

"So, easier?" He swung the girl up into his arms. Grunted, shifted her weight, and headed for the bathroom door. "I thought you said it was going to get terrible?"

Arra snorted, as she retrieved the backpack. "I've only been on this world for seven years, but even I know that if a young man gets caught carrying an unconscious young woman from the ladies' room in a Baptist church, terrible will be an understatement."

She had a point.

♠

"What's with the 'you'?"

Arra twisted around from checking on their two passengers and frowned toward Tony. "The what?"

"Every time a shadow sees you, it says *'you!'* in exactly the same way."

She shrugged. "The shadows are all cast by a single source; this makes their reactions less than original."

"Makes sense."

"Thank you."

Ouch. Sarcasm that cut. "In the dream I had, the shadow didn't want to go back to the Shadowlord; it didn't want to lose its sense of self."

"So?"

His turn to shrug; his shadow, dark against the pale upholstery, shrugging with him. "So maybe we can reason with them."

"Reason with them?" She sounded surprised.

No, he decided, pulling out to pass a line of Sunday drivers heading home to the city, surprise wasn't quite enough. Astonished.

"They're still evil, Tony, even if they're only bits of evil. And you don't reason with evil!"

"Granted. But you can, you know, reform it. During the war on your world, didn't anyone ever try to . . . ?"

"No!"

"Why . . ."

"Because that's not the way it works!"

Rolling his eyes, he tried again. Old people often had trouble with new ideas. "But . . ."

"If you want to meet your Nightwalker at 9:30, you'd best concentrate more on driving and less on suggesting perversions!"

She had a point although *perversions* seemed a little harsh. "It's just . . ."

"When I said concentrate less, I meant not at all!"

Right.

♠

"Arra, you don't have to go with us tonight. We've got the potion; Henry and I can handle things at the studio. There's only the one shadow left."

Eyes locked on the spider solitaire game, Arra grunted something that might have been *good*. Or *sure*. Or *get stuffed*, were "get stuffed" only a single syllable long.

"You can move that black jack."

From her tea cozy position on the dining room table, Zazu hissed at him.

"Or not."

The wizard's concentration on the game—games, since she was running one on each computer—was a little disturbing.

They'd dropped Ben and the caterer off two blocks from Ben's condo since neither of them knew anything about the girl and she was carrying no ID. Arra had woken them and then they'd driven off before they were noticed.

"Oh, crap. Their cars. We left their cars behind; no way they got that far south walking."

"It's a minor point."

"Not to them, it won't be."

"They have a forty-eight-hour hole in their memories. I think it will be."

Put like that, Tony'd admitted she had a point.

She'd been pretty quiet the rest of the way to the co-op, and had said next to nothing while she made a new batch of potion. Too busy eating the burger and fries he'd picked up to worry about the silence, Tony hadn't really noticed something was wrong until she'd capped the second thermos and headed straight for her computers.

And essentially disappeared.

Scratch a little disturbing. It was definitely freaking him out.

He swung his backpack up onto one shoulder, taking what comfort he could from the familiar feel of the thermoses smacking him in the kidneys just above one of the bruises Mouse had left him. "I'll just meet Henry out front."

This time, not even a grunt. One game ended. She started a new game immediately.

"I'll see you tomorrow morning at work."

"Tony."

He paused and turned to face her again.

"Remember that the gate works both ways. You have to stop the shadows returning to him, but you also have to make sure nothing worse comes through."

All of a sudden the lines of electronic playing cards took on a new menace. "Is that what you're looking for? Something worse?"

"I don't know."

♦

"Something worse," Tony muttered moving the lamp into place. "Way to be specific."

"Let it go."

"How?"

Henry wisely decided not to answer. "The gate's about to open."

They were alone in the soundstage. The gate opened and closed and they were still alone. Wherever—whoever—the last shadow was, it wasn't going home. Not yet. Tony had no idea what the hell he was going to do tomorrow morning. *Not going to be as simple as turning on a light,* he acknowledged, his hands shaking as he rolled up the cable.

"Are you all right?"

"Sure. Fine." He'd never felt the pull of the gate so strongly. Had actually found himself stepping toward it, his body practically vibrating with need. New call, familiar feeling. Only a white-knuckled grip on the sound board had held him in place. Not moving—not answering—hurt.

"This shadow-taint of yours; did the wizard mention how we can remove it?"

"No, because that would require a lack of ambiguity." Cables stowed, he straightened. "Just takes time, I guess."

In the dim glow of the emergency light, he saw Henry frown. "It seems stronger than it was."

"Seems stronger or *is* stronger."

The vampire shrugged.

"Okay, then, let's not worry about it." Plastering on a fake smile, Tony added *shadow-taint getting stronger* to his list of things to worry about. Right under *something worse* and *more terrible options*.

He briefly considered adding *finds dark comforting* to the list but comforting wasn't quite the right word. Walking back to the rear doors, he felt hidden, safe, and hyperconscious of the man walking at his side—but then Henry'd been on his list for a few days now.

The circle of light on the back wall announced trouble of a different sort.

Crap. Security.

They hadn't been seen yet, but they were seconds away from discovery.

Grabbing Henry's arm, Tony threw him against the wall, hooked a leg between his, and locked their bodies together at mouth, chest, and groin—realizing too late that Henry might not understand the game.

Fortunately, Henry seemed willing to play regardless.

"Hey! You there! Break it up!"

Pulling away, Tony turned, faked surprise at the sight of the rent-a-cop, and murmured, "Wait here, babe." As red-gold brows flicked up, he turned and stepped forward, launching into a low-voiced and urgent, "this is who I am and I'm trying to impress this guy with the whole working in television thing."

The security guard rolled his eyes but allowed that he understood a guy doing what a guy had to do to get laid. "Just don't fucking do it here!"

"We're on our way out."

"Good." He'd clearly already dismissed them and was anxious to move on. He had a script waiting, after all. "Lock up behind you."

Henry said nothing until the door was closed and locked, then he smiled, his teeth too white in the darkness. "Very clever."

"Thanks." Tony just barely managed to resist the urge to wipe his mouth. He'd kissed Henry a thousand times, but this was the first time he'd tasted blood. Kate's blood, Tina's blood, his blood . . . older blood.

He knew it was all in his head.

It was nothing but . . . shadow-stuff.

♠

The shadows had surrounded her, a ring of darkness she couldn't break. Trapped. No escape. If she banished one, the others would attack. She drew herself up to her full height and began to gather power, determined to make them pay as high a cost as possible for their victory.

As they moved closer, she could hear their voices in her head.

Help us.
Don't let him destroy us.
Help us.
We want to live.
Help us.
We need you.

"So I'm to be responsible for your lives as well?"

In answer, faces began to flicker around the circle. Lee. Mouse. Kate. Ben. Tony . . .

. . . Kiril, Sarn—eyes bulging, tongues protruding as they were nailed to the boards—Haryain, heavy white brows raised above his glasses.

"What's your damage?" he asked in another's voice. "You knew the job was dangerous when you took it."

"This . . ." She waved a hand around the circle, the shadows bending toward the gesture. ". . . isn't my job. I won't let it be my job."

Haryain snorted. "Who says you get a choice?"

Arra jerked awake. Squinting up at the pair of monitors, she reached for her mouse with one hand while wiping away drool with the other. There was always a choice.

There was always another gate.

Fourteen

"SO HOW'D the date go?"

"Date?"

"With Zev? Friday night? I was going to call you, but I had a busy weekend." Amy laid a salacious emphasis on *busy* and waggled her eyebrows in Tony's general direction.

"Barry?"

She punched his shoulder. "Brian! Dipwad. Now tell." Setting her extra-grande mochaccino on the corner of her desk, she dropped into the chair and grinned up at him. "Mama wants all the gory details. Make this Monday morning worth her while."

"I had hamantaschen."

Heavily kohled eyes widened. "Kinky!"

"Cookies."

"You had cookies? What are you, twelve?"

Tony shrugged. So much had happened since Friday night he'd almost forgotten about his non-date with the musical director. "We went out for coffee."

"*I* was drinking coffee at twelve," Amy told him with a pointed slurp from her cup. "That was it?"

"And we talked."

"Jesus fucking Christ. I always thought gay men were supposed to be getting more than the rest of us. Don't you guys have a quota to keep up or something?"

He felt himself smiling for the first time in what seemed like days. "Not since the eighties."

"The eighties?" She smirked as she reached for the phone. "I guess *you* were doing more than coffee at twelve. CB Productions, how can I help you?"

Maybe it was Amy's "the world wouldn't dare fuck with me attitude," maybe it was her electric-green hair, maybe it was the familiar sound of her answering the phone—whatever it was, he felt energized, anticipatory. Like he'd been waiting for something big, something amazing, and that wait was almost over. The fear and doubt that had haunted his dreams and his ride to work were gone.

"Tony!"

And they're back. He turned in time to see Arra emerge from CB's office. She still looked like crap, full sets of luggage under both eyes and her hair sticking up in uncombed gray spikes—exhaustion creating the same hairstyle Amy had probably needed a liter of gel to achieve. Obviously, a good night's sleep hadn't been in the cards.

Given that she'd probably spent most of the night trying to define the future by way of spider solitaire, that could have been an amusing observation. Except that it wasn't.

She took him by the arm, her fingers hot through the sleeve of his jean jacket, and walked him toward the basement door. "I spoke to CB . . ."

"So he knows?"

"Knows what?"

Fully aware that Amy could listen to half a dozen conversations simultaneously, Tony dropped his voice to a low murmur. He'd deal with her opinions on him keeping secrets from her later. "Everything. You said you were going to tell him everything."

"Oh. Right. No. I told him I need you to work that big carbon arc lamp for me this morning; that I'm working on that ghost effect he wants for later in the season and

I need more light levels. He'll clear it with Peter and Sorge."

"I don't . . ." He didn't want to go anywhere near the gate. He didn't want to be within a hundred kilometers of it when it opened. And it didn't matter. There wasn't anyone else. "Sure. Whatever."

Arra's grip tightened for a heartbeat, as though she'd known what he'd been thinking. "I did a search for the last shadow this morning. It's in the studio."

"Who?"

"I don't know and it doesn't matter. Be careful. It'll know the others have been destroyed and it'll be desperate to get back through the gate."

"What about stuff coming this way?"

"I doubt it. Not yet. The Shadowlord hates to move without information; it's his strength and, to a certain extent, his weakness. He likes to be sure. Worry once this last shadow is destroyed—although by destroying some of them away from the gate, we may delay his reaction."

"Swell. That gives us time to prepare."

"There's nothing to prepare!"

"Yeah." He sighed. "I knew that." When she released him and reached for the basement door, it was his turn to take hold of her. "Arra, I was wondering, why do they need to bring the people back to the gate? I mean, one of them followed us out to that location shot last week so obviously the shadows move around fine on their own."

"No, remember I told you that the more specific a shadow is the more constrained its movement? And these latest shadows are really mobile only before they've taken a host," she continued when he nodded. "After they've experienced physical definition, their mobility is pretty much limited to moving a short distance to another host."

"But they can survive on their own, right?"

Tony saw a muscle in her jaw jump as she clenched her teeth. "You cannot reform them!"

"That's not what I meant." Not entirely. "I just thought that it might be more . . . I don't know, intelligent if they bailed on the host after they got the information. I mean lurking shadows are a lot harder to spot than people acting like they're disappearing and acting like night of the living pod people."

Her eyes narrowed and she stared at him for a long moment. She'd been doing that a lot lately and it was beginning to get seriously disturbing.

"Don't give them ideas," she snapped at last, shook off his hand, and headed down to her workshop.

♣

For the seven years she'd been his entire special effects department, Arra had made no close attachments among the crew. She'd interacted as much as necessary to perform her job but no more. Now, it seemed, in less than a week she'd made a friend. Or acquired an accomplice. Chester Bane wasn't sure which, but given everything else that had been going on, the timing was interesting.

Standing just inside his office, he watched Arra head downstairs and, after a long moment spent staring at the closed door, he saw Tony Foster disappear in the direction of the soundstage.

It, whatever it was, had something to do with light levels.

There was nothing he hated more than being lied to, so before he asked questions, he liked to make sure he could identify the answers.

About to return to his desk, he paused as the outer door opened and the two RCMP officers who'd investigated Nikki Waugh's unfortunate death walked into the office. He watched as Rachel hurried to meet them and stepped forward as she turned in his direction.

"Mr. Bane, these officers would like a word with you."

"Of course." He indicated they should precede him

into his office. The man, Constable Elson, moved like he was hunting and close to his quarry. The woman, Constable Danvers, rolled her eyes before she followed her partner. There was disagreement between them, then. Not on the larger issues, perhaps, but she was definitely indulging him on the smaller.

Interesting.

"Alan Wu is dead."

About to lower himself into his desk chair, he paused and turned, staring at the two officers. After a moment, Constable Danvers added, "He died Saturday afternoon."

"I'm sorry to hear that." And he was. In a profession with more than its fair share of insecure nut jobs and delusional divas, Alan Wu had been dependable. He sat, indicated that the police officers should sit, and he waited.

Constable Elson made an obvious and obviously unnecessary show of checking his notes. "Alan Wu is the second of your employees to die in less than a week."

Less than a week. *Now, it seemed, in less than a week she'd made a friend.*

"Alan Wu was not my employee. He was an actor who I regularly employed."

"Tony Foster was with him when he died. He told us he'd been driving around with another of your employees, an Arra Pelindrake. They do both work for you?"

"They do."

"Good. And that's not all."

He locked his gaze on the younger man's face. "Go on."

It got more interesting by the moment.

One of his cameramen had been dumped in emergency at Burnaby General with a broken jaw. No record of who left him there. An electrician and one of the caterers both reported missing by their spouses, gone for forty-eight hours only to turn up Sunday night with no memories and their cars missing.

"I flagged anything that mentioned your company and pulled this together from a number of sources."

"You've been busy."

"I got curious. I don't much believe in coincidence, Mr. Bane. A number of very different roads all seem to lead right back here, and that tells me that there's something going on."

No doubt.

♣

"Tony!"

Tina's voice froze him in place. Tina was the last person he wanted to deal with this morning. He'd already seen Kate standing by the camera smiling at nothing, right thumb rubbing over her left wrist. Praying that he'd never looked quite so dopey, he'd tugged his jacket cuff halfway over his hand and taken the scenic route around to the coffee maker.

"Just so you know," Henry announced as they drove along Adanac Street toward Kate's apartment. *"I didn't like doing that."*

"Doing what?"

"Cranking up the sex appeal." He repeated Tony's phrase like it left a bad taste in his mouth. *"The moment you bring sex into it like that, it becomes too much like I'm forcing myself on an unwilling victim."*

Tony snorted as he twisted around to check on Kate sleeping in the backseat. "News flash, Henry; sex is always a part of it."

"Not so overtly. Not under those circumstances." He paused, as though realizing the circumstances weren't usual. *"Not on my part."*

"What's not on your part?"

"When sex isn't actually occurring, I am not always thinking of sex when I feed."

Since they were both well aware of what the other person was thinking of, neither mentioned it.

"So you weren't thinking of sex when you fed on Tina?"

"No."

"Good."

"Which is not to say that under other circumstances . . ."

"I didn't need to hear that."

And now, looking at Tina approach, all he could think of was her and Henry humping like naked monkeys. The visuals were seriously disturbing.

"Tony, don't forget that the *Darkest Night* fan club will be showing up in about half an hour. They'll watch us shoot, Lee and Mason will pose for a couple of pictures, and then they'll . . ."

Be taken over by shadows from another world.

". . . have some lunch. Tony, are you listening to me?"

"Yeah. Sorry." He forced himself to concentrate.

"After lunch, give them each one of the old scripts and get them the hell out of here before we start . . ." She paused, eyes narrowed. "Is there something on my face?"

"What?"

"You're staring at me."

I know how Henry looks when he's come from feeding on you . . .

"Sorry." His life was just too weird.

"Stop apologizing and pay attention. You know how Peter feels about fans in the studio, so this has to go smoothly or we're all in for an unpleasant afternoon."

"Uh, Arra needs me to do some stuff for her this morning."

"I heard. Just don't leave the fan club unattended. I can't think of anything worse than another fan getting locked in Mason's coffin."

Unfortunately, Tony could.

♣

Three of the games had been stopped by fours. *Fixed opinions will hinder your process.* What was she missing? What was she fixating on? On the other screen, two black jacks prevented her from making the last move that would finish the game.

"This is ridiculous!" Arra shoved her chair out from the desk hard enough to roll her halfway across the workshop. "I might as well try to divine the future from a bowl of instant oatmeal."

Her stomach growled. Desperately trying to discover the source of her unease—although unease was far too mild a word for the feelings of doom filling her head like toxic smoke—she'd skipped breakfast. It was possible that hunger was distracting her just enough to keep her from making sense of the cards.

Possible. But not likely.

She'd been able to cast auguries right until the end, unheeding of the destruction raining down around her. She'd seen the fate of the city and of the wizards. She'd known there was nothing she could do to stop it.

Nothing.

But here and now they hadn't reached *nothing*—although they would.

Here and now, she needed to identify just what was going wrong.

If memory served, the Rice-Krispie square she'd grabbed from the craft services table last week should still be in her desk drawer. It wasn't exactly food, but it was as close as she could get without going upstairs.

Slowly chewing the first bite—slowly because the square had solidified into a substance that defied speed, Arra cleared all screens but one. Maybe if she concentrated on a single game . . .

Two black jacks.

And again.

Sucking the last bit of marshmallow off a corner of the plastic wrap, she scowled down at the clock on the corner of the screen. 11:02 A.M. The gate would open soon and the last shadow would make a move for home. The light would destroy it. It knew it was the last on this world, but would *he* know as he . . .

Plastic hanging limply from a corner of her mouth, Arra stared at the monitor.

Two black jacks.

There were two shadows left on this world.

Not one.

Two.

Somehow, one of them had escaped her spell. Exactly how wasn't important right now, she had to warn Tony.

But the gate was about to open.

If both shadows were there . . .

If he needed help stopping them . . .

If she went to the gate . . .

But if she didn't . . .

Using power with the gate open would be like sending up a flare.

A hundred thousand voices cried out for her to save them. Clutched at her. Dragged her down under the weight of their need. *The Shadowlord comes; you are our last and only hope.*

Tony fought without her. When he reached for her, it was to ask her to fight at his side, not to fight for him. He stubbornly held to hope even as she denied it.

Pushing her chair away from the desk, she spun it around and scanned the workshop shelves. There had to be something . . . Yes! One of the baseball bats they'd blown up in Raymond Dark's hands during the batting cage scene in episode three. The hands had, of course, been Daniel's and the ad lib about switching to aluminum, Lee's—although Mason had claimed it the second time they'd shot Lee pulling the bloody shard of wood from Raymond Dark's shoulder. With CB complaining about the expense, she'd bought six bats, practiced on three, blown two for the camera, and tucked the last one away figuring that sooner or later she'd find a use for it.

Stopping the shadow-held from reaching the gate would also stop the shadow.

♣

With half his attention on the time, half worrying at the hundred and one things likely to go wrong as he attempted to stop a shadow from returning to another world while surrounded by people who wouldn't believe that's what he was doing if it came with a director's commentary, and trying to keep seventeen members of the *Darkest Night* fan club out of trouble, Tony was feeling a little overwhelmed.

And the thought of Arra sitting safely in her basement while he was up here saving the world was pissing him off. *She doesn't need to go near the fucking gate*, he growled silently as he counted the fans. *She could just take a moment and turn this lot into . . .*

One short.

Three guesses where the runaway had gotten to and the first two didn't count.

"Excuse me, but this set's off limits."

The fan froze, one leg hooked over the side of the coffin. "I was just . . ."

"Yeah. I know." Tony jerked his head toward the high-pitched squeals coming from the other side of the soundstage. "I think Mason just appeared."

He got out of the way barely in time to avoid being run over.

Emerging out beside the monitors, he could only assume from the sounds of adoration that Mason was on the other side of the group of hysterically bobbing and weaving bodies.

"Great. Just great." Headphones down around his neck, Peter sounded ready to chew scenery. "I am never going to get him onto the set now."

"Sorry."

The director snorted. "You think you could have prevented that? You are suffering from serious delusions of grandeur, Mr. Foster. You should know by now that nothing comes between Mason and his adoring fans. Particularly when they're carrying cameras." Eyes narrowed as he watched the ebb and flow of the crowd. "At least if he's out where we can see him, we have a chance of avoiding lawsuits."

"Do you want me to tell him you're ready to shoot?"

"He knows. That's why he finally emerged from his dressing room. One of the reasons. And obviously not the most important. You try to remove him from that little love fest there, and he'll treat the world to a scene where you're cast as the villain and he's just trying to give a little back to the people who make the show possible. Forgetting, of course, that there won't be a show if we don't get it shot."

"Could we do my reaction shots first?"

Both Tony and the director turned.

"Lee, I didn't see you there."

Lee smiled. "It seemed safer to stay out of the way."

Tony opened his mouth to ask him how he felt and then closed it again. Not his place. It wasn't like they were . . . friends.

"Sorge?"

The DP glanced up.

"Lee's reaction shots; do we need to relight?"

"I don't think so . . ."

As the DP headed out onto the office set, Peter nodded toward the sides sticking out of Tony's pocket. "You can read him Mason's lines."

From elation to depression in less than a second. Probably a new record. "I can't."

"You *can't?*"

He couldn't look at Lee while he explained. "I have to do that thing for Arra."

"Now?"

The feel of the gate powering up was making his eyeballs twitch. He glanced down at his watch. "Three minutes. She, uh, she says timing is everything in special effects."

"Fine. Whatever. Go. Lee, get out there. Adam . . ."

The 1AD broke off a conversation with a boom operator Tony'd never seen before. Seemed like Hartley hadn't made it in this morning.

". . . make sure that lot shuts up when I call quiet."

Trying not to look like he was walking into pain, Tony made his way to the lamp.

Behind him, Peter called, "Quiet please!"

Adam's voice rose over the continuing fannish babble, "If you lot keep quiet until I give the word, Mason'll pose for pictures with you when we're done."

The babble switched off.

"Rolling!"

♣

Grabbing the rack at the last moment, Constable Elson remained on his feet as he finished his accidental dance with a tattered antediluvian ball gown. "This looks like a fire code violation to me," he muttered, untangling the distressed gray taffeta from around his legs.

"I assure you, Constable, it is not."

"There's not a lot of room in this hall." He stepped back, got poked in the ass by the hilt of a cheap replica cavalry sword, jumped forward, and very nearly tangled with the taffeta again.

"There is, however slight, a clear passageway and the fire marshal has given his approval." The fire marshal also had a teenage son looking forward to a career in television, but CB saw no point in mentioning that. "The soundstage door is just ahead."

It was, in fact, a mere dozen paces ahead although impossible to see until the last corner had been rounded and a rack of white hazmat suits passed. He'd picked the suits up cheap from another show's going out of business sale and instructed the writers to make use of them. Their ideas to date had been less than stellar but he knew that eventually one of them would dream up something the show could use—after all, if an infinite number of monkeys could write Hamlet . . .

His hand was actually on the door when the bell rang and the red light went on.

"Why are we stopping?"

"Cameras are rolling," he said, inclining his head toward Constable Danvers. "We'll have to wait."

"How long?"

He shrugged. "Until the director feels he has what he needs."

"Jack . . ." She turned to her partner who shook his head.

"No. I want a look around that soundstage and I want another word with Mr. Foster."

"We could come back."

Elson folded his arms. "We're here."

He translated the female constable's expression to read: *You wouldn't have half as big a bee up your butt if this wasn't television.* She was probably right. Television, invited into homes 24/7 remained a mystery; to add mystery on top of that would be more than such a man could resist. Although the odds of him actually discovering anything were slim; he wouldn't be waiting to enter the soundstage if CB believed otherwise.

Running feet, pounding between the costumes, pulled all three of them back around the way they'd come.

Baseball bat held across her body, Arra stumbled to a halt by the hazmat suits and stared at the red light beside the door. Damn! Had CB been on his own, she'd have taken her chances with a line of bullshit and charged right on in. But with strangers standing there . . .

Put them to sleep; you can call it a gas leak!

"Problem, Arra?"

Now would be the time . . .

Time.

11:16.

Too late anyway. Tony was on his own. She lowered the bat. "No. No problem."

"Arra Pelindrake?" The blond man stepped forward. "I'm Constable Jack Elson, RCMP. As long as we're all waiting here, I'd like to ask you a few questions."

Beyond the constable, CB's expression said much the same thing.

♣

The lamp was in place, a light blanket arranged behind it to prevent any possible leakage into the set in use. All Tony had to do was hit the switch on the lamp itself—the gaffer had plugged him into the board and told him in no uncertain terms that if he came near it, he'd get a light stand up the ass.

Oh, yeah. Things were going well.

He'd seen a PBS special once—or maybe it was a horror movie, details were fuzzy—about this guy who attacked people with vibrations until their eyeballs melted. That was pretty much exactly how he felt. Like his eyeballs were melting.

Definitely time to turn on the last best hope for humankind. *And the part of the hero will be played by a carbon arc lamp.*

As his hand moved toward the switch, his shadow surged up his legs.

He had time to jerk back futilely before darkness slammed into his head and he was no longer in control.

"I did a search for the last shadow this morning, it's in the studio."

Fuck. Fuck. Fuck. It's in me! Except it hadn't been in him, it had been hiding in his shadow. *How long . . . ?*

And then the gate was open and he was walking—being walked—out underneath it.

Déjà vu all over again.

The shadow hadn't taken over so much as pushed him aside. He was in his own mind, he just wasn't there alone. Henry could have pulled him free with a cocked finger, but Henry wasn't here. Arra wasn't here. Just him.

And shadow.

"Hey. If you go back, you'll die. You know that. You don't have to die!"

No response. And time was running out. Tony could feel the attention of the man on the other side of the gate. Could feel the pull. Could feel the shadow beginning to separate.

So he reached out and grabbed it. Not physically, of course. Physically, he was still standing like a total doofus in the middle of the set.

He wrapped his mind around the *concept* of shadow. Contact.

Everyone has dark memories they can't purge. Memories that creep out of mental corners on sleepless nights, perch on the edge of consciousness, and gnaw. Lucky people remembered things they read in newspapers or saw on television; cruelties that didn't involve them personally but still cut deep. People who lived without the security of freedom or justice had darker memories, memories that often fit neatly into the inflamed map of physical scars. Tony had once seen an ancient Egyptian wizard devour the life of a baby while the baby's parents walked on, unaware their child was dead.

The shadows were pieces of the Shadowlord. Dark memories. Memories of a world where those parents would thank the gods that their baby was safely dead.

The shadow had known what he knew from the moment it had entered his body. Now he knew what the shadow knew. It was like seeing a private slide show of atrocities against the front of his skull.

Had Tony been in control of his mouth, he would have screamed.

Then cruel intelligence on the other side of the gate called the shadow home and the slide show stopped.

Somehow, Tony managed to hang on.

"You don't have to go!" He fed it the memory of being absorbed, of becoming nothing once again. Of losing self.

And if I stay.

It sounded like Hartley, the boom operator, had

Hartley been able to list "enjoys inflicting torment" as one of his hobbies. It also sounded remarkably like the voice in Tony's head.

"That was you. The bright lights in the elevator were freaking you out!"

Yes.

He was losing the tug-of-war. He could feel the shadow slipping away.

If I stay, will you give me your body?

Its tone went beyond innuendo. Tony shuddered, unable to control his body's visceral response and lost a little more of his grip. Strangely, the rush of blood away from his brain helped clear his mind. If a lack of information was all that was keeping the Shadowlord from attacking . . . He couldn't . . . He had to. Arra could deal with whatever that made him and Henry could call him back from wherever he'd gone and another little bit of shadow slipped free while he tried to work out the consequences. "Yes!"

Too late.

As the shadow roared free and his world became pain, he realized it had been taunting him, that however much it feared the loss of self, it *had* to rejoin the whole. It had just been indulging itself before it went home—offering a glimpse at hope, then snatching it away again.

Tony regained consciousness to see a familiar face bending over him. Green eyes were concerned and a warm hand had a comforting grip on his shoulder.

"Tony?"

He clutched at Lee's voice as dark memories threatened to overwhelm him. Lee being there when he woke up was a bit of a dream come true and he was damned well going to hang onto it. "What . . . ?"

A slightly confused but comforting smile. "You tell me. You yelled and when Adam came over to tell you to shut up, you were on the floor." He glanced around and the smile faded. "I was on this floor . . ."

Tony struggled to sit up, wondering, if the 1AD had come to check on him, where the hell he'd gone. *Through the gate? No. The* shadow *went through the gate.*

Oh. Fuck.

As his head cleared the floor, his stomach rebelled and just barely managing to turn away from the actor, he lost what remained of his breakfast and half a dozen strawberry marshmallows all over the fake hardwood floor. Oh, yeah, this was how he dreamed of waking up with Lee . . .

"Eww. Is that real vomit?"

Tony didn't recognize the voice, figured it had to be one of the fans, and briefly considered crawling over and puking on her shoes. In comparison to how he now felt, melting eyeballs had been a good feeling. Coughing out what had to be a piece of his spleen, he managed to gasp, "Arra."

"You want Arra?"

From the sound of it, Lee had moved away, but he was still closer than anyone else in his extended audience. In between heaves that achieved nothing more than a thin stream of greenish-yellow bile, Tony managed a nod.

"He was doing some work for her."

Peter's voice. And running footsteps. More than one set.

"Tony!"

"Arra, don't kneel down there!" Peter's voice again. "He's been . . . Never mind. It looks like you missed it."

He felt a hand on his shoulder and . . . something. It settled his stomach, but more importantly it pushed the darkness back to where he could . . . not ignore it but exist with it. Darker than what he was used to existing with, but he'd manage. Not like he had a choice.

Dropping over onto his back, he looked up into the wizard's eyes and felt tears rise in his own. *So much for what's left of my macho image.*

"It's all right, Tony . . ."

"It isn't." He couldn't cope with platitudes, not from her. "He knows."

♣

"I think . . ." CB dropped his voice to a level most of his employees wouldn't have recognized as his, "it might be best if you speak with Mr. Foster another time."

Constable Elson snorted. "Trust me, Mr. Bane. I'm not put off by puke. I've questioned suspects covered in it."

"Have you? And Mr. Foster is a suspect in . . . ?"

"He's not a suspect," Constable Danvers interjected smoothly before her partner could answer. "We just want to speak to him, which . . ." Her voice sharpened as she directed it at the other officer. ". . . we can do later."

CB inclined his head toward her. "Thank you, Constable. It seems that Mr. Nicholas was among the first on the scene. Would you care to speak with him?"

"No, thank you," Elson began. "That's not . . ."

"Yes." Danvers flushed slightly as both men turned to stare at her. Given her skin color it was difficult to tell for sure, but he was fairly certain she was blushing. "I mean, we're here. Let's get something out of the trip."

"Like what?"

"Mr. Nicholas was second on the scene."

"And?"

"It wouldn't hurt to get a statement." Her tone suggested that she'd been promised some one-on-one time with a very attractive actor and she wasn't leaving until she got it. Elson heard the subtext, opened his mouth to protest, and finally shrugged.

He beckoned the actor over. "Mr. Nicholas, if you could give Constable Danvers and her partner your full cooperation." He locked eyes with the younger man, making sure he understood he was to dazzle them with celebrity and get them the hell out of the building.

"Tony . . ."

"Will be fine."

"Peter?"

"I'll speak with Peter. I'll let him know you're doing me a favor." Nothing as crass as emphasis on the second sentence. Mr. Nicholas knew very well for whom he was doing a favor and the director had undoubtedly heard the entire conversation.

When the actor bestowed a brilliant smile on the female constable and she visibly melted, CB nodded once to the now oblivious officers and walked across the set to where his director stood watching Arra help Tony Foster to his feet. The police were no longer his concern. The one would have her full attention on the actor and the other would have his full attention on making sure she did nothing he considered embarrassing. After Mr. Nicholas turned his considerable charm on Constable Elson, they'd leave—if not convinced that they'd gotten what they came for, at least quite sure that their concerns had been taken seriously.

Mr. Nicholas was a much better actor than most people gave him credit for being.

He was destined for so much more than one small, straight to syndication genre program where he played second to a man with half the ability.

Fortunately, CB Productions had him tied up in a contract Daniel Webster wouldn't have been able to break.

"Arra, why don't you take Mr. Foster down to your workshop? He'll be out of the way down there until he's feeling better."

He kept his face carefully blank as her eyes narrowed. "Yes, thank you, CB. I think I will."

"Peter."

The director started, looking from the producer to the two people slowly leaving the set and back to CB.

"I believe it's time everyone went back to work."

"Right." The big man knew what was going on; Peter could see it in his face. He could also see that he wasn't going to get an explanation. Whatever. He just wanted things to stop screwing up long enough for him to get this episode in the can.

"This is not, after all, the first time someone has been sick in the soundstage."

Peter sighed. "True enough." Raymond Dark's filing cabinet was still a little whiff under the lights.

"Can you manage without him?"

"What, without Tony? Jesus, CB, he's just the production assistant. I think I can struggle on. Adam!" The director's voice echoed off the ceiling. "Where the hell has Mason got himself off to?"

No one seemed to know.

"Well, find him, for Christ's sake. And count the fan club, a couple of them were minors! And get someone over here to clean up this puke."

Confident that things were now back as they should be, at least on the surface—essentially business as usual for television—CB turned . . . and stopped as the director called his name.

"Yes?"

"Tony and Arra."

"Yes?"

"Is there something going on with them? You know . . ." He waggled a hand. ". . . going on?"

Chester Bane favored the director with a long, level stare. "I wouldn't like to guess."

In point of fact, he very much disliked guessing. He liked to know.

He intended to know.

Fifteen

"IT WAS . . . It was in my . . ."

"Shhhh, not yet."

Tony leaned heavily on Arra's arm as she walked him down the basement stairs and sighed in relief as they stepped out onto the workshop floor, realizing the significance of the observation he'd made the first time he came down here. There were no shadows.

He stumbled toward a chair, dropped onto it, and didn't have the strength to protest when Arra grabbed a folded space blanket from a shelf and wrapped it around him. The security of something between him and the world actually felt pretty good.

"Now tell me," the wizard commanded as she sat.

So he did.

"It was hiding in your *shadow*?" She frowned. "That explains the deepening of the shadow-taint, but they've never . . . This is new behavior for them."

Tony considered shrugging, decided his head might lose its precarious balance if he tried, and snorted instead. "They were in Hartley for just over twenty-four hours. You said that no one knows how to hide like an alcoholic. I guess they learned a few tricks."

"No . . . I banished the shadow holding Hartley."

"It slipped through the pauses in your banishing spell. You were breathing kind of heavy so it wasn't one long string of syllables like usual."

Her frown deepened. "It told you that or are you guessing?"

"I touched it. Remember, I told you." Unsure of what might be useful *wizardly* information, he'd told her everything.

"Did I tell you what a stupid thing that was for you to have done?"

"You kind of choked when I got to it the first time. So . . ." He was about to ask: *What now?* What happened now that the Shadowlord had the information he was waiting for? And then he realized he didn't really want to know. Not yet. He could use a few more minutes of ignorant bliss. ". . . so what's your story?"

No doubt Arra heard his original question in the pause. Less than no doubt that she didn't want to deal with the answer either. "The moment I realized there was more than one shadow remaining, I headed for the soundstage but was prevented from entering by the presence of CB and the two officers."

"And the shooting light," Tony muttered, wrapping the space blanket more tightly around him.

"The light alone wouldn't have stopped me—it's a social contract, not an impenetrable barrier—but barging in past witnesses would have required explanations I couldn't give. Not when two of those witnesses were police officers whose suspicions were already aroused. While we waited, they interrogated me about what we were doing together on Saturday, but I don't think they believed what I told them."

"May/December fag-hag romance?"

"What?"

"Never mind. What did you tell them?"

"Exactly what you told them. That you were spending your time off learning another aspect of the business, expanding your skill set, and keeping yourself employable."

"And they didn't believe that?"

"She seemed fine with it. He seemed reluctant."

"Why didn't you . . . ?" He snaked a hand out from under the blanket and used it to wiggle his nose. As Arra stared at him blankly, he sighed. "You never watched *Bewitched*? No," he realized, "how could you? You pretty much just got here. Why didn't you do magic? Make them believe what you wanted or forget you were there as you made a run for the soundstage?"

"The gate was opening. To use power so close to the open gate . . ."

"He would have known you were here. Well, he sure as shit knows now." And things fell into place with a nearly audible click. "He was never looking for another world to conquer, he was looking for you." Tony knew he was right. Knew it because of the way the color left the wizard's face, leaving her looking old and gray. Knew it because of the way she turned and walked to her desk and sank down into her chair as though her legs would no longer hold her weight. "You're the one that got away."

"He killed everyone else in my order." For the first time since he'd known her, Arra sounded old.

"And he wants to complete the set." A flash of bodies nailed to a blackboard and Tony thanked God that his stomach was empty. Not everyone had died quickly and before these two were finally allowed an end to pain, they'd probably told the Shadowlord everything he wanted to know.

"They didn't know what variables I'd used to open the gate," Arra said, as though she'd been reading his mind. "They couldn't tell him where I was. He must have had to keep opening gates at random until he got lucky."

"Why didn't you keep moving? Open another gate and another until you crapped up the trail so badly he'd never find you?"

"Opening a gate requires precise calculations and a sure knowledge of how the energy flow of the world works. It took me a little over five years before I thought I might be able to do it and . . ."

"By then you had a life. Cats."

"The cats have nothing to do with this."

"If you gate away, he'll kill them because they were yours. He'll torture and kill everyone who might have known you just like he did before—just in case one of them might know where you've gone."

She stared at him as though she'd never seen him before. "How . . . ?"

"The shadows are shadows of him. When I grabbed this one, I knew what it knew. It didn't know much, but it was pretty clear on that. He's obsessed with finding you."

"He likes to finish what he starts. Vindictive bastard."

That wasn't quite . . . Searching for the right memory, Tony ended up back at the bodies on the blackboard and shied away. He couldn't go there again. Not right now. Enough of the depths, they were dark and dangerous, and he needed a few minutes in the light and safety of the shallows. "Hey, shouldn't I be having my vodka-catnip cooler?"

"It's not necessary; I poured power into you directly. The potion is essentially a battery, holding the power for transport."

"Okay." From the little Arra had explained about the workings of wizardry that made sense. "I could still use a drink."

"I expect your backpack is up by the lamp."

"Right." Crap. "So what was the baseball bat for?"

"I was wondering that myself." CB's voice flowed down the stairs and filled all the spaces not otherwise occupied with a mix of anger and impatience. Arra started and watched through narrowed eyes as he followed his voice into the workshop. Grateful he wasn't between them, Tony decided it might be best if he remained a spectator in this conversation.

"You came through my wards." When CB looked blank, she sighed, her frown deepening. "My protections. They were meant to keep out the people I don't want down here."

"What you want is irrelevant; this is *my* building. My studio. What I want . . ." He stalked out into the center of the workshop and the space seemed suddenly much smaller. ". . . is information. You may begin with the baseball bat." The bat was dangling from his left hand and from the businesslike way he was holding it, Tony realized he was half inclined to use it.

"Uh . . . CB . . ."

"Not a word, Mr. Foster. I'll deal with you in a moment."

Great.

"It's all right, Tony. It's about time CB knew what was going on. It is happening in *his* studio, after all." Sighing deeply, apparently unable to look the big man in the eye, Arra picked up a pencil and doodled on a scrap of paper as she talked. "I had the bat because I suspected Tony was going to be attacked by a . . ." Explanation and pencil paused. ". . . by another member of the crew."

"Why?"

To Tony's surprise, Arra spilled the whole story. From the shadow glimpsed at the location shoot, right down to what Tony had just told her. She'd didn't give up Henry's secret identity as a creature of the night but laid out the details of everything else. CB's expression never changed. Tony had to give him credit for not interrupting unless, as was likely, he was too stunned to interrupt. Tony'd been a part of the story from the beginning and even he found it hard to believe.

When Arra finally stopped talking, he nodded slowly. "So it appears Constable Elson's instincts are correct. There is something going on at my studio."

"The police," Arra snorted, "are less than useless in a case like this."

"Very probably. Why was I not kept informed from the beginning?"

"You were there when I fell through the gate. You would have realized much, much earlier than Tony here that the Shadowlord wasn't planning an invasion—no matter how much I personally wanted to believe that. You'd have realized he was looking for me." She lifted her head then and met his gaze. "Given the destruction he's capable of, I wasn't entirely convinced you wouldn't just toss me back up through the gate."

"It is a solution that occurred to me as you were speaking."

It hadn't occurred to Tony. But then CB hadn't seen the blackboard.

"So. Mr. Foster here has survived two encounters with the shadows; why, then, did they kill Nikki Waugh?"

Arra sighed and ran a hand back through her hair, standing it up in gray spikes. "That was a different kind of shadow; primitive and sent here to gather the information that would allow the Shadowlord to create the more complex shadows that interacted with Tony and the others. The information was Nikki Waugh's life."

"He sent it to kill?"

"Essentially, yes."

"He needed that information—the information that killed Nikki Waugh—in order to continue his search for you?"

"Apparently."

"So your presence here is responsible for . . ."

"For everything. Yes." Arra slumped down in her chair, her tailbone barely on the edge of the seat. "Trust me, I've added Nikki to the li . . . Damn it!" She picked up the piece of paper she'd been doodling on. "I've just scribbled over an invoice for blasting caps."

"Leave it," CB commanded as she reached for an art eraser.

"Not likely. These have to be filed with the local police and they're already not fond of me."

"Us," Tony reminded her as bits of graphite-covered rubber began to pile up on the paper. *Déjà vu all over again* . . . Although he couldn't quite hold on to just what exactly was evoking the feeling. "So now what?"

CB turned his head just enough to catch Tony's gaze and hold it. Before the shadows and the realization that Henry was holding a lien on his life, Tony would have been—had been—pretty near shitting himself in this kind of situation. Things change. Times change. He didn't look away though; no point in being rude. *Particularly to your six-foot-six employer who's not only already pissed off but happens to still be holding a baseball bat.*

"Now," CB growled, "we close that gate. I will not have my studio destroyed or my people murdered because they got in the way of a dark wizard's vendetta."

"The gate can't be closed from this side," Arra pointed out wearily.

He pivoted his entire upper body to face her directly. "Then it must be closed from the *other* side."

"Sorry." Lifting the invoice, she blew the eraser rubble to the floor.

And Tony remembered.

As Chester Bane forgot.

"Ah, you brought me my bat." Arra slipped the invoice into a hanging file. "Thank you."

"Yes, I . . ." He stared at the bat. Blinked once and frowned. "There was something . . ."

"Arra!"

"Be quiet, Tony."

No. He was not going to be quiet. There was no fucking way he was going to let her just blithely go around erasing chunks of people's lives. Taking the easy way out. Refusing to deal. Except, he couldn't speak. Couldn't make a sound. Couldn't even snap his fingers. Couldn't be anything but quiet.

"Tony." CB frowned. "I was wondering how Mr. Foster was."

Gagged. That's how I am. Fucking cow. He glared at the wizard. *Yeah, and I'd trade you in a heartbeat for three magic beans! Hell, I'd trade you for lima beans!*

"He's still a bit under the weather. I'm beginning to

think there's a bug going around. You'd better check
into it before we get a visit from the Public Heath
Nurse. You know how the media's always looking for
the next medical crisis."

"That's not . . ."

"Constable Elson has a bee up his butt about the studio already and he saw Tony was sick. If he speaks to the
wrong person . . ." Her voice didn't so much trail off as
collapse under the weighted innuendo it carried.

CB's forehead creased. "Constable Elson had best
watch himself," he growled. Shoving the bat onto the
shelf, he headed up the stairs. "The constable isn't the
only one who can *speak* to people."

"Have fun."

His response was wordless but explicit.

As the door closed, Arra slumped. "All right, Tony.
Tell me. Tell me that I've crossed a line. That I'm abus-
ing my power; making arrogant and unilateral decisions.
That ability doesn't give me the right to run the lives of
others. That small abuses lead to larger ones, and that all
power corrupts and that I'm already on the slippery
slope to the decision the Shadowlord made—that my
desires are the only ones that matter. That just because
I can, is reason enough."

Shrugging free of the blanket, he stood, too angry
to remain still. "I was going to say you can't goddamned well rip out chunks of people's lives, but
that's good, too."

"I know how CB thinks. He would have solved the
problem in the simplest way possible by dragging out
that old chestnut about the good of the many outweigh-
ing the good of the one—regardless of whether or not
the one agrees with the sentiment—and tossed me back
through the gate."

"You're a wizard! You don't have to let him toss you
anywhere!"

A sardonic eyebrow lifted. "I didn't."

"Don't let him doesn't mean my way or the highway! It means you bring him around to your way of thinking!"

"How do you suggest I convince him?"

He had no idea, but he knew one thing for certain. "Not by running away. Again! You didn't even try!"

"Because trying makes it so? Do your best and happy endings are inevitable?" Her lip curled. "You're living in a fantasy world."

"Hello!" Tony jabbed a finger toward her. "Wizard!" Held up his hand to show her the small scars on his wrist. "Vampire!" A larger gesture to take in the entire studio. "Television! Fantasy's seeming pretty damned real to me right about now. You're just too goddamned scared!"

"You would be, too, if you knew what I know!"

"So what don't I know?"

She was on her feet now, facing him, her hands curled into fists by her sides. "The Shadowlord destroyed my *entire* order!"

"Yeah? Well he didn't get the last two until after you buggered off on them!"

It probably wasn't a lightning bolt because a lightning bolt would have killed him. It was probably just the biggest static shock in history. It slammed into Tony's chest and threw him backward against a set of shelves. They rocked, but held and he slid down them to the floor, pain sizzling along each individual nerve ending. Tony had no idea there were so many of them. He could have stood not knowing.

"Get out!"

Blinking away afterimages, he dragged himself to his feet. Besides pain, he was feeling remarkably calm. "I think we've pretty much established that the Shadowlord will kill us looking for you." He held up a hand as Arra raised her palm toward him again. "I'm going." Half a dozen steps down from the door, most of his weight on the banister, he turned. "This is your mess. Take some responsibility and clean it up."

"Responsibility!" She spat the word back at him.

"Maybe you've heard of it; it's the flip side of power."

Her angle was bad and she missed him with the second shot.

Zev was standing just inside the production office, balancing a pile of CDs in one hand and dangling a set of small computer speakers from the other. He looked up as Tony came out of the basement, his nose wrinkling at the distinct smell of char cut off by the closing door. "What's burning?"

"Rome." Tony touched a fingertip to his eyebrow piercing. The skin felt puffy and the slightest pressure hurt like hell—not surprising, he supposed, gold was a good conductor. "And I was just speaking to Nero."

"Ah." The musical director frowned. "Did you and Arra have a fight?"

"A disagreement."

"Ah, again. I never knew you were that interested in special effects. You didn't mention it on Friday."

"Slipped my mind. We, uh . . ." he began, just as Zev said, "If we, uh . . ."

A moment's silence.

"Go ahead." A simultaneous polite injunction which, after another moment's silence, degenerated into two thirds of a Three Stooges routine as the stack of CDs started to slide. Zev shifted his grip, Tony reached out a hand to help, and the spark was clearly visible even under the fluorescent lights.

The clatter of the CD cases hitting the floor almost drowned out Zev's reaction.

"Bloody HELL!"

Almost.

"Man, Zev, I'm sorry." Tony dropped to his knees and began gathering up the spilled music. "It's that thing that Arra and I were working on. I guess it got me all charged up."

"You guess?" Clutching his right hand with his left, Zev sucked air through his teeth. "What did she have you doing down there; rubbing cats with glass rods?"

"What?"

"High school physics experiment. Never mind." He worked his fingers and, satisfied they were still functional, reached down to take back the stack of CDs. "I guess if it got you on your knees, I can suffer the pain." As Tony grinned in surprise, his eyes widened. "I said that out loud?"

Tony nodded.

The skin between the top edge of his beard and the bottom edge of his glasses flushed red. "Great. I'll just ..." Speakers banging against his legs, he backed up. "Look, I've got a ton of . . . um." Somehow, although Tony wasn't sure how, he got the door to post open with his elbow. "Later." And vanished.

"Do we have to have another conversation about Zev being a nice guy?" Amy demanded from her desk.

"I didn't do anything!" Tony protested as he stood.

"Please. I could see the sparkage from here."

"There's nothing going on. He's a friend!"

"No, literally, I could see the sparkage." She spread her hands, miming explosions. "What's Arra been doing to you?"

Frowning hurt. "Nothing I shouldn't have expected."

"Well. Aren't we obscu . . . CB Productions, how may I help you?" Her expression clearly stated they weren't done.

They were as far as Tony was concerned. He'd have been gone, except that every step brushed a tiny buzz off the carpet and he had a horrible vision of what would happened to some very expensive equipment if he touched it in this state. He had to bleed the residual juice off.

Metal. He needed metal but not something he'd destroy. An old dented filing cabinet just outside the door to the bull pen caught his eye. That should do. A quick laying on of hands and with any luck he and the filing cabinet would survive the experience.

Standing with his back to the cabinet, hoping it

looked as though he was waiting for Amy to finish giving directions back to the studio from Centennial Pier; he reached back and touched the metal with both hands. *Go on, take it all. Someone around here must know CPR.*

The hollow boom wasn't entirely unexpected although the volume was impressive.

Dropping the phone to her shoulder, Amy glared past him to the bull pen. "What the hell are they up to now?"

"Beats me." Tony shrugged. His palms were sizzling, but he didn't seem to have done himself any damage. "You know; *writers.* Listen, Amy, I've got to get back to work." About to step away, he paused. "Who's out at Centennial Pier?"

"Kemel, the new office PA."

"What happened to Veronica?"

"She quit."

"And why's the new guy out at the pier?"

"Rachel got a call from the location scout and sent him out with the digital to get some pictures of North Vancouver Cemetery."

Tony ran over the geography in his head. "Which is nowhere near Centennial Pier."

"He's lost."

"No shit."

"We'll talk about you and Zev later."

"Right." *Or we'll all die by smoke and shadows. Can't think of which I'm looking forward to more.*

He'd never noticed how many shadows filled the hall to the soundstage. No wonder he'd felt safe walking it earlier; his hitchhiker had felt safe. When he realized he was trying to outrun his shadow, he forced himself to slow down.

"Hey, Tony!" Everett's door was open and Lee was in the chair having his cowlick dealt with yet again. "You okay?"

He'd just been nearly electrocuted by a wizard who seemed more than willing to deal with a disaster she'd set in motion by running away. Everyone in the immediate area was about to become painfully dead and he was the last best and only line of defense. Well, him and Henry. And two thermoses still full of vodka-catnip cocktails.

Green eyes narrowed and Tony wondered just how much of that had shown on his face.

"I'm fine."

◆

"Henry, I told you, I'm fine."

"She attacked you."

Subtext: *She attacked something of mine.*

Tony rolled his eyes. *Jesus, Henry, get an afterlife.* "I provoked her. I said some stuff that really pissed her off."

"But you said it in order that she reconsider her position."

"Bonus if she does it, but no." As he remembered it, he'd been so angry, he'd been hitting out at the only thing available. "I said it pretty much just to piss her off."

"Because you have a death wish?"

He elbowed the vampire lightly in the side. "Duh. I'm here, aren't I?" He didn't want to be there. He wanted to be safe at home, safely oblivious, eating nachos in bed and watching one of Lee's old movies. He wanted his biggest concern to be about his pointless attraction to a straight boy. He didn't want to be in charge of saving, if not the world, the immediate area and anyone who might have ever had anything to do with Arra Pelindrake. No one seemed to care what he wanted. "What time is it?"

They were standing so close, he felt Henry lift his arm to check his watch. Standing in the soundstage with just the emergency lights on, he couldn't even see his wrist, but Henry had an advantage in the dark. "It's just turned 11:00."

"Do you hear anything? I mean anyone? Here."

"Only you. Your heart is racing."

No shit. "Just revving up for the fight."

"Of course."

They had the lamp, and the leftover potion, and a baseball bat picked up on the way home from work, and a certain small amount of experience in kicking metaphysical ass. They didn't have a wizard—she wasn't answering her phone or her buzzer—but they were as ready as they'd ever be. If that last shadow made a break for home, they'd stop it and if the Shadowlord sent new minions through the gate, solid minions, impervious to the light, they'd be facing . . .

Crap.

They knew they'd be facing a vampire. They knew what he knew. "They'll come through prepared. Ready to take you out."

"I am not so easy to kill."

Prince of Darkness voice. *Yeah, that'll impress them.* "But you *can* be killed."

"Not easily."

"But . . ."

"You'll have my back."

"Right." Like that made it better. Tony shifted the bat to his other hand and wiped his sweaty palm against his jeans. "You know, this morning Arra was all ready to rush in and take her bat to the shadow-held. I wonder how she would have explained it, you know, after, while she was standing over the body. I mean, you can't call smacking a coworker with a Louisville Slugger a special effect."

"She probably didn't even consider that." He could hear the smile in Henry's observation. "She thought you were in danger and she rushed in."

"Using up her entire stock of helping out." Tony, on the other hand, wasn't smiling.

"Did she tell you she wasn't going to stand against the Shadowlord?"

"Well, yeah. Right from the start she said she wouldn't face him."

"And in the beginning she said she wouldn't help, but she has."

"As long as it was at no risk to her; she's always planned to run."

He felt Henry shrug. "Plans change."

"I can't believe you're defending her. She's not here, is she?"

"No. She's not here."

"A minute ago you were all pissed off because she'd attacked me."

"The two things are unconnected."

Tony opened his mouth and closed it again, sputtering slightly as the dozen or so things he could say to that got tangled on the way out. When it seemed as though he'd been listening to nothing but his own ragged breathing for half an hour he muttered, "What time is it now?"

"11:17."

"Is that all?" And then he realized. "No gate."

"Apparently not. I suspect our enemy has things to prepare."

That sounded reasonable. Not in the least comforting, or encouraging, but reasonable. "Why face you when he can come through in the morning when you're out of it."

"Why, indeed."

"He can come through in the morning when it's just me." And as long as they were speculating . . . Tony lined up another couple of points as Henry moved the lamp back by the light board and rolled the cables. "He's got to have learned that it's harder for us to stop them when we're shooting. All those people hanging around trying to create a television show really screws with the hero's ability to defend against dark wizards invading from another reality."

Henry's smile flashed white in the dim light. "A television hero would manage."

"Fucking television hero's got fifty people behind the camera making him look good. I'm going to get fired. You know that, right?"

"It's not a given."

"Yeah, it is." They fell into step, heading for the rear door. "Even if we save the world, I'm going to lose my job, lose my apartment, and end up turning tricks in Gastown. All of a sudden, I'm feeling a lot more sympathy toward season six Buffy."

"Is that supposed to mean something?"

"Twenty-first century, Henry; try to keep up."

◆

At 9:30, Tony had vetoed the idea of breaking into the wizard's apartment.

"Look, if she doesn't want to come, you can't force her."

"You can't force her," Henry had corrected. *"I can."*

"And can you force her to fight when she gets there?"

"You'd be surprised how many people fight when cornered."

"Yeah, like rats. She's cornered now." Frowning, Tony'd rubbed at his chest. *"If we go in there, and if she's home, she'll fight us. If she wins, there's no one to block the gate."*

"Alone stood brave Horatius, but constant still in mind; thrice thirty thousand foes before and the broad flood behind."

"What?"

" 'Horatius at the Bridge.' Lord Macaulay."

"Fuck that. Just drive, would you."

So Henry had pulled away from the wizard's co-op wondering what had happened to change Tony's attitude toward her from acceptance to sullen resentment. Immortal patience was a godsend as bit by bit the events of the morning emerged. As he pulled into the studio parking lot, he'd learned about the new circular bruise in the center of Tony's chest, purple and angry amidst the not-yet-faded leftovers of the earlier beating.

With the gate unopened and battle delayed, he'd dropped Tony at his apartment and waited outside, out of sight, until he'd heard his heartbeat—too familiar to him to mistake—slow in the cadences of sleep. Henry could see from the street that all the lights were on and he'd snarled, frustrated by a battle that dealt in terror and left him nothing to fight.

At 2:15, after a quick drive into downtown Vancouver, he followed another of the co-op's members into Arra's building.

If the wizard had warded her door, she hadn't warded it against brute strength. With the sleeves of his sweater pulled down to mask fingerprints, one hand on the door handle and the other up by the dead bolt, Henry gave a short, sharp push. The sound of steel flanges punching out of the wooden frame sounded like a gun going off, but he was in the apartment with the door closed behind him before any of the wizard's neighbors had roused. From the hall, there would be no sign of forced entry.

The wizard was not in the apartment; he couldn't feel her life. He searched every room regardless. Who could say what a wizard's abilities encompassed?

The laptop was gone from the dining room table. In its place a stamped envelope addressed to Anthony Foster. On the envelope a Post-It Note that read, *Vera, please drop this in the mail after feeding the cats.*

Henry set the note aside and carefully ran his thumbnail under the seal of the envelope. The cheap glue parted with a minimum of protest.

A steady regard turned him toward the living room. Both cats sat on the sofa and stared disdainfully at him. Dogs always insisted on playing pack politics with his kind. Cats were smarter.

"I need to know what she's told him."

Zazu snorted.

"If you expect me to believe that you've never made a morally ambiguous choice, think again. Cats are all about morally ambiguous."

Whitby yawned.

He'd half expected the letter to be handwritten in flowing black script on thick linen paper, instead it was Times New Roman, 12pt, on 20lb white bond. There was no salutation or signature.

I saw him win. As he advanced on the city, I cast the crystals and I saw he would win. I cast again, and again, and every time the Shadowlord was victorious. I tried to convince Kiril and Sarn to leave with me, but they refused. They refused to understand that there was nothing they could do—that they could not win. Fight for us, the people of the city screamed. Die for us. They walked out to their deaths and I opened the gate.

Even after seven years, my sight is not so clear in this world, but every time I look, I see him win. What point in trying when loss is foreseen—although I no more expect to convince you of this than I could convince Kiril and Sarn.

I can only hope that on some new world this will change.

Now you know what I know.

For what it's worth, I'm sorry.

"It's not worth much," Henry snarled, folding the letter back along its original lines. Then he stood for a long moment with his hand above the phone.

Tony, it's Henry. Don't go into work tomorrow.

Don't be among the first to die.

Wait until sunset when I am there to fight beside you.

Their tie was strong enough that even at a distance he could make it a command, not a request.

But he'd neither asked nor commanded it in the car as they drove away from the studio, both of them well aware of what the morning could bring.

As much as Henry wanted to, he would not take

Tony's choice from him. He stepped away from the phone, hand dropping to his side. "The choices we make, make us," he told the cats.

Zazu snorted. Whitby yawned.

Arra's letter to Tony back in its envelope, back on the table, Henry slipped out into the night.

Sixteen

THE CARPENTERS had been called in at 6:00, Peter and Sorge together having decided that the location they'd intended to use for the streets-of-London-circa-1870 flashback was unsuitable owing to half a dozen junkies who flat out refused to move. A set, therefore, had to be built. By the time Tony arrived at 7:30, the scream of saws and the pounding of hammers could be heard all the way out to the craft services truck.

As he came in through the open back doors, Charlie Harris, one of the painters, handed him a paint roller duct-taped to a broomstick and pointed him at five meters of plywood wall saying, "Get a layer of the medium gray down. I want to start airbrushing the stone on by 9:00."

"Yeah, but . . ."

"We've got time constraints here, bucko, and Peter said to use anyone who wasn't either directly in front of or directly behind a camera."

"Bucko?"

Hazel eyes blinked myopically at him through paint-flecked glasses. "You're the production assistant, right? You got something more important to do?"

More important? Still a little thrown by *bucko*, Tony glanced toward the set under the gate and realized with horror that the nervous bray of laughter still echoing around the soundstage had come from him. "I've got to save the world at 11:15," he announced. Well, why not? At least when the shit hit the fan, one guy might know enough to duck.

"Christ, you've got hours yet, you'll be long done by . . . Hey! Shit for brains! I told you to paint those doors matte black, not gloss!"

As Charlie hurried off, Tony looked down at the roller and stepped up to the paint tray. It wasn't like he had anything to prepare. The world's last line of defense pretty much consisted of him declaiming, "You shall not pass," and everyone knew how well that had worked out the *last* time. Oh, sure, eventually, it was happily ever after and all that, but first there was the whole falling through fire and dying thing. *And if I die, I don't come back.*

If I die . . .

Die . . .

"Hey, Foster! You want to get some of that paint on the wall instead of the floor?"

Paint dribbled off the roller to puddle by his foot. Wet, it didn't look much like medium gray. It looked like liquid shadow.

"Foster!"

"Right. Sorry."

Painting left him far too much time to think. Thoughts of the gate, thoughts of what might come through the gate, thoughts of what he might do to stop it, thoughts of whether Arra might or might not have screwed off and left him alone—*mights* and *maybes* and *what ifs* chased themselves around in his head, but he couldn't get a grip on any of them. By the time he covered the last bit of plywood, he was so frustrated at the complete and total lack of substance that he was starting to look forward to the possibility of the Shadowlord's army charging through the gate after Arra with swords drawn. One thing about an army, it made it easy to convince people that something was going on.

Drop an army through the gate and at least I won't be facing it alone.

Alone.

Fucking great. He knew that *almost* voice. There was still a shadow here on the soundstage! Whirling around, Tony tried to get a good look at his own shadow as it danced with his heels over the concrete floor.

"Foster, what the hell are you doing?" Charlie glared at him over an armload of Styrofoam capstones. "If you're done, get out of my way."

"I'm, uh . . ." Did his shadow look darker? Occupied?

"You're, uh, nothing. Haul ass over to the workshop and bring the box of sticks for this glue gun."

"I have to . . . I mean, there's someone . . ."

The capstones hit the floor; sticky hands closed around Tony's shoulders and turned him away from the wall. "Workshop. Glue sticks. Now. And, Foster, if you're having a nervous breakdown, I suggest you raise your caffeine levels and get over yourself. Today's a bad day!"

Tell me about it. It wasn't in his shadow, he decided— the voice wasn't clear enough for that or maybe it wasn't enough in his head. Any kind of accurate description took a beating around this sort of shit. Relief mixed with apprehension as he hurried toward the workshop. If not in his shadow, where? Or, more specifically, who?

Peter and Lee were running through phone dialogue as he passed the office set, Lee sitting with one thigh propped on the edge of the desk in what had become one of James Grant's signature positions.

". . . is still good and evil is still evil and good people continue to do what they can to negate the effects of evil people. But it's your choice, Raymond; I won't make it for you. After all, you're the one with the centuries of experience." Moving the phone away from his ear, Lee shook his head. "Did that last bit sound as over the top listening to it as it did saying it?"

Peter shrugged. "You're talking to a vampire detective freaking out about a coven of aristocratic witches he's just discovered he didn't destroy back a hundred odd years ago; does it get more over the top than that?"

Tony walked on as the actor acknowledged the point.

"Three minute warning, people!"

Across the soundstage, other voices took up the cry and construction noises began to drop off. With no time to either stop shooting or stop building, the day would be a patchwork of both, carpenters and painters playing statue as the bell sounded, and bursting into antlike frenzy the second after "Cut."

Glue sticks in hand, Tony got back to the office in time to see the first take of the scene.

". . . won't make it for you. After all, you're the one with the centuries of experience."

"Cut!" As hammers and saws started up again, Peter stepped out from behind the monitor and walked as far onto the set as his headphones would allow. "Let's do it again, only this time, put the emphasis on *centuries* instead of *you're* and then put a little sharpness into the way you hang up."

"I'm mad at him?"

"You're not happy."

"Go from the top of the scene?"

"Not this time. Start in at 'morality hasn't changed.' " Heading back, the director caught sight of Tony and beckoned him in. "Where's your headset, Tony? Get it on and get to work."

"Charlie had me painting."

"London?"

He thought about it for a minute. It certainly hadn't looked like London, but this was television so who the hell knew? "I guess."

"You guess? Wonderful." Stepping behind the monitors, Peter moved out of Tony's line of sight. About to continue on his glue sticks delivery, Tony froze like a deer in the headlights as he realized that Lee had been watching him the entire time. Was, in fact, staring at him wearing the kind of speculative expression he'd been seeing on Arra of late.

Honesty, or something more visceral, forced Tony to admit the expression looked better on Lee.

But it did remind him that he couldn't put off the Arra problem any longer.

♥

". . . cowled robes, how hard is that? No, not bathrobes. Kind of a black caftan with hoods. Yes, they have to be black. Because it's an evil coven, for chrissakes, not a freakin' pajama party!" Amy hung up with a studied lack of emphasis and smiled tightly up at Tony. "That was Kemel. He's in town trying to pick up our rental of a dozen cowled robes. But they can't find them. And the six they *can* find are pink."

"Pink cowled robes?" Tony quickly ran through everything that had shot in Vancouver over the last couple of years and came up with zip. "Doesn't wardrobe usually make that kind of stuff?"

"Wardrobe is busy trying to make our one Victorian walking dress look like it's not the same dress we used back in episode four. And, yes, we could rent, buy, or make another one, but since we already have one, CB wouldn't approve the budget. Isn't it amazing what you can do with trim. Did you actually want something or are you just out here hanging around?"

"The door to Arra's workshop is locked." He'd spent a good five minutes rattling the knob; pushing, pulling and getting nowhere. It said something about the level of the cowl crisis that Amy hadn't noticed.

"No, it isn't."

"Yeah, it is."

"Can't be." She smiled smugly. "There's no lock on the door. Every now and then, it just jams and only Arra can get it open."

"Is she here?"

"Haven't seen her, so, no, I'd say she's not."

No real surprise. "Did she call in?"

"Do I care? Wait . . ." An uplifted emerald-tipped finger cut him off. ". . . let me answer that. If she wasn't bringing a dozen black robes in with her, then, no, I don't."

"Amy, this is important."

"Why?"

"I can't tell you." The big clock on the wall read 12:20. His stomach plummeted and then he remembered to glance down at his watch. 10:20. "You haven't fixed the clock yet."

"Gosh." Heavily kohled eyes opened emphatically wide. "You're right, I haven't. Get over it."

It'd be over soon enough; he had a little less than an hour to go.

Soon.

God damn it! He grabbed at his head, his fingers closing over a sticky smear of paint. *Stop fucking doing that!*

Amy frowned up at him, tapping the end of a pen against her lower lip. She might have looked concerned, she might have looked annoyed—Tony was too distracted by the shadow-voice to decide. "I didn't talk to Arra," she said at last. "Hang on and I'll see if Rachel did."

A scribbled note shoved under the office manager's nose brought no pause in her heated discussion with their ISP about a lack of cable internet hookup and a negative response.

"I guess she'll be in later." Amy's tone fell halfway between statement and question. Trouble was, Tony didn't have any answers.

Although he did have more questions. Would later be too late?

"Tony?"

"Yeah. Sorry." About to ask if CB was in, he changed his mind. What would be the point? Anything CB knew had been erased and even if he had time to start an explanation from scratch, Tony had no way to prove any of it. Murderous body-snatching shadows on the loose from another world—it still sounded like a bad pitch from the bull pen. "I've got to get back to work." Really wishing that Amy would stop staring at him, he spun around on one heel, took two steps, and slammed into a warm, yielding obstacle. CD cases clattered against the floor.

"Zev. Sorry, man. I've uh . . . I've got to go." A glance back over his shoulder. "If Arra calls, tell her . . ." What? Get her magical ass in here? "Fuck it. She knows. Don't even bother."

Amy watched Tony disappear through the door leading to the soundstage and shook her head.

"What was up with him?" Zev asked as he shoved aside a pile of uncollated scripts and stacked his retrieved CDs on the corner of her desk.

"I'm not sure, but I think you've been replaced in his affections by a fifty-five-year-old woman who blows things up."

"Well." After a long moment, the musical director sighed. "That definitely sucks."

♥

The big carbon arc lamp was gone. It wasn't by the set. It wasn't by the lighting board.

Tony stared at the empty space as the first vibrations from the gate started the liquid in his eyeballs quivering. *Crap. Crap! CRAP!* Heart pounding in his throat, he raced to the racks where the extra kliegs were stored. It wasn't there either. Back to the edge of the gate, every hair on his body lifting.

"Three minute warning, people!"

Right. They were shooting in the office set. They were using the lamp.

They weren't using the lamp.

"Sorge said we were done with it, so CB rented it to

that buddy of his who's doing that new sci-fi show over in Westminster. Charged him a freakin' arm and a leg, too. He took it out first thing this morning."

When I was painting . . .

The gaffer looked down at his arm and then up at Tony. "You want to let go of me now?"

"Yeah. Right. Sorry." It took him a moment to remember how his fingers worked.

"If Arra was still using it, she should've said something. Not that it would've made any difference if CB had a chance of making a buck off renting it. Good thing I didn't need it," he added turning back to his board as Peter called for quiet on the set. "He'd have me using freakin' flashlights if it'd save him a few bucks."

"Rolling . . . slate . . . and action!"

Lee's voice talking of good and evil got lost in Tony's rising reaction to the gate.

Flashlights? Digging the heels of both hands into his temples, he staggered back to the dining room. Leaning against one of the vertical two-by-fours, he stared into the set. No one there. No one trying to send a shadow home. This was a good thing until he forced himself to consider why the last shadow wasn't heading home. Last minion left in this world could be staying to act as a welcoming committee. Welcoming what; now that was the question. Odds were good that flashlights wouldn't be enough to stop it and the baseball bat was in his bathroom leaning against the sink.

His nose was running.

A quick touch with the back of his hand.

No, his nose was *bleeding*.

Stupid vampire. Stupid sleeping all day. What the fuck good is that?

The actual opening of the gate felt as though the two halves of his brain were being ripped apart. Slowly.

A weapon. He needed a weapon.

And an aspirin, but that would have to wait.

Just outside the set, he found a metal stand and with

shaking fingers unscrewed the upright. Four feet of aluminum, threaded on both ends—after all those years with Henry, he knew the kind of damage a simple stake could do.

Holding the pipe across his body, he stepped back into the set in time to see a man fall about four feet and land facedown on the dining room table.

The gate closed.

The man laid his palms flat against the wood and pushed himself into a sitting position.

Tony could hear hammering, swearing, wood dragging across concrete, and Sorge's distinct mix of French and English as he spoke to the key grip—with two separate crews working, there were easily thirty people in the soundstage and not one of them had seen anything out of the ordinary. No new allies. No one who wouldn't still demand to see proof of an insane-sounding story.

And all Tony's brain seemed capable of coming up with in the way of reaction was, *Your clothes, give them to me.* Which didn't work on a number of levels but mostly because the stranger was already dressed—black dress pants, black shoes, a gray silk shirt, and a black leather jacket. The shoes were a little off and the jacket not quite right, but all in all, it was a good casual business look.

Oh, for Christ's sake; quit being so fucking gay!

In his own defense, it was easy to look at the clothes. Harder, almost impossible to look at the man. Hair, eyes, mouth . . . Tony assumed they were there, but he couldn't seem to focus on them. Not that it really mattered. Lifting the pipe, he forced his right foot forward.

He'd barely completed the step when Mason Reed hurried across the set, both hands outstretched, his shadow trailing behind him like it would really rather be anywhere else.

Mason. Son of a bitch. The last shadow was in Mason.

Tony'd forgotten the actor was in the studio that day. He'd been with Everett, not out on the soundstage; he hadn't been on the list of possibles.

In full *Raymond Dark* makeup and costume, he stopped at the edge of the table and helped the other man to his feet.

"Shouldn't you be kneeling?" Quietly curious.

"It is not done on this world, Mast . . ."

Something twisted. Mason whimpered and dropped to his knees.

"It is now." Tanned fingers lifted a strand of the actor's hair, turning it so the red-gold glimmered in the light. Tony could see Mason shudder and, as much as he'd never liked the other man, he wouldn't have wished this on him. He managed another step forward as the strand of hair was released and a bored voice murmured, "Get up, fool, before someone sees you and leaps to the wrong conclusion."

On *conclusion*, the stranger lifted his head.

His face came into focus. Eyes locked with Tony's.

The pipe clattered against the floor as it fell from suddenly nerveless fingers. Tony recognized the feeling of being studied like an insect under a magnifying glass. This was what . . . who . . . had been peering through the gate. He felt shadows stirring, wrapping around his soul. Found a word. "Shadowlord."

The pale gray eyes widened slightly. "You know me. How . . . interesting. I know you as well, Tony Foster. I hold a shadow of you." A glance down at the pipe. "Seems there's more substance to you than that, though."

Tony tried to flinch away as warm fingers pinched his chin, but his shadow rose up behind him and held him in place. Not the Shadowlord's minions. Or the Shadowlord's army. The Shadowlord. Here. Himself. Why would he do that? Why would he travel to another world just to take out Arra when he'd already fried her entire order?

"Able to question . . ." The grip on his chin tightened

and his head was forced first one way then the other. ". . . but nothing else. As you are, you are no danger to me." The Shadowlord smiled. His teeth were very white and the smile, wreathed in shadow, was intended to be terrifying, but Tony had seen smiles wreathed in Darkness and the joy of the Hunt . . .

And maybe he shouldn't have made that thought so obvious.

The smile snapped off, no longer dangerously charming, merely dangerous. "Where is she, Tony?"

No reason to waste hero points—he suspected he was going to need all he could muster. "I don't know."

The hand not holding his chin reached out, grabbed his shadow, and pulled it forward. Pulled it through flesh. Screaming would have been nice, but the hand holding his shadow also held back his voice. *Holy fuck, that hurts!*

"You're not lying."

The release hurt almost as much as his shadow snapped back.

"But she hasn't run. Not yet. I can sense only one gate. Mine." An amused tone, at odds with the vicious grip. "It was foolish of her to have waited; the moment she tries to open a gate, I'll know exactly where she is and I'll be on her between a heartbeat and her dying breath. Ah, you didn't know that, did you? You didn't know she was trapped. You're wondering if she knows how loudly the gates call to those who use power. Probably not." The grip became almost a painful caress. "Last time she opened a gate, I was regrettably delayed. This time, there's no one to delay me. Oh, wait, I'm sorry. There's a boy and a Nightwalker. I tremble. I truly do. Tell me where the Nightwalker hides from the sun."

Why don't you already know? Why hadn't the shadow taken that information back through the gate? Granted, it hadn't been in his head for very long, but Arra had said they knew what he knew. Seems Arra was wrong about that. The resulting emotion was more *nah nah nah* than hope, but he found strength in it. "Never."

"And that would be the required cliché response. Do you think I'm giving you a choice?" His hand stretched again over Tony's shoulder. "So foolish."

"Master, this boy is nothing. A production assistant. He does what he is told."

A silver eyebrow lifted. "My point exactly."

"He is beneath your notice."

Yeah, Mason always hated it when someone else was getting all the attention. *You want him?* Tony thought above the rising tide of pain. *He's all yours.*

"Would someone mind telling me what the hell is going on over here?"

Released, Tony could still feel the indentation of the Shadowlord's fingers in his flesh. His knees threatened to buckle, but he gritted his teeth and managed to stay standing.

"And who," Peter continued, sweeping an annoyed gaze over the evil wizard, "is this?"

"You know me. Interesting."

Apparently, no one else *knew* him. Although Tony had no idea how they couldn't feel the power writhing around the Shadowlord like smoke.

"He's a friend of mine, Peter." Gone was the whining sycophant, back was the star of *Darkest Night*, a man who knew his friends would be welcomed for no other reason than that they were his friends and he was essential to the continued employment of a great many people. "He's just dropped by to watch me shoot."

"Right. Fine." Peter was clearly maintaining a fingernail grip on his temper. "Then he'll have a lot more to watch if you'd go over to the office so we can start scene seven. Lighting's set and we've been ready for you for a while now, Mason."

"Which is why Tony came and got him."

Peter shook his head, clearly a little confused about why

Mason's friend was speaking to him, defending a member of his staff; his shadow seemed to be on its knees. "Well," he said at last. "Nice to see someone's doing their job."

The Shadowlord held out a hand. "Michael Swan."

A cursory handshake. "Right. Mason, if you would . . ." As he turned, sweeping Mason before him, he added to the soundstage at large, "Let's go, people; we've got another nine pages to get through today!"

"Your thoughts were filled with this . . . television. Shadows made of light. We have nothing similar. I find the whole concept fascinating." His hand closed gently over Tony's shoulder. Under his shirt, Tony's skin tried to crawl away from the touch. "I do hope Arra cowers for a while—just think of what I could do with something like this."

Evil television? Or was that redundant? He'd come to kill Arra himself because Tony's shadow memories had made television fascinating?

That was . . . unexpected.

As the Shadowlord released him, Tony had a strong suspicion that hysteria was one more touch away. He could feel it beating its fists against the inside of his skull. He watched the Shadowlord catch up with Mason. Felt the panic begin to ease with distance. Wanted nothing more than to run. And didn't. And followed. He didn't bother hiding, or skulking, or trying to be anything less than obvious. What would be the point?

Lee had moved to the edge of the set and was standing with his eyes closed, holding a cup of coffee. His lips were moving, so Tony assumed he was running over lines. Mason passed him without acknowledgment, but the Shadowlord paused and glanced back at Tony, his expression clearly saying, *So, this is the one.*

Great. He hadn't given up Henry, but he'd given up Lee. Or at least his attraction to Lee. *Don't . . . Don't what*, he had no idea. *Just don't.*

And the Shadowlord moved on.

Tony released a breath he hadn't known he was holding just as the color drained from Lee's face and his eyes snapped open.

Oh, shit!

Spasm.

But the Shadowlord wasn't touching the actor. Wasn't even near him.

The coffee mug smashed against the floor, coffee spraying against the shadow that stretched from Lee's back to the Shadowlord's heels. It seemed to be driving serrated spikes into Lee's head.

God fucking damn it!

No lights handy.

What else defeated shadow?

Darkness weakened them.

Gray-on-gray patterns flickered across the floor as a camera rolled into position.

Patterns . . .

Half a dozen running steps took Tony to the edge of the set—the edge of the lights. His shadow fell over Lee's and the Shadowlord's, wiping out the definition of the attack, leaving nothing but a formless shape of darker gray on the concrete.

Lee's breath caught on the edge of a scream and then eased out of him in a wavering exhalation. Then Elaine from craft services was there with a roll of paper towels. And Carol, who was on the lighting crew. And Keisha, the set dresser. With Lee surrounded by concerned women and no place on the floor for new patterns, the Shadowlord's shadow now extended no farther from his heels than it should.

Tony moved one tentative step away; moved his shadow one tentative step away.

Lee seemed fine.

As Mason ran over his blocking with Peter and Sorge, the Shadowlord moved up to stare through the camera's viewfinder. He was Mason's friend, no one would move him. No one wanted to set Mason off and lose an afternoon's work.

Tormenting Lee had obviously been nothing more than a way to yank Tony's chain. How long would the Shadowlord just hang around if Arra stayed hidden? How long before he started killing people to bring Arra out of hiding? And would Arra come if he did?

What would he do if she didn't?

Flush her out with destruction?

According to Arra, it took time to learn the energy of a new world. The longer they had to wait for the other shoe to drop, the more the Shadowlord learned, the more powerful he became. Although it seemed as though shadows were shadows—that power he had now.

Bottom line, he had to be stopped sooner rather than later.

Yeah, and now we've come to that amazing decision, we're no farther ahead than we were. There's a big fucking evil thing hanging around being a fanboy—I'm the only one who knows it and I can't do a thing about it. I can't even take out his minion.

Mason was settling into character although he kept shooting "look at me" glances toward his master.

"Tony?"

Heart in his throat, he spun around so quickly he almost fell over.

Lee backed up a step, both hands in the air. "Are you okay?"

"Me?"

"Your nose is bleeding."

Still? He touched his upper lip and stared down at sticky fingertips. "It's nothing."

Arms wrapped around his torso, Lee nodded. "Sure."

"Are you . . ." A wave back toward the damp spot on the concrete. ". . . okay?"

"Good question." The green eyes stared past Tony's shoulder. "There's some weird shit going on around here ever since Nikki Waugh died. The doctor thinks my little memory lapse was something they call Transient Global Amnesia. Except, according to the cops,

I'm not the only one forgetting things and your nose was bleeding yesterday, too—same bat-time, same bat-channel. And if I didn't know Mason was straight, I'd say he was one short step from bending over for that friend of his."

Tony didn't bother turning to look. "You might want to stay away from Mason. And his friend."

"Lee." Adam leaned between them. "We're ready for you."

"I'll be right there."

The 1AD nodded and headed for the monitors.

"I'm about to shoot a scene with Mason." He almost seemed to be asking if he'd be safe.

"That's not Mason, though." Tony nodded toward the set. "That's Raymond Dark."

Lee looked confused for a moment then he smiled. "Right. I wonder if he's going to take his friend to his interview."

"Interview?"

"Yeah, he's on *Live at Five* tonight. Again."

"They're live . . ."

"That would explain the title of the show, yeah. They seem to think Mason's the only actor on the West Coast."

"Lee!"

As Adam beckoned, Lee nodded at Tony and walked onto the set. Any other time, Tony wouldn't have been able to look away as the actor shed Lee Nicholas and became James Grant. Today, the Shadowlord held his entire attention.

"I wonder if he's going to take his friend to his interview."

"They're live . . ."

"Shadows made of light . . . just think of what I could do with something like this."

And it seemed as though shadows were shadows—that power he had now.

Oh, fucking crap.

The Shadowlord wasn't *only* after Arra. It was also an invasion. And Tony'd handed him the weapon he needed to win it.

♥

The production office was empty. Tony could hear Rachel and Amy and one of the writers in the kitchen arguing over who'd emptied the coffeemaker. Keeping his head down, he hurried toward the open door of CB's office. He had to find a way to break Arra's spell because Chester Bane was the only person Mason ever listened to. The only person with even half a hope in hell of keeping him—and by extension the Shadowlord—from that live interview.

He might even know where Arra was.

But he wasn't in his office.

There was an appointment book open on the desk. CB disapproved of electronic calendars, saying paper and ink never got wiped out by a thunderstorm. Tony'd never heard of anyone's PDA being wiped out by a thunderstorm, but he had no intention of ever pointing that out to CB. The book was open to the current date. CB'd had a breakfast meeting with one of the networks, but the rest of the day was clear. Therefore, he was somewhere in the building.

"Lots of help. It's a big fucking building!" Nothing on the desk suggested *where* in the building CB might be; if he was on the move, they could chase each other around all afterno . . .

Tony slid the appointment book to one side and stared down at the sheet of art paper tucked into the edge of the blotter. The pattern penciled on it looked incredibly familiar. A closer look showed that the pattern had been, in fact, redrawn—lines drawn hard enough to etch the paper erased then filled back in.

Lines erased.

But this wasn't the pattern Arra had used to erase CB's memory.

No.

"My memory."

She'd erased it; he remembered seeing her erase it. Even when he'd forgotten everything else, he'd remembered that. CB must have found the paper and filled the lines back in.

Coincidence? Tony's thoughts flicked back to the vodka-catnip cocktails still in his thermos. If CB was also a wizard, he was going to need a very stiff drink.

After erasing it, Arra had slipped the paper she'd drawn CB's pattern on into her desk.

So, logically, in order to return CB's memory . . .

Finally! Something was going right!

Except that the door to Arra's workshop was still locked. Jammed. Whatever. Point was, he couldn't get the damned thing open! *She's probably got a spell on it. That's why it only opens . . .* He braced one foot against the trim and pulled. *. . . for . . .* Again. Harder. . . . *her.*

Fuck!

The argument in the kitchen built to a crescendo. Any minute, the losing participant would stomp out and demand to know what he was doing. Or Zev would emerge from post. Or Adam would come looking for him.

I don't have time for this! Not only was the door rock solid without so much as a wobble on its hinges but the doorknob wasn't even turning. His hands dropped to his sides. *Completely, fucking hopeless!* Breathing deeply, he closed his eyes and banged his head lightly against the painted wood. *Please. Just. Open.*

The latch rattled against the latch plate.

Tony grabbed for the doorknob, twisted, and pulled.

The door swung open without even the expected ominous creak.

♥

Arra really *had* drawn CB's pattern on an invoice for blasting caps which made it just a little hard to retrace.

If he got it wrong, would it just not work or would CB remember things that hadn't happened? He paused, pencil frozen on the paper. If he got it wrong, would he completely screw up CB's brain? Did he have a right to risk it? As far as he could remember a distant and not very pleasant childhood, he'd always sucked at coloring between the lines.

"Screw it." The pencil started moving again. "He redrew me."

And anyway, the alternative was the Shadowlord live at five.

♥

"What the hell is going on?" Stomping down the stairs, CB's voice bludgeoned the silence out of his way. "We had an agreement, old woman, and if I find you've broken . . ." He caught sight of Tony and paused. His gaze flicked down to the sheet of paper, the pieces falling into place so quickly Tony practically heard the click as they lined up. "Ah . . ."

"Yeah."

"Where is she?"

"I have no idea. I was hoping you might know."

"Has she . . ." One huge hand sketched an unidentifiable pattern in the air.

They so didn't have time for obscure. "Taken up Balinese dancing? What?"

"Opened another gate."

"Apparently not."

CB glanced down at his watch. "The original gate has opened. Did she go through it?"

"No."

"Are you certain?"

"Pretty much, yeah." Tony point-formed the events of the morning, stopping twice to remind CB that he wasn't finished and that roaring off to wring necks without all the information wouldn't help. "You've got to stop Mason from doing that interview," he concluded. "If the

Shadowlord gets in front of a live camera, we're talking shadows of light going out into millions of homes!"

"Millions?" The big man snorted. "Their ratings are nowhere near millions, Mr. Foster. Thousands at best."

"Fine. Thousands. Thousands of shadows taking over people's lives."

"But these shadows won't be able to leave the television."

"Wanna bet? My shadow shouldn't be able to get me in a hammerlock, but it did. Mason's shouldn't be able to roll around like a whipped puppy, but it is. Shadows shouldn't have been able to kill Nikki Waugh or Alan Wu, but they did!" Suddenly unable to remain still, he paced the width of workshop and back as he talked, CB's head turning to follow his passing like he was the ball in a tennis game. Which was pretty much how he felt. "I got a feeling that convincing shadows to leave the box is going to be no big. Then we've got mi . . . thousands of shadow-held who'll hunt down Arra for that son of bitch, forcing her to fight them—or save them from doing stupid things like jumping off an overpass. Draining her power until she can't fight him and . . ." Tony ground his palms together.

"Then he goes home and it is over."

Breathing a little heavily, Tony stopped pacing and stared at the older man. "You don't believe that. Powerful men seek power. It's what they do; hell, it's what they are. There are places on this world without indoor plumbing that still have a television and he's fascinated by television. He's going to take the television road to power!"

"He is fascinated by television because the shadow he holds of you is fascinated by television."

"Fine. Whatever. My bad." Man, CB was big on placing blame. First Arra, now him. "Point is, he's not just going to go home. Arra isn't going to be the only casualty. And Arra, by the way, works for you and is therefore your responsibility—at least a little," he amended as CB scowled down at him. "And more importantly, you are the only one who can stop Mason."

"I arranged this interview."

Oh, for . . . "Un-arrange it! But replace it with something good so Mason doesn't suspect—something ego stroking that'll make them both happy. Because if Mason suspects, then the Shadowlord will suspect and he'll take you out. Right now, he's thinking this world is his oyster—whatever the hell shellfish has to do with anything—and we don't want him to un-mellow. He's a lot less dangerous when he thinks he's already won and . . ."

"You've made your point, Mr. Foster. I understand power politics and I have no desire to compete with those who do . . ." The pause dripped with distaste. ". . . magic. While I am confining Mason to the studio, what will you be doing?"

"Trying to find Arra. She's our only chance of defeating him."

"As I understand it, then, not much of a chance."

"Yeah, well, I'm not so sure. I think there's layers working here and I've almost figured what's . . . Damn!" Every time he tried to shove the last pieces into place, they slipped shadowlike from his grasp. "Look, when he got a bit of me, well, I got a bit of him—of the Shadowlord—you know, a bit, and so next to Arra, I know him better than anyone, anyone alive that is. And I know her. And, I'm outside their history, so I've got a whole new perspective on things. I just think he's putting too much effort into finding her if he's that certain she can't hurt him, so I've got to convince her that . . ."

"Mr. Foster?"

"Yeah?"

"Perhaps," CB said slowly, weighting each word, "until this is over, you should switch to decaf."

Seventeen

IT TOOK him forever to get to downtown Vancouver although Tony had to admit that saving the world by public transportation was a particularly Canadian way to do things. By the time he reached the Burrard Station, however, he was well into the "screw it, I'm buying a car" mindset. Or a bike. Something like Lee's. Except he hated getting wet and, most years, wet was the defining weather for the lower mainland. So, back to the car.

He didn't care what kind of a car.

He just needed something that wouldn't take so god-damned long to get him anywhere. *Hey! I'm trying to find a wizard and save the world here, so could you get the fuck OUT OF MY WAY!*

A trio of elderly Asian women shot a variety of worried glances at him and shuffled to one side, clearing his path from the station to the street. He thought about apologizing, had no idea what he'd be apologizing for since he was about ninety percent certain he hadn't actually said anything out loud, and flagged down a cab. To hell with the expense; maybe CB would kick in a few bucks.

There was a police car parked in front of Arra's building when he arrived. Tony threw some money at the cabbie and raced across the road, ignoring the horns and shouted curses. Mason drove a Porsche 911, a very fast car that he drove very fast, relying on his minor celebrity to get him out of tickets, and when that didn't work, relying on the studio to pay the fines. If Mason and the Shadowlord had left just after he had, they'd have easily gotten to Arra's before him.

Hell, if they'd waited half an hour, had lunch, and then drove Zev's aging sedan into the city, they'd have easily gotten to Arra before him.

If I'm alive at this time tomorrow, I'm buying a damned car.

It was good to have goals. It made the possibility of imminent death not so imminent.

Both doors to the lobby were propped open, allowing the police to come and go as they pleased. Tony moved quickly past the elevator to the stairs—in case of trouble, stairs came with a lot more options than a sealed box hanging off cables.

No surprise upon emerging on the fourth floor to see a small crowd of murmuring tenants staring at the bright yellow police tape stretched across the front of the wizard's apartment. Staying tight against the wall, he worked his way past the edges of the audience until he could peer through the open door.

Something—someone—had pushed the metal sockets holding the latch and the dead bolt right out of the frame. And done it without putting a mark on the door. *Fucking great. Evil wizard with super-strength.*

"Can I help you with something?"

Only one profession ever wrapped such a seemingly innocuous question in so much sarcasm. Tony looked up from the damage, got a firm grip on his increasing need for profanity, and asked, "Is there a body?"

On the other side of the tape, the official police glare deepened. "Who wants to know?"

"Tony Foster. I work with the woman who lives here."

"And yet you don't seem to be at work."

No body, then. Cops at a homicide didn't take the time to exchange smart-ass observations with people hanging around the crime scene. Particularly not at a crime scene that involved a metaphysical, inexplicable death. The sudden surge of relief was intense enough to nearly buckle Tony's knees. Which was when he realized two things: One, that there didn't necessarily need to *be* a body; there had to be a hundred different ways an evil wizard could get rid of a rival that didn't involve an inconvenient corpse. And two, the cop was still waiting for a response. Tony shrugged. "She didn't come in, she didn't call. The boss sent me down to make sure she was all right."

"Uh-huh. Can anyone here vouch for you?"

Anyone here? Tony turned toward the watching/listening crowd of Arra's neighbors and spotted a familiar face. "Julian can."

Julian was ready for his close-up. At the sound of his name he pushed forward, Moira cradled in one arm. "He's been here before, Officer, with Arra Pelindrake. They do, indeed, work together." A dramatic pause. "We have spoken together, he and I."

Oh, yeah. Tony thought as the cop rolled his eyes. *I bet that was some Mustardseed.*

"I don't know why Arra didn't inform her employer she was going away for a few days," Julian continued. "We all knew."

"Well, *I* don't know why *he* knew." The new speaker was short and kind of round with her graying blonde hair cut in a bowl shape. "*I* knew because *I* was feeding her cats. I'm the one who discovered the break-in." She clutched at Tony's arm with a small plump hand. "I found it this morning when I went in to feed them."

"Are they all right?"

"Oh, yes. They're in *my* apartment now." The emphasis came with a distinct sneer in Julian's direction.

"Moira is allergic to cats."

Last night. Not the Shadowlord, then. And not Mason—so far being shadow-held hadn't come with super powers, and Mason's muscle was more show than substance. Which left—Henry.

He'd leave the question of *why* Henry had broken into Arra's apartment for after sunset and only hoped that their earlier visits had left enough fingerprints to screw up any kind of an investigation. Had Arra been here when the vampire arrived? Had Henry locked her away somewhere so she couldn't run? Probably not. If she'd been out and around, free to make up her own mind, there was at least a chance she'd have shown up at the gate this morning—Henry wouldn't take that chance away from him. He'd probably just been looking for her, searching her apartment for some idea of where she'd run off to.

"So you have no idea of where Ms. Pelindrake might be, or how to reach her?"

What? Oh, right, the cop. "Sorry, no." He'd hoped she was home, just hunkered down and not answering the phone. Failing that, he'd wanted to do the same thing Henry had—search the apartment for clues. He'd had no plan for actually getting into the apartment, but it seemed Henry'd taken care of that for him—if the police would just haul ass out of his way.

And right on cue . . .

"Right, we're done." Cop number two appeared behind his partner. "Television's there, TiVo's there, computer's there, seventy bucks in a dish on the coffee table—if it was a burglary, they were after something specific and small."

"No way of knowing until Ms. Pelindrake reappears." Turning his attention back to the crowd, he swept it with a patronizing expression although he'd probably intended said expression to be stern. Not the first cop Tony'd ever met who didn't know the difference. "The moment any of you hears from her, have her call the station. You all have the number."

Since Tony had no intention of having Arra call the station if found, the fact he didn't have the number was irrelevant. *Okay, or not.* As he didn't seem to have an option, he took the offered business card and stepped back out of the way as both constables ducked under the tape, pulling the apartment door closed behind them.

"There's a locksmith on the way," Julian informed them. "I'll personally see to it that no one crosses that tape."

"The tape? Right." Cop number two turned and pulled it off the door. "We're done here. Can't just leave this stuff lying around. People use it for the damnedest things."

Cop number one murmured something too low to be overheard and they laughed together in a manly way as they stepped into the elevator. By the time the doors shut behind them, Tony, Julian, Moira, and the woman with Arra's cats were alone in the hall.

Julian's lip curled. "Assholes."

"No argument from me," Tony muttered. Faggot comments had a distinct tone of their own. No need to hear the actual words. And while they were sharing this moment of solidarity . . . "Listen, Julian, there's a chance that Arra may have left something about where she was going in the calendar on her computer. We ought to have a look."

The "we" was almost enough.

"If I don't find her, she could lose her job."

Which was more or less the truth.

"No." The woman with Arra's cats shook her head. "*I* don't think that's a good idea."

And that settled it.

Julian shifted the Chihuahua to his other arm and pushed the door open. "I'm the president of the co-op board and *I* think we should do everything we can to help a neighbor keep her job."

"Well, when I was president . . ."

"You *were* the president, Vera. You aren't now."

Moira growled an agreement.

Tony ignored all three of them and headed toward the computers, moving slowly enough to give the place a thorough once over. No shadows where they shouldn't be. No inexplicable stains. The laptop was gone, but the desktop was exactly where he remembered it although he couldn't remember ever having seen one of Arra's computers without a game of spider solitaire running. And, as it turned out, he couldn't get into her documents without a password.

"*I* think the police should be doing this!"

His escort had caught up.

"The police can't crack her computer without a warrant. I know. I was on *DaVinci's Inquest.*"

"Years ago and you were a corpse!"

Tony tuned out the argument and typed in "ZazuWhitby."

When it worked, there was a gratifying intake of breath from Julian. "How did you know?"

"Those cats are the only things she cares about." Working the mouse with his right hand, he dragged his phone out of his pocket with his left and thumbed the speed dial. Still no answer from her cell. Pity. He'd had a sudden idea that involved telling her he was taking both cats to the Shadowlord. That'd get her thumb out of her ass PDQ.

Nothing on her calendar. It didn't look like she ever used her calendar.

She *was* using 100GB of a 120GB hard drive—although at least 30G of that seemed to be porn. *Didn't need to know that. It's like finding out your parents had sex.* Totally fucking creepy. Literally.

He double-clicked a bitmap file labeled Gate and an almost familiar pattern of swirls and equations appeared on the screen. It seemed to be the same pattern he'd glimpsed on her computer at the studio. It was definitely *not* the same pattern written on the blackboards on the other side of the gate, even given that part of it had been covered by . . .

"*I* don't think you should be looking at her private things."

Smoke and Shadows ♠ 341

"You're right." He closed it out, grateful to have the memory interrupted. No doubt she had a copy of the gate file on the laptop. Probably why she'd taken the laptop with her.

Her wallpaper was a sunset over water. *Yeah, great. Very helpful.* As far as Tony was concerned, all water looked the same.

"What are you doing?" Tucked in behind his left shoulder, Julian seemed to require a play-by-play.

"She obviously likes this picture, right?" He clicked through the control panel and into design to get the jpeg's name, then into Arra's photos. "I want to see if it's local." There were two dozen similar pictures of sunsets in the folder labeled Kitsalano Point.

"Kitsalano Point, it's that part of Kits Beach just west of the Maritime Museum, that part that pokes out into the bay."

Yeah, that would be why they call it a point. Couldn't be Sunset Beach which was maybe six blocks away. It had to be across the fucking creek. Still, it was a place to start.

"Are you going to look for her there?"

"Thought I might."

"Do you want a drive?"

Okay that was unexpected. "I thought you had to wait for the locksmith. President and everything . . ."

Julian dropped his attention to the dog. "Right."

"Look, if you boys want to go off together, *I'll* stay and wait for the locksmith."

"No, that's okay, it's my responsibility." Shifting Moira to his other arm, he held out his hand. "Good luck, Tony. I hope you find her."

"Yeah. Me, too." For all his affectations, Julian's hand-shake was surprisingly firm. *Must've missed that one when he was filling in the stereotypes form.*

"Wait!" Vera grabbed at his arm. "Your name is Tony?"

"Yes . . ."

"Tony Foster?"

"Yes . . ."

"How silly of me." Her giggle suggested they should agree with the assessment. "I heard you tell the police your name, but it never sank in. If you're Tony Foster, Arra left you a letter. I found it when I went to feed the cats, but then this whole burglary put it out of my mind. It's in my apartment, I didn't, of course, have a chance to mail it. Is it short for Anthony?"

"Is what?"

"Tony. Is it short for Anthony?"

"Yes. It is. My letter?"

"Wait here." A pat on the place she'd grabbed. "I'll get it."

Back in the hall, the two men and the dog watched Vera scuttle off to her apartment.

"You're thinking of strangling her, aren't you?" Julian asked conversationally.

"Oh, yeah."

♠

The letter was no help at all. It didn't tell him where she was. It didn't tell him what to do. It didn't offer anything but more excuses.

What point in trying when loss is foreseen . . .

Nice attitude, old woman.

"The point of trying is trying!"

"You have a fortune cookie back there?"

"What?" Tony stared at the back of the cabbie's head for a moment. "Uh, no. Just thinking out loud."

"Do or do not, there is no try!"

"What?"

"Yoda."

"Right." That would make him Luke Skywalker, Amy could be Princess Leia, Henry'd have to be Han Solo riding to the rescue at the last minute, the Shadowlord had that whole Darth Vader thing down although he was significantly better looking, and Arra could be the irresponsible old wizard who chicken shitted away from a fight without even considering that she was fucking taking it somewhere else and now that it had found her was bailing on the whole goddamned mess!

"Please do not drive your fingers through my upholstery."

"Sorry."

Less caffeine might have been a good idea.

Tony had the cab let him off at the corner of Ogden and Maple, which put him west of the museum and shortened his walk out onto the point. He hoped like hell he didn't have to search the whole beach. It was a big damned beach and even given the crappy weather lately, it was still pretty busy. Not so crowded as it would be in high summer when an oiled sun worshiper couldn't change position without flipping the whole row, but there were bodies on the sand, at least one volleyball game that he could see, and, if he listened carefully, he could hear the grunts of the body builders heading for hernias. Squinting into the sun, he could see heads bobbing in the choppy water like sea otters. Oh, wait. Those were sea otters.

He had sand in his shoes, the late afternoon light bouncing off the bay was making his eyes water even behind his sunglasses, and he was in a significantly bad mood by the time he was out on the point.

No Arra.

"God fucking damn it!" He dropped down cross-legged and stared west. Since he was here, maybe he should take a moment to think quietly. To try and put all the pieces together. Yanking his phone out of his pocket, he punched in the personal and very private number CB'd given him.

"Not even my ex-wives have this number. Do not abuse it."

"I won't. I swear."

"Profanity will not be necessary." Tony'd stared at him in confusion. *"That was a joke, Mr. Foster."*

CB answered on the second ring. "Where are you?" he demanded.

Tony swallowed, trying to force his heart down out of his throat. "How did you . . . ?"

"Call display."

Right. Idiot. "I'm at Kits Beach. On the point."

"Why?"

"Arra apparently liked it here."

"I see. And is she there?"

His mouth open to form the negative, Tony paused. Frowned. Changed his response for no reason he could have given except that he suddenly wasn't . . . *sure*. "I don't know yet. Is Mason . . . ?"

"Mason has been taken care of. I rescheduled the interview and arranged to shoot a new pitch piece to take down into the American markets."

"Mason would give his right nut to have the show picked up by a big station."

"Indeed. There's also a photographer coming in to take shots for magazine ads."

"You're doing magazine ads?" The studio had never been willing to spend the money on the glossies before.

"No."

It was amazing how much CB managed to cram into two letters. A negative. A warning of lines about to be crossed. Impatience that Tony had no answers yet. A willingness to take matters into his own hands if it came down to it.

It might.

Tony supposed he should be happy he wasn't about to die alone. Except that he really didn't want to die at all. And CB would likely end up shadow-held not dead—lots more shadow effective to take over the guys in charge. Unless . . . He chewed at his lower lip. Unless the personalities of the people in charge were strong enough to be a threat. *Fuck, I'd hate to be the shadow trying to hold Chester Bane.*

"Mr. Foster."

"Yeah. Sorry." Looked like he wasn't going to be dying alone after all.

"I suspect that many of the people here are no longer in my employ. When Mr. Swan . . ."

It took Tony a moment to remember who Mr. Swan was. *The Shadowlord held out a hand. "Michael Swan."*

". . . wants to know something, the answers he gets are detailed. Fawning. When he makes a suggestion, it is followed."

Peter, Adam, Tina . . .

"Lee?"

"I don't know. As far as I can tell, he seems to be concerning himself mainly with the crew—Mason excepted, of course. He's fascinated with television, how it works, what it can do, and has every intention of going with Mason to the interview tomorrow."

"Then maybe you should have rescheduled it for a little further away!" Tony yelped, his voice shrill enough to garner a response from a passing gull.

"That would have made Mason very suspicious. We stop this tonight. Before he leaves the studio. Find Arra. Bring her here."

Only Chester Bane could cut a connection quite so definitively.

Find Arra. Bring her here.

"Oh, yeah, like that's the easy part," he muttered at the phone before slipping it back into his pocket.

Unwilling to leave—not sure why but trusting his instincts—Tony swept his gaze over the beach, north then south. If asked, he'd probably say he was waiting. Actually, since he didn't know anyone in the immediate area, if asked, he'd probably tell the nosy bastard to fuck off.

What was he waiting for?

"Who the hell knows."

The otters were gone and the water offered no immediate answers. He shimmied himself into a more comfortable position. Seemed like he was going to be here for a while. The sand was dry and warm and Tony scooped up a handful, pouring it slowly into his other palm; then back again, and again, the action mesmerizing. He'd never really watched the way sand moved before; all the tiny pieces falling . . .

. . . into . . .

. . . place.

Amy'd asked the right question. What's his motivation?

"Not conquest—not until I gave him that new and exciting tailor-made for a Shadowlord way to use television to reach the masses. No, if all he wanted was to conquer and destroy and enslave, he could have done that any time to any world the moment he worked out the gates and he hasn't." The shadow had been fairly clear on the whole searching thing. "He's been searching seven years for this particular world. For the wizard who got away."

A young gull, its feathers still mottled brown stared at him curiously, decided the noise didn't involve eating, and moved on.

"And while he's definitely—as Arra pointed out—a vindictive bastard, he's not just tying up loose ends. He's put way too much effort into this for that. It took him seven years to piece together the bits of information she left behind. Getting what information he could from those last two . . ." Tony swallowed, seeing them again, seeing them like he saw them every time he closed his eyes. "A guy like that—a guy who can do something like that—doesn't put this kind of work into a project without a bigger payoff than dotting the i's and crossing the t's. He has a gradational scale of minions, for God's sake, he's very much the center of his own universe! For all this, he has to believe she's a danger to him."

Tony tossed aside the old handful of sand—it had lost that silky, sun-warmed feel—watched the pattern the wind made as it caught the grains, and scooped up a new one.

"He came himself. He didn't trust this to minions. You

know something, Arra. Something that can hurt him. Big magic's complicated, it's all math and patterns and you have to write it down to work it out. Big magic like the gate. Big magic like whatever's written on a blackboard he hasn't erased for seven years."

The sand wasn't enough now. The pieces coming together were bigger. Tony tossed his second handful after the first, then started sifting stones out of the beach and piling them one on top of the other. "What did you call it that day in the car? The light of Your-a-manatu or something? You woke up and yelled it out like it was important. Like it was a eureka moment. You wizards, that order of yours, worked out something you thought could stop him. But you did that crystal ball thing and saw that it didn't work." A hand against his pocket. The letter crinkled. "You saw him win and you believed what you saw and you ran. The last two wizards weren't enough. Self-fulfilling prophecy."

The stone on top of the pile was about as big around as a twonie and maybe twice as thick.

"Just . . ."

The stone felt good in his hand.

". . . like . . ."

Tony drew back his arm.

". . . this . . ."

And threw the stone as hard as he could off to his left toward the water. Off the way the wind had been blowing the sand.

". . . TIME!"

"OW!" Rubbing her shoulder, a hummock of beach became a wizard who turned and glared at him. "I didn't decide to gate until after I cast the stones and saw him win countless times."

"I think that deep down you decided to bail when your eldest got flamed." He picked up another stone. "I think you'd been second to him for a whole lot of years, got used to thinking that he was the better wizard, the best even, and when he was taken out, it all came down on you. They wanted *you* to save them now and you cracked under the pressure. That's what I think."

Arra clutched at her laptop case so tightly her knuckles whitened. "You don't know what you're talking about!"

"Yeah?" The beach had gone quiet. Even the waves were whispering against the shore. Tony stood, walked across the sand, and dropped to one knee so his eyes and Arra's were level. "You know how I survived on the street for five years? I heard all the bits and pieces that everyone else heard, but *I* put them together. *I* figured out what they meant. You tell me one thing I've gotten wrong. One thing."

The silence continued.

Then a gull screamed and noise rushed back in to fill the spaces.

"It's the Light of *Yeramathia!*" Arra snapped. "Not Your-a-manatu."

"Fine." He sat down, yanked some room into his jeans, and crossed his legs. "One *other* thing."

"This time isn't at all like that time. This time there's only one wizard, not three. Or two."

Tony shrugged. "He thinks there's a chance you can beat him or he wouldn't have put this much work into finding you. Besides, new world—new rules."

"What are you talking about? He's evil; he doesn't follow rules!"

"Not those kind of rules." He had to believe she was being deliberately obtuse. "You told me it takes time to learn to manipulate the energy of a new world. You've had the time; you've had seven whole years that he hasn't. All he has are shadows."

"All he has?" Arra snorted.

"Yeah, and if we don't stop him by tomorrow evening, he'll control everyone who watches *Live at Five.*"

"What?"

The expression on her face was everything he could

have hoped for. "It's a two-for-one deal—double your pleasure, double your fun. It's a search for you and it's a conquest. Hell, for all I know it could also be a dessert topping."

"Tony!"

"He'll probably do the people who produce *Live*, too, come to think of it—that'll give him access to their studio, the morning show, the noon show, the news, and a whole lot more people."

"Tony, what the hell are you talking about?"

"Television." He buried his fingers in the sand. "Shadows made of light. Your Shadowlord's going to use it to create enough shadow-held to find you, help destroy you, and then take over the world. Henry said it way back in your apartment: evil is never content with what it has. It has to keep moving, keep acquiring."

"He doesn't know anything about television!"

"He knows what I know. And he's a smart guy with access to everyone in the studio; he's figuring it out."

Her eyes widened. "He's in the studio? He's here?"

It was Tony's turn to stare for that long moment. Arra seemed to be doing her best to make him believe that she wouldn't be sitting here if she'd only known it had gotten that bad. Just another lie to make it easier to live with herself. With what she'd done. *Lie to yourself if you have to, but leave me out of it.* "Don't give me that crap. You had to have felt him come through the gate this morning. You couldn't have missed that kind of an energy . . ." There was a word. He couldn't think of it. ". . . thing. You had to have known he was here while you were moping around getting sand in your knickers." And drawing gate patterns with a stick, he realized suddenly. Reaching out in front of her, he rubbed them out with the side of his hand. "What you might *not* know is that the moment you open the gate, he'll know where you are and he'll be on you like a dirty shirt."

"And you know so much, Mr. Smart-ass!" She shook

her head, looking old as the burst of anger faded. "As it happens, you're right; he'll know, but he won't be able to manipulate enough energy to jump here."

"He doesn't have to." Tony pointed at a gull's shadow skimming over the beach. "He controls shadows."

"Not the ones he hasn't touched."

The shadow of Tony's arm lying on the sand, waved. Tony stopped waving as Arra got the point. "He's touched me. A couple of times. Touched me; touched my shadow. That's why he let me leave, knowing what I know about him. Because of what he knows about me. Why should he exert himself to find you when I will? Especially since *when* I find you, he has a weapon handy."

Arra's pale eyes narrowed as she stared at a darker patch of sand. "So you're a threat to me. I could remove that threat."

"I don't think he'll do anything until you try to gate," Tony told her hurriedly. This was the weak point in his presentation. She could take him out and open the gate and leave this world. Except that running was one thing. Killing a friend . . . ally . . . coworker, at the very least . . . first was something else again. He hoped. Apparently, the Shadowlord thought so. Or at least he thought Arra thought so because evidence suggested he was definitely the kind of guy who'd cheerfully skin a friend, ally, or coworker alive. "If you'd gone before I found you, you'd have probably been fine."

"You knew that and you came after me anyway?" she asked, lifting her gaze to Tony's face. The clear subtext in both tone and expression said, *I don't like being manipulated.*

"Actually, I just figured that out. Just now." He nodded toward his shadow. It had seemed so obvious when he saw it moving across the sand. "Like right now. Thirty seconds ago." When she seemed at least partially convinced, he added, "Why didn't you?"

"Why didn't I leave? I don't know."

"For the same reason you hung around the gate, knowing he'd find you eventually. Because you're basically a decent person and the guilt's been eating at you for seven years."

"Shut up."

The fabric covering her shoulder felt damp under his hand and he wondered how long she'd been sitting there. "You've got a second chance, the chance you've been waiting for. Hoping for. We can take him."

"We?"

"You and me and CB. And Henry." He nodded toward the west where the sun was still a good distance above the horizon. "Sunset's not until 8:00, but that'll give us time to prepare."

"And the Shadowlord will wait patiently while we marshal our forces against him?"

If the level of sarcasm was any indication, she was starting to perk up.

"He might think you have a chance, but he believes he can win." Tony flicked up a finger. "He thinks you believe the same thing and that's what gave him the TKO in round one." A second finger joined the first. "He's already told me I'm no threat to him." Finger three. "And besides, CB waved some shiny stuff in front of Mason that'll keep him on the soundstage until late. He needs Mason to get on *Live at Five*." He folded the fingers into a fist and shook it out as Arra snorted derisively.

"He doesn't need Mason if he has CB."

"Would you try taking over CB if there was another option?"

"Valid point." She sighed and stared out over the water. "I love it here. It reminds me of home. The sky, the water, the smells, the sounds . . . I just look straight ahead and pretend that if I turn around I'll see the city walls and not half a dozen broiled bimbos courting melanoma. How did you find me?"

He told her about the picture on the computer.

"Very clever, but not what I meant. When you were

sitting back there, behind me, how did you know I was here?" One palm patted the sand. "Right here."

"I don't know." Although he'd definitely known she was there when he threw the stone. "I just did."

"Uh-huh."

"Honestly. I have no idea." He made a mental note to get freaked about that later.

The same juvenile gull wandered past again, gave them a dirty look, and took to the air.

Arra watched him fly, her eyes squinted nearly shut.

"You should have sunglasses on."

"Because you know everything." She snorted explosively, then squared her shoulders and snapped. "Do you really think we can beat him or are you just throwing words at me in a desperate attempt to get me to help?"

Yes. "I think this time you're going to have to fight him regardless. You open a gate, he'll come through shadow and stop you."

"Or I could kill you to clear the shadow away and then gate safely."

"And he'll have won because you'll have become him. Like him. Evil.

She raised a hand as he searched for other synonyms. "Yeah, I get it."

"Good. Because if you have to face him, why not go in believing you'll win?"

Tony half expected her to say: *Because we won't*.

She surprised him.

"All right. I won't fight for you. But I'll fight beside you."

"All I'm asking."

"I know."

"It was all I was *ever* asking."

"I know. Now help me up. I've got to get my cats back from that idiot Vera before they convince her that they always have fresh salmon for dinner."

"And yet you were going to leave them with her when you bailed."

Her hand tightened almost painfully around his as he helped her to her feet. "Don't push it, boy."

"Sorry."

She tucked her arm into his as they walked toward the parking lot, graciously allowing him to support more and more of her weight as they traveled. Tony suspected she was making a point, but since he had no idea what that point was, he just braced himself and kept going. Maybe she was just making sure he wouldn't drop her. *Yeah, of the two of us, I'm the only one who's never run out on an entire world. I won't be the one doing the dropping.* Maybe she was just being a pain in the ass because she could.

The latter seemed more likely.

"I know something else about the Shadowlord," he said as the muscles in his arm started to protest. "Something you don't know."

"You have no idea what I know."

"He's gay."

"You're right, I didn't know that." Shifting her weight, she leaned far enough away to sneer up at him. "However, he's an evil wizard from another world; I doubt very much your gaydar applies."

"Never doubt the gaydar," Tony snorted as they stepped over the concrete divider and into the parking lot. "But that's not it. I told you, he's touched me. I mean, talk about queer eye on the straight guy—every time I come in contact with a straight boy that's being shadow-held, they go after my ass."

"Do they now?"

"They do."

"So that would be Lee and Mouse and Ben . . ."

"Technically Ben just winked at me, but yeah." He really didn't like the speculative sound she made as they reached the car. With any luck, it was about the car. Not that his luck had been great of late.

"Maybe it's not them. Maybe it's your ass." Arra leaned back, looked down, and made a small dismissive moue. "And then again, maybe not. Did you happen to mention that CB has his memory back?"

"I didn't, exactly, but he does."

A raised brow invited him to continue.

"I retraced the paper. Like he did for me." Might as well spread the reaction around.

"Did he now?"

"Yeah. He's kind of pissed."

"No doubt. How fortunate, then, that I'm probably going to my certain death."

Eighteen

"UH, ARRA, that's a new lock. Remember, I told you about the break-in."

"I'm not senile, boy." She paused and tossed a twisted grin at him over her shoulder. "At least you'd better hope I'm not, all things considered." The key turned smoothly and she pushed open the apartment door. "You put the supplies in the kitchen; I'm going to rescue my cats."

Wondering whether it was wise for her to waste energy on something that could be solved by a visit to Julian—and the next instant realizing that the thought of a visit to Julian was probably why she'd done it that way—Tony set the two bags of groceries and the single bag from the liquor store on the counter. By the time he heard the door open again, he had the frozen dinners in the oven and the coffeemaker on. A bottle of vodka in each hand, he watched both cats stalk down the hall, noses in the air and tails lashing from side to side.

"I thought they'd be glad to see you," he said as the wizard came into the kitchen.

Arra snorted. "You've never had cats, have you? Put those down; we'll eat first, then you can put the potion together while I try to remember just how the Light of Yeramathia goes."

"*Try* to remember?"

"Give me a break." She pulled the coffeepot out and

shoved a mug under the drip. "It's been seven years, it was a joint effort originally, and it may have to be adapted for local conditions."

"Yeah, but . . ."

"But what?"

Good question. "Nothing." Wait. Something. "*I'm* to put the potion together?"

"That's right. Better make a double batch, we're probably going to have to pour it down the throats of the entire crew. Those that survive anyway."

"But . . ."

"Until the final . . ." A spark leaped off her fingertip. ". . . zap, it's nothing more than organic chemistry—no more complicated than putting together a decent salsa."

"I don't cook," he protested, shooting a wary glance at her fingers.

"You do now." She took a long swallow of coffee and peered at him over the edge of the mug. "I'm not doing this on my own; that was the deal."

"I'll fight with you, not for you."

"Yeah, that was the deal, but . . ." Fuck, he wished people would stop staring at him. If he hesitated, if now she was willing to fight he even once suggested it was all up to her, she'd bail. Guilt or no guilt, she was still on the edge; he could see it in her eyes. "Okay, fine. I'll make the damned potion. What's the recipe?"

Arra shrugged and bent down to peer into the oven. "You know the ingredients, just use as much as seems right to you. How long until these things are ready? I'm starving."

♣

Tony stared down into the pot of heated vodka and took a cautious sniff. Mostly, it smelled like catnip and since that's what this potion mostly smelled like when Arra made it, he supposed it smelled like it was supposed to. What kind of measurement was . . .*as much as seems right to you* anyway?

"So much for wizardry being an exact science."

Arra had paused on her way out of the kitchen. *"It's not a science at all, kid, it's an art. It's like television—art and science blended."*

Knowing how big a part luck played in making good TV, comparing it to wizardry didn't exactly inspire confidence. As far as he was concerned, a world where Joss Whedon got canceled was exactly the kind of world where the Shadowlord could win.

The contents in the second pot weren't quite the same shade of green. He tossed in another bay leaf and a few more flakes of catnip, changed his mind and attempted to scoop them out again. Unsuccessfully. Sucking his fingers, he realized he should have used a spoon.

"I told her I didn't know what I was doing," he muttered down at Whitby.

Whitby stretched out a paw and languidly poked Tony in the ankle.

He sprinkled a few more flakes of catnip on the cat. Getting stoned seemed like a good idea to him, but since that wasn't an option, he'd have to mellow vicariously.

Someone knocked on the apartment door.

Tony checked his watch. Not quite 4:30—way too early for Henry and Julian had already been by. Twice. Which didn't, of course, rule out the fact that this could be Julian dropping by again.

He turned both pots down to simmer and hurried toward the door. Arra had made it quite clear after Julian's second visit that a third would result in the Shadowlord knowing exactly where she was because she'd open a gate to the world of annoying gits and return her unwelcome visitor to his own kind. And his little dog, too.

A second knock as Tony's fingers closed around the door handle convinced him to yank it open immediately. He very much doubted Arra *would* open a gate but, as the lock, the spark, and the incident with the litter box had proven, she could do smaller magics without attracting unwelcome attention.

"Look, Julian, you've got to sto . . ." Propelled by Keisha's fist, the final consonant exploded out of him along with all the air remaining in his lungs. Gasping for breath, he was able to offer little resistance as the set dresser shoved him up against the wall, his head impacting against the drywall with a distinct crunch.

"So here you are." Her forearm up against his throat, she leaned a little closer. Her dark eyes gleamed. "I was wondering who'd find you first."

Shadow-held.

Holy obvious observation, Batman.

"You don't have to do this."

"Do what? Kick your ass?"

As her knee came up, Tony brought his own leg up and around, hooking hers while simultaneously slamming her on the opposite the side of her head with his elbow. Between the double blows she went down. He followed her to the floor, landing on her torso as hard as he dared.

Keisha grunted, reached between his legs, grabbed a handful of crotch, and squeezed.

Tony yowled. Rearing back, he clutched at her arm with both hands and tried to free himself from her grip. Free her grip from him. Stop the pain!

When his balls dragged away from his body with her fingers, he changed his plan of attack. Unless he could knock her out and take the shadow controlling her out of play, just hitting her wouldn't do any good. Catching her free hand around the wrist, he pinned it to the floor then, twisting his body as much as the pain allowed, began to tickle her exposed side.

The release hurt almost as much as the initial grab and he yowled again as blood flowed suddenly back into abused tissue. Bright side, he hardly felt the back of Keisha's fist drive the edge of his lower lip in over his teeth reopening the cut he'd received during his earlier dance with Mouse. Her hips canted up between his thighs, throwing him forward, off-balance. Barely managing to keep from kissing the linoleum, his weight slammed down on his elbow.

"The master says we can't kill you," she growled, her teeth closing around his ear. "But we can hurt you."

If he yanked his head away, he'd lose a piece of his ear. *Jesus FUCK!*

If he *didn't*, he'd lose a piece of his ear.

Tony could feel warm and wet running down his neck and he really hoped Keisha was drooling.

Something was making a strange half growling, half howling noise. He didn't think it was Keisha. He punched her in the stomach. She grunted and grabbed his wrist. Small bones ground together. The noise continued uninterrupted. Nope, not Keisha. Him?

"Keisha!"

A small eraser bounced off the set dresser's close-cropped hair and hit him on the cheek.

"Go to sleep!"

Her mouth separated from his ear with a wet slurp. Her left leg settled slowly toward the floor. Her hand fell from his wrist. Tony clamped it immediately on his ear.

"Stop being such a baby." Arra's voice sounded both muffled and annoyed. "It seems a little over the top after you had someone deliberately jab a hole through your eyebrow."

"Not the same thing," he muttered, checking his palm. Damp but not bloody. As Keisha sighed under him, he pushed himself carefully up onto his knees.

"Zazu, be quiet!"

The growling howl stopped.

Reaching behind him, Tony untangled a long leg from around his. The moment he was clear, he fell to one side, crawling away until he could brace his back against the wall, cradling all his injured bits close. "Is she . . . ?"

"She's fine," Arra told him as she stared down at the

younger woman. "Physically anyway. Unless you did damage."

"I *took* damage." And as soon as he got the chance, he was heading for the bathroom to check things out. They still fucking hurt!

"The shadow-held aren't stronger than they were before, but they have no inhibitions. They have no fear of injury, so they hold nothing back."

He picked the eraser up off the floor. "So what was this for?"

"To get her attention."

"Right." And then he remembered. "You said she's physically fine. What isn't?"

"What isn't what?"

"Fine."

"Ah. Yes." Arra pressed her lips together into a thin line, all color leaching out. "It's like this," she began just as Tony thought she wasn't going to answer him. "Putting Keisha to sleep involved her energies only—it's undetectable at a distance. The shadow is still in there, confined. If I destroy it, the Shadowlord will know immediately where I am and I am not yet ready for him."

"You've destroyed shadows before."

"So it's true, then. Men really do think with those?" She nodded toward his crotch and he covered it instinctively. "Because you're not thinking now. The Shadowlord wasn't on this world, wasn't part of this world's energy flow before. She'll have to hold the shadow until we defeat him once and for all. And if we don't, well, she'll have worse problems than a few nightmares."

"A few nightmares?" Now he knew to look, he could see Keisha's eyes moving behind her closed lids.

"Constant nightmares."

Constant. Babies dying. Rotting. And he was the only one who could see it. Their parents kissed and hugged and played with the tiny corpses until bits started falling off. "You've got to wake her up."

Arra snorted. "And do what? Smack her on the head with a frying pan? You can't knock someone unconscious without doing damage, Tony. There's no such thing as a Vulcan neck pinch or any other tidy television solution. This is war—not everyone comes out ..."

The only sound for a long time was Keisha's labored breathing.

"... whole." Turning on one heel, Arra headed back to the dining room. "Put her on my bed. She won't wake up until I tell her to."

♣

At 5:57, Carol from the lighting crew showed up.

"If another shadow-held shows up searching for me, you'll have to let them in. They're just as likely to grab one of my neighbors and gouge an eye or something out in front of the peephole in order to get a reaction. With my luck, they'd probably grab the wrong neighbor."

"Why don't you let them in? Open the door and nighty-night them?"

"Because they'll see me and he'll know where I am. He'll have something in them set to my power signature."

"Keisha ..."

"Didn't see me. You distracted her."

"Yeah, and she sure as hell saw me!"

"Didn't you tell me that he doesn't care about you? Now go away and let me finish this. Try putting your brains on ice if they're still not working."

Tony sighed. Carol had a black belt in some kind of martial art. He hadn't been paying enough attention to the overheard conversation to know exactly which martial art but, bottom line, it didn't much matter since he had equivalent training in absolutely nothing. Plastering a fake smile on his face, he opened the door. "Hey. What's happening?"

"Don't play dumb," she snapped, pushing past him.

"All right." He grabbed her shoulder, spun her back around, and threw the contents of his mug in her face.

The coffee wasn't exactly hot, but it distracted her just long enough for him to sweep her legs out from under her and send her crashing to the floor.

Really close contact kept her from landing any serious blows, but she still beat the crap out of him.

"What took you so long?" he gasped, not being at all careful of anything but aching ribs as he crawled off of Carol's sleeping body.

"Time is relative. There's one of those gel cold packs in the freezer. Maybe you'd better use it."

"You think?" His voice already sounded higher. The way things were going, by the end of the night only dogs would be able to hear him.

♣

At 7:02, it was Elaine from craft services.

Keisha, Carol, and Elaine—the three women who'd run to comfort Lee. Wiping up his spills, holding his hand, offering comfort, and making it quite clear there was more being offered . . . Tony had to wonder if this was a message to him from the Shadowlord. If his nose was being rubbed in Lee's obvious unavailability.

A sudden chill ghosted down Tony's spine. Or was the message that Lee was at the studio with the Shadowlord, unprotected?

Elaine knocked again.

And, nice change, she went for his eyes not his balls.

"Put her on the bed with the others."

"Yeah, yeah," he muttered, patting the bleeding scratch on his cheek. "What did your last servant die of?"

Arra's eyes lost their focus for a moment. "One of my order killed him while shadow-held. She melted his bones and left him lying in a fleshy puddle in the great hall. Without structure enough to scream, he died gurgling."

Fighting the urge to vomit, Tony reached down and tucked his hands in Elaine's armpits. He had a vague memory of deliberately not asking that question earlier.

Apparently, his instincts had temporarily deserted him. Smart instincts. If he didn't *have* to be around, he wouldn't be. "You suck as a motivational speaker. You know that, right?"

"You asked."

He laid Elaine out as comfortably as he could beside Carol and Keisha and stared down at them for a moment, hating to leave them trapped. Tormented. Keisha had cried out half a dozen times. Carol's head almost continually jerked from side to side on the pillow. Unfortunately, if even the glare of light in the elevator hadn't been enough to destroy his hitchhiker, there was no way anything in the entire co-op would affect, let alone destroy, these shadows. Well, nothing except Arra and she was saving herself for the final battle. At least, that was the benefit of the doubt explanation.

"I'm sorry," he told them, as Elaine began to tremble. "It's just . . ." Just what? He sighed. "It's just, I'm sorry."

Arra was packing up her laptop as he came out of the bedroom, "Have you worked it out, then?" he asked her, as she slid it into the case. "The light thing?"

"Yes, I have. I charged the potion while you were in with the girls; seal it up and let's get going."

"It's still early. Henry won't be awake for another forty minutes."

"You told him to meet us at the studio?"

"Well, yeah, but . . ."

"I won't be using any power during the drive. We'll be moving more slowly than usual."

That was the best news Tony'd had in days.

"And," Arra continued, swinging her laptop case over her shoulder, "the shadow-held will have a lot more trouble finding us if we're in a moving vehicle. Charging the potions may have created enough of an energy blip to alert him."

Made sense, they were anti-shadow potions and if *he* was the Shadowlord, he'd be watching for something like that. Tony sealed up the four thermoses—they'd bought two new ones with the groceries—and packed them quickly away in his backpack. Then he went for the elevator while Arra locked up and set wards.

"Think of a ward like a spiderweb made of energy," she'd explained earlier when he'd asked. *"Some webs warn the spider there's prey nearby, some capture it."*

"And you're the spider?"

She'd snorted impatiently. *"No, I'm the walrus. I thought I told you to put those on ice?"*

The elevator was taking its own sweet time arriving. A door opened. A familiar yap drove through his eardrums and straight into his brain.

"Julian . . ."

Tony spun around, ready to intervene, but the wizard was smiling almost benignly across the hall toward her neighbor. "Would you mind telling anyone you hear knocking on my door that I've gone to Victoria? With Tony." She gestured.

Julian and Moira leaned out of the doorway to look. Tony waved.

"Victoria?"

"Yes. There's no point in them knocking and knocking and knocking and disturbing everyone on this floor, is there?"

"If you're not home, they can't get in," Julian pointed out archly. "You can't buzz them up."

Moira yapped agreement and Tony wondered how the Shadowlord felt about dogs.

"You and I both know there are ways around that. At the last board meeting you were trying to put more money into security."

"You weren't at the last board meeting."

"I read the minutes. Thank you for your assistance." The elevator announced its arrival. "We'll be going now."

Julian followed.

Eyes rolling, Arra shoved Tony inside, turned and hit

the "close door" button. "Remember: Victoria with Tony," she said as Julian's and Moira's disapproving expressions disappeared.

"Do you think he'll do it?"

"He might."

"Why Victoria?"

"Why not? The farther the shadow-held are from the studio, from where he can call on them for help, the better."

"Will Julian be all right? I mean, will he be in any danger," Tony corrected as Arra's lip curled.

"Hard to say. Depends on whether or not they think he knows more than he's saying. Do I have to keep repeating that this is war?"

"No."

"Do I have to make the observation about omelets and breaking eggs?"

"God, no!"

"Good. It's a stupid observation."

Traffic was heavy on Hastings until they cleared Chinatown, then it spread out and started moving a few kilometers above the limit. Tony drummed his fingers against his thigh and tried not to think of what they were heading toward.

War.

Broken eggs.

Around Clark Drive South, he frowned. "You were working that light thing out on a laptop."

"So?"

"So we could have been in a moving vehicle all afternoon. I drive, you work."

Arra nodded agreement. "Yes, I thought of that after Keisha arrived."

"And?"

"And then I realized I work best in a familiar environment."

Tony stared at the side of her face. "I had to beat up girls," he said at last.

"That's a bit sexist, don't you think?"

"No."

"And given the results, not entirely accurate. There're still *girls* at the studio," she added when he didn't respond.

"Your point?"

The brow he could see lifted into a distinctly sardonic arch.

"Never mind." He glanced at his watch. "I'd better call CB. Make sure the Shadowlord's even still at the studio. Maybe he's convinced Mason to take him clubbing."

"I thought CB had arranged to have promo shots done?"

"Yeah. So?"

"So, it would take more than an extraordinarily powerful, evil wizard to keep Mason Reed from having his picture taken."

"Valid point." CB's cell phone rang half a dozen times before he answered. Worried that the boss might be standing where he could be overheard by the enemy, Tony started talking immediately. *Safest if he just has to answer yes or no.* "Hey, CB, it's Tony. Is he still there?"

"Yes, he is." A dark, smooth voice that caressed each word. Definitely *not* CB's voice. "And he's wondering what's taking you so long."

The line went dead.

Tony dropped his phone like it was contaminated. "He's got CB."

"The Shadowlord answered CB's phone?"

"Yeah."

"Tell me exactly what he said." She frowned as Tony told her. "He's posturing. Trying to frighten you. Rattle you."

"News flash. It worked." His palms left damp streaks on his jeans.

"Yes, but if he'd said nothing at all, you'd have kept talking. Probably said you were with me. Said we were on our way." Her voice trailed off and she drummed her fingers on the steering wheel. "This isn't like him," she announced three blocks later. "He could have gathered information, but he didn't—he played boogeyman instead. That's just not like him."

"How do you know?"

"I may not have stuck around for the big finish, but I was there for the rest of the war," she snapped. "I know him."

"Uh-uh, you *knew* him," Tony amended. "You knew him when he was conquering. He's conquered. He's been 'the conqueror' for seven years. He's not the same guy you faced. Seven years—fuck, *everyone* changes over that long a time."

"Your Nightwalker?"

Tony thought of Vicki Nelson's conquest of Vancouver and snickered, amused for the first time in . . . well, since girls started smacking him around anyway. "You have no idea."

"No. *You* have no idea." But it was a playground response and she sounded unsure and Tony figured that shaking up a few of her carved-in-stone opinions about the Shadowlord was probably a good thing.

Probably.

Maybe not.

When Arra turned onto Boundary Road, he closed his eyes for a moment, confronted the fear that had been chewing at him since the call, and said, "Do you think CB's dead?"

"No. He knows too much. He could be too useful. The Shadowlord can't have changed so much he'd throw away that kind of resource."

Which would have been more reassuring had she not so obviously been trying to reassure herself.

At 8:43 the parking lot was still surprisingly full. Zev's car was gone and so was Amy's—Tony thanked any gods that might be listening for small mercies—but Lee's bike was still there.

"They're shooting promo stuff," he murmured, realizing. "Lee had to stay."

"Any new shadows will be for control, not information, so he's probably shadow-held."

Again? Oh, that's just fucking great. The thought of Lee shadow-held came with the memory of Lee's hands on his body, scrambling his responses.

"He survived it the first time," Arra reminded him, misreading his silence.

"Yeah. That's not very comforting."

She shrugged and turned off the engine.

"What do we do now?"

"Right now? We wait for your Nightwalker. No point in going over the battle plan twice."

Seat belt unbuckled, Tony twisted around so that he could see her. She looked unconcerned. Or possibly blank. Nothing showed. He was looking at the last wizard of her order, the one hope to defeat the Shadowlord—he could just as easily have been looking at someone's grandmother, parking and waiting to pick the grandkids up from school. He wanted to know what she was thinking but he couldn't see it on her face.

"So, does a gate have to be opened in a specific spot?"

"No. Variables are adjusted for location."

"So you could open a gate here?"

She turned very slowly to face him. "I could."

He really, really hoped she'd add, *But I won't.* But she didn't. "Hey, I just thought of something."

"Don't strain yourself."

She was under a lot of stress, so he'd give her that one. "If you can only affect the gate on the world of origin, how's the Shadowlord going to get home? I mean, sure this is a great world and all, but his stuff's back there and I expect he'll want to go back and forth."

"He probably has the spell set up on the other side ready to go off every twelve hours."

"He's got the gate on a timer?"

"Essentially."

"Cool. Still evil," he clarified as Arra turned to glare at him. "But cool."

"Less cool if he calls through reinforcements."

"Granted."

Henry's BMW pulled into the lot at 8:47. Tony opened his door as he parked and walked around the car to meet him beside Arra. He'd left the-story-so-far on Henry's answering machine and then sent him an e-mail as well as a text message. The whole instantaneous electronic communication thing had very little relevance to Henry—sending multiple copies of things he really needed to know worked best. Things like, *CB is holding the Shadowlord at the studio, Mason and most of the crew are shadow-held and we have to take him out tonight. Meet us there as soon as you're up.*

They not only had to take him out tonight, they had to take him out before the gate opened at 11:15. They had to take him out before he called through reinforcements. Tony hadn't asked Arra what kind of reinforcements were likely to be called through. He didn't want to know.

Henry frowned and Tony remembered he was both bruised and bleeding.

"You've been fighting again."

He shrugged, didn't bother hiding the wince as new bruises rose and fell. "I had to take down three of the shadow-held."

"Girls," Arra snorted, getting out of the car. "So." She looked from one to the other. "What's the plan?"

Tony opened his mouth to protest, but as Henry didn't seem surprised by her assumption, he closed it again. It was the son of Henry VIII, trained in strategy and tactics and, hell, probably the minuet for all Tony knew, who asked: "What do you need us to do?"

"Keep the shadow-held from taking me down." Arra began rolling her shoulders like an old boxer about to go into the ring. "Keep the Shadowlord from preventing my call to the Light of Yeramathia."

"Which is?"

Figuring he wouldn't understand the explanation, Tony hadn't bothered to ask.

Arra frowned at Henry's suspicious tone. "The Shadowlord gave himself over to a dark power, this is its opposite."

That was it? Okay, he understood that.

"A god?" If Henry'd sounded suspicious before, he sounded distinctly unhappy now.

"We've had a little trouble with gods in the past," Tony explained hurriedly before Arra's frown could deepen. "An ancient Egyptian undead wizard tried to call up his god from the top of the CN Tower. Oh, and the year before that, we had demons."

"You never thought to mention that?"

He shrugged. "It didn't seem relevant."

"It isn't. But *you* had no way of knowing that." She turned her attention back to Henry. "Yeramathia is neither god nor demon, only a power. We need to attract its attention. I will draw the calling in the air; the Shadowlord will try and stop me. The only things he controls in this world are the shadows and the shadow-held, but there are plenty of the former and the latter will fight you to the death."

"How much time will you need?"

"As long as it takes to draw the calling."

Tony rolled his eyes. Right. More obscure. "And that'll be how long?"

"Well, it's not a 1-800 number," Arra snapped.

Henry's hand closed over Tony's shoulder before the snapping could escalate. "And if it answers?"

"When it answers," Tony muttered.

"We hope it destroys the minion of its ancient enemy."

"Hope?" Tony began, but Henry's fingers tightened.

"If and hope," Henry said softly as though trying the words on for size. "Battles have been won with less. Do you believe we can win?"

With both of them staring at her, Arra shrugged. "Tony does."

And then they both moved to stare at him.

Oh, crap. No, I don't. I just think that if you have to fight—which we do—there's no percentage in going in believing you're going to lose. It's not like if we lose we can try again later. This is it. All or nothing. One final roll of the dice. The big chimichanga. And that's just fucking great, now I'm out of clichés.

Were they waiting for him to say something?

Apparently.

He sighed, squared his shoulders, and tried to think of something inspiring. "Right. Let's go."

"Not exactly the St. Crispin's speech," Henry murmured.

"The what? Never mind." He raised a hand and cut off the explanation. Knowing Henry, it was likely to be lengthy, boring, and classical. "Instead of walking in the back door like the Three Stooges, how about we split his attention. Henry, remember that up-on-the-roof-through-the-ventilation-shaft thing you wanted to do earlier?"

"Uh, no."

"Good. Now's your chance. Arra, you go in through the front doors, I'll go in through the back. Henry, you take out the shadow-held—bottom line they're still flesh and blood and you're . . ." Even in the dim light of the parking lot, he could see the vampire's eyes darken. ". . . you."

"I think," Henry said slowly, "at some point, he'll send something through that can't be killed by light. Something physical."

"You sound upsettingly happy about that."

The mask slipped. "If it has flesh and blood, I can deal with it."

"And me, I'll deal with the Shadowlord."

His shadow fell over Lee's and the Shadowlord's, wiping out the definition of the attack, leaving nothing but a formless shape of darker gray on the concrete.

"You will?"

It almost wasn't a question. Tony made a mental note to ask Arra about that later—if they survived this. "Someone has to and I'm all that's left. You . . ." He bent and picked up his backpack, swinging one strap over his shoulder. ". . . just dial."

"I have to be in his presence for this to work." Her eyes narrowed. "How do you plan on dealing with him?"

Tony shrugged. "Maybe it *is* my ass." He held up a hand to stop Henry's question and then waved them off in opposite directions, hoping the gesture was fast enough that neither of his companions could see how badly his hand was shaking. "Can we just . . . go!"

♣

Walking over the gravel made so much noise that Tony half expected a couple of the bigger guys on the crew to be waiting for him at the back door. They weren't. No one was. *See, he's cocky. No security.*

He slipped through, took his backpack off and set it safely to one side, then began moving quietly down the London street set. It didn't look much like London, but with lighting, fake fog, a filter or two . . . it probably still wouldn't look much like London. Good thing Mason preferred a lot of tight close-ups.

And speaking of close-ups, the cameras seemed to have been moved to the dining room set. Thankful for the clutter, Tony slipped across the soundstage without being seen although, the closer he got to the set, the harder it was not to be noticed.

Shit. Shooting crew and *construction crew.* More people than they'd planned on. Henry was fast and strong, but he was still only one guy. The more people he had to take out, the more likely someone would be taken out permanently. Dead.

This is such a stupid idea. What the hell was I thinking? You do this, you do that, I'll take out the Shad-

owlord. First my brain points out that Henry's the one with the training, then it totally shuts down while my mouth flaps. Delusions of grandeur or . . .

Fuck. At least I'm not the only one. Crammed into the eight or so inches between the distant view of the garden and the dining room window, Tony peered onto the set. The dining room table was gone, the cheap Persian rug had been removed, Mason's coffin was up against the opposite wall, and the throne from episode nine's the-writers-are-on-cheap-drugs Charlemagne flashback had been brought out of storage and set up at the far end of the room, leaving the area actually under the gate empty.

On the throne, still wearing the same clothes he'd dropped through the gate in, was the Shadowlord. Problem was, he didn't look like the conquering tyrant Arra made him out to be and he didn't look evil. He looked like he belonged there. Posture, attitude, expression—everything about him said, *This is my right. Serve me.*

He reminded Tony a little of Henry. Of the Prince of Man bit.

Tony felt himself responding. He'd seen something on PBS once that said nine of out ten men were looking for a strong leader to follow. The moment Henry Fitzroy had vamped into his life, he'd known he was one of the nine.

It was a small step from leader to master.

Mason Reed, still in full Raymond Dark costume and makeup was on his knees to the left of the throne, vogue-ing for the photographer setting up his shot.

Lee was to the right of the throne. Also in character. Also on his knees. As Tony watched, the Shadowlord reached out and ran his fingers through Lee's hair. Eyes closed, the actor leaned into the touch.

Tony felt himself responding to that, too. On a couple of levels. Fingers tightening on the edge of a supporting two-by-four, he decided to go with, *Get your hands off him, you fucking bastard!*

Closely followed by, *I don't get to touch. You don't get to touch!*

Where the hell was Henry?

And Arra?

Were they waiting for him?

Did he have to do everything?

Mason froze as the flash went off and the photographer set up for another shot.

He's documenting his conquest, Tony realized. Both cameras were ready to shoot the set. He could see Peter, Tina, and Sorge wrapped in discussion over at the monitors, Everett was waiting out of shot with his touch-up kit, and everyone not actually working was gathered to one side, watching. Watching the throne. Watching the photographer.

Waiting.

For the gate to open?

No, too early.

For the fight.

For him.

I guess that's my cue.

Yeah, like I'm just going to walk out there . . .

"I know you're here, Tony."

Tony's heart slammed against his ribs. *Fuck!* Excellent timing, he had to give him that.

"I have a part of you in me. You have a part of me in you."

You wish! He fought for control as the Shadowlord's voice filled the soundstage, realizing the bastard didn't know exactly where he was or there'd be more going on than just talking. He glanced down at his shadow. It quivered. *Not good.*

"We're connected. I can feel your fear. I can feel your need."

Like I need to hear your cheesy fucking dialogue?

"If you're waiting for Arra Pelindrake, I wouldn't bother. She's an old woman. I've destroyed everything she ever cared about. She's nothing. A remnant. She knows she can't destroy me just as she's always known it. If she fights with you, it's only because her guilt is driving her to end it."

There was more along the same lines, but Tony ignored it. No matter what he said, there was a chance Arra could beat him or he wouldn't be here personally making sure she was destroyed. The speech wasn't directed at him anyway, it was meant to undermine Arra's confidence. To make her run. It might even work if he didn't do something soon. He had no illusions about the depth of Arra's commitment to the cause. She was there because he was, motivated, as the Shadowlord said, by guilt. But what to do? Sneak around behind the coffin and ram him with it? Shut off the main power? Weaken the shadows in the dark? No way the Shadowlord hadn't taken care of that, though, it was way too obvious. The main breaker would definitely be guarded. Or welded.

"Shall I show you what's in store for you?"

That was directed at him again although Tony wasn't sure how he knew.

The Shadowlord gestured, Peter called, "Roll camera," and Charlie Harris stumbled out into the center of the set, clawing at his own shadow wrapped around him like a shroud.

And Tony remembered.

He couldn't move, he couldn't speak, and most importantly, he couldn't breathe. It was like being trapped under a pliable sheet of cool charcoal-gray rubber that covered him from head to foot like a second skin, curving to fit up each nostril and into his mouth. Obscenely intimate.

The Shadowlord held out his hand and the gesture drew a wisp of black from Charlie's skull. It sped across the set and into the wizard, who closed his eyes and murmured, "Just taste the terror."

Charlie fell to the floor, heels kicking against the painted plywood.

"Are you learning from this, Tony? Thousands will die this way."

Yeah, yeah. You're not just blowing smoke out your ass. I get it. His hands gripping the edge of the wall, Tony braced himself for the charge. A solid tackle, knock the air out of the son of a bitch, and maybe Charlie'd have a chance.

He was standing, left foot raised, right leg about to push off when Henry dropped from the ceiling.

Right onto the Shadowlord's lap.

The vampire reached out, wrapped his hands around the Shadowlord's head, and twisted.

The resulting flare of darkness threw him back almost to the watching crowd.

Tony froze. *Wizardy protections. You can't whack at him.*

"Deal with him."

As the shadow-held advanced on Henry, Tony remembered *he* was supposed to be dealing with the Shadowlord. But not just dealing with him, dealing with his power over shadow.

How do I stop a shadow?

Know what's real.

Light was real. Darkness was real. Light and dark. Light and absence of light.

Okay, that about does it for the options.

And then he realized he'd already given himself the answer.

You're not just blowing smoke out your ass . . .

Nineteen

TONY RACED for the back of soundstage, leaped over a half finished set of stairs, and careened around the edge of the London street set.

Unless things had changed after he'd left the studio—changed in reference to the shooting schedule as opposed to changed because there was an evil wizard hanging around—Peter'd planned on shooting the flashback scene first thing in the morning. The fate of the world depended on how much the crew'd got ready before the shadows took them over.

London streets, especially crappy thrown together at the last minute, gray paint on plywood and Styrofoam streets, needed fog. There were two 1400w pro foggers sitting at the edge of the set, a heavy orange one-hundred-and-fifty-foot extension cord curled up beside each of them. The reservoirs were full of fog juice. They were ready to go.

Cables ran everywhere in a soundstage. Praying that the Shadowlord's need to control the lights had kept the whole place live, Tony yanked the lines from the nearest socket, and plugged the foggers in.

With one in each hand, he headed back toward the gate, his palms so slick with sweat that they slid back and forth in his grip. *Don't drop them. Do* not *drop them.*

Over the sound of his new mantra, he could hear fighting.

And laughing.

And screaming.

And a self-satisfied voice enjoying the taste of the pain.

Not hard to figure out what had happened; Henry'd had to hurt someone and the Shadowlord had drawn the shadow back into himself to enjoy it. A clichéd scene that became less clichéd when real people were hurting.

Tony ran faster. And hit the ground hard, his shadow wrapped around his knees.

The fogger flew from his left hand and skidded across the floor, metal chassis shrieking against the concrete. The fogger from his right hit harder, tipped over, and was only just out of reach.

He could see the *fog ready* light on the remote.

All he had to do was reach it.

Dragging his lower body, he clawed his way forward. His fingertips touched metal just as his shadow closed over his face.

You've got a lungful of air! You've got time!

Easy to say. Harder to deal with.

Eyes covered, working in the dark, he scrabbled at the edge of the fogger, fingernails sliding off the casing. Then it moved. And a little more. He stretched past it. Reaching. Touched the remote cable. Hooked it closer.

He'd read once that lack of oxygen created an automatic panic response in the brain.

Like I need another fucking reason to panic!

There were four buttons on the remote.

As he started to thrash, unable to stop himself, needing to breathe, he pressed the largest.

The goddamned thing was too quiet to hear. And his ears were full of shadow. And it came with a fucking microprocessor, so maybe it wouldn't work flipped over on its side.

Then the shadow's grip started to loosen.

Going, going . . . gone.

Arms thrown wide, Tony sucked in a lungful of sweet, moist air. Then another. Then he opened his eyes and started to cough.

Foggers used distilled water and glycerin. It was perfectly safe to breathe except that the brain saw smoke and another automatic response kicked in.

Coughing and choking and telling his brain to shut the fuck up, Tony staggered to his feet, groped for the other fogger, and stumbled with it toward the set. At 7560 cubic-feet-per-minute output—not something he knew; output was stenciled on the top of both machines—the lower half meter of the immediate area was nearly full. There were still places he could see the floor but those places were disappearing fast. Even so, he wanted the second fogger as close to the gate as possible.

The last time they'd needed them, someone— Daniel?—had told him they used a higher density fog juice that kept the fog close to the floor and away from the guts of expensive electrical equipment. But use enough fog, especially between the confining walls of the set, and it would rise. Fill the air.

Fog was visible because each tiny water droplet refracted light. Or reflected light, Tony wasn't positive which. The point was it broke the light up into bits and that broke shadows up into bits. Destroyed their cohesion.

The light was real.

The shadows were an effect.

He thumbed the fog on as the extension cord hauled him to a stop at the edge of the set.

With no shadows, the Shadowlord had only the shadow-held remaining.

As the set filled, Tony set the fogger down in the covering fog from the other machine.

It felt like he'd been gone for hours, but it had only been minutes.

And not too many of them.

Henry still fought the shadow-held, but he moved too quickly and there were too many of them for Tony to see how the battle was going. Henry would win. Henry was very hard to . . .

A crowbar rose and fell. Impact against flesh and a snarl.

Henry might be hard to kill, but those he fought were more fragile. If he was hurt and the Hunger rose . . . If there was blood and the Hunger rose . . . Tony just hoped Henry would—could—remember that fragility.

Still no sign of Arra.

God damn, h . . .

The hair lifting off the back of his neck, Tony turned toward the throne. The Shadowlord stood staring at him through narrowed eyes. Even at that distance Tony could feel the rage rolling off him.

Man, the air is getting distinctly punky in here.

Teeth clenched, lips thinned to pale lines. Evil still looked pretty damned good. "Get him. Turn that thing off!"

Mind you, good-looking evil is still evil, he admitted, backing up.

Mason and Lee rose up out of the fog.

Apparently shadow-held brains had no problem with that whole breathing smoke thing.

Fucking figured.

Mason reached him first. Tony darted left around a blow and realized as both actors followed his movement that they were obeying literally. *Get him.* Then, *turn that thing off.*

All he had to do was keep them busy until Arra ended things.

Right. *All* he had to do. *If* Arra ended things.

He kept moving since closing with one would lead to a beating by the other; dodging, ducking, and finally slamming a bruised hip into the coffin so hard it rocked on its stand. Pain distracted him long enough for both his attackers to reach him. He ducked under Lee's double-handed grab, found himself between the coffin and the wall, and, working with what he had, tipped it over on them.

It hit the floor with force enough to momentarily whoosh the fog away. The lid slammed open. Chester Bane rolled out.

Time stopped.

His eyes snapped open.

And time started up again.

If asked, Tony would have described his boss as strong, powerful, arrogant, controlling, and a little strange. But not fast. He'd have been wrong. He didn't even see the producer move. One minute CB was on the floor, the next he was on his feet with Mason clutched in one massive hand, Lee in the other. White showed all around his eyes, the muscles of his neck stood out like rebar, and he was roaring—no words, just one loud, enraged bellow. It was the scariest goddamned thing Tony had seen all day . . . and given the day he'd had, that was saying something.

Off by the fogger, someone screamed.

Dragged around by the sound, Tony saw the Shadowlord rear back, clutching his right hand to his chest.

To make fake fog, a fog machine's heat exchanger superheated the fog juice and forced the hot mixture out of the nozzle on the front. By their very nature, fog machines got hot. Very hot. It appeared the Shadowlord's personal protection didn't extend to passive attacks by inanimate objects.

Hoping CB would remember he'd need the men he was destroying when this was over, Tony ran for the Shadowlord.

He didn't remember much from his GED, but he remembered some crap about equal and opposite reactions. In order to blast an attacker away, the protections had to apply the same force to the Shadowlord and this time he wasn't comfortably settled on his throne. If Tony went down, the Shadowlord was taking a fall, too.

Unfortunately, magic was one thing and, as it turned out, physics was something else again. Tony slammed into darkness maybe an inch away from his target and was smashed back into the fog.

A fist wrapped in the front of his shirt and dragged him clear.

"Foolish." Only a sliver of gray showed between narrowed lids. The word was almost a hiss. "We could have . . ."

And then the Shadowlord's attention shifted.

Shirt digging into armpits, Tony twisted in his grip.

At the far end of the set, a golden pattern shimmered in the air. As they watched, frozen in place, a new line of light curved around the outer edge.

Tony hit the floor, thrown aside hard enough to slide until he slammed up against the wall. Palms leaving damp prints against the painted plywood, he hand-walked to his feet. When he turned, Mason stood in front of him.

A quick glance showed CB struggling with three of the construction crew and Lee nowhere in sight.

Ducking a swing, Tony tripped on something in the fog. He managed a reasonably coherent, *Not again!* just before impact, then the mist folded over him. A hand closed around the back of his belt as his hand closed around a backpack.

What the . . . ?

Not a backpack, the photographer's camera bag.

As Mason hauled him up, he ripped through the camera bag, finding what he needed by touch. Finally clearing the fog, he squirmed around and triggered the photographer's flash.

The shadow had been in Mason Reed since Friday morning, absorbing all that Mason was. Mason had never met a flashbulb he didn't love. Yesterday, the fan club had delayed him with pictures and it worked again now. Mason's grip loosened, Tony fell free, got his feet under him, and, continually thumbing the flash, kneed the actor in the nuts.

He could almost hear his own giving a little cheer at getting some back.

As Mason dropped down out of sight, Tony ran for the other end of the set, ducking and weaving through the ongoing battle Henry and CB were fighting with the shadow-held. His feet thumped into bodies he couldn't see. Didn't want to see.

The pattern hadn't grown in the last few moments because Arra, laptop open and balanced on one hand, was holding the Shadowlord in place with the other.

"You're only delaying the inevitable, old woman," he snarled as Tony ducked under a flying can of hair spray and slid between them.

"Let him go, Arra. I've got him."

"You?" Simultaneous. From both wizards.

Eyes locked with the one, he snarled, "Fucking bite me! Let him go and finish!" at the other.

He was almost surprised when she did.

But not quite as surprised as the Shadowlord.

"And what can you do?" he mocked, stepping forward.

Tony slid his hands around the other man's face, laced them behind his head, and locked their mouths together. His lips were cool, but Tony was used to that. He changed the angle, made it wetter, more . . . carnal. *We could have* the Shadowlord had said. *We.*

The protective spell didn't kick in.

Hands locked on his waist hard enough to leave new bruises.

Son of a bitch; it is *my ass.*

Under other circumstances, he'd have found that gratifying. Although, even if evil wizards had been his type, any swelling crotch-side tonight was likely to be edema. Passion, pain—fortunately, all moaning sounded remarkably alike.

As a distraction, it worked because it was unexpected, but it didn't work long.

Darkness flared and Tony found himself on the floor again, his skull cracking hard enough against the concrete to cause stars.

Okay, stars are new.

When they didn't go away, he realized it wasn't stars he was seeing; it was Arra's pattern through the refraction of the fog. Which was dissipating. Either the foggers were empty or the sound stage was just too big.

On the bright side, the Shadowlord seemed to be caught on the lines of light like a fly in a web. That brief bout of tonsil hockey must've given Arra enough time to finish.

Yay, me.

And then again . . .

Torso tight against the light, the Shadowlord flung out his arms, fingers extended. Streamers of darkness began to flow into them. He was calling back the shadows. Releasing the shadow-held. Tony could hear bodies hitting the floor.

He was calling back pieces of himself.

He was getting stronger.

In another moment, he'd be free of the pattern.

Where the hell was Yerma-whoever?

◆

It wasn't working. Arra knew it wouldn't work. Knew it. Had known it. Had always known it. She checked the pattern on the laptop, checked the pattern drawn on the air . . . They were identical. It wasn't her fault.

All your fault.

Caught on the other side of the light, the Shadowlord smiled.

They died because of you, the shadows whispered.

They die when you leave. They die when you stay. They die because you fail them. All of them.

"Shut up!" A world lived in shadow because she couldn't stop him. This world would fall to shadow because she couldn't stop him. He was right. It *was* all her fault.

The light wavered.

His smile broadened and he jerked back.

You should never have come here. You doomed this world.

She shouldn't have. And she had. Her heart was pounding and her vision began to blur.

At least this time you'll die with them.

Kiril. Sarn. Haryain. Tevora. Mai-Sim. Pettryn. So many others, all dead.

Reflecting back the pattern, his eyes glittered in triumph and she realized he knew the names of the dead as well as she did.

Charlie. Chester. Henry. Tony.

"They're not dead!" All right, from what she'd seen, Charlie very probably was, but the others . . . CB and Henry still fought. Tony was down, true, but moving. Struggling.

They're not dead yet.

She could see Tony. He was close enough to the pattern that the gold tinted his skin and hair. He was trying to sit up.

"You're right. They're not dead yet and neither am I." Snapping the laptop closed, she tossed it aside and spread her arms, a mirror image of the wizard on the other side of the light, pulling her own power in to support the pattern. "And *if* I die, I'm going out kicking your skinny ass."

If you die?

Shadow laughter danced cold air up and down her spine.

A little over seven days spent in Tony's company gave her the words she needed. "Bite me, you son of a bitch!"

Teeth gleaming gold, the Shadowlord jerked back again, far enough this time to find his own voice. "Maybe later."

◆

Fighting for focus, Tony rose up on one elbow and stared at the lines. He was right. It was the pattern that had been drawn on the blackboard in another world seven years earlier. The wizards had been nailed here . . .

. . . and here.

But here . . .

He shook his head, trying to clear it, and nearly puked.

But here . . . the line was wrong.

The Shadowlord cried out in victory.

Tony reached out and tugged a line of light a few centimeters to the right.

Golden light flowed out of the pattern. It covered his skin, ran up under his clothing, and drifted past each individual hair on his head. It felt like . . .

Like . . .

Pain.

As he fell, writhing, he realized he wasn't the only one screaming.

The screams didn't quite hide a familiar soft *sputz*.

Back arched to the point where bone had to be protesting, the Shadowlord rose up into the air. One by one, shadows were wrenched from him and destroyed.

Tony screamed a little louder as the bit of him went. It looked no different than the others, but he felt its loss.

By the time the last of the shadows were gone, Tony's voice had faded to a hoarse rasp, but the Shadowlord's agony continued to fill the soundstage. With the shadows gone, there wasn't much of him left. A translucent figure of a man with golden patterns etched into his skin, his eyes and mouth dark holes in a distorted face.

Flare.

And nothing.

◆

When Tony opened his eyes, he was lying on the couch in Raymond Dark's office. It was a comfortable couch; he'd crashed out on it more than once during seventeen-hour shoots.

Golden flecks of light danced across his vision. He remembered fog.

Right. The London street flashback. Had they finished shooting it?

Then he tried to sit up. Memory rode in with the pain.

Henry's arm was around his shoulder a heartbeat later, supporting his weight. Tony blinked and managed to focus on the vampire. His throat hurt, reducing his voice to a rough whisper. "Is that a black eye?"

"Yes. I ducked a crowbar and your makeup artist nailed me with a can of hair spray."

Frowning hurt, too, so Tony stopped doing it. "Sort of remember seeing one fly by."

"It was an interesting battle. Interesting finish." Henry hadn't been able to get to Tony until the light faded. He'd had to stand, surrounded by the fallen, fighting restraining hands, unable to do anything while Tony screamed. Yeramathia, whatever or whoever Yeramathia was, didn't give a damn what he considered his. "What else do you remember?"

"Golden light. The Shadowlord . . ." He waved a trembling hand. There weren't really words for having seen a man dissolve in light. "I remember pain."

"That's because you were touching the pattern when Yeramathia answered." Arra's voice cut through the memory. She stood, arms folded, by Raymond Dark's desk. Apparently, frowning caused *her* no trouble at all.

"What were you thinking, boy? Were you trying to get yourself killed?"

Tony shifted in Henry's grip until he faced her. "I was thinking that your pattern was wrong."

"My pattern?"

"Yeah. Your pattern. I've seen it more recently and it was wrong. So I fixed it."

"You fixed it?"

"Yeah." Her expression had begun to worry him. "No big. I just tugged one line over a bit."

"You *just* tugged one line over a bit?" She was staring at him again, only this time her mouth was open. As Tony was about to point it out, she closed it with a snap. "Right. Well. Next time . . ."

"No." He'd gotten his definite back. "There isn't going to be a next time. We barely survived this time. Go home, Arra, you know you want to. Go home when the timer goes off and start a new order or raise chickens, I don't fucking care." Head throbbing, he let himself sag against Henry's shoulder for a moment. Plenty of time to be butch later. "Just go home and close the gate after you."

"Come with me."

"What?" So much for sagging.

"Be the start of my new order. The Shadowlord has been destroyed, but there remains much work to do on the other side. I could use the help of someone who does not run away from a fight. The help of someone who will not let others run away."

"What?" He squirmed around and looked at Henry who didn't seem all that surprised. "What the hell is she talking about?"

"She's telling you that you can be a wizard, Tony. If you want to."

"Me?"

"You," Arra answered. "You see what others do not. You reach out where others fear to. You are able to touch power and mold it to your use."

The lack of contractions was beginning to seriously freak him out.

"I saw this in you from the beginning. There is great potential in you. You could become . . ." She paused, snorted, and rolled her eyes. "Well, I'm not promising anything but you could become competent with training and practice."

"Me?"

"We'll work on articulate as well."

"She's serious?"

Henry nodded. "And abrasive. But I believe her."

He could go through a magical gate to another world and become a wizard. He could learn to work the energy of that world, bend it and mold it to his own ends. He touched the memory of the Shadowlord; he could learn to command shadow.

His throat was dry.

Tony swallowed, dragged his tongue across his lips, and got slowly to his feet. Henry helped rather a lot with the latter.

"Arra." A deep breath. "I'd rather have perpetual root canals."

Arra sighed, reached into the pocket of her hooded sweatshirt, and handed Henry a twenty. "I still say it was worth a shot. He's an annoying little shit, but I hate to see that kind of potential wasted."

"He's not wasting it," Henry told her as he pocketed the money.

"Bull. He's a production assistant at a third-rate . . ." CB cleared his throat from the doorway and Arra adjusted for his presence. ". . . second-rate production house."

"Yeah, now," Tony protested.

"He can go far here as well," CB added. "Eventually. Right now, it's 11:12. If you're right about the timer, the gate's about to open."

♦

There were people sprawled up against every solid surface on the set. Most of them were drinking a familiar smelling cocktail—Tony noticed that every prop capable of holding liquid as well as the coffee cups from the office kitchen had been put in service. People looked confused but docile, content to suck back the potion— the potion that he'd made—and stare around them with wide, bruised eyes. A few of the crew were sprawled but not drinking, their eyes closed and their arms lying limp by their sides.

Consequences.

"Are they . . . ?"

"No," Henry told him. "Just unconscious. Probably a couple of concussions. Arra said she'd take care of them."

"Is anyone . . ."

"Charlie Harris and Rahal Singh."

One for the Shadowlord. "Did you . . . ?"

"Yes."

And one for Henry. "Are you okay?"

The corner of Henry's mouth that Tony could see curved up into something not quite a smile. "I've killed before, Tony."

"I know." He tightened his grip on the vampire's arm, not because he was in danger of falling but because he needed Henry to understand that he *did* know. Even if, in true guy fashion, they weren't going to talk about it. Big difference between killing for food or for vengeance or even caught up in Darkness and killing without intending to or wanting to. "You up for comfort food later?"

That evoked an actual smile and an incredulous laugh. "If you are."

"Date." As Arra made her way around the edges of the set, stepping over arms and legs and cables, he noticed a complex pattern drawn in chalk in the center of the floor. "What's that?"

"Memories," CB rumbled from behind him. "Ready

to be erased. You and I," he raised his voice to the point where Arra turned toward them, "are not a part of it."

She rolled her eyes. "We've been over this."

"Precedent suggests we have no reason to trust you."

"Does precedent suggest what I have to say to that?"

Then the gate opened and Tony's knees buckled. Fortunately, Henry caught him before he reached the floor. He figured he'd used up his lifetime allotment of smacking into horizontal surfaces.

"You shouldn't be so close."

He struggled back into what was more or less a vertical position. "I need to see this."

As darkness roiled down from an empty place by the ceiling—the Shadowlord's reinforcements coming without being called—Arra lifted both arms over her head and rapidly sketched another pattern in the air. She looked like she always did, but she looked like a wizard, too. Acceptance, Tony realized suddenly. She looked like she'd accepted what she was and what that meant.

Pattern complete, she pushed it forward. There was a sizzle and flash when it hit the darkness. A hiss and a flash as it hit the gate. A distant scream as it disappeared and there was a flashback through the gate so bright Henry threw both arms in front of his eyes. Tony sagged back against CB's momentarily comforting bulk.

He felt the gate snap closed. Arra was still standing there. He must have tensed because CB murmured, "She'll go another time. There are things here that need taking care of."

Right. Of course. "The cats."

"Also the cats." Chester Bane looked out over the soundstage and realized he had been a part of something remarkable. The defeat of an invading evil. The more significant defeat of personal demons. The discovery of a hero in an unlikely place. And the whole damned thing had put them seriously behind schedule.

Still, he allowed reluctantly, it could have been worse. They could also be over budget. "Mr. Fitzroy, if you could assist me with . . ."

The bodies, Tony filled in silently.

Blinking away what must have been painful afterimages, Henry nodded at CB and turned again to Tony. "Will you be all right?"

Tony slid sideways until his weight was against the lid of Raymond Dark's coffin. "I'll be fine."

Eventually.

As the two men moved away, another moved in.

Cradling his left arm against his body, Lee stared at Tony for a long moment. *Did people always do this much staring or am I just noticing it now?* He blinked, then asked himself, *"Why not?"* and stared back.

"That was . . ." The actor's brows nearly met over his nose. "There were . . ." He swallowed and, looking as though he was maybe thirty seconds from a total meltdown, jerked his head toward the place where the gate had been. "There was light. What the hell was that?"

"This is television." Tony swept his arm around in a gesture expansive enough to take in both cameras still pointed toward the center of the set. "It was a special effect."

"Bullshit. I'm not stupid, Tony. Or blind. What's going on." He took a step closer, well within Tony's personal space. "Talk to me."

"All right." He raised a hand to cut off any immediate questions. "But not tonight." He touched his throat. "Hurts. We'll talk tomorrow."

Green eyes narrowed. Wrong color but otherwise a dead man's expression. "Promise me."

"I promise."

An easy promise to make since Arra was already erasing the chalk memories drawn on the floor.

♦

"No, CB says Mason's fine."

Arra snorted as they crossed the soundstage. "I can't say that I'm really surprised. If anyone had ego enough to cope with being shadow-held for so long, it would be Mason Reed." She nodded toward the stepladder. "It's almost time. If there's anything you want to know . . ."

She wanted him to ask about meaning-of-life stuff. She'd been rediscovering her wizard roots over the last three days and wanted him in on it. Tony started to shrug but cut the motion off short as Whitby protested the movement. Both cats had been protesting the indignity of the cat carriers since they'd left the co-op.

"Anything at all," she insisted.

Fine. Tony sorted through unanswered questions searching for one he wouldn't mind having an answer to. There were a lot more of the other kind. "If the Shadowlord had no power here, how did he hold CB?"

"I'm about to leave this world forever and that's it?"

"Yeah. Why? Don't you know?"

Arra snorted and turned toward him at the base of the ladder. "Probably a minor binding spell. The close confines of the coffin helped hold it and hitting the floor broke it. Don't forget to get the gas gauge on the car fixed."

"I won't."

"I've left my laptop down in the workshop."

"It's still working?"

"Apparently it landed on Everett and bounced. But that's beside the point; it has some things on it you might be able to use."

"I'm not a wizard."

She snorted again. "Damned right you're not. Here." She handed him the second cat carrier. "Hold Zazu until I'm up the ladder." First step. Second step.

Not very interesting to look at actually. "It would look a lot more wizardy if you levitated or something."

Third step. "And you'd block this area from the rest of the soundstage? Or maybe you'd rather tell a studio audience where I'm going." Fourth step.

"You didn't have to go through this morning. You could have gone through tonight."

Fifth step. Sixth. "I didn't feel like it. The police have finished with me, I'm out of here."

The RCMP investigation into the "special effect accident" that had killed Charlie Harris and Rahal Singh had been strangely vague considering that they were the third and fourth bodies connected to CB Productions in less than a month. In the end, no charges had been laid and the newspaper coverage had given the show a ratings bump. With any luck, Constables Elson and Danvers would get tired of dropping by before CB got tired of finding them in the building. Unfortunately, Arra's wizardry had had less effect on the insurance industry. CB's enraged commentary on the rise in his rates had probably been heard at the company's head office in Montreal—whole sentences were still echoing around the soundstage.

Tony handed the cat carriers up one at a time, the hand-shaped bruises on his waist reminding him of shadows as he stretched. Arra settled the first carrier on the top of the ladder and the second on the paint platform and looked down at him. No, stared down at him.

Great. More staring. He found a smile that was mostly sincere. "Thanks for the car. And the stuff. And the whole kicking Shadowlord ass."

Arra nodded.

Tony waited.

The gate opened. Zazu went through first—he couldn't see her, but he recognized the yowl. It was slightly higher-pitched than Whitby's. The last he saw of Whitby was an orange and white paw poked through the bars of the crate.

Arra lifted one foot off the step and stopped. "It's going to be one hell of a mess through there."

Yeah, there were wizards nailed to blackboards. He wondered if she could see them from where she was standing.

"Are you sure you don't want to come?"

"I'm sure."

She looked down at that, and finally smiled. "You could be great."

He shrugged. "I'm planning on it."

"Great *and* modest. I'm out of here before the sap level rises any higher. Take care of yourself, kid."

"You, too."

Watching an old woman step off a ladder and disappear in midair was a definite anticlimax. Half decent CGI would have given the scene a lot more oomph.

"You're welcome," he muttered as he folded the ladder and moved it up against the wall. Yeah, getting the car was nice, but would it have killed her to thank him. Not for fighting the Shadowlord, that had nothing to do with her, but she could have thanked him for the backbone he found for her. Without him, she'd have been running until the guilt finally crushed her.

He'd been waiting for her to say something for the last three days, but every conversation they had seemed to end up with her trying to convince him to go with her through the gate.

"I could use the help of someone who does not run away from a fight. Of someone who will not let others run away."

Oh. Hang on.

He'd been a little distracted at the time.

Looking up toward the ceiling, he said, "You're welcome" again but this time he meant it.

"Quiet, please!"

As Peter's voice echoed through the soundstage, Tony crammed the jack back in his ear and turned up his radio.

"Let's settle, people!"

He reached the set in time to call, "Rolling!" with the rest and found a place behind the video village as the second assistant camera called the slate.

"Scene twenty-seven, take two."

Lee grinned as Mason settled his shoulders against the padded satin lining of the coffin and said something that caused the other actor to give a less than blood-sucking undead type snicker.

"Action!"

Left thumb rubbing the scar on his right wrist, Tony watched the monitors as the scene unfolded. Stretched out behind him on the concrete floor, his shadow reached out and held up two fingers behind the shadow of the director's head.

Keep reading for a sneak preview of
Smoke and Mirrors,
Tony Foster's second adventure,
coming in hardcover in July from DAW

CAULFIELD House was anything but average.
Built around the turn of the last century by
Creighton Caulfield, who'd made a fortune in both
mining and timber, the house rested on huge blocks of
pale granite with massive beams of Western Red Cedar
holding up the porch roof. Three stories high with eight
bedrooms, a ballroom, a conservatory, and servants'
quarters on the third floor, it sat tucked away in Deer
Lake Park at the end of a long rutted path too over-
grown to be called a road. Matt, the freelance location
finder CB Productions generally employed, had driven
down Deer Lake Drive to have a look at Edgar
House—which turned out to be far too small to accom-
modate the script. Following what he called a hunch, although Tony suspected he'd gotten lost—it wouldn't be
the first time—he spotted a set of ruts and followed
them. Chester Bane, the CB of CB Productions, had
taken one look at the digital images Matt had shot of

the house he'd stumbled on at the end of the ruts, and decided it was perfect for *Darkest Night.*

Although well within the boundaries of the park, Caulfield House remained privately owned and all but forgotten. Tony had no idea how CB had gotten permission to use the building but shouting had figured prominently—shouting into the phone, shouting behind the closed door of his office, shouting into his cell as he crossed the parking lot ignoring the cars pulling out and causing two fender benders as his staff tried to avoid hitting him. Evidence suggested that CB felt volume could succeed when reason failed, and his track record seemed to support his belief.

But the house *was* perfect in spite of the profanely expressed opinions of the drivers who'd had to maneuver the generator, the craft services truck, the wardrobe/makeup trailer, and the honey wagon down the rutted road close enough to be of any use. Fortunately, as CB had rented the entire house for the week, he had no compunctions about having dressing rooms set up in a couple of the bedrooms. He'd only brought in the honey wagon when Mr. Brummel had informed him what it would cost to replace the elderly septic system if it broke down under the additional input.

The huge second floor bathroom had therefore been painted but was off-limits as far as actually using it. The painters had left the window open to help clear the fumes and Tony glanced up to see the bottom third of the sheer white curtain blowing out over the sill.

He frowned. "Did you see that?"

"The curtain?"

"No, beyond the curtain, in the room. I thought I saw someone looking down at us."

Lee snorted and started walking again, stepping over a sprawling mass of plants that had spilled out of the garden onto the path. "Probably Mason sneaking a smoke by the window. He likely figures the smell of the paint'll cover the stink."

It made sense, except . . .

"Mason's in black," Tony argued, hurrying to catch up. "Whoever this was, they were wearing something light."

"Maybe he took the jacket off so he wouldn't get paint on it. Maybe that's where he went for his earlier smoke and maybe he did a little finger painting on my ass when he got back." One foot raised above the top step, Lee paused and shook his head. "No, I'm pretty sure I'd remember that." Half turning, he grinned down at Tony on the step below. "It seems I have a secret admirer."

Before Tony could decide if he was supposed to read more into that than could possibly be there, Lee was inside and Adam's voice was telling him to *". . . get your ass in gefffst, Tony. We don't have all fissssssking day."*

Fissssssking had enough static involved it almost hurt. Fiddling with the frequency on his walkie-talkie as he followed Lee into the house, Tony had a feeling that the communication difficulties were going to get old fast.

"He peeped you. Not the actor, the other one."

"Don't be ridiculous, Stephen."

"Well he looked like he saw you."

"He saw the curtain blowing out the window, that's all. I'm very good at staying out of sight." Her tone sharpened. "*I'm* not the one that people keep spotting, am I?"

"Those were accidents." His voice hovered between sulky and miserable. "I didn't even know those hikers were there and I don't care what Graham says, I hate hiding."

Comforting now. "I know."

"And besides, I never take the kind of chances you do. Truth, Cassie, what were you thinking, marking him a second time?"

She smiled and glanced down at the smudge of paint on one finger. "I was thinking that since I'd gotten him to take off his jacket, maybe I could get him to take off his pants. Come on." Taking his hand, she pulled him toward the door. "I want to see what they're doing now."

"Raymond, I think you'd better have a look at this."

"Cut and print! That was excellent work, gentlemen." Tossing his headphones onto the shelf under the monitor, Peter turned to his director of photography. "How much time do you need to reset for scene eight?"

Sorge popped a throat lozenge into his mouth and shrugged. "Shooting from down here ... fifteen minutes, maybe twenty. No more. When we move to the top of the stairs ..."

"Don't borrow trouble." He raised his voice enough to attract the attention of his IAD ... "Adam, tell them they've got twenty minutes to kill." ... and lowered it again as he pivoted a hundred and eighty degrees to face his script supervisor. "Tina, let's you and I go over that next scene. There'll be a bitch of a continuity problem if we're not careful, and I don't need a repeat of episode twelve."

"At least we know there's ninety-one people watching the show," she pointed out as she stood.

Peter snorted. "I still think it was one geek with ninety-one e-mail addresses."

As they moved off into the dining room and the techs moved in to shove the video village out into the actual entryway where it wouldn't be in the shot, Adam stepped out into the middle of the foyer and looked up at the two actors. "You've got fifteen, guys."

"I'll be in my dressing room." Turning on one heel, Mason headed back up the stairs.

"If anyone needs me, I'll be in my dressing room as well." Lee grimaced, reached back, and yanked at his pants. "These may dry faster off my ass."

Mouse, his gray hair more a rat-tail down his back and physically the complete opposite of his namesake—

no one had ever referred to him as meek and lived to speak of it—stepped out from behind his camera and whistled. "You want to drop trou, don't let us stop you."

Someone giggled.

Tony missed Lee's response as he realized the highly unlikely sound could only have come from Kate, Mouse's camera assistant. He wouldn't have bet money on Kate knowing *how* to giggle. He wasn't entirely certain she knew how to laugh.

"Tony," Adam's hand closed over his shoulder as Lee followed Mason up the stairs and both actors disappeared down the second floor hall. "I saw Mason talking with Karen from craft services earlier. Go make sure she didn't add any bagels to his muffin basket."

"And if she did?"

"Haul ass upstairs and get make sure he doesn't eat one."

"You want me to wrestle the bagel out of Mason's hand?"

"If that's where it is." Adam grinned and patted him manfully on the shoulder—where manfully could be defined as *better you than me, buddy*. "If he's actually taken a bite, I want you to wrestle it out of his mouth."

Mason loved bagels but the dental adhesive attaching Raymond Dark's fangs to his teeth just wasn't up to the required chewing. After a couple of forty-minute delays while Everett replaced the teeth, and one significantly longer delay after the right fang had been accidentally swallowed, CB had instigated the no-bagels-in-Mason's-dressing-room rule. Since Mason hadn't had to ultimately retrieve the tooth—that job had fallen to Jennifer, his personal assistant who, in Tony's opinion, couldn't possibly be paid enough—he'd chosen to see it as a suggestion rather than a rule and did what he could to get around it.

As a result, Karen, from craft services, found herself under a determined assault by a man who combined good looks and charm with all the ethical consideration of a cat. No one blamed her on those rare occasions she'd been unable to resist.

Today, no one knew where she was.

She wasn't at the table or the truck and there wasn't time enough to search further. Grabbing a pot of black currant jam off the table, Tony headed up the staircase two steps at a time, hoping Mason's midmorning nosh hadn't already brought the day to a complete stop.

As the star of *Darkest Night*, Mason had taken the master suite as his dressing room. Renovated in the fifties, it took up half the front of the second floor and included a bedroom, a closet/dressing room and a small bathroom. Provided he kept flushing to a minimum, Mr. Brummel had cleared this bathroom for Mason's personal use. Lee had to use the honey wagon like every one else.

All the doors that led off the second floor hall were made of the same Douglas Fir that dominated the rest of the house but they—and the trim surrounding them—had been stained to look like mahogany. Tony, who in a pinch could tell the difference between plywood and MDF, had been forced to endure a long lecture on the fir-as-mahogany issue from the gaffer who carved themed chess sets in his spare time. The half finished knight in WWF regalia that he'd pulled from his pocket *had* been impressive.

Hand raised to knock on the door to Mason's room, Tony noticed that both the upper panels had been patched. In the dim light of the second floor hall, the patches were all but invisible but up close he could see the faint difference in the color of the stain. There was something familiar about their shape but he couldn't . . .

Hand still raised, he jumped back as the door jerked open.

Mason stared out at him, wide-eyed. "There's something in my bathroom!"

"Something?" Tony asked, trying to see if both fangs were still in place.

"Something!"

"Okay." About to suggest plumbing problems were way outside his job description and that he should go get Mr. Brummel, Tony changed his mind at Mason's next words.

"It was crouched down between the shower and the toilet."

"It?"

"I couldn't see exactly, it was all shadows . . ."

Oh, crap. "Maybe I'd better go have a look." Before Mason could protest—before he could change his mind and run screaming, he was crossing the bedroom, crossing the dressing room, and opening the bathroom door. The sunlight through the windows did nothing to improve the color scheme but it did chase away any and all shadows. Tony turned toward the toilet and the corner shower unit and frowned. He couldn't figure out what the actor might have seen since there wasn't room enough between them for . . .

Something.

Rocking in place.

Forward.

Back.

Hands clasped around knees, tear-stained face lifted to the light.

And nothing.

Just a space far too small for the bulky body that hadn't quite been there.

Skin prickling between his shoulder blades, jar of black currant jam held in front of him like a shield, Tony took a step into the room. Shadows flickered across the rear wall, filling the six inches between toilet and shower with writhing shades of gray. Had that been all he'd seen?

Stupid question.

No.

So what now? Was he supposed to do something about it?

Whatever it was, the rocking and crying didn't seem actively dangerous.

"Well, Foster?"

"Fuck!" He leaped forward and spun around. With his heart pounding so loudly he could hardly hear himself think, he gestured out the window at the cedar branches blowing across the glass and lied through his teeth. "There's your shadow."

Then the wind dropped again and the shadows disappeared.

Mason ran a hand up through his hair and glanced around the room. "Of course. Now you see them, now you don't." *I wasn't frightened,* his tone added, as his chin rose. *Don't think for a moment I was.* "You're a little jumpy, aren't you?"

"I didn't hear you behind me." Which was the truth because he hadn't—although the admiring way he said it was pure actor manipulation. Working in Television, 101—keep the talent placated.

As expected, Mason preened. "Well, yes, I can move cat quiet when I want to."

In Tony's admittedly limited experience, the noise cats made thudding through apartments was completely disproportionate to their size but Mason clearly liked the line so he nodded a vague agreement.

"It's fucking freezing in here . . ."

Maybe not freezing but damned cold.

"Is that jam for me?"

Jam? He followed Mason's line of sight to his hand. "Oh, yeah."

"Put it by the basket. And then I'm sure you have things to do." The actor's lip curled. Both fangs were still in place. "Important production assistant things."

As it happened, in spite of sarcasm, he did.

There were no bagels in the basket but there was a scattering of poppy seeds on the tray next to a dirty knife. Setting down the jam, Tony turned and spotted a plate half hidden behind the plant that dominated the small table next to the big armchair by the window. *Bagel at twelve o'clock.*

Mason had made himself a snack, set it down then gone to the bathroom and . . .

One thing at a time. Bagel now. Bathroom later.

He reached inside himself for calm, muttered the seven words under his breath, and the first half of the bagel hit his hand with a greasy-slash-sticky impact that suggested Mason had been generous with both the butter and the honey.

"Foster?"

"Just leaving."

All things considered, the sudden sound of someone crying in the bathroom was not entirely unexpected.

As Mason turned to glare at the sound, Tony snagged the other half of the bagel. "Air in the pipes," he said, heading for the door. "Old plumbing."

The actor shot a scathing expression across the room at him. "I knew that."

"Right." Except old plumbing seldom sounded either that unhappy or that articulate. The new noises were almost words. Tony found a lot of comfort in that *almost*.

Safely outside the door, he restacked the bagel butter/honey sides together and headed toward the garbage can at the other end of the hall, rehearsing what he'd say when Mason discovered the bagel was gone. *"I wasn't anywhere near it!"*

No nearer than about six feet and Mason knew it.

Although *near* had become relative. These days he could manage to move unbreakable objects almost ten feet. Breakables still had a tendency to explode. Arra's notes hadn't mentioned explosions but then, until the shadows, she'd handled F/X for CB Productions, so maybe she considered bits of beer bottle flying around the room a minor effect. Fortunately Zev had shown up early for their date and had been more than willing to drive him to the hospital to get the largest piece of bottle removed from his arm. His opinion of juggling beer bottles had been scathing. Tony hadn't had the guts to find out what his opinion of wizardry would have been.

The phrase special effects wizard had become cliché in the industry. Arra Pelindrake, who'd been blowing things up and animating corpses for the last seven years, had been the real thing. Given the effects the new guy was coming up with, it turned out she hadn't been that great at the subtleties of twenty-first century F/X but she *was* a real wizard. The shadows and the evil that controlled them had followed her through a gate she'd created between their world and this. The battle had gone down to the wire but Tony had finally convinced her to stand and fight, and when it was all over she'd been able to go home—but not before dropping the "you could be a wizard, too" bombshell. He'd refused to go with so she'd left him her laptop, six gummed up games of spider solitaire that were supposed to give him insight into the future, and what he'd come to call Wizardshit 101; point form and remarkably obscure instructions on becoming a wizard.

He wasn't a wizard; he was a production assistant, working his way up in the industry until the time when it was his vision on the screen, his vision pulling in the viewers in the prime 19–29 male demographic. He'd had no intention of ever using the laptop.

And there'd been times over the last few months where he'd been able to stay away from it for weeks. Well, one time. For three weeks. Right after he'd had the jagged hunk of beer bottle removed from his arm.

Wizardry, like television, was all about manipulating energy.

And occasionally bread products.

Mason's door jerked open and without thinking much beyond, *Oh, crap,* Tony opened the door he was standing by, dashed into the room, and closed the door quietly behind him. He had a feeling *I wasn't anywhere near your bagel* would play better when he didn't have butter, honey, and poppy seeds all over his hands.

The smell of wet paint told him where he was even before he turned.

The second floor bathroom.

There were no shadows in this bathroom. On the wrong side of the house for direct sunlight there was still enough daylight spilling in through the open window to make the fresh coat of white semigloss gleam. Although the plumbing had been updated in the fifties, the actual fixtures were original—which was why they were shooting the flashback in this room.

Weirdly, although thirty years older, it made Mason's bathroom look dated and . . . haunted.

It was just the flickering shadows from the cedar tree and air in the pipes, he told himself.

Whatever gets you through your day, his self snorted.

Bite me.

The heavy door cut off all sound from the hall. He had no idea if Mason was still prowling around looking for him, hunting his missing bagel.

At least if the taps work, I can wash my hands.

Using the only non-sticky square inch on his right palm, Tony pushed against the old lever faucet and turned on the cold water. And waited. Just as he was about to turn it off again, figuring they hadn't hooked up the water yet, liquid gushed from the faucet, thick and reddish brown, smelling of iron and rot.

Heart in his throat, he jumped back.

Blood!

No wait, rust.

By the time he had his breathing under control, the water was running clear. Feeling foolish, he rinsed off his palms, dried them on his jeans, and closed the tap. Checking out his reflection in the big, somewhat spotty mirror over the sink, he frowned.

Behind him, on the wall . . . it looked as if someone had drawn a finger through the wet paint. When he turned, changing the angle of the light, the mark disappeared. Mirror—finger mark. No mirror—no mark.

And now we know where the paint on Lee's tux came from. Next question: who put it there? Brenda seemed like the prime suspect. She'd been upstairs de-lining both actors before the scene, she'd have noticed the marks had they already been laid down, and the result had been Lee bare-assed in her trailer . . . *And let's not forget that she's already familiar with his ass.* He probably hadn't even noticed her stroking him on the way by.

Opportunity and motive pointed directly to Brenda.

Time . . .

Tony glanced at his watch.

"Crap!" Twenty-three minutes since Adam had called a twenty-minute break. Bright side, Mason wouldn't be able to bug him about a rule-breaking snack in front of the others. Slipping out into the hall, Tony ran for the back stairs figuring he could circle around from the kitchen. With any luck no one had missed him yet—out of the benefits of being low man on the totem pole.

As he ran, he realized Mason had been right about one thing. *It's fucking freezing up here.*

"Why was he in the bathroom? Graham said we'd be safe in there, that they wouldn't be using it until tomorrow."

"Be quiet, Stephen!" Cassy pinched her brother's arm. "Do you want him to hear you?"

"Ow. He can't hear us from way over here!"

"I'm not so sure." She frowned thoughtfully as the young man disappeared through the door leading to the stairs between the servants' rooms and the kitchen. "I get the feeling he doesn't miss much."

Stephen snorted and patted a strand of dark blond hair back into the pomaded dip over his forehead. "Good thing we weren't *in* the bathroom then."

"Yes . . . good thing."